If I Tell

If I Tell

GILL PERDUE

PENGUIN BOOKS

PENGUIN BOOKS

UK | USA | Canada | Ireland | Australia
India | New Zealand | South Africa

Penguin Books is part of the Penguin Random House group of companies
whose addresses can be found at global.penguinrandomhouse.com.

Published by Sandycove 2022
Published in Penguin Books 2023
001

Printed and bound in Great Britain by Clays Ltd, Elcograf S.p.A.

The authorized representative in the EEA is Penguin Random House Ireland,
Morrison Chambers, 32 Nassau Street, Dublin D02 YH68

A CIP catalogue record for this book is available from the British Library

ISBN: 978–0–241–99206–7

www.greenpenguin.co.uk

MIX
Paper from
responsible sources
FSC www.fsc.org FSC® C018179

Penguin Random House is committed to a
sustainable future for our business, our readers
and our planet. This book is made from Forest
Stewardship Council® certified paper.

For Mum – who told us we could achieve anything, and who never made you put down the book you were reading. And for Dad – showman and sage. Love, always.

Thank you both.

Author's note

Dear reader

I deal with some sensitive topics in my novel and I sought expert advice when writing. I have done my best to deal carefully and authentically with themes such as anxiety, gaslighting and the legacy of trauma due to sexual abuse. I hope that those of you living with these issues will not find anything in here to add to your struggles. The characters in this story arrive at a stronger place and, though I realize that healing is not something that comes easily, I hope that is a source of encouragement.

With every good wish
Gill

Every movement hurts. Blinking hurts. Breathing hurts.

He tries to focus. It's dark. Is it the same day, or has he slept? There's a shaft of light slicing in under – under whatever the thing is that's covering him. It's all wrong.

His right hand lies across his chest – moulded there, weighted with lead weights. He thinks about moving it. Any second now, he's going to move it. He thinks the thought – *move hand* – and a small twitch happens at the elbow. This brings a crashing wave of hot pain, radiating from the sternum, along the ribs, across the chest and right up into his brain – into the cells of his brain. It feels as if the actual thought cells are shattered, smashed.

He closes his eyes, the eyelids stiff and heavy, caked with something.

He lies still.

Day One

1. Jenny

Inside, my mouth is jammed and crammed with blood and teeth and jagged *help*s that can't get out. It's daytime grey-morning early and I'm awake, but it feels like the nightmare where you scream and nothing comes out. And I'm sitting on a plastic chair and I have weird clothes on and they're waiting. They're waiting for the words.

'Hi Jenny, I'm Laura,' says Laura, with her giant name badge on so it's not exactly a shocker. 'Did the nurses explain that I'd be coming in to talk to you this morning?' And we both know that yes, yes, of course, they said it. How about one of us says something new, Laura? While we wait for the words.

She waits, smiles encouragingly. A second ticks by on the blue plastic clock above the desk. And another. I press my lips together. I'm keeping my mouth shut tight, tight, just in case. If I open it, shrieks might fly out like bats, dripping blood. It won't be words floating soft like clouds. No.

She waits some more. Tries a different tack. Don't trust her; you know you can't trust her.

'So there's nothing to worry about, okay? I'm a special type of garda. My job is just to chat to you, that's all. Every day, I chat to people – women, men, boys and girls – young people just like you.'

Tick. Silence. Repeat. Don't. Tell. I am not telling. Not chatting.

'Jenny? Did you hear me? I want you to know you're safe – okay? You – you seem to be – are you listening to something – maybe someone else? Jenny?'

5

And I see her look at the other one, but they don't see him. She can't see him. Dumb bitch.

No and No. You cannot trust her.

'And there' – she points to the long-haired woman sitting on a chair in the corner wearing jeans and runners, not like a grown-up. The woman does a smiley face – 'that's Niamh. Niamh's a garda as well. She's going to listen and take notes. In case I miss anything. Okay, Jenny? It's just us girls.'

She moves her chair closer to mine. That's probably not a good idea.

'So, Jenny, I was hoping we could chat and we can get to know each other a bit. But first I need to explain how it works, okay? So if I ask you a question and you don't know the answer, then just say "I don't know" – this is really important.'

The tip of her tongue pokes out of her mouth as she swallows. Like she's scared.

'So if I ask you what's my dog's name, what do you say?'

I want to say *bad dog, Laura, haha, because dogs have their names on their collars like you, Laura.* But I don't say that because the words are stuck. Laura does more waiting. Nothing comes out of my mouth. Good.

'Do you have a dog, Jenny?' she says in that stupid grown-up happy voice. And something is hurting in my throat. Maybe it's bleeding. It hurts so much when she says that about the dog, and I think the noise is me crying, but I can't see. The mirror's too far away.

'Do you have a dog, Jenny?'

Waiting and waiting, and she is looking over at the Niamh woman. Niamh is not Niamh Cinn Óir because her hair is all wrong, it only has gold at the ends. That Niamh had long, golden hair.

'Don't worry, Jenny, take your time. What I'm trying to say is that sometimes I make mistakes or say the wrong thing.'

And dumb Not Niamh goes something like *indeed you do el oh el.*

'When I get it wrong,' she carries on with her fake smile, 'you can tell me that I'm wrong. So if I say you're wearing a purple top, what do you say?'

The ticks are ticking and Laura is doing her waiting. I look down and it's not purple, it says 'hospital laundry services' all over it in small writing. And I could read it, but I won't – I told you – I'm not talking. They can't see him. They can't hear him.

'Jenny, can you listen to my voice, please? Okay? There's only me talking now but, soon, when you're talking – when you do decide to talk, it's very important that you tell me the truth, okay?' She sits back in her chair and puts her hair behind her ear: sssh, she's listening.

'Do you know why you're here?'

She pauses then. And I can hear it better now – the voice. It's much clearer. It says *be careful, Jenny. Be careful. Say nothing.*

Three more ticks and, in the quiet, I hear him laughing.

'You were brought in last night, very late. Remember you were in the ED first?'

Eee Dee. Tee Hee. I before E except after C. You can have consonants and vowels. Vowels rhymes with bowels, yuk. And trowels. And towels. Towels soak up blood. It sinks in.

'So this is Abbot's Hill Hospital.' She takes a breath, 'And for now, you're in the adult psychiatric ward.'

I can't hear the ticks now and I can't hear the words. My heart is thumping. I count thumps instead of ticks. Her hair is really shiny. I think about that shampoo – you know the one. Because you're worth it. Dumb bitch. Stupid, dumb bitch – you're not worth it. Tick. Oh good, the ticks are back.

'You were very upset when they found you last night, and everyone is really worried about you. We all want you to get

7

better as soon as possible. Is that what you want too? Jenny? Can you hear me?'

She smiles at me again, peering in under my fringe, going for the eye contact. Snooping around my brain.

'You're the boss in here, okay? You're safe – this is a safe place. So you can talk to me about anything at all.' And then she does this big, stagey inhale of breath, like – *oh wow, I just thought of this*.

'How about we talk about hobbies and things? What do you like to do?'

You don't want to know, Laura.

2. Laura

She sits in complete stillness, her hair masking her features and, bizarrely, probably suggested by the hospital gown, I see myself at the same age, in the hairdresser's, making Mum do all the talking for me. I was so shy I could barely string two sentences together. I'd start blushing as soon as I opened my mouth and Mum would do the 'Teenagers are sooo difficult' routine while I sat there – hating her but needing her to do this – in awe of her confidence yet judging her every gesture. I knew that if I could do it, I'd do it better. But I couldn't do it.

This girl is not suffering from adolescent shyness and, even though she's tired and in shock, it's not 'just' shock. She's not talking. She's barely moving. I know she's listening, but I'm not sure that it's me she's hearing. It's as though her mind has become untethered from her body – it's floating somewhere out of reach.

On the way in, we had managed to get a few minutes with the psychiatric reg, a weary, pasty-looking bloke in his thirties called Diarmuid Connolly.

'She's presenting as a trauma survivor – completely dissociated,' Dr Connolly had said, scratching at a patch of reddened skin above his elbow. *Stress-induced eczema* popped into my brain; a hazard of the job, always classifying, taking mental snapshots, making notes about people.

'Which suggests a diagnosis of Acute Stress Disorder – fairly common after witnessing or experiencing a traumatic event' – He pulled down his sleeve and frowned, clearly

9

angry with himself for giving in to the urge to scratch – 'like an assault –'

'What have you given her?'

Niamh had shot me a look and I realized, belatedly, that I'd cut across him as he was in mid-flight.

'Sorry, Dr Connolly, I interrupted you there,' I'd said, as contritely as I could manage. He gave a little nod of forgiveness and launched into a nice little layperson's lesson on Stress Disorders.

'Well, ASD – not to be confused with Autism Spectrum Disorder, yes? Acute Stress Disorder will, if not treated correctly, develop into PTSD. And PTSD is the, eh, first cousin of ASD.'

I'd glanced at Niamh, who was waiting for him to list the symptoms of PTSD – her smiling face a picture of genuine interest. Thankfully, he didn't. I don't think I could have listened to yet more Psychiatry for Beginners and maintained a pretence of politeness. Instead he began scratching the other elbow.

'What's she on?' I'd butted in, worried she'd be too out of it to tell us anything, chafing against his painfully slow delivery. 'What are you treating her with?' He pushed his glasses further up towards his freckled forehead and glanced at his notes.

'Current treatment options would involve pharmacology, CBT and talking therapies. You know – mindfulness, psychotherapy and the like.' He looked over at Niamh, who was still doing her smiling and nodding routine.

'Really?' she breathed.

'I've prescribed Mirtrazapine. She had the first dose this morning.'

'Will it make her sleepy? I need to talk to her. We don't want her drowsy; we need to get information –'

Dr Diarmuid had let my words, and the garbled way in which I delivered them, hang in the air for a beat.

'No, not necessarily, Guard.' He'd stressed the title.

'Will she be able to remember what happened to her? Will she be able to tell us?'

'It's likely that, at some level, she remembers everything. She may even be, right now, on an interior level, reliving everything that happened.'

He'd shrugged – smiled a genuine smile at Niamh. The nodding thing was good. I made a mental note to try it myself.

'So, yes, I think she'll be able to tell you, but it may not happen quickly, or in the way you expect.'

He'd turned completely towards Niamh, effectively blocking me. 'I will be talking to her again later on this afternoon. I'm making an exception –' He'd paused, changed tack. 'You're not going to question her for long, are you? What are Tusla saying? Perhaps you should liaise with them – they are the experts on children's welfare, after all. Why not wait for them? You are –'

Extra emphasis on 'experts' – patronizing asshole –

'No, of course not!' Niamh had assured him, before I let fly. 'Tusla are on board with us talking to her. We're trained SVIs – both of us. We'll be working in conjunction with them, of course. This is a victim interview. It's what we do – don't worry.' She gave a little twitch of her head in my direction. I took the cue.

'Thanks so much for this, Doctor. We'll take it from here – and yep – we'll be working with Tusla. Don't worry, our approach is –' I'd searched for a reassuring phrase. 'We're non-confrontational, we just let them – we give them a platform, that's all, so they can tell their story.'

He'd listened, pausing the exploration of his elbow area with his long, pale fingers.

'Right. And there's a bag of her clothes for you – from the

forensic exam? The CN Specialist set them aside. In case you need them for an investigation?'

'Brilliant,' Niamh had enthused. 'That's so helpful.'

'They're at the nurses' station.'

'I'll pick them up now,' I'd said. 'Thank you Doctor.'

A small burst of hope had risen in my chest. It's all about evidence. A bag containing the clothes she was wearing is a good start. An early interview is also good. And the fact that they've done a forensic exam is even better. What I didn't tell Dr Itchy is how great it is if we can get in early – if we can record the video when it's raw – all of it – both the visible and the invisible injuries. Nail the bastard.

Looking at her now, huddled into a tangle of elbows and knees, it occurs to me that what Dr Itchy hadn't mentioned is that there seems to be more going on – maybe an element of psychosis. She's hearing things; I'm almost certain of it. Something or someone is talking to her. And the other strange thing is that, in a weird way, she seems pleased about something. There's a self-satisfied smirk flickering at the edge of her mouth.

Clarification meetings usually take a couple of hours. I glance at my diary – we've two other interviews scheduled for this afternoon, but there's no way we're going to get to them. I catch Niamh's eye and nod at the diary. She twigs straight away and draws her finger across her neck, miming, *Cancel it?*

I nod.

The girl stiffens in the chair, her eyes darting to the corner where Niamh is sitting.

'It's okay. There's nothing to worry about.'

She goes back into her silence, shrugging it over her shoulders like a coat.

I knew this was a big deal, the second the call came in. My work phone rang before I'd even finished dressing.

I was standing in the kitchen, Katie on one hip, looking at the washing I'd recklessly hung out the day before in a fit of day-off domesticity. Even though it wasn't yet light – it was about half six – I could make out the tights and tops twerking like hip-hop dancers on the sagging line, buffeted by the rain.

My phone vibrated on the kitchen table. Matt picked it up and we swapped over our respective burdens. I noticed, with a little spark of annoyance, that he managed to find time to roll his eyes and sigh. We'd argued earlier for the bazillionth time about dropping Katie to Sylvia's. Same argument every time. Plus, he'd wanted me to take the day off, or at least go in later. Like that's even an option. He said I'm overdoing it – that I'm stressed out. He said he'd look after her, give her breakfast, drop her over. I replied, as I always do, that I'd rather do it myself, that it's not a big deal and that I don't want to disrupt her morning routine. That's what I said, anyway.

As soon as she was removed from my arms, Katie started wailing. I made as if to take her again, but Matt frowned at me, annoyed that I couldn't trust him to sort it. I scowled back; it's important to leave no slight unanswered, covered the phone with my hand and hurried out of the room, closing the door on her crying. The Super of Seskin West DDU – Shane Murtagh himself – was on the line.

'I need you to go straight to Abbot's Hill Hospital this morning. Talk to a suspected rape victim.'

'Right, sir. What's her name? Age?'

'She's fourteen or fifteen – we think her name is Jenny. But she's not talking. And Detective Shaw?'

I wait – it's a bad line and I don't want to talk over him.

'She's on the Adult Psych ward. No beds in the CAMHS unit, and you're going to have your work cut out.'

'How so?'

'She's said nothing, not a word, nada, since she was brought in last night. Some woman dropping a babysitter home found her at the side of the road and brought her to the ED. They reckon she's in shock. We got a call from the clinical nurse specialist, Ciara Quirke. She flagged it up. You two – go easy, but still, see what you can get out of her.'

He paused, allowing time to hear an extra-loud yell from Katie.

'How old is she now? Must be coming up to the year, yeah?'

'Haha, thanks for that, sir, she's two and a half, actually – hence the tantrum.'

'Right, well, grand. Work will be a nice break for you so. Heh heh! Bye now.' That was a long conversation for him. The Super isn't known for his chat.

I mouthed *got to go* and left Matt holding a roaring Katie. He nodded – the pissed-off nod rather than the friendly one.

The deal is that one of us waits until Sylvia comes to the house to mind Katie, unless I drop her up myself. It's stupid, but I have this thing about other people driving my daughter; I just can't allow anyone to do it. It has to be me or, at a push, Matt. I've been like this since she was born, but it's got much worse since I went back to work full-time, six months ago. Face it – I think, grabbing my jacket and keys; it started long before that. The anxieties had multiplied – breeding like bacteria in a Petri dish – since I came home from hospital with our new baby, but they'd been lurking below the surface for years.

I think of them – the obsessions, the anxious thoughts – wriggling and twisting like maggots at the heart of a shiny apple. They're everywhere. And since I had Katie, it's like they're in overdrive. Every day is a struggle to survive; every room is crammed full of risk. An innocent cup of coffee could scald that soft pink skin beyond recognition, the string of a blind or a poorly positioned cot mobile is a hangman's noose. The stairs are worse than the Cliffs of Moher. Even a pillow is a lethal weapon. I never stop worrying. It's like if I worry about it, it won't happen.

The car judders as I try to take the hill in third, and I force myself to slow down – calm down. I tell myself it's because of the training. In college we saw medical reports that would put the fear of God in you: car crashes and farm accidents, electrocution from overhead power cables and tragic accidents in the most domestic and peaceful of settings. But at night I still lie awake worrying about the risks to come – the lifetime of risks lining up, waiting to catch hold of Katie and tear my life asunder.

She's nearly three – I'll have to get over myself soon. Matt goes along with it, against his better judgement. He's good that way, or at least he was. But he's fed up with it now. It limits us – it limits her. And I know he's judging me.

Now, in this bleak interview room in Abbot's Hill, I look down at the protocol form again, at the bare facts I'm due to record: name, date of birth, family, school, hobbies – the tent pegs to which a life is tethered. I've written one word – Jenny. How flimsy it looks on a piece of A4. How amazing it is that a child survives until fourteen. It seems to me to be against overwhelming odds.

I smooth the page and glance up, trying to make eye contact.

'Do you have any hobbies, Jenny? Can you talk a little bit about what kind of thing do you like to do in your free time?' She doesn't respond. The 'hobbies' section remains empty, and it looks ridiculous in the face of her – I would say, *grief*? Pain? I try to make eye contact. 'Hobbies, Jen?'

She says nothing. It's like she's waiting for something. Or someone. Dark, wavy hair screens her face and she sits hunched in the chair with her knees drawn up, body language screaming *leave me alone*. I bend in towards her and she flinches. I need to find some way to get her talking.

Tell. Explain. Describe. The holy trinity of open-ended questioning which we pursue in our quest for ABE – achieving best evidence.

'Tell me how you're feeling now.' I glance over at Niamh, who is – as expected – rolling her eyes. It's one of her pet hates, the 'tell me how you're feeling' question. But you can't expect words to work miracles, I tell her. Words are just words, tools to help us get inside. If you want to know how someone is feeling, ask them how they're feeling. I don't have time for Niamh's friendly-chat technique. Just ask the question.

The girl says nothing.

'How about family? Could you tell me a little bit about your family? Who's at home?' The silence lengthens.

Though she's a bit old for it, I decide to try the three houses. I rummage in my bag and take out the pad and some markers. Behind her, Niamh gives a thumbs-up.

'So Jenny, we're going to try something different, okay?' I slide the pad across the desk towards her. 'This is something I do with kids all the time. I want you to draw three houses. Use the whole page, because you'll need space to write in them.' I place markers on the pad.

'You draw three houses; one of them is called the House of Worries, okay? And inside that one, you write down all the things that are worrying you – anything at all.' She's watching now, and at least she's stopped muttering. 'Go on, it's easy. Just a box for a house?' I take the lid off one of the markers and actually put it in her hand, pretending she's about to comply. 'Then you draw the other two houses – the House of Good Things and the House of Dreams. I'm not going to explain them to you – not going to insult your intelligence, okay?'

She sits there with the pen exactly where I placed it, staring at the blank page, curved into a comma of weary despair. The clock on the wall ticks on and still the silence stretches. Niamh raises her eyebrows and shrugs. Then, just when I'm about to give up, Jenny takes the pad on to her lap, sits back and starts to draw.

3. Jenny

I draw the tower and the forest and it's good because she goes over to talk to Niamh for ages and they whisper and Niamh does more texting. The tower is black, and I draw the bricks and the small window at the top and I don't think about what's inside. Shut up, I'm not saying. I'm only drawing, and it will all stay inside. So, then I start on the border of dark green leaves. The markers she gave me are thick so you can't get detailed lines, but if I turn it a bit sideways and use only the tip, I can get the leaves curling and follow their twists and turns. Round and round, I go right to the edge because the hedge is more like a castle wall sweeping up and up into a tall arch. I just want to keep drawing the leaves for ever. I don't draw her dumb house.

And she comes back then and goes, 'Oh wow, a tower, like for a princess, in the fairy tales. I like it. Who lives there?'

And then it goes quiet again, except for more of the ticks, and I start to draw the sea, just for a change. The sea is below the tower and I'm drawing the waves and they are easy to draw because you just go round and round, following the same lines, and it looks like swirly sea.

'Who lives in that tower, Jenny? Hmm?' she says, and I think *haha, wouldn't you like to know, dumb bitch?* Then she goes back over to Niamh and I pretend that I'm here all alone and I can't hear them with their secret whispering.

She comes back over and bends low, trying to catch my eye and do the teacher 'let's be honest, here' thing where they make you look them in the eye. 'So, that's the tower?' she says, as if I've just explained it and as if we're mates. 'And there's the sea? Fantastic. Is this the tower of good things, Jenny?'

Dumb dumb dumb. I want to say that, but I'm not opening my mouth. I want to say *look, does it look like good things happen there, bitch?* I look at the picture and I think about the girl inside. Ssh, shut it. I am not saying it out loud. Sometimes I'm the girl in the tower and sometimes I'm the girl looking out her window at the girl in the tower. And when that happens, I hate it because I know what she's telling me, even though she says nothing. I know that he's in there with her and nobody can see him. They can only see her face and she's a princess, so she keeps her smiling face on. Like the ones they'd put on a stamp.

She's telling me that he's crouching down where no one can catch him and no one can see him. And he's hurting her, but he tells her he loves her and she's a princess. But his fingers are hurting her and he bites like a wolf.

And back then – once upon a time – I loved the princess. I was the girl who was going to rescue her.

4. Laura

The notes say that the girl has a mother, younger half-brother and stepfather. Her dad died some years ago. I wonder how much she took in. She was eight; old enough to understand the gravity of her loss, to realize that dead means dead and that it's permanent. Old enough to have a history, to have regrets, to feel guilty or ashamed for the times when she acted up or behaved badly. Yet, at eight, she may not have understood the complexities of family relationships. There could be guilt, pain, grief, regret – any amount of the feelings which death stirs up – whirling about in her subconscious.

She's still drawing intently and, as I watch her, my thoughts drift back to Mum and my own experience of a parent dying. Mum's on my mind so much at the moment anyway, I didn't need this. Yesterday was the anniversary – fifteen years. I didn't do anything to mark it, and Matt didn't remember. Cian didn't text or contact me either, and it's not that I felt he should have – I didn't contact him – but I felt sort of hurt. Which is stupid when you think of it, because he'd have just as much right to feel hurt too. And Dad – he's been completely indifferent to our wellbeing since he walked out – so it's no surprise that he doesn't give a shit either. You're meant to be over it after fifteen years, aren't you? I know Matt thinks so. I am over it. The pain has become an ache, a lacking feeling – like when you're hungry but you don't know what you want to eat. Sometimes it seems like she's been gone for ever; other times I can't believe that she's actually dead. And yes, I still very occasionally go as if to ring or text her. That cliché as well.

After I had Katie, Mum began to appear as a ghost-grandmother at my shoulder. God – she would have adored her! On good days I summon her up and imagine her laughter and it's all fine. I can accept it. But other days I miss her and I just wish she was here and that she could meet her granddaughter.

Granny Justy – Matt's mum, Justina – and his dad, Dermot, they're only up the road. But Justina Thompson, Senior Partner in Stonehouse Flynn Mortimer, one of Dublin's top three law firms, is not exactly a hands-on granny. They're always off on golf trips anyway.

Funnily enough, one of my strongest memories of Mum is of the day Dad left, when she came back into the house after another doorstep grown-up *talk*. She broke into 'Sisters are Doing it for Themselves' and swept me off the stairs, where I'd been sitting earwigging, and danced us both into the kitchen.

'It's just us now, Lauramora; you, me and Cian. And we're going to be all right – better than all right. We're going to be great.'

And we were. I don't know how she did it; she never showed any weakness, there were no tears and no regrets – or none that she let us see anyway. With Dad gone, the house calmed down. There was no yelling or fighting, none of the battles which had become the wallpaper of our lives.

The 'chocolate breakfasts' (a trick to get Cian up in the mornings), the Shaw Team Talks – the classic Mum energy and good humour. How did she do it? I wish I was more like her – that I had her sense of fun.

She worked full-time at the bank, somehow paying the

mortgage and putting us through school and college. She was never sick – until she was really sick. Okay, we didn't get holidays abroad or expensive gear, but she'd make sure we got to go on school trips and do whatever the other kids were doing. How did she manage the finances? Dad was no help to her at all. After that doorstep 'talk', he and his new girlfriend moved to Cork, where they went on to have three kids together.

I see them on Facebook – my half-siblings. Photos of them all rosy-cheeked and grinning with their arms around each other at barbecues and house parties. The girls – Alva and Áine – they must be in their twenties by now and Seán a couple of years older. That's another unhealthy pastime – checking Dad's Wonderful Second Family on social media. I started doing it when I was in college – at a time when I was already pretty low. I'd pore over Charlie's feed, studying the faces of the twins, wondering what magic they had to make Dad stay. They obviously didn't want for anything anyway – there were photos of horseriding and Communion parties, bouncy castles and rollerblading. And, in the corner of the selfies, Charlie with her swishy ponytail and pert boobs.

Maybe Mum resented him and his new life but, if she did, she never let us see. She caught me trolling the photos once and laughed at my expression.

'Ah, love – she's welcome to him!' She nodded at the photo. 'And in fairness, she put manners on him, didn't she?'

Mum had opened a savings account for school fees with a nest egg her own dad had left her – this even before Dad left. All she asked was that we kept up in class and worked hard. 'I'm not doing this so youse can piss away my hard-earned cash,' was a well-worn phrase. 'I'm investing in my future.' Poor Mum. She never got to cash in that investment.

When I look to the future with Katie – when I start to

think about her going to playschool and then 'big' school, and secondary, and doing the Junior and Leaving Certs and college – I get overwhelmed. It's too much – emotionally, financially – in every way. The only way I keep on going is not to think too far ahead.

A thought rises up, suddenly, along with a surge of guilt; I didn't say goodbye to Katie – I should have said goodbye. She might have had a complete meltdown when she realized I'd gone. And Matt looked so pissed off – what if he loses his temper with her? I've never heard him shout at her, but what if today is the day? I close my eyes and breathe – repeat the mantra: *These are just thoughts. They're not real. Do your job.*

I catch Niamh's eye; her head is cocked to one side and she's giving me the wtf look. She's right, I'm all over the place, lacking concentration and not paying attention to what's in front of me. Between the anniversary and Katie screaming her head off this morning, my focus is majorly disrupted.

Jenny's still working on the first picture. She's now doing a frame of dark leaves all around the edges of the page. I change tack.

'What school are you in?' She doesn't answer, but I write 'Abbot's Field High School?' on the page, because most of the local kids go there. There's a big girls' convent school quite near where she lives, about two miles outside Clonchapel, but I'd be surprised if that's where she goes.

'I went to Abbot's Field,' I say. 'Is that where you are? Is Miss Jackson still there?' She doesn't reply and, out of the corner of my eye, I see Niamh smirking.

'Probably not. Sure I'm ancient!' I laugh. Jenny doesn't join in. 'Do you like art, Jenny?' I gesture towards her picture. 'The waves are good. You're good. Are you doing it for Junior Cert?'

The only sound is her wrist moving across the page as she draws the waves. She pauses to change pens and starts drawing thick black lines on the body of the tower, denoting brickwork. Niamh shifts in her seat and it creaks. The clock ticks.

I watch her and my mind wanders as before, probing for painful anxieties the way your tongue probes a niggly tooth. I wish I'd talked to Mum. I wish I'd been a better daughter – closer. Sometimes when I think about it, it seems like there were endless opportunities to tell her, to be honest with her. We could have spoken frankly, honestly. Perhaps she'd have advised me; how would I know the breadth of her life experience if I never gave her the opportunity to tell me? Or perhaps she wouldn't have had the same experience, but now, now I think, why didn't I talk to her? Would it have killed me to give her the opportunity to comfort me – to be with me in what I was going through?

Suddenly, Jenny leaps up as if stung, her whole body shaking. Her hands grip fistfuls of dark hair and her face contorts into a scream. The papers and markers scatter on to the floor. I jump up, too, knocking my chair over in the process. Niamh is on her feet straight away, stepping in between us, arms wide.

'It's okay, it's okay,' she says, like she's calming a nervous animal. 'C'mere to me – here.' Her arms sweep inwards, clasping the girl into the part-restraint part-hug embrace which is her speciality. 'You're grand. There's nothing to be frightened of, okay?'

And I could kiss Niamh, with her mad bogger accent and her mad hugs, because Jenny allows it. She stands with her head resting on Niamh's shoulder, arms bolted to her sides, eyes closed. It's the calmest she's looked since we started.

Niamh hugs her and pats her back, making soothing

noises as she steers her towards the window. She keeps one hand on the girl's shoulder and sweeps the hair back off her face with the other.

'Ah, you poor mite!' she says. 'Sure, maybe you need five minutes? And a bit of air? Laura, Jaysus! Give her five minutes, would you?' I nod.

'It's almost eleven – time for a break anyway,' I say, heading towards the door. The best plan now is for me to get out of the room, hand over to Niamh for a few minutes.

'I'll get us some drinks.'

5. Laura

At the vending machine, I try to work out what prompted the outburst. I didn't see it coming. She'd been drawing – doing the brickwork on the tower. I think back to what I'd asked her about – school, if she liked art, and before that I'd asked about family. I'm annoyed with myself. I'd allowed her silence to continue so I could wallow in my own thoughts and give voice to my own anxieties, rather than using it as a listening tool – making it an active silence. In the early days of therapy, Sam warned me about this. Though he understood my career choice – applauded it, even – he cautioned that, because of my own baggage, I've to be doubly aware of countertransference.

'Don't get their pain tangled up with yours, Laura. You're going to have to be able to hear them clearly – to draw out their stories as though you're unravelling a – a knitted scarf or something. But the moment you drift into your own memories, your own pain – you'll be lost.'

I must contact him, actually. Suddenly I realize just how much I'd value an hour in Sam's quiet study, talking while the dust motes drift and settle. Talk therapy with a kindly psychotherapist who sits there twinkling at you like a wise barn owl can't be beaten – it'd probably help ease things between me and Matt, too. I make a mental note (yet another), to make an appointment.

The SVI training was good. We learned strategies for interviewing victims of all ages – victims of rape and trafficking, domestic abuse survivors and kids suffering from chronic neglect and trauma. We learned in workshops and role plays how to approach from a trauma-sensitive angle. I dreaded the role plays – though I'd worked out a way of keeping myself slightly out of it by that stage. Not out of it in a druggy way – just sort of separate – apart. No way was I going to risk having a panic attack, like I had in training college. The first one. The one that made me think I'd lost my mind.

It must have been October or November – in the first term, anyway – and we were taking it in turns to be Victim and Garda. It wasn't even my turn. I was watching Fiona. She'd been paired with David, and he was good, too, fully committed to the role. I can't remember what triggered it – I just remember being completely focussed on Fiona – her acting was amazing. And her body language – she walked to the chair as though picking her way through shards of glass, holding herself in case she fell apart. I believed her – she was brittle and defensive, her voice high and shaky, like a child's. I bought it – the whole thing. I forgot we were in a classroom still fuggy with the smell of break-time coffees. I just listened; her soft voice stumbled in halting sentences, telling what happened. All other sounds fell away, and it was as though the light changed – and a pale mist fell across my field of vision.

I can't remember; I only know what they told me afterwards. Which was I stood up, and all my stuff, my pens and notes and books, they fell to the floor. I didn't hear them. I left the room. I walked past the reception, out the main door of the building and into the car park. I've no recollection of it.

They found me a couple of minutes later on the ground there – with a graze on my cheek and a bruised shoulder. They thought I'd been knocked down, but I hadn't. I don't remember what happened – I think I just walked until I fell down. I simply had to leave the room before I heard any more of Fiona's story. I can't remember anything else, just silence and the mist.

Our tutor – Mary – diagnosed a panic attack. 'I have to note it,' she said. 'These things are important.'

'Does it mean I can't finish my training?'

'No – of course not. Not necessarily. But you need to find someone to talk to – get some counselling. And you'll need to look out for yourself, all right? When you're on the job – peer support – all that stuff is really important.'

I promised I would. When I was home for Christmas, I told Mum I was suffering from 'college stress' and that the tutor wanted me to get some counselling.

'Definitely you should do that, love,' she'd said. 'And you can talk to me any time – you know that, don't you?'

She'd swept me into a hug then, stroking my hair.

'You're not yourself, are you? What's up?'

I'd hugged her back – resisting the urge to sob into her soft woolly jumper and tell her the whole story – then extricated myself from the embrace.

'It's just pressure of exams and stuff, Mum.'

She paid for the sessions with Sam, never prying – never looking for payback. And later, when I was doing the SVI training – with actors playing the roles – I made sure I never let my guard down. I can do that – now.

Through the glass at the top of the door, I watch Niamh in action. You've got to find an 'in' early in the process – something they want to talk about, something they care about – this is her genius area. She has a sixth sense for finding the 'in'.

I think back to little Robbie Elliot – a five-year-old we worked with a few months ago, just after I came back. He was so gorgeous – all curly dark hair and big brown eyes. I was lead on his case and we played Lego together as part of the clarification process, building rapport, becoming buddies. After the disclosure – physical and verbal abuse by the father, neglect and verbal abuse by the mother – we recorded the interview and sent it to the investigating team. Social services and Tusla were contacted and the plan was that Dad would be prosecuted and some work would be done to help Mum, to give her the parenting skills and the assistance she needed.

Then phone calls started coming in saying that Robbie wanted to talk to 'Lowa'; he had more things to tell. When he arrived in the unit, he ran straight over and grabbed my hand, dragging me over to the Lego. Turns out the afternoons he'd spent playing with me had been the high points of Robbie's five years. He'd just gone and invented a whole load of reasons to come back to the unit to get access to the giant box of plastic bricks.

'I told you not to keep making those fecking Lego castles with him!' was Niamh's comment. 'He's obsessed with them.'

Niamh's brilliant. She's such a natural. I knew she'd be great from the first day she appeared in the unit. She tripped over the frayed bit of carpet in the doorway, did a little stumble into the filing cabinet and just managed to stop herself from falling headfirst into the central workstation by grabbing the nearest chair – which, if I remember rightly, contained a pursed-lipped Edel – the self-described 'longest-serving SVI on the team'. Edel bristled. Undeterred, Niamh patted Edel's bony knee, then her skeleton-thin shoulder, adjusted her cross-body bag, which had turned into more of a cross-throat bag, and tugged her shirt back in place.

'Lap dance is extra,' she grinned, sticking out her hand to shake. 'Niamh Darmody. Pleased to meet ye.'

I was her mentor, but we quickly became friends – Niamh needed very little mentoring. Kids open up to her really quickly – she makes them laugh, or slags herself, or comes out with yet another of her bogger stories and, before you know it, they're best buddies. Same thing with the team – she can take a slagging as well as dish it out. She wears her intelligence lightly, does Niamh. She followed me into the DDU as soon as she could and was buckshee for a year or two. But while I was off on maternity leave, she went for the detective position that came up – and got it. Maybe it's from the camogie or, I don't know, her position in the family, but she's a team player and that makes people warm to her.

She's said that I overthink it, and maybe that's true – I do plan the conversations. I use the tools like the Three Houses or the magic-wand question – anything designed to get them talking. I listen. I wait. It's like a game of chess; your move sets up theirs. Question, response, question, response – we track our way across the floor until we get to the end and we have a full story all ready to record.

But now, with Jenny, it's like an awkward samba rather than a graceful progression across the floor. I question. She takes a step back. I wait. She moves sideways. She watches. She judges. She pushes back against me. Why do I feel like I'm the one being moved across the chessboard? How come she's making eye contact now – with Niamh? They're standing side by side at the window, talking about something.

When I come back in, I see that the clock has been taken down. It's propped against the wall and the batteries are sitting upright like saltshakers on the desk. Niamh catches my eye and gives a little 'it's all grand' nod. I'm annoyed with myself that I hadn't copped on about the clock. That should have been easy to spot. I offer the three cans and Jenny takes one.

'Are you feeling better, Jenny?' I move back to the desk and sit down, literally trying to give her some space. Jenny busies herself opening the can, saying nothing.

'I sorted everything, didn't I, chicken?' Niamh takes a massive slurp of her Coke, then sets it on the window ledge. 'I told her my motto.'

'Oh yeah?' I say, wondering which of Niamh's inappropriate sayings that might be. There's more silence, except for Niamh's next swig of Coke.

'Yeah,' says Niamh, 'it's shit now, but it's gonna be grand,' she burps. 'That covers everything.'

Jenny's looking down, and there's that long fringe hiding her face, but I think I see the tiniest curve of a smile at the edge of her mouth.

'Okay,' I say, 'we should get back to our chat, Jenny, shouldn't we?' I can hear the sickly-sweet counsellor tone in my voice and I feel another jab of anger at myself. I hate those instructions masquerading as rhetorical questions: we'd better do this, hadn't we?; we must get on with our work, mustn't we? Remember how the bullshit detector is on high alert when you're that age, Laura? Don't bullshit her. It's not a chat any more.

'Jenny, how about we start with something easy? Tell me a bit about your friends, okay?' She's drinking her 7Up with one arm folded protectively across her stomach and she's swaying ever so slightly from side to side. It's a self-comforting gesture, rocking the way you'd rock a baby.

'Do you have friends you can talk to – when things get you down?' I sift through my teenage memories, trying to find something we'd have in common. At fourteen, I wasn't allowed in town and the new Dundrum Centre hadn't been finished. We hung around in Bushy Park or the shops up at the village. I remember, suddenly, that was the year our team made it to the hockey finals. We'd matches most Saturdays, and we'd go to each other's houses for team-bonding nights.

So I fill the silence for a while. I tell Jenny about my best friend, Christina. Loud and posh, Christina arrived in the middle of First Year from a private primary school, which didn't endear her to anyone. Even her name set off sniggers – *Christinaah* was how she introduced herself. But straight away Christina volunteered for the job of goalie, a position nobody wanted. I tell Jenny how fearless she was. How she went from being 'stuck-up Christinaah' to the girl who saved five shots on goal in the penalty shoot-out. I feel rather than see Jenny listening, and it's good, but then I realize that, actually, I'm telling myself something. I hear myself say, 'God, she was fearless. She literally stepped in front of the ball. She didn't let fear get the better of her, you know? She faced it down.'

In the silence that follows, I think about the words I've just said. When I was having therapy, Sam used to get me to tell my dreams and nightmares aloud. 'It's all there, in your words,' he'd say. 'Say it aloud so you understand what your subconscious is telling you.' It takes a few moments to realize that I'm not only remembering an old schoolfriend, I'm telling myself to face down my fears. Or perhaps there's a bit of both.

What I wonder now, after everything that's happened, is if that shift was where it began. In the silence of those first hours with Jenny, is that where the lines started to blur? When, instead of seeing her, I began to see me. Her silences became my silences. Both of us waiting.

And so I talk on about Christina. How much fun she was and the outrageous things she said and did. At a time when I was shy and timid, Christina's unashamed loudness held me in thrall. The spectre of Christina strides into the room with us, padded up in her goalie gear, telling me to face my fears and – somehow – finally, unlocking Jenny's voice.

'Amy – she's my friend.'

Her voice is low and the tone is flat but, even so, it's so unexpected I can't help myself – I flinch at the sound. She clamps her mouth shut, as if speaking took her by surprise, too. Niamh literally rolls up her sleeves in the background.

'That's great. Can you tell me a bit more about Amy?' I say, as gently as I can. 'What's she like?'

'Amy's –'

She stops and I will myself to stay quiet, not to ask another question, to wait.

'One time, we nearly went to this party. Philip – a guy in our year. It was in a yacht club.'

'But you didn't go?' She shakes her head and bundles her limbs together, rests her head on her knees. It's like a door closing.

'Can you tell me –'

'That's not the world I live in,' she says, her voice muffled by her knees.

'Jenny?' I lean in towards her, trying – and failing again – to make eye contact, speaking to the top of her head. 'Tell me about your world.'

'There's only him.'

'Who do you mean?'

She doesn't answer.

'Okay, can you describe your world? What's your world like, Jenny?'

There's another long pause, during which she inhales as if she's about to speak, her body tipping forward imperceptibly towards me, only to sit back and close her mouth. Her eyes flit about; she's listening to the unseen speaker. I glance at Niamh to see if she's noticed. She nods.

'Not my world. His. Mum is sick. So there's only him. It's all ruled by him. She's in bed most days or she might watch TV. She sleeps a lot.'

'Your mum's sick? I'm sorry to hear that. It must be difficult, worrying for you. Are you worried about your mum?' She's gone back to the picture and started going over and over the border of leaves she drew earlier, blackening them until the page is crispy and crumpled.

'Jenny – who do you mean when you say "him"? You said, "It's all ruled by him". Who do you mean?'

She ignores me – taking a different marker and starting on the archway.

'Yeah, we were invited to Philip's party. But he wouldn't let me go and Amy's mum didn't want her going on her own. So I wrecked it for both of us.'

'And you think you wrecked it for Amy? Did Amy think you wrecked it?'

I wait a bit. But she's disappeared into her thoughts again. She picks up her can and takes a sip.

'So that's your friend Amy. Good. But I'd like to know a bit more about "him". Who wouldn't let you go to the party? Can you tell me?'

I'm gabbling, flinging random questions at her like confetti. Behind her, Niamh mimes a smoothing action, her expression puzzled. I take a breath, make myself hold it. But I'm frustrated – the moment's gone. She's clammed up again.

'Jenny, I need you to keep talking, okay? Tell me how you're feeling.'

Niamh opens her palms upwards and gives a little shrug, like she's saying, *What? Again?*

6. Jenny

Keep it shut up tight, dumb bitch. She shouldn't ask about the party because now all I hear in my head is *we'll have our own party, won't we?* And that means another time, and so I looked at the tower and this time I'm the girl in the tower. I pray I'll escape, but he keeps me there. But that is over. Hah, that is over, that's over. I am pressing my teeth down tight and it's keeping my tongue squashed. And Niamh squashed it all in in in with her squashy hug and it feels okay because no truth will come out and no lies will come out. Poor Laura, waiting, waiting.

She's given me a can of 7Up and I fiddle with the ring pull so I can think, and they talk a bit but I can't hear what they're saying. I draw the dark leaves all around, hidden. And then Laura is back with her questions. They go on and on. And you think that it's easy to shut up say nothing, dumb bitch. But it's not.

And I think that maybe I will – or maybe I will not talk to her. Talk and tell. *Tell Me a Story*, that's a book we had at home. If it's a story, it's not difficult. You can choose what you show and what you hide when you tell a story. It's not difficult. You can choose to make it tumbling little words, like teddies jumping over each other. Not the jagged, sharp ones that make you bleed.

And my voice was so croaky and, haha, she nearly fell off her chair when I started to talk.

'Just a story.' A little bit of Laura's make-up is slipping below her eye, like she rubbed it. But she doesn't know and she doesn't fix it. She does a shiny 'encourage the child' smile.

'I like stories.'

It's like I gave her a present. Get a life, Laura, and I want to say *dumb bitch* but a little bit of me likes her because she is trying so hard and because she messed up her eye make-up. Amy and I tried to do the flicks with eyeliner, and it's really hard. You can do one eye but the other is not as easy. But stories are hard, too, especially if they are too tangled up, and so I say nothing and the words go round and round, round and round inside.

And a lot of time happens because next she says tell me something you don't like to do and I think *haha, that is a long list*. Think you're so smart, bitch? Shut up shut up. She's not tricking me with that one.

'Okay,' she says with her shoulders shrugging and her two palms up. 'You're the boss, Jenny. You spoke about Amy. That was good. But you can start wherever you like. You came in here yesterday, so how about you start there? Tell me everything that happened yesterday. Start with yesterday.'

And that's so funny, and I think *oh thank you, Dad, you love that song*.

'That's by The Beatles,' I say. 'My dad loved them. He said there's a Beatles song for everything.'

She's listening now like those spaniels, the ones that king liked – the floppy-ears ones. Her head's on one side and it's something you can almost touch, the intensity of her listening. It's freaking me out. It comes off her like waves of heat, and it smells. It smells of the pink deodorant. Be careful.

'Be careful of the king's dog.'

'Jenny? Let's talk a bit more about your dad, yes? Tell me some more about him.'

I can do that, Laura. I can do that easy peasy.

'One morning, it was lashing rain and the wind was mad and Dad was singing "Fixing a Hole". That's the song for if

36

you're fixing something. And then he –' I stop. She lifts her head, opens her big eyes wider. That's when I see the formula. They can't trip you up with maths. But still, be careful. So I say –

'If A equals Stormy morning and B equals Windswept rooftop and C equals Broken bracket on rooftop and D equals Dad without a safety harness, what is the sum of A to D?' She doesn't answer. I mean, I think she's worked it out all right, but she doesn't answer.

'I'll tell you,' I say, to help her – though she's meant to be helping me.

'A plus B plus C plus D equal DD. Dead Dad. He died.'

Her ears are still pricked up like a puppy's and she's doing a lot of smiling – the serious smiling, not the happy one. The 'oh dear poor you' smile, and I hate it. They say be careful what you wish for, don't they? Maybe she's wishing I wasn't talking any more. Maybe she thinks I'm a dumb bitch, too. Shut up, you dumb cow. You can shut up now. Nobody cares. But Laura smiles some more, even a bit with her eyes, and she says, 'Go on.' And she doesn't say *dumb bitch*.

'I'm very sorry to hear that, Jenny. When was that? How long ago?'

But that could be a trick. She probably has all that stuff written down. There's a big, thick file on her desk underneath the clock. I can see it. It's probably full of stuff about me. I hold up five and one on my fingers. There's a brown line under my nail, in the letter C bit. It looks dirty.

'So your dad was very important to you, I can see that. He could go in the House of Good Things.' She points to the page, to my picture of the tower. 'Or we could make it the Tower of Good Things?' And I go, 'No!' and maybe I shout, but how dumb can you be?

'Bad things happen in the tower,' I say, and I shut my mouth tight then because it might get out. And then she does loads of stuff like 'What bad things? What do you mean, bad things, is there anything you want to tell me?' Of course she does, dumb bitch.

'Okay, that's fine, Jenny,' she says. 'Park that for now, yes? Let's go back to talking. Just talking. How about you talk about a normal day for you? Let's say you're going to school, start with that?'

I'm looking at my hands – the brown bit is gone, I sucked it till it went away. My fists are closing and opening, like flowers. I see a smudge of black on my knuckle. I lick that away, too.

'There's a fancy stove in the kitchen. Stuart lights it every morning.' If the stove is lit, Mum might get up. Sometimes, anyway.

'Who's Stuart?'

Wait. Boom!

Wait. Boom!

I've never heard a gunshot, not a real one. But when I wait there's a beat of silence and in the silence I hear it – Boom! The kill shot.

'Mum's husband. Mr Perfect.'

Boom! Bang! You're dead.

'Okay,' she says slowly slowly, because she's doing her thinking. 'Stuart, right? Your stepfather?' And I'm not saying *right* because no way – there's no way he can have the 'father' word. Our father who art in heaven blah blah blah blah blah.

'So Stuart lights the stove and then what happens? Tell me about it – a typical day?' And I want to say it, *there's no typical day, there's just days when it's bad and days when it's really bad. And you wake up and you wish you didn't.*

'One time, I was wearing this old shirt that was Dad's. And Stuart goes – "What are you wearing that for?"'

And right away, I knew I'd made a mistake. Dumb, dumb, dumb. He lit the firelighter and he held it in his bare hands, even though it was on fire. Then he put it in the stove, really carefully. And when I saw how carefully he did it, I got more worried. That's bad. Laura's still waiting.

'Go on,' she says.

'Yeah, well, I wanted to say *because it belonged to Dad, who I still miss every day*. But I didn't say that. That'd be suicide.'

I kept those words inside my mouth, I swallowed them down quickly – makes it easier. Though they were like sharp pebbles and they hurt. And I hear Niamh scribble then, like a crazy rat. And Laura nods.

'Then?'

'Then he got up and stood in front of me and his big, giant, meaty hands were scrunching and squeezing his hips.'

There were smudges of soot across his knuckles and his fingers were the claws of a T-Rex. They were twitching and reaching. They could tear the flesh from your body.

'So I told him – "Oh, you know, it's just an old shirt that was lying around," but he goes, "No, take it off now."'

And he stepped closer. And he moved as if to touch me. I tried to go out the door, but he was blocking it, and he said it again – *take it off now*. I lifted it up and I closed my eyes like it would stop him looking. And I felt the cold air on my stomach, and he stared at me: fox – rabbit. He held out his hand to take it like the way the teachers do with chewing gum, like they hate you. And he stuffed it in the bin.

'And?' says Laura.

Dumb bitch.

And Karl was looking really scared. Karl's always sitting, just watching. He was at the kitchen table. He stopped eating his Rice Krispies and he stirred the spoon round and round in the bowl, round and round, with this small, grating sound.

'He put it in the bin.'

And Karl was staring at me; his eyes were huge. He stirred

two more circles in his Rice Krispies. I weighed it up. It wasn't worth it.

'And then?'

And now I have to stand up – I feel like I'm not breathing. I jump up quickly and my chair knocks against hers. And she jumps. And it makes me jump. I didn't do it on purpose. Maybe I should say that? But I don't. Niamh is on the edge of her seat, too, getting ready to hug me again. I walk over to the window and lean my forehead against the cool glass. I imagine the cold paralysing my thoughts, freezing them into jagged icicles. I'd like that. You can stab someone to death with an icicle and they die and there's no murder weapon left because it melts. I know that.

'How did you feel when Stuart put your dad's shirt in the bin, Jenny?'

She waits again. I have to admit, she's pretty patient. She must do it all day, sit there, waiting for people to tell her stuff. But, seriously, she's worried about the shirt? I sigh.

'It was just an old shirt.'

'But it meant something to you, didn't it? It meant a lot to you.' I wait. It's very quiet and I can't even hear the voice. And then I say:

'I felt –'

'Yes?'

She sits forward in her chair and her dark hair swings forward eagerly, as if even her hair wants to join in the chat. She tucks it back behind her ear. I turn from the window and walk slowly back to the chair. She follows me with her eyes. And the words are coming fast now, hissing like snakes. *Don't tell her don't tell her don't tell her.*

'I felt –' a word pops into my head – *hate*. I see it hanging there in the air, written in blood; you know, those horror letters from old movies. HATE.

'I felt like –'

'Yes?'

It's still just hanging there, and there's blood blobbing down off it in slow, heavy drops. I count while the blood drips. Drip. One. Drip. Two. Drip. Three. Be careful.

'I wished we had rubber gloves, so I could get it out of the bin.'

She sits back. Disappointed, but hiding it well. Hah! Haha! You tricked her.

But I'm bored with that. I'm not thinking about the shirt. I'm thinking about blood. I'm thinking that blood is redder than you think, and much thicker. It's shiny, too, but not for long. After a while, it goes brown, then black. And if enough of it spills out of you, you die. That's what happened to George Washington. He had a cold. And his doctors were doing bloodletting on him. They let out too much blood and he went into shock. Then he died.

'Jenny?' Laura's saying. 'You were telling me about your stepfather?' I wasn't, though. Bitch should listen, but I know she's playing games inside my head. And so I say nothing for a long, long time and the ticks carry on for ages. And even the voice is quiet. Laura drops it.

This is easy. I can do it.

7. Laura

She didn't fall for that line, and I'm kind of glad. I'd think less of her if it'd been that easy. She sits with one leg tucked underneath her, hiding behind the dark hair, glancing out every now and again as if to check how it's going down. It's strange – I can't shake the feeling that she's taking the lead – she's choosing where we go. It's like she's spinning gossamer strands and I have to follow them. But I should be leading the way – I'm meant to be shining a light so she can tell me what's in the dark corners. It's what I'm trained to do. I know Niamh will be on at me later – I can see her noticing everything – and I'm already justifying myself. Maybe I'm just tired, out of sync. I hate fighting with Matt – every time it happens, I feel like I've failed, like I've bored another hole into our little rowboat. And it's about Mum, too – the anniversary. Why should it matter? A date is just a random date. But it does.

When Mum died, I was twenty-two. I lost the mum you're aware of when you're twenty-two, the mum of your childhood memories – making you wash your hands and tidy your room. The mum of your teenage years, nagging you out of bed, turning off the TV and forcing you to get on with your studying, giving out to you when she catches you drinking, prying you for information – always trying to be a part of your life. And I thought I was fine – that I didn't need *that* Mum any more. Sure, of course I loved her to bits. But I was an adult. I was fine. I had my career, my friends – everything was under control. Her work was done.

When she died, everyone told me how lucky I was and how lucky she was, even though it was desperate that she died so young. But still, wasn't it great that she lived to see me graduate? And bloody hell, how proud she was when I got the Commissioner's medal! She told everyone. Like everyone – her bank pals, the woman in the post office, Brenda in the café, her hairdresser – everyone. I'd be going in to buy a paper and some random stranger would congratulate me on the medal. You'd think I'd been awarded the Nobel Prize.

But as the years pass and now, as Katie develops and learns new things every second day and I find new things to love about her, it adds a new something to the list of things Mum will never see.

I wasn't even there when she died. I'd visited the previous afternoon and stayed a couple of hours. Her breathing was desperate – she was coughing every couple of minutes and I was planning to leave at five when they would put her on the nebulizer. So I did all the talking, updating her on all the goings-on at work, the characters in the station. It was my first posting and I was doing well. I was getting better, too; that day, I was really pleased because I'd been able to drive through Terenure – past the bank, even – without any panic. Mum loved hearing all the stories I'd come home with as a young garda on the beat. I had made her laugh with a story about the mum who I'd caught pulling into the taxi rank outside Liffey Valley Shopping Centre.

It was a Saturday afternoon and the car park was jammers. This poor woman had a car full of young girls who'd obviously badgered her into bringing them all shopping. She was apologizing before the window was even fully lowered.

'I'm so sorry, Guard. I know it's a taxi rank; I'm only pulling in here for a second – just to let them off. Then I'll go and find parking. I know I can't park here and –'

I'd given her my most serious expression and leaned into the car.

'Yes, Madam, this is a taxi rank,' I said, and I waited a couple of moments for the girls in the car to become silent before continuing, 'but isn't this Mammy's Taxi you're driving?'

The woman froze, not sure what I was getting at. I stepped back. 'Mammy's Taxi can park here,' I said, waving the other cars on. 'I'll guide you in.'

Mum's face was priceless, hearing that. She beamed – told me I'd made the woman's day. In her eyes, I was always making someone's day. When the nurse came in, she was in a rush to get the mask on her and Mum didn't get a chance to say our usual goodbye.

I stood at the doorway so she could see me – said, 'Bye Mum, love you.' Through the mask, I saw her mouthing the words, her usual response, which was always *Love you more*. I smiled, shook my head to discourage her from speaking, said, 'Don't worry, Mum, I know you love me more,' and hurried off.

I said it then, and I meant it. But now I understand. She always loved me more. That's how it is.

The room comes back into focus. I feel Niamh's stare boring into me. Her head is cocked to one side again.

'So and anyway,' she says. It's another of her phrases and she knows it annoys me. Especially as she pronounces it *annieway*. 'So and anyway, Laura? I think you were asking Jenny about that afternoon, *after* school maybe?'

I nod my thanks, embarrassed. 'Yes, that's right. What do you do after school, usually? What did you do that day, the day Stuart put the shirt in the bin? Can you tell me about that?'

8. Jenny

That is three questions, Laura. One, two, three. One two too many. Maybe Laura is running out of time. She tries again – let's take it from the top.

'You put the shirt in the bin, yes? And – was it a school day? If it was, presumably you went to school and saw your friend Amy?'

She waits for more about Amy, and there is loads more 'cos Amy's fun. As well as eyeliner, Amy knows about drink. She got cans for us that time and we drank them in the park after school. Mine was mixed fruit and I loved it. It went into my brain and it swept everything else – all the bad shit – it sort of swept it to one side or down the stairs. All the stuff I don't want to think about, the Kopparberg swept it all away and, even if I wanted to, I couldn't think about it. It was great.

'What about your other friends? Can you tell me about them?'

I don't have a lot of friends, Laura. But Luke – I'm thinking about Luke, that time he put his arm around my shoulders when we were walking out the school gate and he sort of squeezed and we walked in step two three four steps, rolling side to side, like pirates. And he was going, 'Aargh, me hearties,' and stuff. If you did Luke's genetic profiling – seriously, like 90 per cent of the DNA would be nice-guy genes. And the rest would be funny. He is funny. And kind. I'm thinking 80 per cent nice guy and 20 per cent funny. But he's funnier than 20 per cent. And really he's more like 98 per cent good guy. So that doesn't work.

She pushes her hair behind her ears, this time both hands both ears, and she does double listening. Double. And there are no marks anywhere on her that I can see. Definitely no bruises. Her hands are thin and her wrists are bony. He'd be able to snap them – Snap! Like twigs. She does the sadface smile.

'So you're the boss here, Jenny. What would you like to talk about?'

'Luke's a good guy.'

But I'm sad now, thinking about him. I can see his face like someone scribbled hurt and surprise all over it. And the hot shiver feeling comes back.

'Who's Luke?'

And then I remember where I am. The dumb office, the blue clock with no batteries any more. Niamh over by the window.

'Guy in school,' I say. Be careful be careful now.

'That's all.' I say it like bad dog, Laura. Bad dog, you drop it now, Laura.

'Right,' she says, all business-like, 'let's go back to that day. You went to school, and what did you do afterwards?'

'I picked Karl up from Val's.'

It was freezing and, as usual, Karl didn't want to leave Val's house. We trekked up the hill past the SuperValu. Change Charlie was sitting on his usual corner at the car park. His hood was up because of the cold, but he must have seen us, because when we stopped in front of him he was already grinning, but his nose and cheeks were purple from the cold. He always says, 'How's tricks?' And I was going to say, *grand, how are you?*, but he's homeless and he's no job since Dad – since the bike shop closed. He used to help people find a parking place and they'd give him a bit of change.

When I was little, I thought his name was Changed Charlie, that someone, a bad witch or sorcerer, had changed him into

46

a beggar. Dad laughed a lot at that, and he said, 'Charlie's the fool on the hill, Jen-Pen.' And I thought *fool* was a bad word, but Dad says the fool is wise.

'Jenny?' She's still waiting. 'You were telling me about the afternoon. You picked up Karl from Val's? Is Val the childminder?'

And I wish she was, because no one messes with Val, but she's on the no-visit list. Top of the no-visit list.

'You picked Karl up? Then what happened?'

Val is Mum's best friend – only friend. I never thought that before – it's the same for her; no friends allowed. But he can't stop Val. Nobody can stop Val. And anyway, she knew Mum from before, when Mum was an actual person. Like a proper person, not a – a ghost.

'So you picked Karl up, then what?'

That was the first day on the island. And I can tell some things about the island, but some things are secret, re-member? Don't let her trick you. But I can remember that first day, and Socks.

'We were walking along, near the spooky house, and we saw this dog. He was just standing there. And he –'

There's a scrunching feeling happening in my chest, like a giant hand rummaging around inside. I can't – I don't want to remember all of it. But she's waiting and moving her head, first to one side then the other, as if the questions are too heavy to stay still. Like they're rolling around in her brain.

'A dog? Tell me about the dog.'

'He's dark brown but he has gold bits. Like toffee.'

Niamh's not writing that down, nor is Laura. No scribbles. She doesn't know – they don't know anything. Hah. She doesn't even know what to write down.

Laura's blinking like a patient dog. She's waiting for more. I can do this, though. I can choose what to tell, remember?

'And this was where? You said something about a spooky house?'

I think about the house – hidden, hidden. I like the word *hide*. I like the way the tiny 'i' hides in the middle of it, like it's sheltering between Mummy *h* and Daddy *d*. Gigantic trees, the really dark ones that look like a wall, are all around the house, even the gate. It's a secret house. Be careful and be careful. Shut up and that secret won't give you a headache, not if you shut up.

It was Mrs Ambrose's house. She used to teach in our primary school for about a zillion years. There was a party for her when she retired. We had a giant chocolate cake. She was really nice to me after Dad died, I remember that. Like when everyone was talking in these special voices, Mrs Ambrose was just normal. She gave me jobs to do in her classroom and stuff.

Laura does more nodding and nodding. Niamh's stomach does a gurgling growl, and she tries to turn it into a cough and then she goes, 'Whoops – beg your pardon, lads. Must be getting close to lunchtime.'

And I remember Mrs Ambrose. Poor Mrs Ambrose. She'd got really thin – like she was made from rulers.

'It's Mrs Ambrose's house. My old teacher. She said she was looking for someone to walk her dog.'

I stop then and squeeze very hard inside my brain in case the tears come out. The scrunching feeling's gone – it's more like ripping. I'm remembering the feel of Socks's fur and his soft face against my cheek. And it's bad bad, and there's something really bad. My heart's beating so fast and my mind circles round and round, round and round, like Socks deciding where to lie down. Be careful. Careful careful careful. We are not going there, you dumb bitch. Nobody says anything. No secrets come out. Poor Laura. Poor, growling Niamh.

'So you met your old teacher and made a plan to walk her dog?'

Haha, this is good. She's going nowhere. Nothing more about the island, right. All locked up safe. So there is a bit more quiet and no ticking.

And then there's buzzing from the corner where Niamh is sitting and I jump because it's loud after the quiet. And Niamh's all like 'Yeah' and 'What?' and 'Right, sir,' and she's all antsy and Laura looks over at her. And Niamh is beckoning.

Laura gets up and I like her trousers. She's slim, like Mum. She goes over to Niamh and it's whisper whisper look over at me. Dumb bitch, I'm telling you – I keep telling you shut up. Then she comes back and sits down and I can see she picked up questions when she was gone away and they're sitting in her brain like cakes in a tin. But Laura doesn't eat cakes, I'll bet. She'd only cut a little piece off the edge.

'Jenny?'

On the hill outside the window, there's a line of trees, and they're bending and shivering together like they're cold. It's raining and they probably don't want to lose their leaves, but they have no choice. The wind takes what it wants. He's gonna strip them bare.

'Jenny?' she says, and she makes my name sound different. She sounds different, like her words are not teddies or clouds. They're splinters of broken plates.

'Jenny. I want you to listen very carefully. Things – things have changed. We – we've just got some new information –'

She stands up, gets out from behind the desk and walks close. Dumb bitch. She does the peering thing, trying to look in my brain, and I can smell her.

'Do you remember yesterday – Sunday?'

'Sunday Bloody Sunday', that's U2, not The Beatles, but

Dad liked that, too. It's on the CD with the scowling little boy who looks like Karl. And Mum used to laugh back then when she laughed, and she said, 'Your dad is a time traveller, Jen, he only likes the music from before he was born.'

'We just heard that your stepfather is missing. Jenny – Stuart is missing. He hasn't been seen since yesterday. Do you know anything about this? Do you know where Stuart could be?'

No can do no no no, Laura. No way. Be very very sssh secret and careful now, bitch. Laura does the waiting while I choose the words. I will choose carefully; it's fine and I'm getting the hang of it now. I make her wait and I make her think what I want her to think. What do you say when people are looking for someone? Like if they're not glad he's gone?

'Oh dear,' I say. 'That's strange.'

I think she hates me then a little bit because I think she sees me hiding inside the words – the slippery-fake words the dumb grown-ups use all the time for their lies. And I go, 'Oh dear,' again because it's funny. And she throws a look at Niamh, like she wants her to help. Dumb.

'Do you know where he is, Jenny?'

And I go, like, looking all around the room, into the corners and up to the ceiling and even move my head side to side like I'm trying to see out the window to where the trees are crying laughing.

'No, I can't imagine where he might be,' I go. 'Don't *you* know where he is? I thought you'd know because you're a special type of police officer, Laura.'

I turn around in the chair and point at Niamh. Niamh isn't writing anything. Hah.

'Maybe *she* knows?'

And Niamh is not so scared. But Laura is getting narky and that means she's scared.

'Niamh doesn't know where he is, and nor do I. That's why we're asking you. When was the last time you saw him?'

It's a secret. And it happened long ago and far away or was it once upon a time? They're both waiting.

'I think,' I start, and it's so funny because now they both sit up and they're leaning forwards listening listening and I could say anything and Niamh will write it down, haha, and Laura will do her V frown like a seagull on her smooth forehead and I will hear her heart beat tic-tic, tic-tic, light as feathers.

'I think he's maybe gone away,' I say, 'for a few days – because he's not very well.'

And that's true because he's not very well at all. You don't feel very well when your blood leaves your body and your brain is bashed. That's funny.

9. Laura

Jesus, that weird smirk she did at the end made me shiver. I've never been so glad to step out of an interview. I stand there for a second, my palms pressing the door firmly closed, and I lean my head back against it as if I'm trying to push something inside. A nurse passes us on the corridor.

'We're going to get some lunch,' Niamh answers, her eyebrows raised.

'Oh right, I'll go into her now so. You two go on.'

'We're not finished,' I blurt, more forcefully than I mean to. 'Don't bring her back to the ward yet. And don't leave her alone.'

The nurse is young and blonde, with that nursey combination of smiley innocence and steely resolve. Her expression registers surprise and maybe even disappointment at my sharp tone.

'Of course.' She smiles again. 'I was going in to see her anyway.' She presses the buzzer to let us out of the ward. 'Café's on the second floor,' she says.

I watch Niamh's bag bump against her hip as she tramps down the stairs ahead of me; we're completely in sync by the time we reach the bottom. I get to sixteen before I catch myself counting and stifle the impulse. Niamh goes up to get the food and, quickly, before she turns round, I take out the wipes and sweep the table. It has that brown, sticky look to it and any amount of thumb prints and grease splodges smear the surface. I don't even want to think what might be on the underside.

'That's what I like to see. A proper organized Mammy.' Niamh is back. She grins, taking in the sight of my snack box and the packet of rice cakes. I glance down and move the packet to make it look less symmetrical, feeling foolish.

'You're gas,' she says. 'But don't feel bad, my sister Siobhán went a bit like that after she had her first. Leaving the house was a military operation. Her bag weighed a ton with all the snacks and baby shite. Here.' She slides a plate across the table. A dense wedge of lasagne squats in the middle of a ring of grizzled-looking chips which huddle together, looking up at it, like groupies. I think of it sitting in my stomach like a boulder – impervious to the acids of digestion – and suppress a shudder.

'Don't judge the mammies,' I say, with what I hope is a carefree smile. 'We like to be organized. You have that.' I nod towards the plate and begin opening my snack box. 'I brought something.'

'Fair play.' She starts ripping open ketchup sachets, spurting their contents on to her plate. In a matter of seconds, a small pile of empty and half-empty sachets lie like fallen comrades, oozing crimson blobs on to each other and on to the sticky table. I long to gather them up and bin them, then wipe the table. I resist.

My wrap has held together well, and I feel a lurch of gratitude for the sight of the tidy, colourful swirls. These days, anything organized or orderly can give me that hit of serotonin – a well-constructed sandwich, a neatly made bed.

I'm pathetic.

'Look, do you want me to do this one?' Niamh pushes some escaped curls out of the way of her fork. 'It's not too late. We can swap?'

'No!' I put down the wrap. 'What? Why?'

'All I meant was, it's not going to be an easy one, is it?' she says, between mouthfuls of lasagne. 'It's gonna be a long day and, I don't know, but you look a bit stressed is all, like more than your usual "I haven't slept since Baby was born" stressed?'

Now she starts on the sachets of brown sugar – ripping the tops off three of them simultaneously, then tipping them into her coffee. Sixty calories. Plus eighteen for the milk. The empty sugar packs drift down like pale sheets to lie on top of the fallen ketchup. The table looks like a battlefield.

She's frowning again.

'You didn't make contact with a counsellor, did you?'

'For what?' I play for time.

'Come on, Laura. Last month – Mitzi?'

I sigh.

'I don't need to talk to anyone. It was sorted – at least she pressed charges. He'll do time – she'll get away from him. Job done.'

I won't forget the sight of her, though – not for a long time. The woman had barricaded herself into the bathroom and called 999 from there, screaming in terror that he'd killed Mitzi and he was going to kill her. Niamh and I responded first – we were actually patrolling the same estate when the call came through – a quiet Sunday night up till then.

Neighbours were already thronging around the gate and on the doorstep, claiming they'd heard a bang, when we drew up. When back-up arrived, they cleared the crowd and we prepared to enter – but the guy came out with his hands up almost immediately – smirking for the cameras. Not press – neighbours and their phones. Uniform took him in while we went into the house, bracing ourselves for a dead child and a devastated mother.

'It was an armed incident,' Niamh is saying, and she's right; we had drawn our weapons and we did recover an air rifle from the scene. 'And it was fucking traumatic, yeah?'

In the front room, a cream leather sofa was dalmationed in blood spatters, but no body. The woman's name was Dona. It took us fifteen minutes to talk her into opening the door of the bathroom – to believe us when we told her that her partner was in a squad car, in handcuffs, heading for the station.

We'd heard the key turning in the lock and the door opened. I recoiled instantly – Dona's terror had loosened her bowels – and the smell of human faeces hit us full in the face.

'C'mere, pet.' Niamh strode past me and grabbed the woman – who was still convulsing in terror – firmly by the shoulders. 'You're all right.'

Wrapped in a bloodstained bath towel was a white cat – Mitzi. Mitzi was dead. He'd shot the cat first and – judging by the marks on Dona's throat – if she hadn't escaped to the bathroom, he'd have killed her next.

'It's not mandatory,' I say, though I know she's right. It's recommended that you attend for counselling following any traumatic incident – a shooting, a fatal accident, a bad crash, even upsetting victim interviews. I've screened calls – three or four, at least – from the company they use for counselling. The woman – Jackie – left messages to call her. I didn't.

'I'm grand – really. He shot a cat. He's a bastard. But when you think – you know – we thought there was a child in-volved? At least that wasn't it. So, in answer to your question, no, I haven't made contact – because I'm grand.'

Niamh sighs.

'Bollocks.'

For all the jokes and the ramped-up culchie act, living up to every cliché about home-spun country girls, Niamh is the best SVI I've ever worked with and a bloody sharp detective. She can read people, and that's not just clients. She watches. I know she's seen the shake and the lapses in concentration. I know she knows something's up – something else. She probably even knows I counted the stairs. She sighs again and sweeps her hair around to the other side of her shoulders, leans forward. She's dropped it – for now.

'Right – with Jenny, there's going to be a lot going on, yeah? Her dad died when she was eight, so there's the grief of that. Added to which, we're going to have huge issues around trust. I mean, what, she's fourteen and this stuff has been going on a long time. We both saw the X-rays. The photos.'

She gulps her coffee and sets it down, sloshing it on to the table. I let it sit there.

'Yep,' I say, thinking of the bruises, the remodelled fractures – places where broken bone had healed and thickened – two in the right arm and one at the base of the skull.

'You're right. It's going to take her ages to trust us.'

'To trust you.' Niamh points her sandwich at me. 'I'm background this time. Good cop, invisible cop.'

My phone lurches into a full vibrate 'n' ring combo and I jump to answer it, recognizing the number. It's the Inspector, or Cigire – he prefers the Irish title.

'It's Cig. Hang on.'

As I listen, the food in my mouth separates into distinct and equally indigestible clumps. Niamh is chewing and miming, *What?* at the same time, which should be funny but isn't.

'Right, Cig, yeah, got it.' I hang up, then I look at my veggie wrap; the beetroot-and-spinach mix has jumbled and smashed together, pieces of beetroot seeping into the napkin like blood. It looks like something medical. Swallowing down the nausea, I gather up the whole lot. Then I ram it back into the box and snap the lid closed. My hands have begun to shake, but I keep them hidden. Niamh gulps the last of her coffee and finishes off the chips.

'What happened? What did he say?'

I put the box back in my bag and find the disinfectant.

'First off, there's still no sign of the stepfather. He's vanished off the face of the earth.'

Niamh dips the last chip in ketchup and brings it for a spin around the plate, gathering up the remaining particles of pasta and flakes of chips. She eats it, wipes her fingers on the paper napkin, scrunches that into a ball and sits back.

'We know that – go on –'

I spray more sanitizer on my hands and rub it in, my voice sounding a lot calmer than I feel.

'They think something happened in the car. It's – Cig said it was a bloodbath. They've taken samples.'

'Oh,' she says, her face slack as she processes the information.

'So they can test against the clothes she was wearing.'

'And something else,' I say, finally giving in to the compulsion and sweeping the pile of ketchup-oozing sachets into the napkin and wiping the red smears off the table. 'They found a knife.'

10. Laura

It's been a miserable week of rain and wind – and today is no different. Niamh follows me as I move towards the automatic exit doors instead of heading back upstairs. Outside, people wrestle umbrellas and coats, scurrying into the warmth of the hospital as fast as they can.

'We'll check in on the mum first,' I say, gesturing to the main hospital in the distance. Niamh nods her agreement. Word from Cig was that they'd called in earlier but got nothing. The little boy is in the children's ward – intensive care also. She's in a medically induced coma so I know we won't be able to question her, but something drives me. I've got to see her. I'm looking for answers to mother/daughter riddles. Where is she in all this? Why isn't Jenny talking about her, asking about her? I've no idea where she fits in Jenny's story or what she's like. I need to see her – even if she can't speak.

We are blown across the square, buffeted by wind and rain. At the pedestrian crossing there's a battle of wills taking place between a guy in a car who had obviously thought he could make it over before the pedestrian – an elderly priest – stepped on to the striped tarmac. Now the priest is staring him down, shaming him into looking away and taking as long as possible on the crossing, his hands outstretched like Moses parting the Red Sea.

I know it's unfair to taint them all, but still. Maybe they're not getting away with it any more, or locking up pregnant girls and selling babies, but you can still rely on the odd one or two of their victims coming in. My very first case was one where the priest was the abuser. Classic, in fact. Mark was nine and had been an altar boy for a year. Father Seán got Mark to come half an hour before Mass so he could inspect him, make sure Mark was clean enough to serve at the Lord's table. 'He told me I had to do what he said because he's basically standing in for Jesus,' Mark said in our first meeting, rubbing at invisible stains on his jeans. 'I thought I had to do everything he said.'

'Everything' included inspecting the boy so comprehensively that no orifice was left unexplored, in case he was hiding things from Our Lord. It included allowing the priest to suck the poison out. Matt says I'm biased, that I see it everywhere. Perhaps he's right.

We use the priest's hold-up to get across the road, and Niamh yells, 'Thanks, Father!' back at him. 'What?' she says when I raise my eyebrows. 'Some of them are decent people trying to do some good in the world, Laura.' We shake off the rain and do our hands with the wall-mounted sanitizer. 'So you can stop scowling now, okay?'

Get a grip of this, Laura, don't let the anger take over, I counsel myself as we wait for the lift, barely aware of Niamh's chatter. It's starting up again. I know the signs – the sense of being removed from people, even from Matt and Katie. It's like everyone is snuggled up by the fire, laughing and having fun, while I'm on the outskirts, over by a draughty door. I'm standing guard. I'm always on duty, watching out for danger. And you can't laugh and joke when you're on duty. Matt says I'm no fun any more and, even though he says he's joking, I see now that he's right; this has been coming for ages.

Last night's row is on my mind, too. We were standing in the kitchen at that blissful moment when Katie had gone to sleep and the evening was ours. He switched on the baby monitor – although it's kind of obsolete now – and held it up to my ear so I could hear her soft snores. I moved to the sofa and he joined me, handing me a large glass of wine.

'What's wrong?' he said.

'I'm fine, there's nothing wrong.'

He wasn't convinced. 'Are you worried about Katie – is that it?' With his free hand he put his arm around me and pulled me close. 'It's just a cold or something, she's grand.' Wine sloshed over the top of the glass on to my lap.

'Fuck's sake, Matt, look what you did!' I leapt up and stormed over to the sink for the cloth. 'I'm fine! I'm just tired, and now I'm covered in wine, thanks to you.'

I saw myself reflected in the kitchen window as I scrubbed at the trousers, my face a pale coin of bad humour. The fabric was black, so it didn't even matter.

'I'm doing my best, but you're not making it easy. Do you think –' he turned towards the TV screen, deliberately not making eye contact – 'like, maybe you should go see someone – just for a few sessions?'

'Oh yeah – of course, Matt. It's me – my fault.'

'We can both go, if you like.'

Poor Matt. He'd put Katie to bed, even though it was my turn that night. He'd opened the wine – he had the crisps and Netflix all lined up. He *was* making an effort. Why the hell couldn't I do the same? I arranged my features into a smile and turned away from the sink, preparing the apology. But he'd already switched on the TV and started watching something.

He's impossible to fight with, and it's not like I'm worried he's going to leave or anything, but recently, it's like we're both Katie's employees, rather than a couple. He does his job; I do mine. We co-parent. God, I hate that phrase.

We're outside ICU. Niamh flashes the badge, the buzzer sounds and we enter. There's a kind of energized hush in the air and immediately we're whispering.

'Can we look in on Melanie Cullen?' Niamh asks the nurse, a tired-looking fifty-something woman with a hairstyle at odds with her weary face and greyish skintone – all angles and bounce – who motions for us to follow her. The hair bounces jauntily and we track it, past screened-off cubicles and around a corner, arriving at Melanie's bedside.

I've seen all sorts of broken and injured bodies. I've stood calmly watching mothers identify dead children and I have not shed a tear – trying to impart strength by my own reaction, or lack of it. But the sight of Melanie makes me stop. Her hands lie bandaged by her sides, the manicured fingernails like weird blossoms emerging from the wrapping. Her chest rises and falls, rises and falls, accompanied by the whispering oxygen machine. Her face – Niamh and I exchange a look. I know that it's mostly swelling and that the facial tissue can balloon like crazy, but it's a puffy, livid mess – she looks like a pink jellyfish in bandages.

'You wanted to see her?' Jaunty-hair tries to hide her impatience. 'She's clearly not going to be talking, you know?'

I realize that I'd been expecting something different, but I don't know what. She's like Sleeping Beauty in the glass coffin or something; a young mum, skinny and frail, her short hair sticking out from under the bandages in tufts, dried blood still caked on her eyelashes.

'When was she brought in?'

'I wasn't on – but as far as I know, it was yesterday evening before nine. There's a daughter – she wasn't with her. We heard that she was found later on?'

'Uh-hum,' Niamh says noncommittally, leaving the question hanging.

'What are her injuries?'

'How long have you got? She lost a lot of blood from the neck wound, then there's the head injury, suspected $C2$

fracture, lacerations to her hands and arms, punctured lung – that's just the start of it. Apparently, the little boy is almost as bad.'

'Jesus Christ,' breathes Niamh. We don't need words for us to know what we're both wondering.

Melanie's neck is slender, even in bandages her collar-bones prominent and frail-looking. I step closer to the bedside and bend down to whisper.

'I know you can't talk, Melanie, but things are going to be okay. We're going to take care of you all now. You and Jenny – and Karl.'

Niamh nods a thank you at the nurse and we head out.

'At least she's safe now.' I pat my hands with the paper towel to absorb the hand sanitizer. Niamh watches me closely.

'Safe from who?' she says, with a small shrug. 'Nothing is certain yet.'

I turn away so she can't see my anger and walk back down the corridor towards the main entrance. I count fifty-eight steps before I stop, trying to get a grip. Niamh is right behind me. Jesus! I hope I wasn't counting out loud.

'You okay?' she says, placing her hand on my arm and giving it a squeeze. The movement makes her handbag swing forwards to hit me on the thigh. 'Oh! Sorry.' Her bag is open and I glance inside – a reflex. It's more like a big drawer full of knick-knacks than a handbag – I see a pair of sports socks, some snack bars, a half-eaten apple – there's even a whistle. She sees me looking.

'I'm coaching the under-16s later,' she says. 'As opposed to fending off rapists by loud whistling.' She laughs. 'The rapist would get a bit of this –' she smacks her fist against her palm – 'and this!' She mimes a knee to the crotch.

I know what she's doing. Trademark Niamh – funny-girl routine. We're just inside the entrance and every move we make activates the automatic doors. Niamh plucks the sleeve of my jacket and pulls me aside.

'If you want me to take over – even just for the last hour?' She looks at the digital clock hanging above the twenty-four-hour shop in the foyer. 'I'm happy to do it, yeah?'

'It's fine, Niamh.' I'm bristling at her anxious tone – like I'm fragile or something. Or not capable of doing my job. 'I can handle it. I just need to get her talking again – so we can find out what happened to her.'

'Yeah – but we should look at this from every angle.' Niamh takes a step back to let a woman with a buggy in the shop doorway. 'Especially now.'

'You don't think – come on! You can't think her capable –'

She shrugs again, gestures with open hands.

'We don't know, Laura. We don't know anything yet. What about the stepfather? He can't have just vanished –'

An image from Jenny's file photos flashes into my brain – a big thumb-print-shaped bruise on her skinny hipbone – and I'm shot through by a bolt of white-hot anger.

'Jenny's the victim here, right, Niamh? Never mind him! Let's do what we always do – let's get her story?'

'I –'

'We do the usual, okay, Detective Darmody? Focus on the victim – provide the platform.'

Niamh exhales a long breath, searching my face.

'Hohkay,' she says, drawing the word out. 'Let's cool the jets, okay?'

'Come on.' I start walking through the entrance towards the psych unit. 'We need to get back to the girl.'

11. Niamh

She's got fair skinny. I watch her clanking her way across the concourse – every step jarring, her body rigid. I hang back deliberately.

'You go on,' I say, pointing towards the shop by the entrance. 'Gonna buy some snacks.'

It'll do no harm to put a bit of space between us, just a couple of minutes even, for her to compose herself. Christ but she's het up! If she could see herself sitting there at lunch – all angles and anxiety folded in on itself – bony fingers clasping her bony elbows, trying to stop herself cleaning up the table! She's fierce painful to look at.

I get some more cans from the fridge and a packet of Hobnobs, bringing them up to the till. The young fella is tall, gym-buffed, the way they all are now. He checks me out – the up-down sweep – and goes for the lazy smile. A boob man so. He rings in the drinks and the biscuits, watching me.

'Hob*knobs*,' he grins, stressing the last syllable. 'Anything else you want?'

'Yeah, actually.' I can't resist messing with him. I do a straight-girl head tilt. Almost but not quite batting the eyelashes. 'Can you give me, eh –'

'Yeah?' Now it's his turn to tilt the head. He's good-looking, all right. If you like the high cheekbones/grey eyes combo. Polish, I'm guessing.

'Can I get, eh – two packets of those?'

I point to the sour jellies. I'll give them to the girls halfway through training later. He takes them down from the hook, scans them.

'For my kids.' I smile – ending the moment. He nods. Disappointed, bless him.

'That's seven-sixty.'

I pay him and he places the change on the counter. No handies, then. I take the two-euro coin, leaving the others. 'Stick that in the box,' I say, nodding towards the ISPCC container. 'Thanks.'

A blast of icy sleet hits me as I make my way towards the psych building. It'll be Baltic tonight at training – but I know they'll all turn up because of the league match next weekend. A surge of affection for the team warms me – probably because they haven't a fecking hope against St Teresa's. But they'll give it their all. If I've taught them anything, it's that – commitment. I hope.

I ram the sweets into the top of my handbag so I don't forget them then take the stairs to the ward – allowing myself a bit more time to think. Laura's worrying me. She's not herself. The Laura who trained me – who was my mentor – was brilliant. Quirky and uptight? Yeah, sure. Inclined to take things too seriously? Absolutely. But she was sound. Christ, how I looked up to her! She was always the smartest person in the room, always a step ahead. I watched her in the interviews – steadily unpicking the information strand by strand, never rushing the client. You could see she had the destination in her sights from the outset, but she allowed the victim to make their own way there.

That was then. Before she had Katie? As I make my way up the final flight of stairs I try to remember when the change began. She took an extended maternity leave and came back in a flurry of activity, leaving me to be partnered with Edel while she was gone – thanks, Laura. Next stop, if she wanted it, could be sergeant – but not the way she's going on now.

I slow down on the last few steps, trying to finish the thought. No. My gut tells me it's nothing to do with career stuff. It's as if something's been asleep inside her for a very long time – something that was always there.

And now it's woken up.

12. Jenny

I want to get out. I've got to get out. I need to see Mum and Karl. I need to tell them. But then I stop and I don't know – I can't remember what I need to tell them. And there's something else bad – really bad – but I can't find it in the place where the thoughts are. It's not there. What is it? Why can't I find it? Dumb. What have you forgotten now?

Laura said I could get out, but not properly out, like not outside. She said I could go and eat in the dining room. And Smiley Nurse is here, watching me, so I can't run away. But tonight, maybe – when it's dark.

Laura's gone out the door again and she was talking on her phone earlier and she said no a lot to whoever it was. No not yet. No way. Not fit at all. That's what she said. Niamh was all, like, you can go to stretch your legs a bit, pet, do some star jumps, heheh, but no way. I'm staying here, 'cos there's no way he can come here, we're too high up. My choice. Niamh said I get to choose. Anyway, I don't want to be where they all are – it said 'Day Room' on the door – shuffling around and staring at me. Why do they stare? And why don't they walk or sit down? Why are they sliding around each other with those little, tiny steps that are more like the dancing that old people do, or the one where you stand on your dad's shoes and you hold his hands and he dances around but you have to go slow or you fall off?

That's what dads do. Stu said he's my new dad, but that's another lie, and he's even pretending to himself. He is always pretending, and he was pretending even in the beginning. He called to the shop and he bought bike things, and his mouth was wide like a letterbox but his eyes were darting, swish-swish, like he was taking tiny bites out of Mum. And he said, 'Nice to see you, Mel.' After Dad died he called more and more and more, and the letterbox smile shivered on his face – fake and bright. And he said, 'You know I'm always here for you, Mel. And Little Jenny.' And he didn't buy any more bike things and, later, when we moved to his house, I knew. He didn't have a bike.

'How's my buddy, Jenny?' he'd say, standing at the door. 'You're looking so pretty today. Aren't you going to let me in?'

And nobody said *not by the hair on my chinny chin chin.*

I don't remember much of those days after the funeral – it was boring and quiet after Granny Marie stopped coming over and all the other visitors went away, too, and there were no more cakes and apple tarts. And Stu came over in his car and he brought us up to his house for afternoon tea, and Mum was all, 'Oh, this is a palace, Stu, it's amazing.' But I didn't like it because it's empty and bare and the floors are cold stone and there's nowhere soft to sit and no cushions. And the pictures on the walls have no pictures on them – they were like slabs of brown and grey.

At home, you know which chair is yours because Dad painted them different colours and my pictures are on the wall beside Mum's, and Dad says we're both artists and you can play anywhere and make messes and you don't have to wash your hands in the bathroom with gold taps.

But Stuart was walking around like a king and saying, 'Oh, now I've got two princesses to keep happy, don't I?' And he had a big chocolate cake sitting all on its own on the giant white table.

And that was the first day he bought me a dress to wear. And Mum goes, 'Oh no, Stu, that's too much, you're too good,' and he goes, 'Har har, no, I couldn't resist, could I?' And they made me put it on. I remember it. I thought it was a sailor outfit at first – it was white with a navy trim and a bow thing at the neck. And my legs were bare, and he said, 'What you need is knee socks,' and the following week Mum got them for me. And Stu started buying clothes for Mum and for me, and dumb princess bitch goes, 'Oh thank you, oh thank you.'

And that day I ate the chocolate cake wearing the white dress and I didn't look at his wolf face. But I got chocolate icing all over me and he brought me to the bathroom with the gold taps and he squirted the soap all over my fingers, though I told him I could do it myself, and then he rubbed it and swirled it everywhere, right the way up to my wrists, standing behind me, smiling at me in the mirror with his shivering bad-wolf smile and his chin poking down on my head, and he was stroking and squeezing and rolling my hands inside his hands, and they were all covered in soap and bubbles then he added more water and snuggled closer closer closer until he's pressing against all of me, laughing. 'Isn't this great fun, look at the bubbles we're making, I bet our hands have never been so clean ever in their lives' – and I knew then.

And Mum did not say *Jenny can wash her own hands* and she did not say *Jenny, why don't you and I visit the gold taps bathroom together, just us two?* Mum smelt our hands when we came back and put on her shiny eyes and said, 'Oh yes, clean as a whistle.'

I smell my hand, and it's still got the smell of cheese sandwiches, like school.

There's a cheese sandwich sitting in front of me. Smiley Nurse brought it in. I'm looking at the little brown specks in the bread. Like freckles. Stuart has freckles all over the back of his neck and on his chest. They make me feel sick. They're like flakes of brown dandruff that can't fall off – they're glued to his clammy, oily skin. I imagine them sprinkled over my sandwich. He's everywhere, even in the food I eat. And there's relish or chutney or something smeared on the slices of sweating cheese. The relish looks like clumps of dried blood, like blood clots. Clots. Lots of clots.

Clots of clots. Blood is crucial. I googled this before the – before. In the library at school. *The primary function of the cardiovascular system is to provide oxygen to the body. When someone is in a state of shock, the blood volume is decreased and the supply of oxygen to the organs is compromised. In irreversible shock, it's just as it sounds.* That's what it said. Irreversible means no going back. No going back.

'You're not eating your sandwich, Jenny? Do you want something else?' When did they come back in? I shrug. Actually, it's barely a shrug. I'm so tired.

'I'm tired,' I say, like a little kid. But it doesn't work.

'Okay, Jenny, things have changed a bit. We need to talk. Let's start with Stuart.'

No, actually, we don't. No thank you, no, no, Laura. I watch her as she sets her stuff out on the desk: biros and a pencil and a ruler. She puts them in a line across the top of her page. It makes me think of school.

'Earlier, you spoke about home and your life at home' – she pauses – 'in a world ruled by Stuart?'

She waits for a bit, but I say nothing now because, anyway, that wasn't even a question. But she doesn't give up.

'So that brings us back to Stuart. Jenny, Stuart is missing. You said he went away. Do you know where he is?' She doesn't even wait. 'Do you know what's happened to him?'

And that *is* a question. And I think of all the ways she could say it: listen –

a) Do you know what's HAPPENED to him?

b) Do you KNOW what's happened to him?

c) Do YOU know what's happened to him?

d) DO you know what's happened to him?

But it's okay, it's okay. She said it all in small letters – like she knows she hasn't a chance.

'And I think you might know something about this, Jenny. If there's a risk to human life – it's very serious. It's the kind of situation where you have to speak out.'

'I've told you loads,' I say. Even I can hear how whiny that sounds. Ssh. Shut it.

'Yes,' she says. 'You have. But there is more, isn't there?' She waits. She waits more. More more more. Please, sir, I want some more, but that didn't work out so well for anyone.

'There was blood on your clothes and all over your hands and arms when they found you. They cleaned it off in the Emergency Department. They thought you were bleeding. But you weren't bleeding. It wasn't your blood, Jenny.'

I look down at my hands. Be careful and slow, Jennifer. I turn them over. They look pale and kind of small. There's a tiny red line still under my nail. But no blood. 'Soft hands like a princess,' Dad said. I put them on his hot forehead when he had the headaches. 'Thank you, princess.' And I loved when Dad put his hand on mine and he patted it and he said, 'Great girl,' and I knew he'd never hurt me and that he loved me.

And Stuart says he loves us, but that is a lie. Everything that comes out of his mouth is lies – they tumble out like slippery snakes. At the wedding he was all smiling, but I looked behind his teeth and I saw. And Mum was a princess for that day. Her hair fell down her back to her waist like a sheet of gold shimmering.

'It's a fishtail dress, Jen-Pen. Isn't it lovely?'

I couldn't see the fish tail, but it sparkled like water. My dress sparkled a lot, too, because in the middle of the white

71

flowers there were tiny pearls and sequins. And I loved it at first because back then it was still me and Mum. And I told her she looked like a princess, and she said, 'We're both princesses today, Jen.'

The dress was scratchy on my arms because the shiny bits were scratchy. And when all the people were talking to Mum, I was sad because it wasn't me and Mum any more. And I was scratching because of the sharp bits in the dress and he turned his big teeth towards me and peeled his lips away from them.

'You carry on, darling,' he said, and he lifted me up, though he's not my dad. 'I'll bring her outside to get some air.'

And I didn't get air outside. He brought me into the room with the wheelchair on it where you shouldn't go, and he locked the door. And that was the first day, and it was too late because now Mum was already his princess – not mine.

'Let's take that scratchy dress off for a bit.' And it scratched my face going over my head. He folded it the right side out and he hung it where the towel was meant to be. 'Do you need the loo?' And his eyes were hungry.

'Show me where it's hurting you and I'll rub it. Is it here?

'Here?

'Here?'

'Tell me about the blood instead, Jenny. Can you tell me a bit more about that?'

I know it's exactly what she wants, but I can't stop myself. I think of blood and I think of Stuart. I think of him lying there, and the blood, so red, so shiny. Like crimson syrup instead of golden syrup. Gross. A squeezy bottle of crimson syrup. The big giant picks him up like a bottle of ketchup and squeezes the blood and guts out of his body.

'No!' I must have shouted that because Niamh and Laura both jump like they got a jolt of electricity. But you've got to

72

be careful. How many times do I have to say it: be careful. There's only one way now, and it's the waiting way. No more thinking and remembering about his tricking. He's not in school – think about school.

'School is okay. I don't mind school.'

One time in art class, we did the pictures where you cover the whole thing with paint. Amy did this parrot in a rainforest and we hung them up in the hallway outside the art room. Hers was brilliant. She said mine was, too – but Mum is the only artist in our family, like Dad said. Mine was shit. Socks looked like a ghost – you could hardly see him at all.

'So – you say school is okay? And you're smiling, now – that's good.' Laura smiles back at me – safe behind her shiny hair and her shiny teeth. I bet her house is shiny and smiley. I bet nothing dirty is allowed in her shiny life. Nothing bad. No bad smells, no dirty places.

'What about home? And Stuart? Let's stick to that for now.'

You're lucky to have a home; you've no idea. Lucky I took you and your mother in. You'd have been on the street if it wasn't for me. But that's not true – it's not true shut up. Mum – the mum from before had a job and she was real, like a real mum. There used to be an ad for holiday homes near the sea or something and when it came on, Dad would go, 'Tell me, love, is that the one you worked on?' even though he knew it was, he just wanted to make her smile. We both knew about it and I thought Mum was famous. She was in art college before she met Dad – in England. 'We met on a shoot,' is what she said when her friends asked, and that was when she had friends. And later I learned that a shoot is not shooting, it's filming a film. And it's not true that we were beggars. If Mum – and now my heart begins to pound again and I want to see her.

73

'Can I go home?' I say, but even before she opens her mouth I see the no.

'Soon,' she says. 'But we've to talk a bit more first. Talking helps, Jenny. If you let it. So come on, tell me a bit about normal life for you at home?'

'Our normal. Our normal isn't normal. Like it's not the same for Amy, or Luke. Amy's mum thinks she's brilliant.'

I mean, she is and all – but her mum comes to all the plays and debates and stuff and, when she looks at Amy, it's like Amy's a movie star and her mum's her biggest fan.

'And Luke's dad is a doctor or something. Last year, when the exams finished, his dad arrived at the gate dressed as a cowboy. It was a roasting-hot day and he had a cowboy hat on and he was carrying this big bucket full of ice pops. And he doled them out as we came out the gates, saying, "Yee-haw" and stuff like that.'

She laughs at that.

'That's fun – what a nice thing to do. But for you – your normal, then. What's that like?'

She has no idea. Our normal is different. I think back back back. Back way back. It's been like this for ever. It's not even, like, we're not even surprised any more. It's normal. And then yikes and oh shit it pops out.

'He hits Mum.'

There, hah, I said it. I said it and my heart is beating very fast. You've done it now. But I don't care. The first time – I remember every bit. He was watching the TV. Mum was kneeling on the floor with Karl, baby Karl – before he could walk. I think she must have been well then, or in good form anyway; she was playing with him, stacking little wooden bricks. Karl was laughing, knocking over the bricks every time she stacked them up. She was laughing, too. And he was sighing. That's the first warning.

74

Mum looked up and said, 'Look at him Stu, he loves it.' All smiles. She went back to the game and started stacking up the blocks again. And she didn't hear the sighs. She was saying, 'Not yet, not yet,' while she added a block, then another and another. Karl was rocking, opening his chubby arms wide, then clasping his hands together, then springing them open again, dying to be allowed to knock down the tower.

And Mum was going, 'Wait, Karlie, wait,' and Karl was squealing and squealing, trying to say now – Nuh! Nuh! Nuh!

And then, so sudden, Stu grabbed the mug from the table – the I Heart London mug. And he fired it at Mum. At her head. Blam! Side of her head. Boing! Into the tower of blocks. Smash! Down on to the floor. Karl screaming. Mum sobbing.

He said it was an accident and he did this fake laugh, and he goes, 'I was aiming at the tower.' And I stood there oh very very still. Behind him, where he couldn't see me. In my hand was the other mug of tea, the one I'd been bringing in for Mum. My knuckles clenched around the handle. And I wanted to smash it – Blam, Boing, Smash – over and over on his head. But hahah, no way can you say that out loud dumb bitch.

'Once he threw a cup at her and it hit her in the face.'

'He hit your mum. That's not okay, Jen,' she says. Big revelation. She hands me the box of tissues. But I'm not crying. I'm not crying.

'You're safe here, Jenny,' she says. 'You can tell me anything. And you'll feel better.' I wait and wait. And if the clock was still ticking, that would be a lot of ticks. I look at the splashes on my sleeve – three of them. One for each lie.

1. I'm not safe.
2. I can't tell her.
3. I won't feel better.

'Tell me what's been happening, Jen.'

Oh yes of course. I'm going to blurt it all out right out now – all the stuff I couldn't say before. Not to Amy or Luke, not to Val, not even to Ms Wilson, our English teacher, who is actually really easy to talk to and always says we can tell her anything. Laura, who I only just met, thinks that after years of squashing it all up smaller and smaller – squashing it and stuffing it inside the locked box where it can't hurt anyone – that I'm going to burst open the box now. Doesn't she know that the longer you don't tell, the harder it is? You can't trust her at all. I keep telling you. She's going to mess up the whole thing and it'll be your fault. You'll only have yourself to blame. Dumb bitch.

She's looking at me and shaking her head a bit, though maybe she doesn't know she's doing it.

'You don't know what he's like. Everyone thinks he's brilliant and, like, Mr Nice Guy.'

Didn't he rescue us after Dad died? He says he saved our lives. And we just drag him down, we ruin everything. I can't stand this – it's such a mess. And then I go blurting blurting.

'He hits us, too – me and Karl. For nothing. It's – it's just what he does. And nobody knows.'

Stupid bitch. You know what happens now. What if he comes to get me here? If he gets out and he's downstairs and Laura hands me over and he says, 'I'll take it from here,' with his fake smile. He would trick Laura with the winning smile, saying, 'You've been such a great help, thanks.' And then outside, when no one's watching, he says, 'Get in the car, bitch.'

And Laura is talking – she's been talking for a while. She is leaning forwards and it's double hands smoothing shiny hair behind double ears. That's her extra-hard-listening face. And she's saying thank you like a talk-show host.

'Thank you, Jenny – you've told me so much and this is good – but it's not enough. We really need to know if you – if you know anything about Stuart. Do you know where he is? Can you think of anything that could have happened to him?'

She gets up and walks over to the window. It's getting dark outside and she pulls the blind closed. She turns back towards me.

'We're going to talk again in –' And there's a huge noise and I jump but it's only Niamh pushing back her chair and standing up. And she goes, 'Sorry, that was clumsy, heheh.'

And she points at her phone and I don't know what she's saying but there's more of their whispering and Laura starts tidying up her pencils and stuff.

'Okay,' she says, 'that's enough for today,' and I don't know if she means for me or her. And now I don't want them to go because – because I want to go home but only if he's not there.

'Am I going home? Can I go home?' Niamh puts her hand on my shoulder and it feels like a hot-water bottle.

'Not yet, chicken,' she says. 'You've to have some rest, all right?'

13. Jenny

They bring me back to the ward. A different nurse is at the door and she stares at me when we go through the doors. And she looks like a witch because her hair is very black. She looks like she hates me and she knows bad things about me.

'She'll be here for tonight anyway,' Laura says in a whisper voice.

'Ah right,' says the nurse, not in a whisper voice. In a voice which says *you're an evil little bitch and don't think I don't know what you've done*. Maybe she is the black witch from the island and she knows. Laura looks over and sees me doing my not listening and now I don't know if she hates me, too. Maybe they all hate me. Her caterpillar eyebrows huddle together in a frown and I think that everyone knows. And when people say the walls have ears, maybe it's true – everyone knows.

'Just until we know a bit more,' Niamh says in her smiley voice, and she squeezes my shoulder again.

'What were they thinking anyway?' says the nurse. 'She's not meant to be here. She should be in the Sunbeam Unit.'

And Laura says, 'No beds,' and looks narky, and I am wondering what the sunbeam unit is like and I'm thinking all the beds have yellow duvet covers. But Laura's not listening to her. She's reading through the chart like she's lost in her head somewhere and so Niamh steers me over to the counter where all the nurses hang out and hands me over.

'See you tomorrow, chicken,' she says.

It's warm on the ward and it makes you feel sleepy. And I am sleepy, but I've got to stay sharp. That way they won't catch me. When it's really quiet later and they're all asleep – they have to go to sleep, even the really bad ones. That's when I'll do it. There's a door at the end of the corridor. I saw it on the way to the interview room. It leads into the stairwell – so that won't be locked because, otherwise, how could you go up and down stairs? I've got to get out. It's like I can't remember stuff in here, I'm not going to be able to think straight until I'm outside.

I'll go straight home. Mum and Karl and Socks – they must be dying for me to get back. They're probably waiting for me. They're sitting in front of the stove and it's all cosy and warm. Karl and Socks are snuggled up on the sofa. Mum is reading a magazine and she's drinking tea, no – hot chocolate out of the I Heart London mug.

I'm definitely going to get out tonight, because I have to see them. Because they're all waiting for me. But not him. He's not there.

The nurse is doing the drugs round. That's what they actually call it. And it's crazy, she has to wear this red vest which says 'Don't talk to me – drugs!' and I asked her why, but she just pointed to the vest. Luke will love that.

When I tell him that, inside here, the nurses wear a vest which says 'Don't Talk to Me, I'm Doing Drugs'. I mean, it doesn't say the second bit, but that'll make him laugh. She pushes round the trolley, which is like a mini-cupboard on wheels. And she doles out the tablets in paper cups. Emer is her name, the nurse in the vest. The nurse that does the drugs.

'You're in here,' says Barbara, the nurse that is a witch, too. 'We moved you.'

But I can't remember where I was before. I was with Laura and Niamh today – all day. But before? I just can't remember. Laura said the emergency department and I remember bright

bright lights and the sick feeling and my hands so sticky and dirty. And the kind nurse who held my hand. And later she washed the blood away. I put my hand to my wrist and turn it over to see the marks. But it's clean.

This room has two beds and one chair. The curtain is half around one of the beds but you can just see a crumpled skinny old woman lying there asleep, like a pile of Tesco bags.

'That's Catherine,' says Barbara. 'Don't wake her or she'll cry.' I walk around the curtain and sit on the chair beside the empty bed.

'Sit there now – you'll be going back to bed after the drugs round,' says Barbara. 'You missed the tea – do you want anything?'

I don't answer because I only want to get out, that's all I want, and I'm doing that later when it's quiet, but I am not telling Nurse Barbara. Be careful and don't say it out loud. And when I get home I can have tea with Mum and Karl and Socks. Barbara looks less like she hates me now, but I don't know why and she passes me a box of tissues. The box is nearly empty.

'Dry your eyes,' she says. 'Go on. Then get into bed. That's the best thing for you now. You can take your meds and go straight to sleep.'

Do you know 'Lucy in the Sky with Diamonds' is not about taking drugs, though everyone says it stands for LSD? John Lennon's little boy brought home a picture he'd drawn in school of his friend Lucy; she was swinging on a swing. He'd given her these diamond-shaped eyes. 'Lucy in the Sky with Diamonds' was the title of the picture, that's all.

Sometimes when Stu hit me, that's where I went, in my head. I put myself on the swing, like Lucy. One Saturday morning I'd been up before anyone else and I went down to watch TV. I made myself a bowl of cornflakes and brought it inside to the sofa. And I was sitting on the sofa with the half-empty bowl of cornflakes resting on the arm, watching that mermaid series, wondering would she manage to rescue the guy in time and what would he do when he came back from being unconscious and realized she was actually a mermaid. So, I only heard the creak of the last stair and the bang of the kitchen door.

'Ah, for God's sake!' That got my attention. I grabbed the bowl off the sofa, but it was too late. In two strides, Stuart was across the room, in front of me. He ripped the bowl out of my hands and the milk sloshed on to the floor and across his shirt. With his free hand he hit me across the head – whack. But whack is not right because I heard other noises, like clang and burn and ring ring ring in my brain.

'Get into the kitchen and clean up that mess. How many times do you have to be told something? Huh?' He grabbed my wrist and dragged me across the room. I stumbled because the clanging and ringing make you stumble. Into the kitchen. There was the evidence. Number one: Open box of cereal on the table. Number two: Loose cornflakes spilt on table and, oh no, on floor. Rookie error – he'd only got to follow the trail of cornflakes to find me. He flung the bowl into the sink and spun me around to face the evidence.

'Clean it up.' He let go of my wrist and gave me a shove. That's when I started the song. In my head I could see these bright orange trees. They were waving and the tangerines bobbed about like balloons. I floated in the sky and it was the colour of marmalade. I picked up the cornflakes off the floor, nine cornflakes. I tidied away the box into the cupboard. I put the bowl in the dishwasher. There were slaps and a thump in the back while I did, but I didn't count. I was with Lucy in a peachy orange sky. And anyway, at least Mum was okay. At least Karl was still asleep. So everything was fine. Fine.

That was why I made the island. I made it so he couldn't get us – me and Karl. I blocked the door and we were quiet quiet. The red boat to sit in, bobbing up and down on the waves. And the tall cliffs all jagged. And the beautiful white horse. And that first day we saw Niamh Cinn Óir on her white horse and she was amazing. I thought I could do anything that day. I could be like her. She doesn't hide from anyone. Her name means Brightness and her long, golden hair whirls in the wind when she gallops across the land on her huge white horse. Men see her and they're afraid and they don't dare touch her. No man would touch her. I think I hear horses' hooves and I wonder has she come from Tír na nÓg to rescue me, but it's not horses, it's rain pummelling the skylight.

It's the middle of the night, but there are still lights on in the corridor. I heard them talking earlier. I'm meant to be in the children's unit, but there's no beds. I wish I was there, and then it'd be easier to get out. But I'm lying here now. I have on the hospital gown, but I have tracksuit bottoms underneath. And I see little boot things under Catherine's bed. I could fit into those. And there's a cardigan on the chair. It's purple and a bit sparkly like old women wear, but I'm going to put it on to hide the gown. I'm getting smart.

I wake up with my heart blam-blamming fast because I thought he was watching me. I thought Stu was sneaking into my room. I could hear his breathing right over my head, and I shot up out of bed, but it was just a nurse and she put her finger to her lips and turned away. I'm going to stay awake and wait now. For the chance to get out. All the Tesco bags rustle then and Catherine says in her sleep, 'When's the bus coming? Did you see the bus yet?'

14. Laura

I take the outside lane on the bypass, heading back towards Templeogue, already snarled in the evening rush hour.

'Erm, turning left here? Left!' Niamh shrieks, grabbing the door handle as we lurch across two lanes and take the left for the station.

'Oh God, sorry! Sorry, Niamh. Jesus! Thought I was going home – wish I was!'

I pat her arm, glance over at her. Niamh is a grand girl, as she says herself. She's tall and athletic – like a warrior. I realize suddenly, I've never once heard her mention her weight or use the word 'diet'. It's just not on her radar. I'm still patting her arm – it's like warm stone to the touch. Solid and timeless.

'Sorry about that,' I say, pulling into a parking space outside the station, a vaulted modern building – all angles and glass – the single word 'Garda' hewn into the cube of granite marking the entrance Seskin West Gardaí have reason to thank the Celtic Tiger for – for both the fancy building and the crime rate to match.

'You're grand,' she says. 'Once I've changed my knickers, I'll be fine.'

In spite of everything, I laugh. We're almost in the incident room when she stops.

'So – what are we telling them? We don't have a lot.'

I bristle. 'What are you talking about? She disclosed the domestic stuff – she spoke a good bit about home –'

'She's completely dissociated, Laura – what was it Dr

Connolly called it? – Acute Stress Disorder or whatever? So we can't take everything she says for bleeding gospel truth. Wait –' She studies me closely. 'She's a tricky customer, yeah? And she's sick.'

'Yeah, but I know – I – I know she's going to tell us more. Come on – you know how it's going to pan out? He'll have been abusing her –'

She puts her hand up like a stop sign.

'Yes and yes and maybe that's true. But this was just a clarification meeting and –'

'Well, yes, but we need to know –'

'I agree. But – I don't know.' She starts walking again, shakes her head. 'You're being a bit weird on this one is all. Like there's too much at stake.'

It's my turn to stop. We're in front of the main desk. Declan's the Unit Sergeant on duty today and beside him, Sorcha, the new trainee, is setting papers ready for the briefing. I turn so they can't see my face.

'How much more do you want at stake? She's been raped. She's been beaten. Her mum and brother are in intensive care. Jesus, Niamh! We've got to help her.'

She looks at me strangely.

'And a man is missing, yeah? I agree. We've to build up a picture, get the statement – find out what happened.' She pauses again. 'But it's not as if we're doing it by, like, seven o'clock tonight.' She tilts her chin, considering something. 'Did you notice her looking at you? She's doing these sneaky looks all the time. She's watching to see how you're taking it. She's testing you.'

Again, we're used to that. It can take three or four clarification meetings – over many weeks – for a child to trust you enough to tell you what's happened to them. They rarely launch into it. Niamh is right, though. I have an image of her sideways look from under the long hair – a sneaky sort of look. She was watching me, measuring.

'All I'm saying – and I can't believe it's me saying this to *you* – is be careful. Slow down.'

Niamh waits and, over the top of my head, I see her make eye contact with someone. She grins.

'How're ye?'

I turn. Declan is watching us. He'd better not have heard that, I think. I don't want him seeing her 'handle' me, like I'm an idiot. I turn, switching on the smile.

We head into the incident room, which is buzzing already. It's set up like an open-plan office, with information, photos, statements and job lists all displayed or about to be pinned up on the various noticeboards lining the walls. There's a bank of phones, a load of computers and a large screen being used by other detectives and, supervising it all, Detective Inspector Don Not-on-My-Watch McNeil – the Cigire – stands by the main window, looking rumpled and cranky. He nods in our direction.

'Let's look at what we have – try to work out a timeline. What have you got from the girl?'

'We don't have a whole lot yet, Cig,' Niamh says. 'She's really confused. Still in shock.' She opens the folder. 'Here's the report from last night and the notes from the clinical nurse specialist.' She passes it up to him. 'It shows sexual assault – in the last forty-eight hours – and there's evidence of physical abuse, old and more recent.'

Niamh is composed, sticking to the facts. There's no trace of emotion in her voice or demeanour. That used to be me. I used to pride myself on keeping cool in the face of this stuff. I take a breath, try to remember the training. Give the victim a platform. Don't get swept up in it.

I try to visualize myself sweeping a stage, lining up the

chairs, training a spotlight centre front, on Jenny. She needs to be heard. It's Jenny in the chair, Laura. Not you. Get a grip. Niamh is still talking.

'She disclosed domestic violence at home perpetrated on her mum and both kids.' She looks at me, giving me the cue.

'Yeah, we got a disclosure of ongoing violence at home, emotional and physical. Is there anything on record here – domestics? Call-outs?'

Denise shakes her head. 'No, I checked already. Up to now, we've absolutely nothing on them in the books. No complaints, nothing.' The Bookman – well, it's technically Bookwoman today, as it's Mairéad Scally – is taking notes, making the list of what has to be done.

'He works in town – an ad agency near Baggot Street.' Denise glances through the pages in front of her, shaking her head. 'Don't know much about the mum – Melanie. Neighbours say she's very quiet. Used to work in film production.'

'Right, I need boots on the ground – house to house. Talk to the neighbours. I need more on where they found the car, see if we can work out what happened.' Mairéad types it in.

He stops, presses a stubby finger against his temple as though prising information out manually.

'Did you get any results back yet from the clothes?'

Niamh and I glance at each other. Shit! I never picked them up from the nurses' station!

'I –'

Before I can finish, Niamh steps forward. 'Sorry, Cig – I was meant to do that earlier. I'll go back now –'

Cig looks like he's about to explode. He stares at her, shaking his head in disbelief; phrases like 'Basic policing! Simple bloody tasks!' squeeze through his compressed lips.

She opens her mouth to speak, but he holds up a hand, turning away from her, as though she's not there. I try to catch her eye, wanting to thank her, but she stares straight ahead.

'And I want the search team to extend the search area as far as the family home, in case he went back there,' Cig goes on, blanking Niamh. 'We've got to find him. Judging by the amount of blood in the car, if he's not dead already, he soon will be.'

'Do we have reason to believe he's badly injured?'

Cig looks at me as if I've sprouted wings.

'We've a car drenched in blood and two people in intensive care!' he snaps. 'If his injuries are half as bad as hers, he's not going to survive more than a couple of days.'

He turns to give Niamh the full benefit of his scathing look.

'Of course, if we *had* any blood results from the clothes the girl was wearing, we might know whose blood was all over her – but we know jack shit because someone *forgot* to do the most basic bit of policing, which is to gather evidence!'

Wisely, Niamh says nothing.

'Right,' he says, gathering up papers, 'search the house, too. Check for passports.'

'The airport?' says one of the new recruits.

'Yeah – the airport, bus and train stations, doctors' surgeries, even the Emergency Department here. They're busy. He could be unidentified. People make mistakes, *don't they?*' Another glare in Niamh's direction.

Disgusted at myself for letting this continue, I take a step towards him. 'Eh, Cig –'

'Could there be CCTV footage at home?' says Niamh, literally stepping in front of me. 'Or neighbours? We'd be able to see if he went back there.'

Cig turns to the Super, who's been tucked into a corner by the radiator, literally taking a back seat. Heavy-set with hooded, lizard-like eyes that miss nothing, you'd easily forget he was there. He was watching me.

'Can I've more bodies to check that out?' Cig says.

The Super nods.

'Murder/suicide gone wrong?' Seán is on a roll. Clearly nobody told him that the Cig is not a fan of speculation.

'Missing person is what we have at present. That's all we have. Missing person, presumed injured – and two victims who can tell us nothing.'

'Three victims,' I say. 'The girl.'

Cig looks at me closely.

'Who is potentially a suspect – yes.'

He turns away, fixing Seán with a look, 'So, we're not going to go leaping to conclusions, are we?'

It's coming. I know it.

'Not on my watch.'

Niamh and I make eye contact. She does the tiniest wink.

Thirty minutes later we're in the cramped room in the unit where we have our desks, Jenny's clothes spread out on the table in evidence bags. Niamh went up to the hospital to pick up the bag of clothes while I started on the paperwork. I'd tried to thank her as soon as we left the incident room – but she shrugged it off.

'You're grand.' She nodded. 'He can't give me too much of a bollicking because I'm coaching his first-born later. One of the perks, don't you know?' And then she was gone to get the clothes.

Now we're looking at them, wondering what to say.

'Isn't that a bit – have you ever seen a fourteen-year-old

wear something like that?' I point to the dress. Beneath the bloodstains, it's a pale pink-and-grey skater-type dress, with long sleeves and a flared skirt. Girly and childish.

'No? They wear track bottoms and hoodies! Or – at a push – jeans and a nice top. Look.' She lifts it carefully in its plastic and holds it up to my shoulders.

'She's about your height.'

We both look down to where the dress ends – midway down my thigh.

Niamh holds up an ankle boot with a low heel and a dia- manté buckle along the side and, in her other hand, a pair of ankle socks – bloodstained along the top. She shakes her head. In my head, I assemble the outfit – a girly dress with long sleeves – demure. But bare legs and ankle boots – that's a lot of bare flesh for a fourteen-year-old. Don't they usually cover up?

'There's no way she chose this outfit,' Niamh says, voicing my thoughts.

I don't answer. I've just spotted her pants and bra. The bra is cotton – peach-coloured and soft – no under-wiring or anything. It's one of those starter bras – more of a bralette. But it's the pants that get me. They're a shade of mint green with a peach trim and on the front is a picture of a princess. They're like something a seven-year-old would wear. A rust-coloured bloodstain butterflies the crotch. And just like that, I'm blindsided by memory – pain, ripped fabric, torn flesh. Hands yanking and grabbing.

'Laura – are you okay? Did you hear what I said?'

Niamh steps closer towards me. 'I've been talking to you for about ten minutes, for feck's sake! Did you hear any of it at all?'

She grabs a pen and labels the evidence bags – ND1, ND2 – all the way through to five.

'I'll drop these across to the lab tonight – hopefully, they'll get to them tomorrow.' She nods in the direction of the hallway. 'It'll be on the nine o'clock news later – missing man and the Help number.'

'What are they saying?'

'Nothing about the girl at this stage. Just the usual – name, description – man missing following a road accident. Nothing about helping with enquiries or anything.'

'Right.'

'It might shake out a few witnesses, or friends of the family or whatever.'

She grabs the apple from her bag and bites – holding it between her teeth while she ties back her hair. All of a sudden, she looks about eighteen instead of her thirty-plus years – the fresh face with no make-up, the long, untinted hair – natural highlights from being outdoors – the strong features and piercing light green eyes. She tries to speak.

'I ga-ah gah.' She removes the apple. 'Sorry, I gotta go. Why don't you go on home? First get yourself a big drink of water – keep hydrated, bitch! Then go home. Take the notes with you – get your hours in. Have your dinner. Have a rest and – you know – your nightly shag or whatever? Or is that only at weekends?'

She grins. 'That ride you're married to – he deserves better,' she goes on after seeing me attempt to smile.

'Fuck off,' I say, feeling a lifting inside. This is what I love about Niamh.

'Thanks,' she says, as if I'd wished her well. 'I will. I'll be home after ten – ring me if you want, yeah?'

She zips up her jacket and steps into the corridor.

'And I mean it – get some sleep or rest, or whatever it takes. You look wrecked. I'll see ya in the morning.'

'Thanks. Bye,' I say, sitting down and firing up the computer.

'Let's go out on a sesh – we haven't done that for ages,' she shouts down the hallway, without turning. 'Tomorrow night, okay?'

The door bangs before I can reply.

15. Laura

I shuffle the pages, smooth them flat. I've been at this for forty minutes and my head is killing me. Niamh's right: I should drink more water. Then again, maybe if she'd write a bit more neatly, I wouldn't get such a headache trying to decipher her notes. Even before I finish thinking that, I know I'm being a bitch. I'm just tired and it's late and I haven't had any food since I abandoned the spinach-and-beetroot wrap.

I check again. I've a five-page report from the multidisciplinary team in the emergency department and nowhere in it – nowhere – is there a single word uttered by Jenny. But by the end of today it's a different matter. Now I know where the phrase 'word salad' comes from.

> Amy – schoolfriend. Not allowed to attend party by S. Control issues.
> Dad (A+B+C+D=Dead Dad). Beatles songs. Died in fall from roof.
> Stuart – controls everything. The T-shirt – made her take off. Then binned.
> Scared? Mum too.
> 'big, giant, meaty hands scrunching and squeezing'
> Mum and Karl
> He hits Mum.
> Amy/Luke – nice. Good guy. Schoolfriends.
> 'There's only him.'
> 'Not my world. His. It's all ruled by him.'
> 'He hits us . . . for nothing.'

'Our normal isn't normal.'

'That'd be suicide.' Niamh had underlined that one. Then she'd put a bubble and several arrows (in case I'd miss it) around this bit: 'I think he's maybe gone away for a few days – because he's not very well.'

Val minds Karl pm. (N.B. interview?)

Mrs A – retired teacher living nearby. (?)

I take a fresh sheet and get started.

Clarification – Initial meeting:

J presented at first meeting: shocked, confused

Initially not speaking – then torrent of ~~info~~ garbled facts & info re: family, Mum, brother (Karl), Stuart, schoolfriends. Interested in The Beatles (Dad)

Concentration: very poor/intermittent

Memory: seemingly poor/could be suppressing memories/refusing to remember or refusing to say what she remembers?

Pressured speech alternating with long silences

Auditory hallucinations – seemed to be listening to another voice(s)

Depressed mood

Flat affect – psychosis? Schizophrenia?

DISCLOSURE: Discloses physical abuse – J, K and Mum

'He hits Mum.' 'He hits us, too . . . For nothing.' S threw a mug of coffee at Mum.

DELAYING: J talks slowly, long silences – making herself wait before replying. Playing for time?

A search of rip.ie threw up the listing for her father's death.

The death has occurred of Ben Davies of Clonchapel and Ben's Bikes Rathgar.

Passed peacefully at the Beaumont Hospital on 20/03/13 following a tragic accident at home. Very sadly missed by his wife Melanie, daughter Jenny, mother Marie, sister Georgie, brothers-in-law, nieces, nephews and his many friends and customers.

My eyes linger over the phrase 'tragic accident at home' and, in spite of the heat in the stuffy room, I shiver, remembering 'Dead Dad', said in that flat voice – as though reading a list of spellings. And then when we told her Stuart was missing, all she said was 'Oh dear.' They call it flat affect: when the patient has no expression in their voice or on their face. It can be another aspect of trauma or it can come about through shock. I remind myself that it's also common after a psychotic episode and in schizophrenia. It's as if a person gets no access to the emotion that should accompany the event. It's simply too big to get close to it. Grief after death. The rage and pain after an assault. That can happen – I should know.

Yes, sometimes you say things with no emotion when you're making sure that no emotion leaks out. And other times you could be aiming for sarcasm. Like: 'He's not very well.'

I get another lurch of tiredness and check my phone. Ten thirty-eight – shit. First, I'd hoped to be back in time to take over from Sylvia. Then I was just looking to make it before Matt puts Katie to bed. And *then* I was thinking it'd be fine if I get in before Matt goes to bed. But after half ten, he knows not to wait up, and he's a man who's fond of his sleep. Anyway, it's a bit easier if he's already asleep. I don't have to talk to him. After last night's exchange and this morning's squabbling, I doubt we'd even manage two words without fighting. So that's that.

On a normal day, when everything is pretty straightforward, Katie and I get to play her current favourite game of Trash the House before bedtime. But this is not going to be straightforward. Although, let's face it, it's not as if interviewing traumatized victims is ever straightforward. My phone buzzes and I nearly leap out of the chair. I see Matt's text.

Didn't wait up. K good. No wars with Damien/L! Nite

Back in the day, there'd have been an *x*, or maybe even two. And I'm the same. Since when was ending a text with two xs an over-the-top display of affection?

That was funny, though, about Liam. Liam, at three and a half, is the terror of the neighbourhood. Matt and I have taken to calling him Damien, after the son of Satan child in *The Omen*. That way, Katie doesn't know who we're talking about. He's the only other three-year-old who lives locally, so we often see him. A chorus of 'No, Liam! Dána! Tá sé sin an-dána! Put that down, Liam. Liam, I said no,' follows him, as his mums Shauna and/or Lucy sprint around after him, doing damage limitation.

The most recent war was a few weeks ago. We were in with Shauna and Liam, picking up the spare key because I'd managed to lock us out of the house. When we arrived, Shauna had that cabin-fever look I recognized, so we went in for a cup of tea. Liam was playing in his play kitchen.

'Liam, féach! Katie's anseo!' The plan is that Liam will be enrolling in the Gaelscoil up the road, so Shauna and Lucy are always working on increasing his incidental Irish. I'm not convinced it's working; all I've ever heard him say is a big loud 'No!' But the girls' Irish is definitely improving. Shauna took hold of Katie's hand as she was hanging back and brought her over to the 'cistin'. Liam scowled.

Even though she's lively enough at home, Katie can be

very timid with other kids so, for a little while, she stood watching Liam arrange his plastic pots and pans, but she was dying to get at them. A toy saucepan fell to the floor and she seized her opportunity.

'Here,' she said, picking it up and making as if to hand it to him. Liam let out a bloodcurdling yell of 'No!' and at the same time there was a yell of 'No, Liam!' from Shauna. Liam grabbed the plastic pan with both hands and simultaneously kicked Katie as hard as he could. She fell backwards, banging her head against the edge of the table. I leapt up and gathered her to me, trying, unsuccessfully, to hide my rage.

'Jesus, Shauna! He kicked her!'

'Oh my God! Oh, I'm so sorry, Katie! Sorry, Laura,' Shauna said, mortified. 'Liam, that is very, very naughty! An dána! You're going on the naughty step right now.' She grabbed his hand and dragged the now-wailing Liam into the hallway, where she plonked him on to the bottom step of the stairs.

'Don't move!' she yelled, coming back into the kitchen and closing the frosted glass door, which did nothing to muffle the sound of Liam's screaming. Meanwhile, I was surreptitiously checking Katie's head for bumps, fearing concussion. While Liam roared and Katie hiccupped, Shauna apologized again and plied her with biscuits. I said all the correct Mummy things about kids will be kids and he didn't mean anything by it, but I was surprised by the strength of my own reaction. If I'd been closer to him, I think I could easily have slapped him – hard.

We don't do the naughty step – but I think the rule is that the child spends one minute per year of age on it in time out. Liam was inconsolable; those three minutes may as well have been a life sentence. He got off the step and pressed up against the door, his two podgy little hands flattened on the glass, wailing. Through the glass, you could see the grief-stricken face – it was like *The Scream*.

Then a strange thing happened. Katie slid down off my knee and ran over to the door, still clutching the biscuits. She placed her hands against Liam's, through the glass, like some bonkers prison-visiting scene in a movie, still holding the biscuits, so it was more like her fists on the glass.

'Him tired, Muma,' she said, turning back to look at me. 'Him tired.'

'Oh my God, isn't she the cutest?' said Shauna. 'She's forgiven him already!'

'That's what Matt says when she's misbehaving.' I laughed, hearing his well-worn parenting phrase. I say she's being bold. Matt always says she's tired.

'Liam, you can come back in – tar isteach,' Shauna says, opening the door. 'And say thank you to Katie for maithiúnas. You're a lucky buachaill – she forgives you.'

Liam was let back into the kitchen and in no time both victim and perpetrator were eating biscuits, which the victim had promptly handed over.

'That little anti-Christ needs manners put on him,' laughed Niamh when I told her the next day. 'And she needs to work on her rage.'

'But that's the funny thing – she wasn't angry with him. Once she'd stopped crying, it was as if nothing had happened between them.'

'That's exactly what I mean,' Niamh had said. 'She needs to work on that.'

At eleven o'clock, I can't do any more. I'm ready to call it a night. It's weird – I feel her presence – as though Jenny's at my shoulder watching what I write, watching me give up for now, just for now – and head home. There's a darkness about her – that heavy hair with its curtain of fringe; I was practically on my knees, trying to make eye contact beneath it. The wiry frame draped in the baggy hospital-issue top, the cuffs damp from her sucking and chewing them. Her face was thin, gaunt even, and her eyes were deeply shadowed and seemed to glitter – not with the brimming tears of a tragic victim. It was more like they were tracking movements, measuring the room – roving like a night owl.

What if she's the attacker here? What if Stuart's crawled off somewhere, injured, losing blood from a wound? He's not going to last long in this freezing weather. He could bleed out from a stab wound in a matter of hours, or he could die from exposure.

Twelve years of practice means nothing is strange any more, but in terms of age, Jenny seems both ancient and childlike. When she was talking – well, gabbling with the pressure of speech – she was like a little kid of nine or ten. But then, when she stopped herself and you could almost see the feverish thoughts racing, eyes darting – she seemed calculating in an adult way, devious and cunning.

She's small but athletic-looking – stronger than she looks. And she definitely knows where he is.

Day Two

16. Laura

The radio is on in the kitchen and I can hear Katie rapping her spoon against the table of the highchair, impatient for food. Neither of them has seen me, so I get the Sig out of the safe and holstered under my jacket before entering the kitchen. Matt hates having a gun in the house – doesn't want to know about that side of detective work.

'Morning,' he says, over Katie's excited babbling. The announcer is talking about implementation of recent budget measures – including 'hundreds' of additional gardaí. He mimes a thumbs-up.

'That's good news,' he says, getting ready to switch it off. Then the appeal for information comes on. I motion for him to leave it.

Gardaí in Clonchapel are appealing to the public for assistance in tracing the whereabouts of a local man, Stuart Cullen, forty-three, who has been missing from his home in Dublin 14 since Sunday, 3rd November. Mr Cullen was last seen at about 6.30 p.m., getting into his 18 D registered silver BMW. The car was later involved in an accident. He is described as 5 feet 11 to 6 feet in height, of medium build, with light brown hair and blue eyes and was last seen wearing a navy puffa jacket, blue shirt and black trousers. Anyone with information is asked to contact Clonchapel Gardaí.

Matt raises his eyebrows as I switch it off. He knows better than to ask – I can't talk to him about my cases, but he gives a little nod of recognition. I watch him butter the toast for

Katie. He goes all the way to the edges with meticulous attention to detail, ignoring her drumming fists and kicking heels as she vents her frustration.

'Jesus, Matt! Give it to her already, would you? She's hungry.'

'One minute,' he says mildly, inserting the buttery knife into the centre of the toast and withdrawing it slowly. This is his technique for cleaning it, before putting it into the jam, or, in this case – because all standards have been abandoned – Nutella. I'm filled with rage – as I always am when I see this. It's so – so devious. Why doesn't he get a clean spoon? It annoys me. Matt knows it.

He uses the knife to scoop out a blob of Nutella and, before he begins spreading it on the toast, he passes me the jar for inspection.

'Exhibit A,' he says. 'The suspect failed to use a clean spoon for the chocolate spread and left crumbs in it. Oh, no! Wait. There are *no* crumbs in the Nutella. Would you believe it? Case closed.'

He smiles. I sigh – he's taking ages – then reach across the table and grab the bowl of blueberries, tipping some of them on to Katie's tray. She looks at me suspiciously, then carefully starts bursting the berries one by one with her thumb. One spurts a jet of fruit jelly into my hair.

'Katie!' I snap. 'Don't do that. Naughty.'

At the mention of the word, her face begins to fall apart; it's like watching a demolition – I wait for the crash. She starts to wail and flails both hands angrily all over the tray, scattering the berries right and left.

Matt doesn't look at me. He cuts the toast into a butterfly shape and picks it up.

'Look, Katie! Butterfly!' He flies the toast butterfly above the cups and plates, making aeroplane noises and swooping it over my head, across the top of the coffee pot, bouncing it off her ears, nose and chubby fists. Finally, he lands it on the tray in front of her. Katie beams.

Matt turns to me. He wipes the Nutella off his fingers then takes out his mobile.

'Did you reply to the text from Gemma?' He's obviously decided not to criticize my child-rearing skills, then. Always so bloody patient.

'No – shit. I didn't see it,' I say, although I guiltily recall seeing *Gemma/Richards W* appear on my screen at some stage yesterday. 'I was caught up –'

'It's fine,' he says, already absolving me and saving me from making up an excuse. 'I accepted anyway. We're not doing anything on Saturday, are we? And you're off Sunday?' He's right but, even so, I sigh.

'What's it for? What's the occasion?' Already I'm wondering what I'll wear and who'll be there. I hate myself when I'm like this.

'Just dinner – no – supper,' he says, and like that, I'm right back where I belong, wondering what's the difference between them. Does one have more cutlery than the other? Better wine glasses? Different dress code?

'Smart-casual,' he says, reading my mind. 'It's the twins' birthday party – the supper is afterwards. Gemma said to bring Katie in the afternoon, then they're ordering pizzas and wine in the evening.'

He wipes Katie's sticky hands with a cloth. She immediately picks up another half-chewed piece of Nutella toast and gets to work on it.

'But –' I'm trying to think of excuses. I don't want to go. And if I did want to socialize, I'd way prefer to see one of my friends. Maeve – she's just had her second and – Christ! I realize I don't even remember if she had a boy or a girl. I'm such a crap friend. I've completely lost touch with Lucy, too, and now, with Christina living in Spain, that's another friend I never see. Christ.

I want to come home after work on Saturday and close the door and I don't want to talk to anyone – except Katie and Matt. Plus, I've no idea how this case will pan out. I've to drop everything to get to grips with it. So, I really don't want to have to sprint home, shower and choose something bloody smart-casual to wear to a pizza party in Richard and Gemma's fuck-off mansion in Ballsbridge, where even the traffic noise is on a different level.

Richard is a friend of Matt's from way back. They played on the same rugby team even before they ended up in UCD, where they played on the college team. So, when I'm with Richard and Gemma listening to 'the guys' (as she calls them) reminisce about great matches of yore and slag each other with a never-ending supply of Fly-Half versus Wing jokes, somehow it's like *I'm* the blow-in. The fact that they've twin boys – Harry and Jamie – means that the rugby jokes can now be traded over the heads of the next generation. Things like 'Let's hope his passes are as pretty as his face – not like his father's,' or 'All I want is for them to grow up happy – and not become Wingers like their Uncle Matt.'

Gemma and Richard are both doctors – she's a cardiologist, he's in gastroenterology – and, notwithstanding their brilliant careers and twins (twins!), they live in this amazing hundred-year-old three-storey house with an immaculate garden in which they are constantly socializing. Constantly. If we don't go on Saturday, it'll be the third or fourth time we've declined.

I like them both – that's the other thing. When I was on leave after having Katie, we met up regularly and Gemma and I got on really well. I was the oracle on baby issues and,

I suppose, I actually liked being the one who knew the score. Matt and I would warn them about the sleepless nights and the teething. I gave Gemma the full low-down on childbirth and – yeah – now I think of it, we were both probably patronizing as hell.

And I needn't have bothered with the dire warnings; childbirth, like everything else Gemma touches, turned to gold. The twins were fed on a strict regime where everything was timed and measured. They were weaned by six months and now, at just one, are both reportedly taking their first steps along the marble hallway (underfloor heated) of their D.4 mansion.

The only time there was ever anything not right between the guys was when Rich chose his property-developer buddy Jonno – not Matt – as godfather. Though Matt told me he was fine, I could see he was gutted.

'Smart move, actually,' he'd smiled bravely. 'Jonno's loaded. He'll probably give them each a nightclub for their eighteenth.'

I was stunned. Matt was best man at their wedding. Before that, he was roommate on rugby trips and teammate on the pitch. He was a shoulder to not cry on when Gemma briefly broke up with Rich (to put manners on him – all part of her plan) and we were the first friends they told when they were expecting.

Jonno doesn't even play rugby – too busy sailing. At the christening, we drank cocktails and ate complicated-looking finger food passed around by 'girls' who came with the caterer. I stood in front of the massive marble fireplace, listening to the shrill laughter and South Dublin accents, discussing skiing and au pairs, the best place to get sushi, rugby trips and, oh God, already – the best secondary schools. I wasn't drinking, as I wanted to pick Katie up early from Granny Justy, and I had that left-out feeling you get when you're the only one completely sober.

I'd told Justy I was surprised they hadn't chosen Matt.

'Oh dear,' she'd said. 'Poor Matt. That's a shame. Gemma – I know her parents, actually; he's a consultant at the Mater – Gemma's a strategic thinker.'

She'd handed me Katie, then went back in to get the changing bag. Her gold bangles clanked as she placed her hand on my shoulder and mimed 'mwah mwah' kisses on each cheek. Katie copied with a wet kissing noise.

'Bye, darlings!'

I had stood there for a moment – wondering if I was missing something – what did she mean, *strategic thinker*?

'Bye – eh – sorry, Justy, what do you mean about Gemma? I'm not sure I follow –' I'd said, then began walking down the front steps.

'Oh Lord! Nothing at all – just that Gemma has it all planned. Lovely to see you, darlings.'

I'd turned and begun walking down the granite steps, Katie clasped to my hip, wriggling in her efforts to do a full-body wave for Granny.

'Bye, Justy, thanks for minding Katie,' I'd called, in a voice that sounded bright and optimistic and clear. A lying voice.

Jonno and his latest stunning girlfriend will be there on Saturday, no doubt. And Gemma's friend from college, Leah, who had a little girl around the same time as the twins were born. Leah's a quantity surveyor – so she and Matt can enjoy chatting about economics and the recent budget. Matt would probably have a much better time without me, I realize, and I *do* have the excuse of being at work for most of the day.

'Why don't you bring Katie to the party in the afternoon,' I say, 'then when I get home from work, I'll come and pick her up and leave you to enjoy the rest of the evening? You can have a few drinks and get a taxi back later?' Matt looks at me as though I'm speaking in a foreign language.

'We're invited – *we* – both of us are invited, Laura. The party ends at five. I'll bring Katie home and give her tea. Then, when you get home, you can have a bit of time with her, your glass of special medicine' – he looks at Katie when he says this – 'and I'll drive us over. We can always leave the car there and go back on Sunday, okay?'

I wait too long to answer and, in the silence, Katie starts to bang the table again. Suddenly, Matt stands up and begins brushing crumbs from the table on to the plate. I notice his hands – a whitening of the knuckles – and there's a stony set to his jaw. He's raging.

'Are you trying to push me away?' he says. 'Can you even hear yourself?'

'I'm not – it's –'

Why is he pushing and pushing at this? I feel like screaming. I'm tired – I want to come home at the weekend and curl up behind a locked front door, not stand talking shit with bloody Richard and Gemma with her bloody masterplan for her bloody perfect life. Matt is still holding the plate of toast crumbs; he's like a Labrador waiting for an instruction! He has no idea! I'm working full-time in a job where it's up to me to pull people – kids, women, babies even – from the barrel of shit that is their life. Shit layered on top of shit dumped by shitheads from one generation to the next since the shitting dawn of time.

'Laura, I –' I can't hear him over Katie's banging. He steps closer.

'Come *on*, Laura,' he pleads.

'I don't have to justify myself to you,' I say coldly. 'And we're not joined at the hip, are we? You go to the party if it's so important.'

17. Niamh

I sit at the junction of Castlewood Avenue and Rathmines, watching the traffic inch its way towards the city centre, glad to be going in the opposite direction, literally heading for the hills. It's still dark, but the shops are open and people are about – buying their breakfast coffees, queueing at the cash machine, waiting at bus stops – anonymous ants scurrying about the grey buildings. Mammy thought I'd never last in Dublin.

Mammy was wrong about that – and a few other things. She didn't know, still doesn't – let's face it – that the scale of Dublin is what drew me away from home and what keeps me here. The anonymous confusion of city life is where I can be myself. In Knocknabo, the village where everyone knows your name, I'd always be Niamh – *Ah, you know her dad Lorcan and her mam Martina from up at Moyvale Farm? She's the younger sister – went off to Templemore to become a guard, you know.*

Even dirty old Rathmines and the house share with a pair of primary teachers – my former teammate Lisa and her beardy boyfriend, Max – the couple who win the award for loudest, most regular sex ever – can't put me off. Of course, when we first moved in, Lisa was single and determined to stay that way. But Coppers and Max had other plans.

My stomach rumbles. Typical. I had a big bowl of porridge before leaving – what? – less than twenty minutes ago. Mam would laugh if I told her that the Dublin traffic is so bad you've time to get hungry again between leaving home and arriving at work.

Or maybe she wouldn't. Dad would laugh. She might smile her soft, regretful smile – the smile of a woman who wishes for a little bit less of me in so many ways.

I stop to get doughnuts for the coffee break, but still arrive in the incident room ahead of Laura for the daily briefing. There's a chorus of 'Wells?' from the gang – ripping the piss out of the Tipp greeting.

'Well?' I nod back at them, then, more quietly, 'Ye feckers.'

They've put photos and info on the noticeboard – a family photo, a print-out of Stuart that looks like it's from his work website, the car at the scene, including interior shots of the bloodstains along the doors and in the footwells – both the driver and passenger sides – and all over the airbags. There's a shot of the knife – a standard kitchen knife, serrated, small – like you'd use for chopping meat. It's in the footwell of the back seat – behind the driver. I bend closer, trying to see if there are stains on it, then hear Cig's voice behind me.

'Nothing.'

'No?'

''Course, she could have cleaned it before chucking it –'

'She? You reckon –'

'I don't reckon anything yet – just a theory?'

Cig sighs – the kind of sigh you do at the end of the day when you're knackered, even though it's not even nine – and hitches up his trousers. He's lost weight. I remembered the chat after training last night – Leonie told me they were all on a 'no carbs till Christmas' kick at home. Linda's idea.

'And he's only eating once a day – you know?' She'd roared laughing then. 'Thank Christ he does the fasting on workdays – it makes him narky as hell.'

I'd told her I'd bear it in mind.

We stand side by side, looking at the pictures.

'Where'd you get this one?' I point to the dog-eared photo.

It's from a few years ago. Stuart and Mel and Jenny are wearing matching Christmas jumpers – white with red reindeer and red snowflakes. Mel is holding baby Karl to her chest, as though afraid someone might take him, an unfocussed look blurring her expression. Stuart is grinning broadly – he has a strong jawline and white, even teeth which he's baring like he's in an ad for dentures.

'Do you – did you guys do those family photos' – I nod towards the picture – 'for Christmas and stuff, when your kids were small?'

'Did we feck!' He shakes his head. 'None of them would sit still long enough – or the baby had a teething rash or Linda was feeling too fat – you know? Women!' He stumbles to a halt abruptly. 'I mean – Christ – don't quote me. Haha!' He stops, flustered, worried he's fallen into a soup of political correctness. In a louder voice he goes on, 'Fecking expensive, those studio shots anyway.'

We look back at the photo. Stuart's right hand squats on Melanie's shoulder, claiming her – but it's the left hand that I focus on. It's grasping an anxious, haunted-looking Jenny on to his lap. She's wearing the matching jumper and a little red kilt, her bony bare legs dangling awkwardly in mid-air. The span of his fingers extends from her hip to her armpit, the index finger across her left breast. There's no sign of puberty – she's only about nine and flat-chested – but something about it is deeply unnerving. I remember her talking about his 'big, giant, meaty hands'.

I do a little hunch and release of my shoulders – as though shrugging the hand off on her behalf.

'It was in the handbag,' says Cig. 'We think it was the mam's – Melanie's. Although it's so small – the bag – it could have been the girl's, I suppose. There –' He points to another photo of a small, circular handbag covered in silver sequins.

'Feck-all inside it – I thought you women carried the kitchen sink? This only had a lipstick and the purse. Less than twenty euro in notes and coins in the purse – and this photo.'

'Well – I suppose if they were going to a party – maybe she only needed –'

I stop, realizing even I don't believe that explanation. She's a mammy – I think of Siobhán and even neat-freak Laura – there'd be a phone, a few pens or a biro, tissues, wipes; stuff that would come in handy if your kid kicks off.

'Not even a mobile phone?'

'No. She mustn't have brought it.' Cig shrugs. 'Or maybe she doesn't have one?'

Everyone has a phone, I think. Certainly, every mammy. But maybe you don't need a phone if you live in a world 'ruled by him'.

Cig's still talking.

'I have Seán on that – he's calling the office to see if we can get a number for Stuart, at least.' He pauses. 'I'll cover that in the briefing. No point in –' He pauses, looking about the room. 'Where's Shaw?'

'She'll be here any minute,' I begin covering for her. 'She – she said she might call to his workplace – Stuart's office – on the way in –'

Cig shoots me a sharp look.

'Save it,' he says. 'And I want to know if' – he lowers his voice – 'if this is – if there's anything I should know, right?'

'How d'you mean, Cig?' I'm not being smart – I'm genuinely baffled.

Cig looks uncomfortable. He swallows, and the sagging stubbled flesh below his jawline judders in time with the action.

'Forget it,' he says. 'Just keep an eye on – on everything.'

Clearly, I'm not the only one who's noticed the difference in her. It irks me – her stubbornness. We're entitled to six sessions with a counsellor for free; it doesn't go on your official record – no one would even know. I've got a lot out of mine – unlike Laura, I actually attended after the whole Mitzi incident. We didn't even talk about that – we talked about Mam and how she's still angry with me – and it helped.

But no way will Laura go for counselling. It's like she'd be admitting weakness or something. Which is all fine and dandy – until she cracks and gets us both in trouble.

It's another five minutes before Laura appears. She's lorried on the foundation today – and straightened the bejaysus out of her hair. It's like a helmet, and she stands in the doorway like she's about to enter a battle. I watch her take stock of the room. I'm in the far corner, and it gives me the chance to see her almost as a stranger – literally, a bit of distance. Her eyes flicker – I can nearly hear her internal checklist: Cig, Mairéad, Seán, Sorcha; the two uniforms on this today, Scully and Flynn; and St Bernard – Bernard Dooley, one of the dog-handlers. She's doing a weird thing with the fingers of her left hand – tapping each one in sequence against her thumb, like she's counting.

'Good morning, Shaw.' Cig's tone is sarcastic. I will her not to let him get to her, but she's flustered.

'Sorry – sorry, everyone. Yes – I –'

Dabs of violet underscore her eyes. Has she been crying?

'Are ye using the dogs today?' I nod at St Bernard, desperately trying to break the tension. 'How're ya, Bernard?'

'Dooley, can you get to the family home,' says Cig, glancing at him. 'I've a uniform down there. Get whatever you need, and then I want a thorough search of the area.' He holds up his hand, pre-empting protest. 'Yes, I know it's been done already – but not with a victim recovery dog.' The dollied-up name for cadaver dog. So, he thinks there's a possibility the guy is dead already.

His gaze slides across Laura, effectively dismissing her and settling on me. 'You two get back to the hospital.'

'Yes, Cig,' she says.

'And I want calls made to the school – the priest – the local Tesco – the nearest garage – just get me more info on this family. Someone must know something about them.'

There's a general murmuring of assent. I grab Laura's elbow and pull her aside.

'How are you doing? You all right?'

'Of course! Just got delayed at home this morning – blueberry-juice emergency.' She laughs – it's more like a cough. She's not meeting my eyes.

'Haha, oh yeah, that's bad. Listen, you go on to the hospital – I'll follow you. Gonna make a couple of calls – check up on the clothes, okay?'

She nods agreement.

'Grand. See you down there. Listen.' I turn, reckoning I'll just ask her outright. 'Is there something going on? Are you okay – really?'

Her face closes completely – as though someone threw a switch. She presses her lips together, the sinews in her neck twitching – and I think she's going to yell at me, but she swallows it down.

'I'm fine.' She inhales a long sigh, then exhales. 'Ready for action,' she says in a bright voice.

'See you in a bit.'

18. Jenny

I fell asleep properly, like the whole night, even though the light was on in the corridor. Dumb dumb dumb. It must have been the tablets. The nurse with red hair brought me a tray of breakfast stuff and arranged for me to have a shower, and that was good. And she says I've to talk to the doctor later – the one with the flakey skin – but that's in the afternoon. And I looked at morning TV and recipes that only take ten minutes, and then the red-haired nurse comes back and brings me down the hall to where Laura is waiting and there's lots of smiling. I sit down on my chair, being a very good girl. Stay still and it won't hurt. I'll have to wait until the lunch break and then I can try. I could get out the door into the stairwell and then sprint sprint run down the stairs and out to the trees. I look down at my feet. I have striped socks and slippers and they're not mine. I'll have to find my shoes or it won't work.

'Well?' says Niamh, coming in the door with bags and jackets and scarves falling off her. 'Wagon,' she says, nodding at Laura, and red-haired nurse looks embarrassed and I want to smile, but you can't trust her. Keep it shut up.

'Niamh –' Laura is sighing, and her frowning face is all stitched together in disapproval. 'I think we need to re-member the type of words we should use. What about –'

And Niamh goes, 'Oh sorry, bitch. My bad,' and a snort nearly comes out my nose because she's funny and I like her.

Laura comes closer. She nods at me, as if we're both in this together, like we're a team. Both working on a case. I wonder if she can actually read stuff inside my head, like a mind reader. If you do this job all the time, you'd get good at that. If you watch someone closely for long enough, you can see what they're thinking. Sometimes I can see the pictures in Stuart's head better than he can. I hate that. When I can see it coming even before he does.

'How are you doing today, Jenny?'

'I want to go home. I need to see Mum and Karl.'

'I know,' she says, and her eyes dart – zing zing – over and back to Niamh. 'Of course you do. That's completely understandable. We just need to talk a bit more. Do you remember we agreed you were going to start at the beginning and tell me the whole story today?'

No, I do not remember, Laura. Say nothing. I can't remember anything and I just need to go home. But she's saying other stuff, like 'It's okay to tell me if you don't know or you don't remember, but what happened the last time you saw Stuart?' and 'When was the last time you saw him? Can you remember?'

Wrong wrong wrong. All wrong. The train is going down the wrong track there. And now an image comes into my mind: Stuart lying face down. His eyes are closed and there's blood in the folds of his shirt, on the back of his head, in the creases of his neck. Like someone tipped a jar of blackberry jam over him. I say nothing. You've got to be so, so careful. This is her trying to trick you. This is not the plan, dumb bitch.

'Why do I have to stay here?'

'It's best for now,' she says. 'It's just for now.'

'I'm not mad,' I say. 'There's nothing wrong with me. I told you. I'm not even angry or anything any more.'

'Any more.' She holds out a little brown paper bag. 'That's interesting. Any more. So you were angry, were you?' She rustles the bag. 'It's a croissant – one of the chocolate ones. Better than breakfast on the ward, yeah?'

Porridge stuff and cornflakes and toast that had gone so bendy you couldn't even chew it. And everyone sat there or shuffled around, and they had their little cups of juice and their little cups of tablets.

'We've work to do, Jenny. You need to talk to me some more, tell me what's been going on. Do you remember? We said we would meet up today and you'd tell me everything, from the very beginning?' I take the bag and put it up to my nose to smell it. It smells amazing.

'I can make sure that the bad stuff, the things we were talking about – we can make sure it doesn't happen, that it never happens again. Now that we know what's been going on, we can do things. It will never happen again.'

And I think *stop lying, stop saying happens and happening*. Be careful and shut up, bitch. Shut up. It's not done yet.

'Jenny, did you ever hear that saying, "the truth will set you free"?' she says. 'I'm not sure who said it. But I agree with the thought behind it. You know, the truth being liberating?'

Seriously? Truth with a capital T. Truth comes along with his big old golden key and sets you free. What does that even mean? Doesn't she know that nobody tells the truth – no one? And then I think maybe she does know about the island and it's all a trick – to trick me. Maybe I already told her something. Because I feel like I just talked and talked yesterday. Shut up, Jennifer. Shut up, you stupid bitch; if you can just shut up, it's not long now.

I eat the croissant. That was kind of nice of her, but it could still be a trick. It has the real dark chocolate in it. The real deal.

'Nothing is real,' my dad said, and I didn't know what he meant. But now I know. He meant that everybody lies. And he was right. Every one of them, all the grown-ups, at some point they all sign up for the lying. All of them are in on it.

And I am so sick of them lying. Tooth Fairy and Santa Claus and Easter Bunny and God watching from hahaha heaven, and that's just the start of it. And everything's gonna be all right, I'm here, I'll always be here. Lies.

Fairy tales are way more honest. Bad things happen. For every handsome prince, there's a hideous ogre. Trolls lie in wait under dark bridges. Wolves hunt dumb kids who stray from the safe path. Act stupid, get punished. Do nothing, get punished. Be good, get punished. Stupid bitch Mummy Goat goes out for the afternoon and Big Bad Wolf comes to the door, tricks his way in and murders all your brothers and sisters. People lie. People are greedy and jealous and sneaky and out for themselves. They hurt other people, too – even little kids. They enjoy it. They take what they want and they don't care.

People die. And they don't come back and they don't live happily ever after. I can see them all here, right here. Right now. The troll is under Laura's desk. Cyclops is crunching a baby's skull in the corner where Niamh is sitting – fragments of blood and bone litter the floor. He's going to start on her next.

We had this lesson with Ms Wilson where she went through all the fairy tales and she made us analyse them. Like, she said Hansel and Gretel is all about learning to control yourself and stuff – not a story sponsored by dentists to warn you off sweets, which was what Freddy said. His mum is a dentist – hah. Ms Wilson said it means you have to stick to your goal. And Cinderella is about having patience and being resourceful – but we were all laughing too hard after Amy said, 'It tells you that if you want to get ahead in life, you need really good clothes, really good shoes and a really rich man.'

Then we had to choose our favourite and write about it. And loads of girls picked the Ugly Duckling or Cinderella, but I picked the Wolf and the Seven Little Kids. Where, after the worst bit has happened, the Mother Goat cuts her babies out of the sleeping Wolf's belly, then she piles in rocks and stitches him back up. And she's so calm and ladylike in the picture, stitching his stomach, using her hooves like hands. When he wakes, he feels so bad he staggers to the river to get a drink of water. And then he falls in and drowns. Haha. And Ms Wilson said there's not a whole lot of analysing needed for that one.

'Classic revenge story, Jen. Classic.'

And after class she called me over to her desk and she said all that teacher stuff, like 'I'm here if you ever need to talk.' And 'Is everything oh kay at home? Is there anything you'd like to talk about?' And I looked at my shoes – they're black runners, but you're meant to wear ones you can polish. I hoped Ms Wilson didn't notice that. And then I remembered to look at her face and smile. She was smiling, and her cheeks really do look like apples. So I said, 'Thanks,' and 'No, I'm fine.' Because – I don't want them all knowing and looking at me, like it's a disease spreading – like a creeping cancer inching its way up my body, crusted, weeping sores covering the skin that used to be the smooth, clean skin of a little girl.

The croissant was nice, but I'm thinking about the rocks in the wolf's belly. Now the croissant is inside my body – what if that's a trick? Laura could have hidden tablets in the – in the chocolate bit – and it might be like a truth drug and all the stuff will come out and I won't be able to stop it. I told you not to trust her. Dumb dumb dumb.

'Did you – are there tablets hidden inside – in the croissants? Did you put something in there?'

'Jenny, listen – of course not. The croissant is just a – it's just a croissant. You've got to trust me – talk to me. I can help.' She sits back in the chair and sweeps her shiny hair off her shiny face and does a smile. You cannot trust her.

'You're still confused, Jenny – you're in shock. And at the moment, your head is full of worries and anxieties and bad memories and, listen, Jenny –' She comes round to me and kneels down so she can see my face. 'You've got to trust me? Yes?' Then she sits back on her heels and smiles again. 'Do you know what I did last night? I went home and I listened to some Beatles songs.'

If this is a trick, it's a good one, 'cos I'm listening. I'm wondering which ones.

'What was it?'

'Oh, it was the *White Album*.'

The *White Album* was Dad's favourite.

'And I listened for a while and the song I really love is "Here Comes the Sun".'

She goes back to her desk and just leaves me thinking about it, and I do, and I know why she wants me to think about it. She wants me to think everything's going to be all right.

'Tell me happy memories for a bit, okay? You could talk about your friends?'

That makes me smile a tiny bit because I'm remembering Amy and her Deadly Plans. Amy has the best plans. We were outside the music room and she was, like, flicking my hair from one side to the other, frowning. And she said, 'Well, apparently, he thinks you're really pretty but, you know, standards and all that. We're still gonna need a plan.'

'Amy tried to set me up with this boy – Luke. She told him I was some kind of expert on dogs and he tried to get us to walk our dogs together – but he didn't even have a dog. He said he was going to get one, though.'

'Good planning by Amy.' She does her Laura Laugh and she thinks I don't know how fake it is.

'Well, yeah, but oh my God, she's so embarrassing. It was so embarrassing.'

And I think about how he was at lunchtime that day. He'd even brought a notebook and pen.

'What's the best type of dog to get?' He sat down opposite us, clicked the top of the biro. 'Amy said you'd know.' So I began telling him that I didn't actually have a dog but, under the table, Amy nudged my knee.

'Ask her anything you like, Luke. I told you, she's an expert.'

'Well, okay then. Number one, what's the best type to get, like I said, and two, where did you get it? From a breeder or the internet or what?'

Amy kneed me again. 'Well, um, Socks – Socks is a collie-type dog. You know, the black-and-white ones?'

At this point, he actually wrote something down in his notebook.

'Luke, are you really getting a dog?' This got me another knee-knock under the table.

'Hey!' said Amy, like she'd been struck by a lightning bolt of inspiration. 'Luke, you could help Jen walk the dog – Sockie, or whatever its name is?' I stamped really hard on her foot. I was mortified. But she just squeaked. Luke nodded.

'Not a bad idea, um –' So he looked at me – you could see him kind of steeling himself to go for it, and a blush began creeping across his cheekbones.

Laura's listening hard and watching – always watching. I remember the blush. I shrug to shake it off.

'And he was just about to, you know, ask me out or something, and then the bell rang – before he could say anything.'

And Amy had called me the densest person she'd ever met and she zipped up her schoolbag like she was punishing it.

'Aw,' said Laura, all sadface.

'Yeah, and I told her, "He's not my dog. So it's not true."' And Amy said, "Who cares? The truth is overrated. What matters is how you feel."'

'And was that true? Was Luke really going to get a dog?'

Laura's still waiting. I look at her.

'The truth is overrated,' I say.

She smiles at that. And then she changes fast, and I told you, I keep telling you, she moves fast and she'll trap you. Dumb bitch.

'Do you know where Stuart is, Jenny? People are very concerned. People are looking for him.' She waits. Niamh waits, too – her pen in the air, like I'm about to give the actual map reference or something.

'Jenny, you need to tell me – if you know anything about where he is or what's happened to Stuart, you need to tell me. I can help.'

I think about that. I think *shut up shut up shut up. Keep your stupid trap shut, stupid bitch, just for once.* I think it's too late for that.

I turn to see how it's going down with Niamh, but she's looking at something on her phone. I think it's a phone – but maybe it's a voice recorder or something. Is she allowed to do that? I'm talking too much. I'm forgetting to be careful. But sometimes I don't even know if I said something out loud. Sometimes I think I'm stuck in my head and no one can see me in there. And sometimes I think my head is inside out, spread out like a grapefruit you carve, and everything is there and everyone can see it.

Then it's quiet for a long time and, haha, I shut up and close my eyes. I hear Laura get up and go over to Niamh, and it's whisper whisper and Niamh says, 'Go back to the dog.' That's not good.

'So tell me more about the dog-walking, Jenny? Where do you usually go on the walks? Is it just you or did you say you and Karl went together?' And I know what she's thinking because it's always people walking dogs who find the body, isn't it? The body was discovered by a dog-walker in the early morning. But haha, I am not an early dog-walker. But I could make her brain go for a walk, hah.

'Sometimes we bring him up the hill behind the town. He loves that.' And Niamh goes, 'Gorse Hill or the Hellfire?' and I think *yes, that sounds good*. Good place for him, the Hellfire. The devil came to play a game of cards there and the house burned down. And so I say, 'The Hellfire,' and Laura looks at me funny.

'How do you get there?' she says. 'It's – it must be about five miles from your house?' Have you never heard of fitness? Dumb bitch Laura.

'Oh, it's a bit of a hike,' I say, 'but it's worth it when you get there,' because that's the kind of shit grown-ups say. And now I'm laughing inside and I think of loads of gardaí climbing the Hellfire, walking their dogs. It will be nice for the dogs to get out, though.

Then I think of Socks sniffing with his wet, black nose and a big, huge howl comes up my lungs, but it is not coming out. I turn it into a cough and Niamh brings me water and tissues and doughnuts, but I'm not crying. And I think my head will burst and I wish I had the grapefruit knife, no, the bigger one – the steak knife. And wham I would slice that sad part out of my brain.

'And what about Mum?' says Laura. 'Does she come on the walks, too?' And I like that picture so much better than the Mum picture in my head. I think more about it and there's Mum and me and Karl and Socks and you can see our silhouettes going up Hellfire Hill. We're in order of height with

Mum at the top and Socks at the bottom. But we all walk up together and the sky is orange with those V-shape birds flying across it.

'Oh yes, sometimes,' I say.

And I don't think don't think of the other picture with blood all black and scrunchy stuck in her blonde hair.

'That's great,' says Laura, with her 'I don't believe one word' face which I now know. 'We'll take a short break so you can get some lunch, okay?'

Luke's mum and dad are never in and, one time, when he was making us snacks, I looked up the medical books in the study. Luke thinks I want to be a doctor but, haha, it's because of other reasons. The best book is *Trauma* Ninth Edition. The chapter called 'Outcomes' tells you how long it takes.

You can die of dehydration and another thing you can die of is irreversible shock.

I learned it off – I wrote it on a Post-it and stuffed it in my pocket. Irreversible shock means that even if you try to fix the injury, there's a drop in blood pressure. And then there's organ failure and death 'despite any heroic attempts to resuscitate the patient'. That's exactly what it says, haha: no heroes no heroics no more prince.

Irreversible shock and dehydration are in charge.

19. Laura

'We've an address for the childminder,' Niamh clicks out of her phone and puts it in her bag. 'Val? So I'm gonna head back now.' Before I can answer, she continues, 'No point in us both going. Give me a text when Dr Connolly's finished with her, okay?'

They've taken Jenny back to the ward and she's to be seen by him before we can talk to her again, though I've requested another meeting as soon as possible.

'Right, that's good,' I say. 'She might know something all right. If anything comes up that we can use, ring or text straight away, yeah?'

Niamh looks confused. 'Well, no – I won't – because you're not meant to question her on her own? Clarification meeting protocol, eh, yeah?'

She zips up her jacket – rain and thunder are forecast – and rummages in her bag to find her car keys. We arrived separately today.

'You get some lunch, do your notes or whatever. I'd say I won't be long. I'll text you when I'm on the way back.'

'Right,' I say, unable to shake the feeling of being managed – handled. Is it that obvious? I head to the canteen and queue for coffee, find a corner table, wipe it and sit down. While the coffee cools, I google Beatles albums and lyrics. She definitely perked up at the mention of 'Here Comes the Sun'. And, as I'm scrolling through titles – just like that – the dark thoughts begin to creep in – stealthily, sneakily – like the thieves they are.

I don't know how they do it – against my will – when I'm

thinking about something else. I was on my phone, for God's sake! But here they come – my worst thoughts: Katie lying dead on the road outside our house, knocked down by a car, her body mangled and twisted, her face a mass of blood. Or this one: Katie pale and lifeless, electrocuted or poisoned or hanged by the cord from the blind and Matt bending over her, pumping her chest, trying to restart her heart. And this: Matt bending over her and he's not saving her life, he's choking her, his big rugby fingers pressing her airways closed. That's a new one. But it's always Katie and she's always dead. And I'm always too late.

What scares me most is the one I hardly dare to think – that if she – if – that if the worst had already happened, I'd be free of this agony. I cannot believe I gave birth to this thought.

Confront the thoughts. No matter how bad they are, you must confront them. Challenge the compulsions.

Yes, I will, thanks, Sam. And yes, I remember that this is a chronic disease and that it never completely goes away. And yes, I remember that getting better is only 50 per cent of the job. Staying well is the other fifty.

So, I make myself stay with the anxiety – the many anxieties: what if something happens to Katie when I'm at work? What if Sylvia takes her eyes off her while opening the front door to someone and she runs out on the road and is mown down by a car? What if there's a paedophile watching our house and he snatches her when Sylvia's not looking, or what if Matt comes home early and he takes her out for a walk by the river? The river's really high at the moment and she never holds his hand, because he doesn't make her, and what if she runs down the riverbank and trips into the weir and drowns?

Sam always says you can't be bored and scared at the same time, so I think up more scenarios, each worse than the one before, until, at last, it happens. I run out of possibilities and the compulsion fades. I've succeeded in exhausting the crop of anxieties. For now.

I'd been seeing Sam once a week for almost a full year, before I actually got the hang of it and accepted that OCD is a disease you live with – like diabetes or asthma. There really is no magic wand or tablet, although tablets can definitely help. You have to ask yourself: what is the likelihood of your fear coming true? The answer is always slim to nil. Then you have to challenge the logic behind the fear. And when you do this, you find that there is no logic.

Matt is not going to come home early to take Katie out in a storm, bring her dangerously close to the raging torrent/ muddy stream that is the Dodder and, bizarrely, fail to hold her hand or supervise her. It makes no sense. It is not going to happen. Sylvia is the most sensible and brilliant childminder in the country. She managed to rear her own kids to adulthood before minding Katie. She has never once opened the front door and let her run out into the road. And now that I think about it, Katie's sprint is not that fast, it's more of a podgy drunken-puppet run, and if she did make it out the door, Sylvia would catch her easily before she reached the gate.

And Matt is a great dad and the kindest of men. He'd never hurt her. He loves her. I love her – with every strand of my being in every molecule. I'd never hurt her. Never.

I find a ragged piece of skin at the side of my thumbnail. But instead of ripping it I stand up and make myself head up to the counter to buy some actual food. Keep on track, Laura. Or, as Niamh would say – fuck this shit, let's eat.

I do well over lunch – managing to eat chips and beans off the hospital plates – and when I'm halfway through the mug of coffee, it occurs to me that I could take a run out to Sam.

If I'm quick, I might even catch him before his afternoon sessions. That way, I can tell Jackie from the counselling team that I've made contact with a therapist privately – they can stop ringing me.

Sam's house is about three or four miles north of Clonchapel, up a winding mountain road – the kind of road they use for car adverts. It's impossible to drive it without channelling your inner rally driver, gearing down for the corner, accelerating out of the bend. It's years since I've been up here, and I'd forgotten the feeling, the other benefit this drive gives you. With each bend and each gear lowered for the climb, you get the feeling of escaping the grey depression of the lowlands. You drive higher and the brown-greys of the Tesco car park disappear, the dank ditches turn into green hedges, the tattered, rain-lashed estates into rolling fields bordered by ancient stone.

I pull into his driveway, adding a flourish of gravel-crunch as a sound effect to my car advert – already feeling stronger at the thought of seeing him. It's only as I ring the doorbell that I think it's a bit cheeky, showing up without a phone call or even a text in advance. I should have brought biscuits or a cake or something.

I wait, freezing in the chilly breeze, for what seems like an age, and it comes flooding back to me – the countless other waits on this exact doorstep. Different Lauras each time. Thanks to Sam, each Laura a bit better than the last – a bit stronger, a bit more confident, a bit less of a mess.

'Well, imagine my surprise!' He beams, throwing the door wide open. 'If it isn't Detective Garda – or is it Superintendent Garda Laura Shaw of the flying squadron?'

'Damn professional etiquette, I'm giving you a hug, Sam,' I say, doing exactly that.

Except now it's me being the fantasist, because none of

that happens. I stand on the doorstep, rehearsing exchanges exactly like that one for about five minutes, then realize that the house is empty and Sam must be out. I take out my key and am just about to get back in the car when I hear a shout.

'Hello? Hello? Who are you looking for?'

'Hi, Cora.' I close the car door and retrace my steps towards her. 'I'm really sorry for not calling ahead, I was looking to speak to Sam. I know I should have called first – sorry!' I'm nineteen again and in full nervous, babbling mode. Cora – Sam's university lecturer partner – was always terrifying. Even though she was lovely to me, insisting – if she was there – on giving me tea and biscuits after the sessions, I was intimidated by her forthright, challenging stance on just about everything. 'Change the system,' she'd say. 'Don't be afraid to make mistakes – just do better than we did. We're relying on your generation of young women.' No pressure then, Cora. Although she'd been well impressed when I told her I was thinking of applying to train as an SVI. 'You'd be amazing at the job, Laura,' she'd said. 'A natural.'

A smaller, thinner Cora smiles at me now. She's wearing one of her usual hand-knitted jumpers with a giant roll-neck which emphasizes her weight loss. She's ill, I think.

'Come in, Laura,' she says, reaching to hug me and then ushering me into the darkened hallway. 'Better do this inside.'

I follow her into the kitchen, making my way to the Aga, grateful for the warmth as I lean against it. Cora and Sam never received the memo on the whole kitchen-cum-laboratory style which is currently in fashion. Stripped pine gleams yellow against dark green walls that are covered in photographs and paintings. Wall-mounted fancy plates glint in the weak November sun and a seventies cork board wilts under the assault of what looks like hundreds of postcards.

Cora fills the kettle, switches it on and turns to face me.

'Laura, I'm sorry to tell you this,' she says, gesturing for me to sit down. 'Sam died.' I pull out a chair and sit down heavily, the chair creaking in protest.

'Oh no,' is all I can manage. 'How? Like, I mean, when?' Cora busies herself taking out the mugs and a carton of milk. She spoons tea into the teapot – Sam's favourite type, Lapsang.

'Almost two years ago now. I'm sorry, Laura. I thought you knew.' She stirs the same teapot with the chip in the spout, replaces the lid.

'I'm so sorry, I didn't even know he was sick. If I'd known, I'd have visited and – or sent a card or something.' Cora pats my hand.

'He wasn't sick long, which was great. From the diagnosis to him going it was less than two months. He didn't want chemo and it wouldn't have bought him much time. He didn't even stop working until about three weeks beforehand – he was finishing an article and he didn't want to let them down. Although I told him that was his ego talking – he didn't want to leave the world without having the last word, that's what it was really about.'

I smile at that. One of Sam's most charming characteristics was his giant ego. That would be exactly right.

Cora passes me a mug of tea and I inhale the fragrant steam. Tears well up behind my eyelids – the tears I'd been fighting since the row with Matt, since Mum's anniversary – they're unleashed. I cry like a kid. I suppose I cry like the kid I was when I first started coming here. And I cry at my childish belief that I could grow up and get a job and reproduce and, meanwhile, the grown-ups would stay the same. Idiot.

Cora waits, then reaches across the table and pats my hand. 'I know,' she says.

After a few seconds, I manage to stop.

'I'm sorry,' I begin, but she cuts me off.

'Don't be. He asked for copious tears at his service of re-membrance' – she laughs – 'so, he'll be very flattered at these. Anyway,' she says, taking hold of both my hands and leaning forwards as if to stand up, 'I am finally – finally – getting around to clearing his study, so this is excellent timing.'

She motions for me to follow. We pass along the silent hallway, and it's just the same as it used to be: the further along the corridor I go, the calmer I feel. The space is narrow and the walls here are painted the same dark green. Framed pictures are uplit with soft yellow lights at shoulder height, detailed prints of plants beckoning you to study them – a fern, a dandelion clock, orchids. The study door is padded with green baize – the kind of stuff you'd see on a snooker table. 'So they can't hear your screams,' Sam would joke. Then the whoosh of air, the creak of the door, and we enter his study.

'Book-lined' doesn't even begin to cover it. Bookcases at hip height line three of the walls and ceiling-height double bookcases stand duty on either side of the stove. Books are laid out on the roll-top desk, books on top of the books in the cases, lying across them. Books open on the windowsill and the three coffee tables.

'I've given away two boxes already.' Cora gives a crooked smile. 'Honestly.' She bustles over to the bookcase behind the desk and, picking up an empty cardboard box from the floor, hands it to me.

'I'll leave you in peace for a bit. Fill this with any books you'd like – anything that'd be useful for you, or maybe for the job? You're still doing some SVI work, yes?' She points to the shelf nearest the window. 'Loads of children's stuff there, from when he was teaching the Master's.'

With Cora gone, her lively energy leaves the room, too. It's still and silent, as though time has stopped. Outside, the sky darkens and I watch a posse of oak leaves take an exploratory whirl across the garden, skimming the bare branches and skipping across the bird table. I sit in the client chair and face Sam's empty one across the desk.

I try the usual techniques, the ones he taught me himself. I tell myself it's just a feeling and that feelings pass. I tell myself that he wouldn't want me to feel guilty – his most hated emotion. I tell myself that having Sam alive and sitting in this chair is not what was keeping me well, that I am in control of my thoughts and that they are exactly that – just thoughts.

I tell myself all these things. But now – sitting here in the client chair – I realize I'm struggling. Matt's right. My love for Katie has warped into a fungus that feeds on itself – destroying relationships, sucking the joy out of life. It's not love – it's terror and responsibility and fear. I'm out of control – that whole thing with the car – it's ridiculous. I'm a mess, and Sam is gone. Mum is gone. Matt's fed up with me. The anxieties are mounting. Sad, sick, angry Laura is ready to take over.

20. Niamh

I'm outside the childminder's home – a neat semi-d in Clonchapel Grove, the estate nearest to Clonchapel Primary School. A beaten-up-looking Yaris – 08 registered, with tax, insurance and NCT up to date – is parked in the drive and a pair of scooters, one big, one small, lean against the side passage gate. Before I can ring the bell, my head knocks into the wooden wind chime hanging in the porch, announcing my arrival.

The front door is opened by a short woman – early forties, one of those dark redheads with a freckled complexion.

'Hi?' she says, taking in the badge and opening the door to invite me in before I'm finished introducing myself. Her right wrist is bandaged.

'Would it be all right if I come in and ask you a few questions, Ms –'

'Val – please,' she interrupts. 'Come in – of course!'

She smiles an open, flustered smile, stepping back into the hallway and ushering me in. The smell of fresh coffee greets me, along with evidence of busy family life: small wellington boots and runners are stacked on top of a storage unit. Jackets, bags and coats hang above it and, on each of the first ten steps of the staircase is arranged a small pile of stuff which I'm guessing is to be brought upstairs at a later time – folded clothes, toys, two boxes of toothpaste, slippers, towels. The sight gives me a pang of homesickness – Mammy used to do that, too. And woe betide you if she saw you going upstairs with empty hands.

'How is Mel? The kids? God – when I think –' Val stops suddenly. 'Sorry – I was just making coffee. Would you like some? I make sure to get a hot one before the school pick-up.'

'I'd murder a cup.' I like her already. No artifice and, I'm guessing, no bull. And coffee.

The kitchen looks out over a small back garden dominated by a kids' soccer goal net. If there ever was grass, it's been trampled to mush.

'Boys,' she says.

I nod – but don't add that our back field was the same – tracked into mud by myself and Tom practising our striking, hurling the ball from one to the other until it was too dark and Mam would yell for us to get the hell inside.

'Thanks –' I take the steaming cup of coffee. 'Brilliant.'

Val is forthright, transparent, open. In less time than it takes to get to the last mouthful of coffee, we've established that she's been worried about Mel for a long time – thought she was suffering a chronic depression – since the death of her first husband, Ben. On the subject of Stuart, she was equally honest. No love lost there.

'Look – I don't know what went on between them – and I couldn't get to talk to Mel alone. The other day we went shopping – when we chose her new image and arranged the haircut – that was the first time I'd been alone with her in months.'

'What day was that?'

'Saturday?'

I nod.

'And what did you talk about then?'

'Well – she was actually in great form. I got the feeling she was more confident, you know? She talked about getting back to work – earning money. She said it was time she –' She paused then, looking up at a point in the ceiling in recollection. 'Yes. I remember her words, because I thought it sounded strange; she said: "It's time I take back control of my life," and I said – well, I can't remember exactly – but I was all for it, and we talked about setting up a business together.'

'Oh?'

'Before she married Stu, before Ben and the bike shop even – we worked together. We go way back – video production. We worked for a company called ClearView – they're gone now. Mel was art director – she sourced locations, props, styled the shoots, that type of thing. She was really good.'

'And then? Did she give up the job – what happened?'

Val paused, narrowed her eyes in concentration.

'Not immediately – no. She had Jenny, and then she and Ben – well, Ben inherited the bike shop and they moved in. But she was still working part time when she met Stu. I remember because we were filming scenes for an Iron Man challenge and his company – Stu's – were our clients. Ben was providing the bikes.'

'And so Melanie met Stuart at that stage? Before Ben died?'

She nods vigorously, gulping her last mouthful of coffee.

'And was he friendly – Stuart – with Ben?'

'Not sure,' she frowns. 'I think Mel was the attraction.'

'Would he have been involved in their lives at all, like, would he have known Jenny?'

'Uh-hum – yes. She would have known him from when she was very young – and he was brilliant with kids. I think it's why Mel was so quick to –'

She breaks off. 'That sounds judgy – sorry – I didn't mean that. I just meant that she and Stuart got together fairly quickly after Ben died. I was worried' – again, she pauses – 'I suppose I was worried it was too soon. But like I say, he's a popular guy. In the office, too, there was a big fan club for him – old Stu is quite the charmer. But –'

'Yes?'

'Look, I don't want to – well. I've no proof or anything, so maybe my radar is way off – but I just never warmed to him, you know? And believe me, the feeling is mutual. I think he can't stand me.'

She sits back, adjusts her waistband. She's wearing a long, brightly patterned woollen jumper with black jeggings – the ones that look like skinny jeans – tucked into a battered old pair of Docs.

'This' – she gestures towards her boobs and midriff – 'holds no currency for a guy like Stuart –'

She stops, places the mug on the table.

'Actually no, that's not it,' she says. 'If I was prepared to make an effort – you know, do the whole make-up, clothes.' She mimes squeezing her boobs in and up, opens her eyes wide like a doll's. 'If I tried a bit harder, I wouldn't be so offensive to him – it's the fact that I clearly don't care, that's what he doesn't like about me.'

I know exactly what she means. You're allowed plenty of leeway with men – as long as you look like you're trying. Stu sounds like a right dick.

'I've tried to be a good friend to Mel – she knows I'm here. Jesus! I'm always here for her – and the kids. But I gave up calling to the house –'

She shakes her head.

'Will Mel and Karl be okay? No one would tell me anything at the hospital – I'm not next of kin.' She hesitates. 'I mean, that's fine, of course. It's just I want to help – is there anything . . . I heard – I heard Jen's in the psych unit. Is there anything I can do?'

She's getting a bit upset, so I tell her they're improving,

that she's been very helpful – that I've a clearer picture of Stuart and the family dynamic and that she's a good friend, which is true. I ask her for background on Mel's family; turns out there's only the brother, Gareth, and Val doesn't have a number or an address for him. I make a note to get Uniform to look for an address book at the family home. I ask about other friends – mums at the school, friends of Mel's from work – all are met with a headshake and 'no'.

After that, Val and I are quiet for a moment – both realizing the extent of Mel's isolation. Her dad's dead, her mum lives in a UK care home, with dementia, and the brother is somewhere in the UK – for now uncontactable.

'Does she have a phone? It wasn't in her bag –'

Val shakes her head – lips pursed.

'She said she liked not having one – that she didn't want it to rule her life.'

We both let that sit. Jenny's phrase comes back to me again – *it's all ruled by him*. Stuart ruled Mel's life. Stuart was king of his kingdom and ruler of all. What a pity Mel didn't confide in Val. I let my gaze travel the messy, cosy kitchen, through to the sitting room full of books and toys, then back to Val's clear-eyed, frank, make-up-free face. This home could have provided sanctuary – Val is warm and wise and kind. Strong and feisty, too. No wonder Stu kept them apart.

I put away my notebook and thank her for her time – and the coffee. Crouching so as not to bang into the wind chimes again, I step out the door on to the step.

'Thanks – you've been very helpful.'

She shrugs. 'I wish I could do more. Will I bring stuff to the hospital – nightclothes, wash things – that kind of thing?'

I shake my head. 'Not yet, though I'm sure in time that'd be great. Tell me' – I point to her bandaged wrist – 'what happened there?'

Val looks sheepish. 'Bloody scooter!' She indicates the larger of the two. 'Jack wanted me to scoot beside him going to school – and so I did. And went arse over tit for my troubles!'

'Fair play to you,' I say, trying not to laugh.

Back in the car, away from the warmth of Val's personality, a thought occurs to me – she didn't ask a single question about Stuart. She didn't ask if we'd found him. She didn't ask about leads. It's as if she doesn't care if he's alive or dead.

I'm in the car on the way back to the hospital when Cig calls. I update him about the visit, but he's more concerned with the missed calls to Laura.

'I've been calling Shaw for the last half-hour,' he snaps. 'I need to talk to her.'

'Right, sir – Cig – I'm nearly there now. I'll get her to call you asap.'

'Make sure you do. And, Detective, they found something else at the house – a medical textbook. Full-on gore, photographs of wounds and injuries – the type of book a medical student would use. Not a fifteen-year-old.'

'Fourteen – she's fourteen.'

'Noted. Thank you, Darmody.'

'Could it be his?'

'It could – in theeeory.' Cig draws out the vowels with an edge of sarcasm. I remember he's probably still fasting. 'Only they found it hidden in the girl's bedroom – in her bed.'

'Right.'

'Right – exactly,' says Cig. 'Get Shaw to phone right away.'

'Yessir – I –' But he's cut the call.

What does he want with Laura? I wonder. Usually, information on cases is shared or passed to either of us, as though we're interchangeable. And – why's she not answering her phone?

21. Jenny

Laura's weird. She doesn't look right. Her hair is shiny and swingy and she's wearing the same clothes from before – black jacket and a grey top. But her face is not the same. She looks like she's been crumpled, and her face is red. Niamh says, 'Are you okay?' but not to me and I hear Laura go, 'Grand,' and nod over at me. So I talk and Laura listens and it's like when you feed the pigeons and they peck stuff up really quickly – frantically. She sucks it up, like, whoosh. We're getting into a routine. And if I keep talking she keeps nodding and smiling, and that's good. There are no secrets squeezing out and soon Laura's head will be full and it will be over and I can go home. She wants something true. Though I already told her the truth is overrated.

She asks about the dog and if I ever brought him to Bushy Park. And it's quiet again and Laura tells me about the dogs in Bushy that she used to see when she had a dog. She talks and talks like she is filling up the silence.

'One woman used to bring her dog in a buggy, can you believe it?' And I look at Niamh to see if she's laughing. They could be tricking me. And Niamh just says, 'That's gas.' So maybe it's true. But Bushy Park is too near and so I tell her about the sea.

'It wasn't like us taking Socks for a walk, it was the opposite. He bolted. We had to run to keep up and we ran for ages. Miles. Out of Clonchapel. We ran till we reached the sea.'

'You ran to the sea?' She's looking confused, and I see it then – the look between them. Like a little flash. Haha. Hah.

'Yeah, because you – because you can only reach the island by boat. I told you that. And we all got in the little red boat. But when we got there it was pouring rain and the wind was howling.'

'You were going to an island? Go on.'

'So we just kept running and we left the beach and scrambled up the cliff. Then down the other side and then –' I shiver then because I remember the tower. And she sees it and yes, of course she does, she asks why I'm shivering. And she shouldn't ask me – she must know already. She's got forms and papers in front of her. It's written there, I bet it is.

They wrote stuff down and they took photos and they looked at the marks. I remember now. It was very bright and I was lying on the white bed and eight lights on the ceiling, but minus one 'cos it was flickering and a young nurse shook her head side to side to side so sadly. 'Just another stitch or two and you're done, pet.' And the cream felt soft and cool and made the stinging go away. I don't have to say it. She knows.

'Is there something upsetting you? You look scared, Jenny. Are you scared?'

'The tower.'

'Tell me about the tower.'

'Bad things happen in the tower.'

And then she says, 'What bad things and where's the tower?', and don't pretend you didn't know she was going to say that. Dumb bitch. And I think about the story from the island. Just a story. Quickly now, a story. And I said that out loud, because her puppy spaniel ears prick up.

'Jenny, you say it's just a story? Tell it like a story then – a true story?'

Don't tell don't tell, but I don't care now. Only words. Only a story. Hah. And then the story rushes out like a river, but it's okay. It's a story. Nothing is real.

'Once upon a time there was a princess with long golden hair, like Rapunzel, and she was kind and good and everybody loved her. And her country was an island – far out in the sea.' And she's nodding, 'Aha' and 'Right' and saying the same as me. Things like – 'An island? Right, I see.'

'The princess had a pet owl who perched on her shoulder and went everywhere with her, and her name was Minerva. The owl. The princess really loved her.'

This is easy – I know every word of this story. Niamh might need a new notebook.

'And she had a baby mouse, too, with big, shiny eyes. She kept him in her pocket.' And I want it to be safe for the princess and her pets. I don't want to say the next bit. I want them to stay there, in the palace, just the three of them. I hate him. But she goes, 'Go on, Jenny. What happened?'

'One day, the evil prince from the next kingdom came calling. He was rich and big and strong and he always has to have whatever he wants. And everyone thought he was great. He took one look at the princess and her kingdom and he said, "That's mine. I'm taking that. We're going to get married." And because the princess was good and kind and gentle she agreed.'

And I stop then because the princess is dumb dumb dumb. And I'm so angry at her – dumb bitch who let him in. And Mum sits in her room and she drinks her wine and she straightens her long hair and fixes her make-up. The thick one with a sponge covers everything, even the black bruises. Flawless. 'There,' she says, sweeping pink blush across her cheek. 'All fine.' And I hate her then because Karl is hungry and I am, too. But we can't go back down to the kitchen. We have to wait for another day. Or for when he goes to work. And she's pretty and, there – she's putting on perfume and she's in multicolour but we are black and white and grey and Karl has wet his pants again. And I know that later, later in the dark he'll come and I'll be trapped in the tower. While she sleeps. Bitch. Dumb bitch. And that was when I knew that she couldn't save me.

'Go on with your story, Jen.' I can hear that Niamh has stopped writing and now Laura has her pen poised, too. 'You said the princess agreed to marry him?'

'Yes, but Minerva knew it was a bad idea. She was not calm and happy any more. She wouldn't settle. She tried to warn the princess. Every time the prince came near, Minerva hopped closer to the princess, flapping her wings and blocking him, or flew up into the air and found a high perch to sit on.'

Now she's saying nothing but she's wearing her special Laura sadface – it looks real, though, not like a mask.

'The prince really hated the owl. He hated how the princess kept her on her shoulder and he hated how they whispered with their heads together and how much they seemed to love each other. He hated that Minerva could see the truth, because owls can always see the truth. Did you know that? Their vision – like they can turn their heads all the way round so they see everything. And he hated that.'

'So the owl sees everything? What does she see?'

But no way, Laura, no way. I'm not telling the things in the tower. No way.

'On the morning of the wedding, the princess woke early and put on her wedding dress and the owl locket which she always wore. Then she went to get Minerva from her perch – but Minerva was gone. The princess ran all over the castle, looking for her. All the – the villagers and everyone looked everywhere, too, but she'd disappeared.

'The poor princess was broken-hearted. She was frantic, but she had to go through with the wedding because everyone – all the kingdom was there. But as soon as it was over, she raced out and started searching again.'

You can say anything you like in a story. As long as it's hidden inside, they won't know and they can't find out. Laura has her listening face on, and Niamh is on the edge of her seat – cliff-hanger for her. Hah.

'And, go on, did she find her?' says Laura.

'After hours and hours she got a message from the prince that he had a surprise for her and she was to go to the tower. So she didn't even stop to get help, or even to get out of her wedding dress, she just dashed to the tower and climbed up the stone steps to the top. Round and round she went, climbing the staircase. She was sure that Minerva would be waiting for her inside.'

And I'm sad then – even though it's only a story. I'm sad because I know what happens next. Not a happy-ever-after kind of story.

'The princess climbed in through the tiny window at the top of the tower. The room was bare and cold and empty. There was no sign of Minerva. She ran back to the window and looked out. And there was the prince, far, far below, standing at the foot of the tower, looking up. He had a strange smile on his face. And then she saw why. He was holding Minerva – roughly, with his giant fist. Brave little Minerva was pecking and struggling and twisting, trying to escape. But he had big leather gloves on and he couldn't feel a thing. And he didn't care anyway. And the princess stared. She couldn't understand what she saw. She couldn't understand what was going to happen. Dumb bitch.'

Don't tell don't tell. But I think *shut up. Now YOU shut up, dumb dumb shit. You can shut up. I will tell in my story.*

'He held Minerva tight and he ripped out one of her tail feathers with his giant, meaty hands. Then another, and another. And the little bird struggled and struggled and fought and twisted and turned. And the princess was screaming,

"Please, please don't, please don't," but who cares when a princess says please – he didn't care, he wasn't scared. He just laughed more and then he grabbed the bird by the neck and stuffed her into a sack so he could keep her there, for whatever he wanted. And he rode off on his horse.'

And I do feel bad now, I do. Laura is not laughing the Laura Laugh and her shiny hair is in a messy position, some behind her ears and some hanging loose. She looks very serious. Even though it's just a story. I twist around to look at Niamh and she looks serious, too – though she tries a grey wet-washing smile. I turn back to Laura.

'And then?'

'Then *smash!* The prince smashed the stone steps with – with – he smashed the steps so no one could get up or down. There was no way out. And the princess lay down inside the room and she didn't look.' And she did nothing and she didn't stop it.

And now it's weird because, in my head, I can see Laura on the island, like as if she came with us in the boat. That's not right. I didn't put her there. But I see her now and she's looking up at the tower and she looks sad. This could be another trick. Maybe she's in charge of this. Maybe she's telling me what to say and she made me tell that story. I'm so tired. It's tiring trying to think what to say and what you can't say. And I feel something bad now about Mum and Karl. There's a sad feeling, and my heart is suddenly pounding.

'Mum and Karl will be waiting for me – they must be really worried. I need to see them. I need to get home.'

'I know you do – soon you'll be home. Soon. Your mum and Karl are fine – are going to be fine.'

Niamh moves around in her chair and checks her phone again. Why? Then she looks at Laura and I don't know what that means.

This is so hard. Dumb dumb, why did I say this is easy? I want to tell her. I want to tell Laura the rest – about the tower room and the marsh when you're choking underwater and the screaming wind and – and I could hand it all over to her like a package. She would reach across the table to get it. She might have to stand up to take it. It's so bulky and it's not wrapped properly. Bits – sharp bits – are sticking out and you could cut yourself, you'd have to be careful and the tape is sticky. But maybe Laura could take hold of it maybe, just shut up for one second, I'm only saying maybe. And she'd put it down on the table. She could put it down on the table to sort it out and then it wouldn't be mine any more.

But Laura doesn't do that. Instead Niamh says we have to leave it there, again. And Laura says 'No' and stuff like 'Not yet'. She says – 'We've got to at least try.'

'We're going to have to leave it there, Jenny,' says Niamh, even though she's not the boss of me or Laura. 'Thank you, you were great, and you told us lots today.'

Laura stands up and she picks up her briefcase. It looks heavy; it's bulging with papers and plastic folders.

'Jenny,' she says, all innocent. 'Now would be a good time to tell us what you know about Stuart's whereabouts. If you know where he is, you must tell us. Do you understand that?'

But Niamh said, 'We will leave it there,' and that's better. Yes, we will leave it there and we will leave him there and he is never ever coming back from there. Hah. And Laura's question has to fly off and find a new home.

22. Laura

Dissociative amnesia. Defined by memory loss that's more severe than normal forgetfulness and can't be explained by a medical condition. The sufferer cannot recall information about themselves, or events and people in their lives, especially from a <u>traumatic</u> time. Dissociative amnesia can be <u>specific to events in a certain time</u>, such as intense combat, or, more rarely, can involve <u>complete loss of memory</u> about yourself. It may sometimes involve travel or confused <u>wandering away</u> from your life (dissociative fugue). An episode of <u>amnesia</u> usually occurs suddenly and may last minutes, hours or, rarely, months or years.

I underline the last bit again. Sam's notes on dissociative disorders are spread across my lap. There are two more boxes of books hiding behind the sofa. I've no idea where I'll put them, and I ignored Matt's raised eyebrow when he saw me carting them in from the car. It seems I now have my own library. Their scent reminds me of the study, and Sam. There's a kind of peppery tobacco air off them and I find myself holding one of the hardback tomes up to my face, closing my eyes and inhaling deeply. It puts me in the familiar battered leather chair in the warm study, being studied kindly – always kindly and without judgement – by Sam.

If that sounds like an idealized picture, it's because it is. I can't explain, even now, why I always felt so safe in that room, with him. We could be talking about distressing things: shameful details from that night, fears, nightmares – anything – but with Sam listening it was like they had no power over me. They were just words.

I knew I had to get help when I basically stopped going anywhere near the bank in Terenure, and then I began avoiding Terenure itself, which is pretty limiting as it's on the way into town. And, finally, I stopped going anywhere. Then there were the endless flashbacks – really detailed – of the worst bits of that night. And the intrusive thoughts – violent and graphic and always involving people I cared about and my adored Bobby. I'd check and re-check that his harness was on properly before taking him for a walk. I'd visualize him being run over by a massive articulated truck. Literally, I'd imagine his head bursting; I could even hear his yelps of pain. No detail was spared in these intrusive thoughts. It took months – endless sessions with Sam – to get the thoughts under control.

'It seems to me you're standing on the edge of an abyss,' Sam had said more than once. 'A traumatic event will do that to you. It rips the ground from under you and hurls you down into the pit. And you claw your way back out, as you have done, Laura. You've made your way back – look at what you've achieved. But the abyss is still there, just behind you – in your past. What we have to work on is to keep you from falling back; we need to give you the tools to step away from the edge. But you're going to have to do it again and again.'

With Sam, I was brave enough to do it. Sam showed me how to step away from the edge. But I realize now that I'd glossed over the phrase 'again and again'. I hadn't accepted that post-traumatic-induced OCD is ongoing, and that I'll need to step away from the brink over and over and over. It will always be there, and I will never forget it.

I wish I could ask Sam about Jenny. 'Go step by step,' he always said, but you need to know which steps to choose. I speed-read his notes and various articles, expecting him to have conveniently left the answers there for me. Is it dissociative amnesia? A fugue state? Jenny's remembering some things – she hasn't forgotten who she is, and she was able to tell me about friends and family members. But she seems to have no knowledge of that night – the night she was admitted. She's no idea what happened to her mum and Karl – and I'm choosing not to tell her – yet. I think I'm getting better at reading her; and there's a difference between the way she is when we talk about Stuart and when we talk about her mum and Karl. But I could be way off. Another thing Sam always said is that you can never know what someone else is thinking.

I can't get away from the feeling – more than a feeling – I'm certain she's lying when it comes to him. But the question is, does she know she's lying? Is the whole fairy tale her trying to obscure the truth, or is it the only way she's able to tell the truth?

'Muma! Muma!' The mini tornado that is Katie blasts into the room, clutches the legs of my trousers, my good work trousers, yelling 'Horsey, Muma! Peeze, horsey!'

'She did say please,' says Matt, reaching down and lifting her up as I quickly stack the notes and books together and place them out of harm's reach on the floor. He doesn't mention this morning.

'I thought you were bringing her up to bed?'

But he plops her firmly on to my lap. 'Oh, but you're such a great horsey.' He grins. I don't respond.

'Muma's legs are about to fall off. Mum's very tired, Katie.'

'Bad tired. Bad Muma. Do it again. Again, again.' She doesn't even bother to make eye contact, just grasps the trouser fabric in her dimpled little fists and stares straight ahead in readiness. 'Now!'

I sigh and begin to bob her up and down, chanting the rhyme: 'This is the way the lady rides – trit trot, trit trot – no!

Stop it, Katie!' She's grabbed on to my trousers so tightly that the seam is beginning to rip. 'Don't pull it!' I lift her off my lap, ignoring her wails. She looks stricken, fat tears welling up in her eyes.

Matt turns and looks at me. He'd be entitled to sigh or make a comment, but what's worse is his silence, a kind of long-suffering patience.

'Here, Katie,' he says. 'Muma's tired. I'll do it.' She stops crying straight away and allows herself to be repositioned on Matt's lap.

'And this is the way the gentleman rides – a-gallop, a-gallop, a-gallop,' he says, going faster. She squeals in anticipation. 'And this is the way the farmer rides – a-canter, a-canter, a-canter, and he –'

'He FALLS OFF HIS HORSE!' screams Katie, clinging on and shrieking with delight.

'See? Daddy's the best, isn't he? Dada had a very busy day at work, too, but still he plays horsey.' He pats my head, making the surge of guilt even worse. I hadn't even thought of it – he's in the middle of a big project – a merger or something.

'Mummy horsey is just too old and cranky.' He smiles, and I think just maybe – maybe – it will be okay between us.

'Very funny,' I say.

I know I'm lucky. Matt sweeps Katie up off the floor and into piggyback position, fastening her hands around his neck. He's a kind husband, a great dad. I am so lucky – it's all there, within my reach. Why can't I just take it? Why can't I feel it? Why can't I return Matt's grin with one of my own? Squeeze his hand on his way past? Why do I feel like I'm watching them, watching us, from a height? As if I'm seeing us through one of those nanny cams mounted in a corner.

'Say "Goodnight, Captain" to Mummy, Katie.'

148

'Goodnightcaptain to MumaKatie.'

'Goodnight, Katie, I'll be up later for the fast-asleep kiss.'

Katie gives a serious nod.

'And you'll be?'

'Fat asleep?'

'Fat asleep!' Matt agrees, with a thumbs-up.

I watch him negotiate the doorway, careful not to knock his two-and-a-half-year-old burden against the sharp edges. One arm curves underneath her so she doesn't slip. With his other hand he holds both hers, so she can't let go. He giant-steps up the stairs and she screams with delight at each one. As they reach the top, I hear him shout down.

'Enjoy your meeting with Kay,' he says, ladling on the irony. 'Meeting Kay' is our code for going out for a drink, so called in honour of poor old Kay, one of our neighbours and frequent callers, who holds you in a vice of conversation when she manages to catch you in the park or on the doorstep, nailing you in place with dire warnings about criminal gangs targeting our neighbourhood, or beggars calling to the door, or migrants, or travellers, or asylum seekers – basically, everything is a cause for her concern. And that's before she starts sharing her childrearing tips. Before she could speak, Katie recognized a rival. And so, we're allowed meet Kay at nighttime – and Katie considers it sufficiently boring not to want to come along. She knows she won't be missing anything.

'I will – thanks,' I shout back. 'Won't be late.'

With a surge of energy, I bundle the pages together, stuff them into the briefcase and stand up. There's no way I'm going to chance going upstairs to change into something a bit nicer – if Katie catches me, that'll be it. Instead, I grab my make-up bag and tiptoe through the kitchen and into the small bathroom off it. Yet another paint job needing to be done, I think, looking at the peeling skirting boards. Time.

Maybe Matt will do it at the weekend. Yeah. Time. Don't think about it.

After Mum died and the house was sold and Dad had taken his cut, the money came through and we were able to get the mortgage for this place – a three-bed former council house backing on to the river, in Clonchapel. Cian used his to add another wing on his Canadian mansion, as I call it. But still. We'd enough money to buy this and add a few licks of paint, and now, even though Matt's income is increasing – now we have the money for improvements and repairs, we don't have the time.

I rummage in the little cabinet to find my old make-up bag and – result! My dangly earrings are still there. I add a layer of make-up and a bit of eyeliner, noting a new crease at the corner of my eyes. Then I press the earrings through my ears, wincing as they bite into me – I haven't worn earrings for weeks. Some lipstick and – I pause, looking at my reflection hopefully, as if I'll have magically Cinderellaed into attractive-ness in the intervening moments – but no. Serious, sad-looking Laura scowls back at me. They talk about RBF, Resting Bitch Face; this is more ABF – Anxious Bitch Face. I try to sum-mon Sam, or even a kind comment. The best I can come up with is the earrings, at least, look good. Mum brought them back from Spain on her last trip. Little silver pomegranates – the symbol of Catherine of Aragon, apparently – dangle from delicate leaves. I love them – and, somehow, they've sur-vived rented flats and house moves and messy motherhood.

I hear Matt's voice upstairs. Katie's gone quiet – so she must be listening to the story. Hurriedly, I send Niamh a text.

Text when u outside
DON'T ring doorbell
! xx

Then I turn my phone to silent, protecting the peace, and sneak back into the kitchen, where I can keep an eye on the front-door glass panels, through which I'll be able to see Niamh when she arrives. I potter around the kitchen, tidying up, closing the cupboards, making sure the locks are working. In the hall cupboard I reopen and lock the gun safe. Protect and maintain. A parent's first duty is to protect and maintain the child. When I think of the preparations before Katie arrived: the stair gates and cupboard locks, sterilizers for the kitchen and blinds for the car windows, a baby monitor in case she'd cry unheard upstairs for a nanosecond. Car seats that you'd need a degree in engineering just to strap her in, a pressure-sensitive mattress so we'd know if she rolls on to her front – or was it her back? Cups of coffee drunk standing up at the counter in case the sleeping infant could reach the table and pour it over herself.

I remember leaving a restaurant – the first time we'd braved the outside world with new-born Katie – because cigarette smoke had drifted in like the serpent of doom, through the open window. I couldn't finish my food, thinking of the poison entering her pristine lungs. I left a perfectly good pizza uneaten. I even made Matt leave his steak, though he asked them to doggie-bag it, of course. From now on it would be our fault. My fault. Anything bad that might occur – the tiniest scrape or bump – from now on, I had to ensure it didn't happen.

In the SVI training, they said we have to be aware of our own issues, that we need to recognize our biases and assumptions, our injuries and neuroses, so that none of these can taint the evidence. And all fourteen of us in the class, we all knew to watch out for the cases and the clients who might trigger something. The training was intense. We took turns playing the child's role – answering the interview questions and those in the cross-examination. I can't think of a single person who emerged unscathed – who didn't crack at least once. You weren't allowed to get cosy; we had to change partners each day. The failure rate varied between 30 and 40 per cent, so it was by no means a done deal that I'd pass, but thanks to Sam and thanks to big brother, Cian, who said I'd never hack it, I smashed it.

Provide the victim with a platform, Laura. Maintain the structure, Laura. Set appropriate limits. And beware one's own unresolved conflicts. Right, Laura? They have no place in the interview room.

But tonight, instead of looking forward to a night of fun with Niamh, I'm worse than ever.

Jaysus! That hideous story about the little owl. What was it she said – something about him tearing out the feathers one by one while the princess watched? Then he smashed the steps so the princess was trapped in the tower. It doesn't take a genius to work it out. Though that's not exactly how I put it to the Cig at the meeting – I'm still smarting from the conversation. That's the thing about Cig – if he's on your case, he's on it, big time.

'If you take the story as a fantasy, a fairy tale which she's developed as a coping mechanism, or if you think of it like a dream sequence, it begins to make sense.'

Of course, he'd just stared at me, not agreeing or disagreeing.

'A man is missing – presumed at the very least injured, yeah? All I'm asking, all I'm saying, is that we don't have time for interpreting dreams and faffing around with fantasies, Officer.' *Not on my watch* was unsaid, but we'd all heard the ghost whisper of it. He'd turned back to the map.

'I'm sending a team down to check the harbour. See if anyone saw her take a boat out. See if anyone remembers her, or them.' He'd frowned at Niamh's notes. 'If she did take a boat or if they were both in it together, then she comes back without him, and then she somehow walks all the way back to the village, to Ely Gate, where she's picked up at –'

'Eh, 01.26, Cig.'

He had frowned again. 'I mean, that's at least a four-mile walk, isn't it? Which would explain the exhaustion and dehydration.' He'd glared at me then, his finger marking his place on the page. 'So the island – do you reckon she means the west pier there? You know, the smaller part of the harbour, with the manmade dock where they tie up all the small craft. It's got boulders and cement and that type of thing. I suppose it could conceivably look like an island.' He'd sighed. 'To a kid.'

'I still don't think she meant an actual island,' I'd told him, 'I think the whole concept of the island is in her head – it's the place where everything is playing out.'

'Thanks for the psychoanalysis, Shaw. That's good, coming from you. Well, I'm not having a missing man die or drown or whatever because we didn't get a team four miles down the road to the harbour.' Then he had said it. 'Not on my watch. Do it,' he'd added.

'Yes, Cig.'

'And get the sub-aqua guys on standby, too, in case.'

I can still hear them upstairs – Katie's questions, Matt's laughter. Idyllic sounds of family life. But the world is full of risk, and nothing stops the anxious thoughts, the memories and images that linger like crime stains.

Jenny's photos showed bruises, freshly flowering in shades of red and purple, and older ones like splotches of tea, brown and yellow. Bruises in the shape of thumbs and fingers. The tear which needed three stitches.

And then I think of Sam. Funny, annoying, kind and brilliant Sam. Who made me do my homework, who made me work hard at getting better, who helped me turn away from the abyss.

But I don't turn. Instead, I sit at the kitchen table and let them come. I don't even try to fight them. There's no point. They prise open any locked door with their bony claws. They slip under the cracks in the floorboards – wisps of despair. They cluster in gangs, overwhelming my defences.

I can hear Matt – he's actually singing to her. But I don't think about that or how lucky I am. I take another step closer to the edge and I remember instead a rainy night and him with his fake concern and his 'You-look-like-you-could-do-with-some-help' Good Samaritan routine. 'I was just driving home from work – you're in luck.'

23. Jenny

It's much later now, and I've been careful. No tablets or drugs for me, haha. They're in the toilet. I'm staying awake. The lights are finally off in the corridor and it's dark. Agency Nurse – I thought it was her name earlier because she said, 'I'm agency,' but now I know what it means – has gone to the nurses' station, and she must be sitting down there behind the counter but she can't see me over the top of it. I'm crawling along the shiny floor to pass by.

I have an invisibility cloak like the one the giant's wife gave Jack and it's the same as Harry Potter's. It's Catherine's sparkly purple cardigan. I've stuffed the gown into my jeans and I'm wearing Catherine's booties which have fur inside and they're really warm. I wish they were the same as the ones Hermes wore with wings on the sides so I could fly, but that would be just too lucky. At least they're warm.

Quiet – don't make a sound. I'm tucked into the doorway of the bathroom. I peep around the corner and count: two more doorways until the stairs. I can do it.

'It dries really quickly in cold water, apparently,' Agency Nurse is saying.

There's some murmuring, but I don't know what it is or what she says. And I must be getting so stupid because for a second I want to go back and find out what it could be. What dries in cold water? How can you dry something in water? Stupid stupid. I ignore that and keep going. Stick with the mission. Mrs A says everyone has a mission. But sometimes it takes a while to find out what it is. On the island, there's only one mission – kill him.

This is my mission now – get out of here. New mission. Get out of Abbot's Hill. Get home to Mum and Karl. Mission accomplished. I creep along in the shadows, crawling on my hands and knees along the shiny floor. Past the doorway – that's doorway number one. Past doorway number two. I have to cross over now to the stair door. I peer over my shoulder before I do it and I see the nurses at their desk and they're in a spotlight. They're not looking at me. It's going to be okay.

Hardly daring to breathe, hardly daring to believe this could work, I scuttle across to the door and push it. And a thought comes in, zap, into my brain – a question: why am I bent down on my hands and knees like a small child, crawling underneath the nurses' station? How is this even happening? I'm fourteen. What the hell is going on? Then I remember the mission – I have to get out. I push against the door again. It's so heavy I straighten up a bit, then put my shoulder against it and heave. Nothing happens. I heave again, much harder. Still nothing happens.

'You have to press the door-release button,' says Agency Nurse with a frown. Abort mission. Abort due to Frowning Nurse. The frown is way worse than before and I don't think she even means what she says. Like she's not really telling me how to get out because next thing she takes hold of my elbow and her thumb is digging in and she sort of steers me back down the hallway towards the spotlight station. 'Come on now,' she says. 'Enough of this nonsense.'

As we pass by the station Other Nurse waves at me with her sandwich. 'Ham and mustard,' she says. 'Want some?'

'She's getting into bed,' says Agency. And it must be true because in a minute I am in bed and the invisibility cloak is back on Catherine's chair and the mission is over.

And I lie there and I can't even cry. I'm too tired. Dumb stupid bitch and your dumb mission. The smell of Other Nurse's sandwich is wafting through the doorway – I can smell the vinegar in the mustard. I'm kind of hungry now. I would like the ham. But no mustard.

There's a man in India who claims he hasn't had food or drink for, like, seventy years. But I looked it up and it's supposed to be three days. Just three days without food or water. I am counting and it's been two sleeps in here, haha, so only one more sleep and then he will be dead.

The only Beatles song I don't like is 'Mean Mr Mustard'. Mustard is a disgusting colour, like a mixture of baby poo and banana and milk. And it has the word *must* in there. Like musty old clothes that are damp and smelly. Like *must*, you must do something, you don't have a choice, you must do what I say or bad things will happen. And you have to do it. 'Mean Mr Mustard' has a mustard moustache and mustard-coloured hair and they match his mustard freckles all over his body – even his legs and his chest. Once I told Karl about Mean Mr Mustard, and he listened and his eyes were huge. I told him what happened. But he didn't really understand, though he whispered, 'Mean Mister'. I didn't say it again. I didn't want Karl getting caught.

Mission aborted, and then Drug Nurse said I had to have two of the blue tablets and I swallowed them because it's easier. But in the night my mind was fighting sleep like a boxer in the ring. Jab, duck, jab, punch – remember, remember. But the thoughts kept slipping and sliding, ducking and diving out of reach, and I just couldn't hold on to them.

Then much later in the really dark part of the night, Catherine called out – 'Help! Help! Come here!' – and she stretched out her hand, which was all skinny and knobbly. She did it for ages, and nobody came. I think she wanted me to take her hand; it was waving around, like a snake or something, trying to reach me. But I stayed put.

'What is it?' I whispered. She looked straight at me.

'I'm dying,' she said, and her eyes looked all black and glittery. 'Why is it taking so long?'

And her voice was full of longing. And then she turned over and pulled the waving snake arm back inside the bed-clothes and closed her eyes. And I seriously thought she'd died. But she was asleep.

How long does it take to die?

24. Laura

Niamh lifts her cocktail – a medicinal-looking mixture of rum, cinnamon, raspberry liqueur and Prosecco, topped off with a clove-studded lemon – winks, then downs almost the whole thing in one go.

'Sláinte.'

'Cheers – right.' I take a sip of mine through the rim of crushed gingernut biscuits – 'Gretel's Fizz', they call it – vodka, blackcurrant cordial and gingerbread syrup. It's delicious. We're in a 'secret' cocktail club in Temple Bar – Niamh's idea.

'Come on, it'll be fun. Better than the fecking pub, plus more drink in less time,' she'd wheedled, bundling me into the taxi in Rathgar with the same precision and skill she shows loading the squad car. 'I know you're going to be a pain in the hole about getting back by midnight, so no argument – it has to be cocktails.'

Midnight? More like eleven. She squishes in beside me, her leg pressing against mine. I wait a beat before moving away.

'You know I could get an hour of childcare, nearly, for the price of this?' I say, taking another sip, feeling the vodka hit.

'Yeah, and if my aunt had balls, she'd be my uncle,' quips Niamh. 'So what?' She leans forward, a halo of light behind her emphasizing her dark eyebrows and dramatic features. She's swept her hair over one shoulder but, even so, it's like a creature in its own right, there's so much of it. It's that great shade they talk about – bronde. Brown with blonde highlights. Only hers are natural. She nods at my glass.

'Go wan,' she says. 'It's nine thirty already.'

'I've to drive in the morning,' I say. 'I can't have more than one. Don't you –'

'Exactly my point.' She laughs, turning to summon over the waitress. 'Could we get some soakage – I mean, food?'

The girl returns Niamh's grin and brings menus, but Niamh orders for us both. In ten minutes, two heaped bowls of butter-fried diced potatoes, topped with chilli sauce and melted cheese, sit in front of us. Vast.

'Niamh – we could have shared –'

'Shuthefuckup and eat it, Laura.' She sits forward and starts on hers. 'I'm not sharing – I'm bloody starving. And you – Jaysus! Just eat it!'

I start to eat and realize that I am absolutely starving. It's delicious – hot and salty, spiced with fragrant jalapenos and chillies, so I'm knocking back the cocktail like water. Niamh orders another round and the smiling girl is back like magic with fresh concoctions.

'What did you get?'

'I told her to surprise me,' grins Niamh, pushing the glass towards me. 'You should stick with vodka – so this is yours.'

I sip, tasting grapefruit, lemon, mint – and more vodka. It burns pleasantly on the way down. I sit back against the velvet, luxuriating in a bath of wellbeing: the overheated room, the cosy corner, the rich food and sweet cocktails. We're upstairs on the top floor of the building, tucked into a corner near the fire. Most of the other tables are occupied by couples and there's a group of tourists who are quizzing the waitress about whether they'd be able to visit Kerry and take in a show in Dublin in one day.

'Glad to see you made an effort,' says Niamh, indicating the earrings. 'You weren't wearing those earlier.'

'Yeah – I know. Sorry – I didn't want Katie to know I was going out so, er, my options were limited. You look nice,' I add. And it's true. She's wearing a sheer top in a plum shade with a high neck and long sleeves. The colour brings out the gold tints in her hair.

'Yeah, thanks. I went the whole hog – waxing, the lot!'

She leans towards me. 'And if you swear never to tell anyone on pain of fucking death, I'll tell you what happened.'

'Pain of fucking death, I swear,' I say.

'So I hadn't booked in advance because – ah – just because I'm not organized like you. So, I walked into the place – you know the one with the purple sign in Rathgar? Alpha to Omega, or whatever it's called?' I nod.

'Very posh,' I say.

'God,' says Niamh. 'That's very true. Anyway, I hadn't rung in advance and I wanted to get the whole lot done – brows, legs, bikini line – you know?'

'I did think your brows are looking really nice – I meant to say it, actually,' I say, feeling bad that I hadn't noticed.

'That's not it – shut up for a second. So I walked up to the girl on the reception and she's sitting in front of a screen and – you know what it's like. And I go, "I'm sorry, I haven't made an appointment, but I want to get a bikini and leg wax –" and she's a bit snooty, and she goes, "Oh, I'll have to see," and so I think, well, in fairness, I suppose you'd need to know what you're getting into, so I put down my bag and –' She mimes opening the button of her jeans. My mouth falls open.

'No way – you didn't – tell me you didn't!'

She pauses for effect – takes a long, slow gulp of her cocktail – savouring my horror.

Then she smacks her lips together, her eyes sparkling with mischief – and she shakes her head regretfully.

'No. But I fecking should have – she was some dose!'

I'm blushing on her behalf – in fact, I wouldn't put it past her to have done it.

'I was fair tempted,' she says, swigging the last of her drink, then crumpling into laughter. 'Oh Christ! You should have seen her face!'

I begin to laugh – and that sets her off again.

'What knickers were you wearing?' I snort, feeling vodka burn its way down my nose as I collapse into giggles. I haven't laughed in so long, it's more like crying.

'Fuck off!'

We have another round of drinks.

'So going back to something you said earlier,' she says, 'why didn't you want Katie to know you're going out?'

'She has separation anxiety – or, well, she would have if she knew and – oh, it's just easier is all.'

Niamh considers this. 'She has her daddy. She has a mammy who needs a night off every now and again. She might cry for a bit when she sees you go out, but then you come back? And the next time you go out, she'll cry less because she'll remember that Mammy went out one time before and then Mammy came back.'

'I know – you're right. I – I don't want to upset her.'

'Why not?' says Niamh. 'It's not like it'll do her any harm, is it? She's not going to fucking explode, you know.'

An angry burst of flame – like marsh gas – ignites. What does Niamh know? She doesn't have kids. I take another sip of my drink, wanting to drown the anger. It's empty. I look around for the waitress. Suddenly, it's important to have more.

She appears at my side like an elf. She's tiny.

'I just need one more – like the first one – the Hansel and Gretel one, okay?'

Elf Waitress smiles and looks to Niamh for – I don't know – confirmation? Permission?

'Don't be looking at her,' I say, wagging my finger. 'She's not the boss of me. I'm her boss, actually, in actual fact.'

'Really?' says the girl, her gaze slipping away from me to Niamh once more. Niamh gives the tiniest of smiles and a barely perceptible nod of permission.

'Right you are,' Elf Waitress says. 'One Gretel Fizz coming right up.'

Niamh watches her as she makes her way easily through the maze of tables on to the stairwell. Cocktails have to be brought up from the bar downstairs. I listen to her footsteps – she sounds like a little pony trip-trapping down a hill – and then I scan the room, filled with a kind of drink-fuelled benevolence. Alcohol simplifies things, I realize. We're all friends here. That's good.

In an instant, the girl is back with the drinks. I'm blown away by the precision with which they're assembled – I can't get over the dusting of gingerbread, the pretty glass stirrer. Elf Waitress twinkles her smile and tiptoes back down the stairs. When her ponytail is no longer visible, Niamh turns to me with a smile. And suddenly, I understand – or think I do.

'Oh,' I say. 'You know her.'

'I do,' says Niamh drily. 'You're on top of your game, Detective Shaw.'

'No – but you know what I mean – you know-know her. Like you and her –'

Niamh watches me with great interest, stirring her cocktail. She still has half of it left.

'I do know her. Her name is Sophie,' says Niamh.

I try to choose my words carefully, but they're not ready.

'I knew it!' I say, waving my glass cocktail stirrer at her. I decide I'm going to keep it for stirring my drinks at home. We don't really drink cocktails at home, but we should. I decide we will. The thought makes me very happy.

'You know that girl and she knows you. That's why you brought me here!'

'Holy God! You're on fire tonight, Detective.'

'And she – are you two together?' I blurt. Loudly. I look over to see if the Americans have heard, but they're gone. Actually, I realize, everyone's gone except us.

'God! No – friend-of-a-friend thing,' says Niamh.

'So, the elf – whatshername – she's not your girlfriend?'

'The elf?'

'She looks like one.'

'Yeah, she does a bit,' Niamh agrees. 'No, she's not. She used to go out with a friend of mine.'

'And what about you? Are you seeing anyone? Why don't I know anything about –'

I stop talking, realizing I'm about to cry. What kind of friend am I? I know nothing about Niamh's life – I never even asked her.

'Are you crying?' Niamh puts her hand on mine and, with her other hand, shoves my glass out of reach. 'Shit. Laura – you're – don't cry. What the hell are you crying for?'

I shake my head as though I can shake out all the sadness – about Sam and Mum's anniversary and fighting with Matt and about my friend, who has a whole life I never even think about, never ask about. I'm a shit friend. I'm a shit person. A shit wife and a shit mother. And I can't even – and I'm so sad for Jenny. But I can't tell her that.

'Sam died.'

'Who's Sam?'

'He's a – a friend,' I sigh, not knowing where to begin. 'I went to see him today, but he'd died and I didn't know –' I inhale a series of sobs. 'And Sunday was Mum's anniversary.'

'Christ, Laura! Why don't you talk to me?' she blurts. 'Jesus! Your friend dies and you don't tell me. And it was your mum's anniversary! Why didn't you tell me? That's hard.'

164

'And you never talk to me!' I snap, angrily. 'I know nothing at all about your life!'

'For God's sake, Laura!' It's Niamh's turn to be angry. 'You're *impossible* to talk to sometimes! You – since you came back after Katie – you've been so weird and closed off. You say I never talk to you – well, you never ask! You don't ask me anything! Not about home, or my family, or the camogie and how the team are getting on. You're in your own world and I know – I know from Siobhán that it's difficult when you have kids – so I've let you be. But don't you *dare* give out to me for not talking when you're like a bloody brick wall. Walking around counting and wiping all the surfaces with your fecking antiseptic wipes, your anxiety like another person in the room!'

She reaches down and picks up her handbag.

'Annie way, this is going nowhere, and we need to get you home.' She sighs, passes me my bag. 'I'll look after the bill.'

'I – but –'

'You can get me back tomorrow.'

Elf Waitress appears from thin air with the card machine, a question in her expression. 'Thanks,' says Niamh, punching in her code. The girl tilts her head – I'm reminded of a robin watching humans with interest.

'Bye now – come again.' She smiles.

We murmur goodbyes. I walk as steadily as I can towards the bathroom – deflated, defeated, sick of myself.

'I'll wait for you at the stairs, yeah?' says Niamh.

25. Niamh

She fixes her hair, still clasping her front-door keys, before turning to wave me off. From the back seat of the taxi, I shake my head and mime a key-twisting action, and she nods her understanding. I watch her battle the lock, thinking I should probably have opened up for her. It should be funny, but it's not.

'Hang on,' I say to the driver, 'I'll just –' I'm about to get out, but then Laura's in – stepping up into the hallway and waving another goodbye. She mouths a regretful-looking 'thank you' – already ashamed. A pang of sympathy hits me – she's going to be mortified tomorrow.

I'm the one who should be sorry, I think. Perhaps a night on the lash was not what she needed – but, otherwise, how do you get her out of herself? She doesn't play a sport, she and Matt hardly ever go out. I know she goes to the gym – or she used to, but don't tell me that Pilates and mat work shite does anything for – for whatever demon is eating her up inside. She doesn't mention any friends – there's work, and home, and that's it.

'Where are we going?' the taxi driver glances at me in the rear-view mirror. Narky as hell – even though not a speck of puke touched the cab.

'Castlewood Avenue, thanks,' I say. 'Sorry about earlier,' I add. 'She's going through a rough patch.'

His eyes flick back to the road ahead. He nods, but I can feel his disapproval. I want to tell him to shove it – that the woman who just puked her guts up over someone's hedge and not on his car got a medal for bravery, that he's lucky to have her in his bloody cab. He should be honoured. Fucking git. I ignore the hostility and remember that day – wallowing in the memory like a cosy dressing gown. Christ! Laura was a fucking legend back then.

I'd been about three weeks in the DDU. It was going fairly well; I was holding my own with the slagging – what Laura called the ritual hazing. Bastards. But sure, it didn't really bother me – not after Edel. Tongue that'd clip a fecking hedge, that one.

We were actually on our way back to the unit when a call came through telling us to get to a garage on the M50 – that a child abduction/hostage situation was going on. As the details emerged over the radio, she stared straight ahead calmly – taking the U-turn, indicating to merge into the traffic, nodding as each fact emerged – as though logging them.

Suspect has taken a child . . . crèche . . . believed to be his daughter

. . . spotted on the M50 and followed

. . . Texaco garage – vacant lot

. . . squad car and Uniform at scene

. . . doused himself and child

. . . stand-off

'Do we have a name?'

. . . Paul . . . the child is Kayley . . .

'What are you going to do?' I couldn't believe how calm she was. 'What's the plan for something like this?'

'We'll see,' was all she said, swinging the car out to overtake a line of traffic.

We arrived at the scene and I remember thinking it looked fake – like an episode from *Fair City* or something. Three squad cars had pulled up on the forecourt of the garage behind what must have been his car – a Ford Focus – abandoned at a crazy angle beside the petrol pump, two of its doors still open. Fuel was spilt over the ground and you could see a trail of wet footprints from the pump across the front of the forecourt and on to a vacant lot beside the garage, where, just to make matters worse, someone had built a pile of pallets – ready for –

'Christ, look!' I hissed. She barely glanced at the gouger – he was young, maybe only in his twenties, skinny and desperate-looking. He had the child – a little girl of about two – clamped awkwardly to his narrow waist with one hand. She was clinging on like a baby koala, roaring her head off. Both of them were drenched in the fuel. The child's eyes were clamped shut and her hair – what might have been pretty curls – was plastered on to her forehead, dripping down her face. It must sting like crazy, I thought. In his other hand, in white-clenched knuckles, the man held a lighter – thumb ready to click the flame into being. Dickhead.

Laura closed the car door and walked around behind it, making her way towards the nearest uniform. Calm as you like, her eyes roving carefully right to left and back again, she took in the scene. This was not how I pictured it. Why wasn't she running over to him – where was the megaphone? The garda marksman?

Delicately, as if whispering a secret, she said something to the uniformed garda, who nodded and ran into the shop. The crowd that had gathered around the sliding doors parted to let her through.

Slowly – maddeningly slowly – she walked across the forecourt and on to the waste ground. She gave a little nod of recognition to the assembled gardaí, then stopped about five metres from the pile of pallets.

'Hi, Paul.' She smiled, pushing her hair behind her ears with both hands – that thing she still does. 'I'm Laura – I'm –'

'Get away! Get back!' he yelled. 'I'll do it, I'm telling you – get back!'

She gave a little nod as if to say, 'Fair enough,' then took a couple of steps back, her hands in the air in front of her, palms facing him.

'Nobody's going to do anything to harm you, Paul.' She shook her head, as if the idea was unthinkable. 'But we need you to come down from there – get the baby – get Kayley cleaned up, okay?'

At the mention of her name, the child's cries grew even louder and she began wriggling to get out of his grasp. He pulled her closer, his eyes – I've seen that expression on a frightened animal at the mart, or the abattoir. I came closer to her and leaned in. I'd an idea of tackling him – the child would tumble, but at least she'd be out of his grasp. I'd easily a stone on him.

'I could –' She shook her head at me. No.

'Get back! Get back! I – I'll do it. I just –'

The garda who'd run into the shop came running back out. Laura tilted her head to listen to whatever it was she whispered in her ear, then nodded and began walking towards Paul.

'Okay, Paul, I'm going to come and take hold of Kayley now, right?'

'No! Get back!' his thumb clicked against the switch. Mercifully, no flame appeared.

'It's going to be fine, all right, Paul? You're going to come down peacefully and give me the –'

She spoke softly to me. 'Move to the other side of me – take your coat off – and get ready to catch the child.'

I did as she said, terror gripping me. Adrenalin coursed in my body – my whole arms shook as I took off my jacket. Christ! Could I do this?

Beside me, Laura had taken off her jacket, too – the navy linen one she was fierce proud of – and held it loosely in her left hand. For a mad moment, I thought she was going to throw it over his face – or wave it like a crazed bullfighter. She motioned for me to slow down.

'Get back!' the man screamed again, clicking frantically now, working his thumb up and down, up and down. Then the flame burst into life.

I stared at Laura. Why wasn't she running? She was nowhere near close enough to grab the child. They'd both go up!

I kept staring at her. Laura kept walking. Two metres away. One and a half metres – one metre – less than a few steps now. She kept her eyes on him.

'I'm gonna do it! I –'

A horrified gasp tore through the crowd as Paul held the lighter against his body, the flame licking against his sodden jacket. At the sound from the crowd, he screamed, too, staring down at the flame.

Laura began climbing the pallets.

To this day, if we're in the pub with the team, someone is bound to toast a round with *No worries, lads – it's only fucking diesel.* It wasn't exactly what Laura said, but that was the drift.

That's what I mean – that's Laura. Or that was the woman who trained me. That Laura was a strategist – a clear and unemotional thinker. Calm enough to send an officer to check the CCTV footage of the pumps to find out what he'd covered himself and the child in. Calm enough to remember that diesel is less flammable than petrol, and that she only needed a few extra seconds – plus the shock factor – to take the child calmly from her father's grasp and pass her to me.

We pull up outside the flat and I pay the taxi guy, stifling a yawn. I'm in the bed in a couple of minutes, drifting off to sleep, when another image from that day makes me snort with laughter. Paul was holding Laura's hand as they clambered down from the pyre together and she cuffed him with particular gentleness.

Where's that Laura gone?

Day Three

26. Laura

'Muma tired! Sssh!' yells Katie at the top of her voice as she clambers into the bed. Her ice-cold bare feet scrabble their way down my side and she snuggles against me. 'Ssh, Dad!' she roars in my ear. 'Me an' Muma sleeping.'

I groan. A bolt of pain jabs from behind my left ear through my brain, emerging somewhere over my left eye socket. I don't dare lift my head. Instead, I fix my gaze on Matt's knees, focussing on the sharp and indestructible crease in his suit trousers. A mug of tea glides across my line of vision and he places it on the bedside table.

'Big night with Kay?' he says, with the kind of cheer that someone who went to bed at half eleven possesses.

'What time is it?' I moan.

'Quarter past,' he says. 'The tea's too hot to drink. Have your shower, I'll bring Madam downstairs and do breakfast.' He stage-whispers, 'We have Coco Pops, ssh! Don't tell her.'

I wince as Katie basically walks across my kidneys in her haste to get out.

'Toto Tops!' she screams.

'Thanks,' I say, forcing myself upright and waiting for the pounding to settle.

'Want a fry?' He pauses in the doorway. 'Runny egg?' My stomach heaves.

The night before assembles itself in fragments – the bar, the drinks, Niamh and Elf Waitress – oh, Jesus, the big platters of fried food. Niamh made the taxi guy stop – oh God – the shame as I remember throwing up behind someone's hedge on Rathmines road. Niamh wiping my face and hands – she must have come home with me then gone back to her flat – even though it meant doubling back on herself. Wincing with a combination of regret and self-hatred, I stumble into the shower. I try not to let myself think about it.

Ten minutes later, there's a rare calm in the kitchen. Matt's looking at me with a fondness I don't deserve – I think it amuses him to see me in this state.

'What are you smiling at?'

'Nothing – it's just a long time since I've seen you like this. Don't beat yourself up – it's good for you to loosen up every now and then. You were like an elephant trying to tiptoe getting into bed.'

'Muma efilint,' laughs Katie, miming a trumpeting action. My head throbs but, just for a second, I'm in the moment. In a warm kitchen with the two people I love most in the world. I begin to feel a bit better after some toast and more tea. Meanwhile, Katie sits in her chair shovelling Coco Pops into her mouth like a ranch hand after a gruelling morning rounding up cattle.

'You missed a call from Mum last night,' says Matt.

'Oh, really? Sorry,' I say, trying to sound it. But conversations with Granny Justy are like trying to navigate a room full of expensive crystal vases wearing hobnail boots and a sumo-wrestling suit. I lurch from one spectacular fail to the next.

'Why was she calling?'

'She's put Katie's name down for the tennis club.'

I swallow noisily, trying not to choke on the hot tea. 'You're kidding.'

'Nope,' he says mildly. 'Apparently, it's impossible to get in if you leave it till they're in primary school, so she paid them a visit yesterday and got Katie's name added to the list.'

'But we don't even know – we haven't even decided where she's going to school, for fox's sake!'

Matt passes me over the box of paracetamol. 'Don't get it out of proportion,' he soothes. 'She's trying to do something nice. She queued for two hours. And she paid the deposit.'

'You have to queue? You have to pay a deposit? For a two-year-old to join a tennis club? Ah, Matt! Come on! You're winding me up.'

He takes back the box of tablets and replaces them in the top cupboard, out of reach. A certain rigidity in his shoulders tells me he's becoming defensive. He's always like this about his parents. It's like he feels guilty for everything they did for him.

He turns and, just for a second, we're teenagers again – the rich boy and the daughter of a single mother. Not my words – but I felt like they hovered over me in neon writing from the moment I first met Justy and Dermot in their terrifyingly big Rathgar mansion. I'll never be good enough for him in their eyes. That's what it feels like – though Matt says I'm paranoid.

'It's important to her,' he says. 'And she paid three hundred euro.' He makes his way towards the hall to let Sylvia in.

'Three hundred euro?' I'm flabbergasted. 'Why didn't they just give us three hundred euro?'

'Don't,' he says.

I hear him greet Sylvia and the clatter of her car keys landing in the dish on the hall table.

'Sil-va! Sil-va!' yells Katie, banging her heels against the chair in glee.

Matt steps back into the room and puts his hand on my shoulder. He's trying.

'You should be happy that she had to queue for two hours,' he says. 'We're lucky she doesn't charge us for her time – that'd be another five hundred. Bye, baby.' He kisses Katie and heads out.

27. Jenny

'Morning, Jenny, how are you doing?' Niamh slaps a file on to the desk and marches over to her chair kind of briskly. I like that word; it sounds as if it has biscuits in it. No nonsense and biscuits. Niamh is mega-brisk today. She pulls her chair closer to me without standing up, like she's riding a horse. Although maybe I think that because of the boots she's wearing. Like a cowgirl.

'Sit down, pet, why don't you?' She frowns. 'I thought Laura was in. Never mind. We'll wait for her before we start.'

I walk to my chair and sit down, although I'm thinking I'm too tired. What I really want to do is stay on the floor and lean my head back against the wall and close my eyes. But when my eyes are closed, he's still there – I told you, I told you there's nothing you can do and you need to shut up. I glance over at Laura's empty chair.

'She's on her way,' says Niamh. 'But – well, why don't we start with this, while we're waiting?'

She smiles and hands me a paper bag. I look inside. Some doughnuts. Hah. Give them nice food to make them trust you. Don't trust her. Stay sharp.

'Quick! Eat up before the boss gets here,' she grins, handing me a tissue for the crumbs.

Then Laura comes in and she's all apologies and stuff about traffic. Niamh does this big grin at her like she's won a prize.

'Good *morning*,' she says. 'Did you sleep well?' Laura squeezes her lips together instead of answering. Her hair is messy at the back – not the shiny you're-worth-it hair. It's still wet in parts, like she didn't blow-dry it. She has some black eyeliner outside the edge of her eye and she winces when Niamh's talking, like it's too loud. They have a look between them while Laura lays out all her pens and stuff. She lines them up.

'Okay, Jen, let's talk today. Let's really talk. Okay?'

I take a bite of the doughnut, and it tastes lovely. Sorry, Laura. This is easy, you can keep a secret easy when you're eating. No words will be spilling out. Only doughnut sugar. And you can count chews. Twenty-four before she says, 'Going back to your mum and stepfather Stuart – can you tell me a bit more about living in the middle of that relationship? Were you scared? Did you ever think about trying to escape?'

She hasn't got a clue. Scared is nothing – scared is for when you dress up at Halloween and scare the grown-ups. And it's over at bedtime. She should try living my life for a week – for a day. See how she likes the soundtrack that is always running. That sound – the one which isn't like anything else, the sound of a fist thumping flesh. You hear sounds and you don't think *oh my goodness, the door's banging in the wind* or *oh dear me, was that a book falling off a table?* You think – *was that Mum falling backwards into the sideboard? Or being slammed into the wall? Was that a thump in the back?* And that's when you might sing 'Hey Jude' in your head so you don't hear it.

'Yes, it was a little bit upsetting,' I say, and I'm major sarky. 'It's a teeny bit upsetting being hit and watching your mum get hit. And Karl. You could say that's upsetting. And stressful.'

And Niamh – smiley Niamh in her cowboy boots – is not far away, and I wish she came to the island because I think she would hit him.

'Good – well done, Jen. I can see you're angry,' and Laura's like, *You go, girl!* Cheerleader Laura. It's quiet then and I think about the other times – when there are no noises and it's shush shush silent. When you come downstairs and Karl is hiding under the kitchen table in a pool of wee, too scared to move. And the wee pools outwards, slowly slowly slowly, in a yellow circle.

When it's not happening to you, it's happening to someone else. You learn not to be glad when it's not your turn. So I don't say any more. I don't feel like talking now. Shut up, bitch. Both of you.

I'm thinking about Irreversible Shock. Discoloured skin, rapid pulse, bluish lips and nails, weakness. He hasn't found me and he can't get out and – shut up. He can't get out. And I see an image then, but I don't want to see it. I see his arm reaching out the window and it's the tower window and he's stretching and his hand is covered in blood but it's all dried now. And his big thumb and his big dirty fingers fumble like blind worms and they grab hold of the slippery stone and they pull and strain. And I'm standing up again and I walk to the window and I look out. Shut up shut up. Shut up, bitch. Not much longer.

'Jenny, I know you understand what's been happening. Deep down, you know, don't you?'

Laura comes and stands beside me at the window, and she's only a tiny bit taller than me and now we're both looking out at this wide, green sweep of grass. It's immaculate and neat, with little hills and dips and those broccoli trees. She nods towards it.

'A golf course, would you believe it? All that beautiful space, all that green, and it's a golf course.'

And I look at it and I wish I was out there, running. On the island when he's not there. If he wasn't there, the island would be beautiful – all the birds would come back and the princess and her owl and the little mouse would sit under the tree, that tree right there – I can see them.

'Can I go out there?'

My voice comes out like a baby's. I'm getting so weak in here I'm pathetic. It's pathetic. I want to be outside under that tree. Luke and I could climb it – there's even a good branch to sit on and dangle your legs and I could dare him to jump down. He'd probably do it, too. I would – I know it now, I'm brave. There's stuff I had to do that most fourteen-year-old girls shut up shut up you dumb bitch how many times just shut up about it.

'It's ridiculous,' she's saying, and Niamh is joining in. 'It should at least be available for the patients – wouldn't you think they'd offer it? Even if it was only for an hour a day?'

Niamh nods. So that's a no then.

I turn away from the window and I think *well, let's see what happens if I just go to walk out the door.* So I walk to the door. My hand is on the handle and it's actually turning, and she says –

'Well, if you want to go out, that's fine, Jenny. But I'm afraid I have to follow you and we've to do a bit more talking – so we may as well do it here.'

'So I'm a prisoner? Till – till when?'

'You're not a prisoner, Jen,' she says, and she's not smiling. She's shaking her head. 'But we have to make some progress – you need to talk to me. And you do need to tell me about Stuart – if you know where he is, you've got to tell me, Jen. I can't stress this enough. If he's –'

And in my head there's a neon sign flashing STUART DEAD STUART DEAD STUART DEAD STUART DEAD STUART DEAD STUART DEAD STUART DEAD.

'If something bad has happened to him or if he's harmed or injured – it doesn't help you, Jen. It's not what you want. Believe me.'

She should say *please*. She should say *believe me, please* or maybe *please believe me*. Dad loved 'Oh! Darling', from the *Abbey Road* album and I love it too. Paul wrote it and did lead vocals. And he got up really early every day for a week to go and sing it and wreck his voice; he wanted to make it sound really raw and cracked, to suit the song. One time when Mum was cranky, Dad came racing into the kitchen and he did a big skid on to both knees and he looked up at her and he sang it just like that – 'Ooooh! darling' – and she laughed and flicked water at him with the washing-up brush.

And then I realize I am back sitting down in the chair like a good girl and, haha, it's not funny, I am crying. But I don't know why. And I'm actually taking three tissues out of the box on her desk even though I said I never would, and it feels like she's winning so be careful. Three–nil to Laura. But ha, I still haven't said anything bad so that's okay. Nil all.

But she's still looking at me closely and her wet hair is drying and I know she's going to keep unravelling and unpicking.

'John Lennon wanted to sing lead on "Oh! Darling", but he couldn't because Paul got to decide. Because Paul wrote it. Did you know John was actually brought up by his aunt? I'm not sure why, I think his parents just couldn't keep him or something.'

I used to think about that: I wished we had an aunt because then the three of us could run – could have run away to her. Maybe. But Mum only has a brother, Gareth, and we never see him. Well, we saw him at the funeral. And his wife, Susan – she had really black hair, I remember, and it was shining and swishing against her leather coat. I don't think she liked us. They only stayed a short time, till after the tea. Said they had to get to the airport, saying that 'if there's anything we can do just call' shit, and we've never seen them since. Stuart slithered into the picture, and that was that.

Laura is saying nothing. I look at the clock, but even though she put it back up it's still stopped. It says twelve. Well, two minutes past. Then she opens the desk drawer and checks something. And I think *what's in the drawer? What could it be?* But that's what she wants – it's all tricks. Shut up and listen to the quiet. But of course, eventually, she speaks.

'So that stuff about The Beatles, that's interesting, Jenny. Not many people would know that type of thing.' She grins her Laura grin. 'You should go on *Mastermind* – if they still have it. Specialist subject – The Beatles.'

And I don't know if I'm meant to laugh but I almost do, because Luke once said the same thing – well, he said I should study History of The Beatles in college. And I never got to check if he was just messing or if you really could.

'Yesterday, Jen, you spoke about Stuart hitting you. Can you tell me a bit about that?'

Don't answer that. Shut up and keep it shut up. She shouldn't even ask something like that, with her shiny hair and her smile. The words want to pop up; they're in my mouth ready to pour out. Swallow them and shut up. Burning hot and icy cold at the same time, but don't tell her that. It burns like nettles and, at the same time, it freezes. Everything freezes over and you can't let it crack. That either. Shut up.

'Jenny? Try to tell me about it, okay?' I grab the water glass and drink. Even though the water's warm now, I don't care. It's real, I know, because I can feel it. There's drops on the outside of the glass and they feel wet against my palm. I don't think I said anything out loud. I look at her to see. But Laura's just looking at me and it looks like she actually wants to help.

And I think *what if I tell her – just one more small thing, from the island?* That would be okay, wouldn't it? But I don't want to go back. I'm scared to go back to the island, and I need Socks to go with me anyway. My mind is rummaging around; it's scurrying and scrabbling and I can't find what I'm looking for. Like Socks rummaging through the piles of wet leaves with his pointy nose, but why is it sad so sad thinking about Socks? What's hidden in the leaves?

'Socks is really called Socrates, that's his full name. It's on his collar tag and Mrs A has this book about him – Socrates the man. Not the dog.' And she likes that. I nearly say 'fetch' to make her go after it. But I don't need to.

'Greek philosopher Socrates?' she says. 'That's good. And did you read the book?'

'He said there's two worlds.'

Poor Socrates – they sentenced him to death. He had to drink poison – and he did it, too. How brave is that, to lift up the cup or glass or whatever and bring it up to your mouth and open your mouth and drink it down and all the time you know you're going to die? And I wonder if it would taste disgusting and could you feel it burning and twisting up your insides? Or would it be like poison berries or the poison apple – delicious but then you fall down dead?

'I didn't know that,' she's saying. 'Tell me about the two worlds.'

I sigh because I hate when it's all so obvious and you know what she's going to say though you've only yourself to blame, you started it. Dumb.

'One is the world you can see and feel, like the real world. And the other is the world of ideas – all the ideas people have. He said the ideas world is the most important one.'

'That's very, very interesting for us, Jenny.' She stands up and does a kind of tippy-toe stretch. 'I say that because we have two worlds going on here, don't we?' She walks a little tour of the room, past her desk and the window and Niamh, who, yes, is still just sitting there, writing and writing.

'Here we are in Abbot's Hill Hospital and there's you, me

and Niamh' (who actually nods at this point – dumb) 'and the window and the desk and the shabby carpet,' and so we all look at the carpet. 'But equally real to you is the other world of – of your thoughts, Jenny, and your fears and your memories. All these ideas and thoughts, like the island with the princess and –' She sits back down and looks straight at me.

'How about we play a game called Truth and Lies? So we can start trying to separate the two worlds. Because I was hoping that today will be the day that you tell me everything, your whole story from beginning to end. And then we could record it – video it. Niamh and I are all ready to do that, when you're ready.'

And I'm staring and my mouth is probably open, like, what the hell because she's going, 'No, okay, no, listen. Listen, Jen.

'You're in charge – I promise. When you're ready – only when you're ready – we can record your story so that it's there for ever: the truth. It's your statement. Nobody will interrupt you, you'll be able to tell the whole story. And when he's charged and brought to court, the judge and the lawyers will see that video and he won't be able to lie and twist things, because the truth will be out and they will hear your words. Would that be okay with you – if the DVD is used in court some day?'

But I'm thinking *you can't charge a dead man and a dead man can't go to court to twist things*. And before I can think, hah, I think *what if they have found the island and they've found him?* and my throat is tight and I feel hot and there's no way no way no way I can go on. But she's already started on her truth and lies.

'So if, for example, if you're in school one morning and the girl sitting beside you takes your schoolbag and empties everything out in a big heap on the teacher's desk. And then the teacher comes in and says, "Who did this?", and she says, "Jenny did it." Would she be telling the truth or telling a lie?'

I've seen those court-case things on TV – *Judge Judy* – where everyone is fighting. And I think she wears loads more make-up than a real judge would wear. Like, tons. But what would the judge be like here and does he really sit up high, like in a box? I can see Stu coming in with his sick smirk and the blue shirt and he's flicking back his hair and he's going, 'There must be some *terrible* mistake – Mel and the kids are *everything* to me. I have no idea what she's talking about, but then again she is dumb, a dumb, lying, ungrateful bitch.'

'We need to talk about reality – what is real and what is not. So your two worlds, Jenny. Which one is real for you?' And that is dumb and I'm not saying.

And then she sighs. She's not Cheerleader Laura yelling, *Go, Jenny!* It's more like *You're a pain in the arse, Jenny*, and she says, 'Come on, Jenny, you can tell the difference between truth and lies, you're fourteen. You need to tell me. Tell me what's been going on in this world – the real world.'

But she knows nothing. Nothing. There's only one world and it's all around you. You bring it with you wherever you go. I see them – Mum and Karl – all broken and bloodied. And I don't want to see it but dumb bitch who cares what you want?

'There *is* no real!' I shout that like a crazy bitch and I don't want to shout at her but it's like with Mum – I hate them when they're meant to be patient and talk soft to you and look after you but they're just angry and disappointed and useless.

'Nothing is real! I don't know what you're talking about! You said tell the story and I can go home. I told you now. I told you, Laura. I need to go home!'

I can't stop now – my heart is swish-thumping and my ears are full of the roaring wind. Maybe, just maybe, she's right and that picture isn't real. And maybe there was too much shouting and roaring because Niamh is squashing me in a hug and Smiley Nurse is in again and she gives daggers looks to Laura and her hand is holding mine.

'Will I bring her back to the ward?' Smiley Nurse says at the same time that I'm saying I want to go home. They don't even bother with no. What have I done that they don't even answer me? I'm a prisoner.

'We'll take a coffee break, how 'bout that?' says Niamh, and I don't know which of us she's asking. And Laura's picking at the skin on her hand and her eyes don't look at mine. And now I see red bits in her eyes; they're bloodshot. She looks shit. And she says, 'Yes, that's a good idea, and when we come back, Jen, we need to talk about reality. It's time.'

And I think it doesn't matter what's real, what's lies and what's the truth. If someone put down the cup in front of me now – the cup of poison that Socrates had – I would drink it down in one go. I know how to do it quickly. And then it would all be over. And that would be real.

28. Laura

'We're going for coffee,' says Niamh, pretty much shoving me off the ward and on to the stairwell. 'Or are we on Solpadeine?'

'Both,' I say, making my way to the table which seems to have become ours. 'Thanks for last night – eh – bringing me home and everything. You didn't have to do that –'

I'm just about to take the antiseptic wipes out of my bag when I remember. I might have been pissed, but I wasn't too pissed to remember her words.

She's sick of me – my anxiety like a – what did she say? Something about another fucking person in the room. All this time, she's been watching me, judging. She probably laughs about me with her girlfriends. I'm a joke.

'I'm going to get a coffee,' I say, getting up. 'What'll you have?'

She laughs. 'So that's how we're playing it? Okay.' She sits down on the chair opposite and opens her folder. Her gaze slides down to my hands and I tuck them out of view and stop picking. 'I'll have a cappuccino. Thanks.'

She starts to read, and I feel like I've been dismissed. I walk up to the counter and order the coffees, watching her while the waitress wrestles with the noisy machine. Niamh can't see me. She's bent over her phone, or her notes, checking something. There's nothing in her manner to suggest a hangover or tiredness, though it must have been after one before she got to bed. Her long legs are stretched out under the table and I'm reminded of – a racehorse or something, shut up in a stall. Her hair falls loose down her back – glossy and wavy. She looks as if she could stand up any moment and sprint five miles. I remember her telling me – way back, that her mother was raging she didn't do Medicine. She'd got enough points. She's so smart. Instead, she plays this smiling country-hick act. It hits me then, as I bring the coffees, that I failed some kind of test last night. I'm gutted. I want to be her friend – I thought I was. More than anything, I want her to like me.

I place the coffee in front of her and sit down.

'I'm sorry about last night. I don't get out much,' I say – meaning it.

She puts down her phone and looks squarely at me. 'Thanks. I was a bit hard on you, too. I was –'

'No, you're right. I've been –' I sigh, genuinely frustrated at myself, my lack of interest in anyone except basically myself and Katie. 'Maybe I could come and watch your next match with the girls? Are you – they in, erm, division one of the league?'

Niamh snorts into the foam on top of her coffee and a piece of it lands on the table in front of me.

'Like you know a fecking thing about the league! Jaysus! Don't overdo it.' She shakes her head, wiping the foam from her top lip. 'I keep forgetting you went to your posh Proddy hockey-playing school and you haven't a clue.' She smiles. 'But it's nice of you to suggest it.'

'And I'm sorry I never even asked – about –' I pause, and she leaps in.

'About my love life? About me being gay? Yeah.' She shrugs. 'It's not a big deal. It's not a secret.' Her face clouds over. 'I mean, a few years back when I came out at home, different story all right. Mam wasn't happy. And one of my brothers – yeah. But Dad's cool, and yeah, it's grand. It is what it is, as Edel would say.'

She glances down at the thick file in front of her, pats it. 'Getting back to this, yeah? We have a disclosure – she trusts you. Or, at least, she's beginning to trust you. But it's early days yet. You can't push her.'

'I know.' I give a self-deprecating eye roll. I'm pleased we're back on track. 'You know me – always rushing things.'

But Niamh doesn't laugh or acknowledge the eye roll. She sighs.

'Laura – this is what I'm talking about. Stop talking shite. You *don't* rush things, actually. Ev-er. You build rapport and you build more rapport and you lure them in. I've watched you. You make them comfortable and then you build more rapport, with a purpose, and then – then they disclose. I watched you do this for two years – when I was training, re-member?' She taps the file with her fingernail. 'You're the Jedi master of this – usually. So, what's going on?'

I wait, realizing I'm the same as Jenny. Waiting.

'Do you want to talk to me about it? Is it your mum? The anniversary? Or the friend you told me about?'

I shake my head. 'No – that was just – look, I was drunk and knackered. Never could hold my drink anyway. I'm fine.'

'So what's going on? Why is she getting to you so much?'

I look to switch her focus. 'The Cig's been on to me at least five times already this morning. He wants to bring her in for questioning,' I say.

'There's no way she's in a fit state for that.'

'Which is what I said.'

She takes a bottle of water out of her giant handbag and swigs, then offers it to me. 'Just messing with you.' She smiles. 'Here.'

I take the new bottle she's holding, break the seal and drink.

'So? What did you tell him?' she asks.

'I told him that she wasn't being taken in for questioning. She's not ready and she would tell him nothing anyway.'

'All true.'

'What did you get from the childminder?'

'She's gutted. They wouldn't let her in ICU. Said there's no point in calling Mel's mum – she's in a care home in the UK. Gave us the name of her brother, though – Gareth. We'll put in a call. She'd no idea – none – of any problems. Or rather, she says she knew Mel suffered from depression and she's no great love for Stuart, but she'd no idea of any stuff going on. She asked to see them.'

'And you said?'

Niamh shakes her head. 'Too soon.' She picks up her phone, clicks a few buttons, scrolls and then passes it over to me. 'There's your Prince Charming,' she says.

It's a photo and paragraph from Stuart's work website, part of the 'Meet the Team' page. It shows a handsome guy in the edgy, hipster tradition of those kinds of pages. He's wearing a bright pink shirt with the sleeves rolled up, faded denims and the obligatory trendy runners. His arms are folded to match the tough-guy stance, but everything – the bright photo, the energetic pose, the self-deprecating grin and tousled hair – make you think, what a great guy.

I study it, reading the lines underneath: ' "Stuart Cullen – Strategic Business Director. I lead a team that uses ideas to stimulate debate and provoke interesting answers in defining future direction for our clients. For me, strategy is about framing the brand in –" '

'He doesn't look like a baddie, does he?' Niamh takes the phone back. She shrugs.

'They never do,' I say, thinking, *what do I know, anyway?* I've not exactly shown myself to be a great judge of character.

'Street angel, house devil, as my nan used to say,' says

Niamh. 'Mind you, she said a load of other stuff that you can't rely on.' She laughs. 'Like, it's the quiet ones you need to watch – that's another one. And that it's only a matter of time till you – that's me – get raped and murdered in Dublin. Oh, and she said Dublin people have to keep their pets in at night because fur traders are lying in wait on the dark corners of your streets, waiting to seize your beloved cat and skin it – for a pair of gloves or a scarf.'

I laugh.

'Right,' says Niamh. 'A laugh, thank Christ! So now I'm asking you again, what's going on? Why are you coming at this like a freight train? Where's Garda Shaw's famed cool and clinical approach?' She smiles at me, studying me exactly as if I were the client, missing nothing. 'We touched on this yesterday evening,' she says, in the long-suffering-counsellor tone we both hate. 'Something's up?'

There's a reason people talk about sweeping things under the rug or burying your feelings and hiding your emotions. It works. I'm aware of the irony of this view when you consider my job and the fact that, every day, I try to get kids to talk to me, to tell me the things they've never told anyone else. My job is to help them bring it all out into the open, to shine a light in the dark places. But, for me, it's a different story.

'Look, she reminds me of someone, that's all.' How can I tell her it's teenage me I see when I look at Jenny? I grew up not far from where she lives. I even went to the same school – Abbot's Field Comprehensive. I picture Jenny walking the same streets, hanging around in gangs of hormoned-up teens, jostling and jeering each other outside the SuperValu, or the older end of the village, or Bushy Park, like we used to. I picture her smiling and saying nothing, working on the tough image, hiding her home life. I picture her trapped in her own home, desperately trying to find a way out of the situation she's in, without getting hurt. I know some of that struggle.

'I understand her – that's what I'm trying to say. I know she's going to tell us – she feels –'

'Laura, you don't know how she feels!' Niamh interrupts, frowning at me like a schoolteacher. 'Don't start talking like you're best friends, okay? You've got to take a step back. She's sick. She's hiding information –'

'I know! Do you really think I don't know that? But it's working – I'm getting through to her. She trusts me.'

Niamh sits back. 'You're wrong there. But that's not the question. The question is, do we trust her?'

A moment passes. I reach across the table to take Niamh's phone. 'Here, let me look at that again.'

Niamh passes it over.

'Why don't we nip down and talk to them? *Eureka!!!Agency* with three exclamation points?' I scroll down. ' "For all your advertising needs." ' I wait. 'It'll take twenty minutes, maximum thirty,' I say, thinking how's that for a distraction technique? Works almost as well as denial.

Niamh's on board, or perhaps she's letting me off the hook. 'Fine! Let's do it.'

'You should try Truth and Lies again, when we get back,' she says afterwards, pulling out of the parking place. We'd found a space just across from Stuart's office, on a residential street, and spent a worthwhile half-hour inside talking to the team.

'You got to her. That might be the angle to take. You could see she was thinking about it.'

I turn the framed photograph over and open the back, removing the picture. *Sunny days and happy people*, written on the back. I replace the picture in the frame. We'd taken it from the wall behind Stuart's desk in his office. Nola, his assistant, had scurried about in circles of panic, trying to help us.

'Still no sign of him? I helped on the search yesterday, but I couldn't get out today, what with –' she had gestured at Stuart's pristine clean and organized desk – 'all of this.'

'Can you tell us a little bit about him?' Niamh kept her talking while I nosed around the office.

'Anything at all, nothing is too inconsequential, Nola. Often the smallest detail cracks the case, you know,' Niamh went on. I glanced at her, then looked away quickly in case I caught her eye.

'Well, I don't know, I mean, I really – it's just such a shock! I mean, he has the perfect life and the perfect family – well, apart from, you know, his wife's illness. But she's stunning and she's getting better, I think, and oh –' She stopped and gulped, patting at her long, straightened hair in a nervous manner. 'You're writing this down?'

'Absolutely!' Niamh nodded. 'This is just the type of thing that helps. We're building a profile.'

'You were telling me about his wife, Melanie?' I pointed her out in the photograph. 'Her illness?'

'Oh, well, she – you probably know this anyway.' Nola lowered her voice to a piercing whisper. 'She has some issues, mentally speaking. Doesn't leave the house – I mean, like, she never leaves the house. We haven't seen her for years, although – yes – she did come to the Christmas party all right, with the kids.'

'That's where you saw Stuart last, yes? At the Christmas party on Sunday?'

'Yes. They were all there – all four of them.'

'Great,' said Niamh. 'Do go on, Nola, you're most helpful.'

'Oh well, that's it, really. They left the Leisure Centre in a bit of a rush – I'm not sure why. It could have been a problem, you know, for Melanie – with the eh.' She stops, looking sheepish. 'Sorry, maybe it isn't my place to say or to pass on, but as his assistant I'm the recipient of private information.'

'It's important, Nola,' said Niamh. 'Anything which can help the investigation, anything at all?'

Nola smooths her hair either side of her shoulders. 'Her agoraphobia. Melanie is agoraphobic. Stuart often has to leave early to go home and get dinner or do the shopping or bring the kids places. He really is a saint. I mean, he adores his family. He's either in work or at home or at the gym. That's his routine.'

'Tell me, Nola,' I butted in. 'Is there anyone who would wish him harm? Does he have enemies? Rivals?'

'Enemies? Rivals?' Nola was so aghast I thought I'd over-done it. 'Nooooo, not at all! He was –' She hesitated. 'He *is* really popular. He's the life and soul of this place, always smiling and – you know, charming everyone. The clients love him. He's Mr Perfect.'

Funny, wasn't that exactly what Jenny had said? I sit back in the warm car, listening to Niamh grinding the gears, and study the photo of Mr Perfect and his perfect family; Mum and Dad and the two children.

At first glance, they really do look the part. Melanie is sort of crumpled in against Stuart's side, long blonde hair falling to her waist, his arm around her shoulder. She's wearing a bright summer dress of pink and yellow flowers on a white background. They're in a suburban garden, bathed in a ray of golden afternoon light. Behind them on the grass under a small tree, there's a table with what looks like the remains of an outdoor lunch – maybe a barbecue. Wine bottles, a jug and an assortment of serving plates, salad bowls, glasses, plates and colourful napkins are strewn over the pink-and-white checked tablecloth. I feel like I've seen the photo before, and then I realize it's like the ones you get from your local supermarket advertising the bank-holiday summer specials. It's like an ad. Mel is stunning. Stuart looks tanned and fit. Jenny and Karl look like the perfect big sis and little brother for this perfect portrait of the perfect family. Yet Jenny's smile is not quite there. Her eyeline is not on whoever's behind the camera; she's looking down. Karl is only a toddler and he's clutching on to his big sister's leg, smiling up at her. No – it's as if only Mum and Dad are fully on board with the charade. And maybe I'm imagining this, but now I think I see a kind of desperation in Melanie's smile, and is that the shadow of a bruise on her wrist?

'What's it say on the back of the picture?'

'Sunny days and happy people,' I say.

Niamh snorts. 'Right. Of course it does – the perfect family at the perfect barbecue in their perfect life.'

Neither of us says anything for a few moments. We let that sit. We've just gone through the junction at the Dodder bridge when Niamh changes lane suddenly and pulls into the garage.

'Picking up a sandwich for later – do you want anything?' she says.

I shake my head and sit back to wait for her, noticing how quiet it is in the car without her. That's the thing with Niamh – it's like her presence is bigger than your average presence. I watch cars and customers come and go.

The problem with sitting in a garage forecourt is that there's a high probability of seeing a van. And there's an equally high probability of seeing a white van. So many people have vans – the ubiquitous white van of your electrician or carpenter, the van which transports flat-pack furniture or a football team. Florists and gardeners have vans, Laura.

Vans are not evil in themselves. Nobody bats an eyelid if the van's windows are blocked out. You pay less tax if they're blocked out; it means it's a trade vehicle. I know that now. I checked it all out afterwards, back when I still thought about finding him and reporting it.

I kept seeing the van. Any time I saw it, I'd take out my phone and – shaking – try to get a photograph. Once, the van was parked outside a house and the driver's door was open. I was sure it was him. But then a woman came out with three small dogs. They were leaping about, tangling their leads, and she chivvied them into the van and shut the door. As she drove away, I realized it said 'Walkies!' in giant lettering on the side.

There are two vans on the forecourt today, the classic white and a blue one. Neither of them belongs to the bastard who raped me eighteen years ago.

29. Jenny

They're both already there in the room, when brown-haired nurse brings me back. I wanted to stay with Smiley Nurse but she had to go somewhere else. She's young, like maybe twenties, and she brought me down to the café and they gave me hot chocolate. She even paid. Because I'd no money.

'When am I going home?' I kept asking her. 'You can tell them I'm fine, can't you?' But Ellie – that's her name – she just kept smiling and saying stuff like 'It won't be long now. I'm pretty sure you'll be home soon.' I thought I liked her, but that's more lies, Ellie. But she got me hot chocolate, so I didn't say anything bad.

And now Laura and Niamh – Niamh who is cowgirl Niamh today – they look like stormtroopers or something. They've been outside and you can smell that outdoors, crisp, smoky smell off them. It's like crackling little sparks on their clothes. They know something. That's what it is. They're looking at each other like they're the team, but it's meant to be me and Laura, our team to find the truth. Dumb dumb of course, here you go, dumb bitch, liking Laura with your dumb girl crush and thinking she's going to fix everything.

I see now, they're buddies, pardners, like the cop shows. Of course they are. And I'm just the day job. Bitches.

'Is there a band in this hospital?' I say to Laura, and I play a little rat-a-tat on the chair before I sit down. She jumps. She's still jumpy. It's funny because I think she'd like to say, 'What a dumb question,' but she can't.

'I don't think so,' she says – true professional. 'Interesting idea, though.'

'When Ringo was thirteen, he had TB and he was in hospital for ages, like a year or something, and that's where he learned to play the drums – in the hospital band. He used the cardboard tubes from the inside of bandage containers as his drumsticks. And he'd thwack them on the lockers and stuff.'

'Is that one of your dad's Beatles facts?' And there, just like that, she ruins it. Luke found it on the internet, but I'm not telling her. Haha. That's right.

But then maybe she is pissed off, like really pissed off, because I can't believe what she does and Niamh just lets her. She says I can trust her and I am sick saying it, no no, don't trust her. She gets the clock and snap snaps the batteries in, then she hangs it back up on the wall.

'I know you don't like it, but the clock is ticking, Jenny.'

Hahstupidhah, she probably thinks that's funny and I thought she was nice but now it's like, bring it on, bitch.

'Sunday. Stuart's been gone since Sunday, Jen. But you saw him on Sunday, didn't you? There was an office party?'

His smartest outfit for the party. And I nearly puke then; it surges up when I remember the blue shirt. But it's okay, I don't puke. Why can't they leave it alone? It's not real. It's not real. It's a story. Once upon a time there was a bad prince and he hurt people and then something bad happened to him and he never came back and they all lived happily ever after. The end.

One time, I came back and Mum was up. She'd done her hair really nicely and she was sitting at the kitchen table, reading a newspaper. And it was so great to see her up and looking pretty and just reading. Karl was sitting opposite, drawing. Perfect. And she said, 'See this?' And she pointed to an article on Evening Classes in Havelock College. She'd circled one – Introduction to Video Production – a one-year part-time course.

'I could learn all the production stuff – start with the basics. It's all changed since I was working. Loads of new technology – but I could do it, couldn't I?' Her eyes were shining.

'I was art director before,' she said. 'It was my job to, you know, find the location, get the props and set it all up – make it believable. But this – this might actually lead –'

And then, the front door slammed, and we heard keys being flung into the dish. We jumped.

And Mum went into her full-on perfect-wife routine – 'I was just putting the kettle on, Stu, I'll make you a nice cup of tea.'

And I hated her for her little-girl voice and for being so dumb. Dumb bitch. It was already going to happen. We all knew it. He put on his fake patient smile. Then he saw what she'd been looking at. Why did she circle it? Dumb bitch. Dumb.

'I hope you weren't thinking for one second about that, Melanie.' He stared at her, shaking his head from side to side in a show of disbelief. 'They're only after your money, first off, and second, how do you think you could possibly man-age it when you can't even get the dinner on the table and you've all day to do it? I mean, what time did you make it out of bed today? And, let's see, is the shopping done? No. Is the fire lit? No. No. No. Of course not.'

And she started whimpering stuff about 'Oh, I was going to, Stu' and 'I'm sorry', all the while watching him. He walked across the room, got a slice of bread from the packet and put it in the toaster. Then he stood facing the window, checking his reflection, both hands spread wide on the counter. And he drew in a huge breath: I'll huff and I'll puff and I'll blow your house in. The chair scraped as Mum stood up. Karl slid down off the chair and bolted into the sitting room, crying. I stepped closer to Mum, but Stuart whirled round, stepped in between us and shouldered me out of the way.

'What were you thinking of, Melanie?' With both hands, he grabbed her shoulders and rammed her back down on to the chair. 'How could you do that kind of thing when you can't even do the dinner?'

He bent close to her face, squeezing her shoulders, pressing down and down. Mum bent her head, cringing and shaking – waiting for it to end. Not answering. Just waiting for it to end, like a stray dog. Her face was all crumpled in and she kept looking at his shoes. And still she waited. He waited. He had all the time in the world, and he was loving it. I could see how much he was loving it remember, don't tell. I'm not telling, Laura, but I could see because there it was in his trousers, hard like a stick, and he moved his hand inside his pocket to make it even better and he kept staring at her.

I was right beside the chopping board – and, behind that, the knives. I was beside the knives. They live in a wooden block with slits in it. Six soldiers all ready for duty. Paring knife. Boning knife. Carving knife. Bread knife. The little sharp one. And Sergeant Sharp Steak. And a question began to grow in my chest, filling it up up, filling it right up till it might burst. His back was to me – he couldn't see me. I could just take – I could just grab –

Clack! The toaster popped up. Crash! He pushed, and Mum's chair toppled backwards over on to the floor. Back-flip time; Mum's skinny legs with her little black boots sticking up like the wicked witch from under the house.

And he left her on the floor and went to get his toast. And that day, I was brave. Maybe not brave enough to call on

Sergeant Sharp Steak, but brave. Haha, stupid bitch brave. I yelled at him.

'I hate you! I wish you were dead. I wish we'd never come here –'

Dumb dumb dumb. I stopped. With one hand, he grabbed my hair – my ponytail, wrapped it over his fist and tugged me to him. Oh yeah goodbye brave hello fear.

'Do you know what? I'm in no mood to listen to your moaning. You're so full of it – with your perfect life that you lived before. You never question it, do you? Do you ever wonder if it was really that perfect?'

He yanked my hair again and pulled me down, down. My knees bent and buckled until I was on the floor like Mum. And she did nothing nothing. And I was kneeling at his feet and he pressed himself against me and I could smell it.

'Ask yourself. Mum and Dad, always happy, holding hands, singing their Bee Gees songs? In their little shop which was making loads of money and your dad without a care in the world? Everything was brilliant and everyone was happy. Really?'

I tried to twist and get away, but now his knee was pressing me down. Behind me, Mum was scrabbling and getting up and crying and saying stuff like 'Stu, don't. Please don't.'

'When are you going to grow up?' he said, shoving me backwards. I landed heavily – and the jarring as I hit the stone-tiled floor went right up my spine. And then he turned and began buttering his toast. 'Try a bit of gratitude and manners, Jennifer,' he said, biting into the toast. 'Try helping your mother out – look at her. She could do with some help. She needs all the help she can get.'

And I must have put my head down on the table then because Laura is on her knees. Haha, trying to get the old eye contact going. She sweeps her hair back again and that's when I see her fingers have all these red bits and little raggedy white bits of skin. Not all of them, just the hand I can see. She sees me looking and hides her hand. And I feel worse because I've seen that. But I don't know why. She's talking in the serious voice – I don't know what she's done with Good Joke Laura – and she says, 'Jenny, it's my job to protect you and keep you safe. That's what we're here for.' She gives up with the eye contact and pulls her chair over, sitting knee to knee with me.

'I can't undo the things that have happened to you – but I can help make sure that it stops. You need to tell me.'

Lying Laura, haha, that's a new one. Lying Laura goes on and on then, saying that she has to protect human life and we have to find Stuart and tell the truth and do you know where he is and blah blah same script.

I hate him. I hate him so much. I hate, hate him. Shut up shut up. Shut up, lying bitch Laura.

'Jenny?' She passes me the box of tissues. 'You need to tell me the truth. We know you were with him on Sunday. In the car. We know you're a witness to the truth. You need to tell me what happened to Stuart. You need to tell me what happened to you. Time is running out.'

But that's the problem. Time is running out and truth is running in. Socrates was sentenced to death for telling the truth. He drank the poison. Why did he say that about Dad, without a care in the world? Now I see him – Dad – with his head in his hands, at the kitchen table. Dad often sat like that. I'd forgotten. I never think about that. I only think about the Beatles stuff, the happy stuff. She waits. I wait. And the stupid ticks tick.

'Jenny?'

I don't answer. My head is hurting. I'm hearing him say 'When are you going to grow up?' and he's looking at me, he's always looking at me. Fox and rabbit. Fee fi fo fum. He has pictures, too – on his phone. The swimming pictures.

When Karl was little – just a baby – he said Mum had to rest and why don't we go off on an adventure? And I was dumb dumb dumb. But I liked the swimming costumes he bought for me – a new one every time. Pink with yellow sea-horses and a frilly skirt – that was the first. It matched my armbands and he took photos on his phone to show Mum, but he never showed them – never. And the bikini for me because I was a big girl now – it was orange and silver sparkly sequins. I – I loved it. Dumb bitch.

And he always had to check that it was tight enough so the water couldn't get in and then I smiled and did my diving pose and he held me in the water because big girls don't need armbands.

One time not long ago, I was standing behind him and he was watching TV and flicking through the pictures on his phone and I saw me in the sequin bikini – my dumb little face smiling and smiling. Dumb bitch.

I always knew when he was nearby on the island, especially in the dark. I could feel his thoughts and I could smell his smell on the wind. It smells of rotting things and caged animals. It stinks. This is all wrong and I want it to stop. I want him to stop.

I'm going to think about something else. I'm going to think about dehydration and shock – the twin angels of death. I'm going to think about infection which can mess up the blood flow to the organs and that can lead to clots and gangrene. I'm going to think about the blood pressure dropping and the respiratory organs – the heart and lungs failing. Failure of these organs leads to death. *Trauma* Ninth Edition.

She's messing up my thinking with her talk talk questions and I want her to shut up. Shut up, bitch.

I said that out loud and it's funny because it works bam, like magic. She shuts up.

'What day is it?' I say, all wide-awake sitting-up now. And she has to check with Niamh, which is pretty worrying for a garda if they don't know what day it is, haha.

'Wednesday?' she says with a big question. She leans forward in the chair; she's nearly on top of me.

'Jenny, where is Stuart?'

And I sigh again because she's so dumb with her questions, always looking over at Niamh, always asking, 'Where's Stuart, where's Stuart?'

'On the island. On the island. He's on the island, like I keep telling you.' I told her loads of times, and I even heard Niamh write it down. But shut up now because remember, they're a team, a crack detective team. And you're not on their team, dumb bitch.

And Laura waits doing her waiting thing, then she says tell me more about the island, Jenny. What happened to the little owl, Minerva? And what happened to the princess? And so I tell her the next bit of the story, but it's sad too.

'So once upon a time there was a princess and she was locked in a tower and she couldn't get out because she was a dumb bitch and she didn't care for her little pet mouse and he died. He shrivelled into a little ball of wrinkles and she sits every day in her stupid bitch tower and she brushes her long, long hair over and over. And she waits for stuff to happen but nothing ever does. Well, nothing good.'

I'm so sad, thinking of the little mouse. We never even gave him a name in the story, we just called him Mousie. But he's fucking dead now anyway.

'Who's dead?' She's glancing over at Niamh like she has the secrets of the world written on her face. Then she bites the skin of her fingertip and straight away squeezes her hands into fists so she can't do it again.

'Mousie is dead and it's sad because he didn't even live long enough to get a proper name or even do anything.'

And it really is sad. Inside my throat I feel the tears gathering together, all jumbled up with the yells. I want to say *stupid bitch, it's all your fault*. You sit there brushing your hair and sleeping and the thorns grow and he comes in. Every night.

'He left her in the tower with her dead pet mouse. And he takes what he wants. He has Minerva and he keeps her and any time he wants he can take her and rip out her feathers or do whatever he likes to her. And the princess does nothing. She sits in the tower she does nothing and all the time he's hurting Minerva. He's ripping out her feathers and squashing her. And she stares at the tower window and she's waiting for the princess to scream and get help and do something. But she does nothing. And then he's finished and he goes to the tower and says, "Oh princess, oh princess, let down your hair that I may climb without a stair." Like in the story. And she tosses her golden hair out the window and he grabs it with his giant slab hands and he climbs up into the tower and then he does whatever he wants.'

I am so sad then because I remember when the dumb bitch princess saw what he did to Minerva and she did nothing to stop him. She just cried her princess tears.

'This is a really sad story,' she says. She puts her red bitten hand very gently on my knee. It looks very pink.

'Minerva tried to help. Dumb bitch princess did nothing but Minerva tried to help. She pecked him, but his giant hands didn't feel it. He grabbed the little bird and he tore out her soft feathers and he threw her up in the air and the princess sat in the tower window and held out her arms and she cried, "Come on, come on, fly up here to me." And Minerva tried to fly but her wings wouldn't flap because all the feathers were gone and she flapped and flapped and bam! He shot her clean through her chest with an arrow and –' I stop because all the screams very nearly leap out of my mouth, but I swallow them down. 'And she fell down.'

And there are loads of ticks then. Laura does her silent nod and she looks at me and we both listen to the ticks. And to Niamh's scribbles.

'Is that the end?' She straightens up and takes a breath. 'Is that the end of the story?'

No no no, Laura. That's not the end because Minerva wasn't dead. Now it's time for the last chapter – the best one. The chapter where the prince dies.

30. Laura

She's clammed up again. I shouldn't have asked her if that's the end and I shouldn't have called it a story. I need facts. Courts deal in facts. Lawyers trade them like golden coins. She's so small and vulnerable, wrapped in anger and bravado like a flak-jacket. She's put it all together into a story where it can't hurt her, or that's what she thinks. And somewhere along the line, I'm getting my story mixed up with hers. I'm so busy trying to draw hers out that something is happening to my own. It's begun seeping through, like blood through a bandage.

Mum hadn't wanted me to go. In fact, unusually for her, she'd actually told me not to.

'I don't like you out late on the bike. It's bad enough you trekking over to see him in daylight! All the way into town.' 'Town' meant city-centre Dublin, a cycle of less than five miles. 'It'll be dark, the roads could be wet, you'll be tired.' She stuffed her cosmetic bag into the small case and began zipping up her suitcase, wheezing with the effort.

'Let me, Mum.'

'Well, you're an adult now, I can't stop you –'

'No, I mean this.' I reached across and took the case from her, zipped it shut, then put it by the door. We sat on the end of the bed while she got her breath. She and her buddy Marie were due to head off to Spain, leaving me alone for a whole week. Cian was in the states for the summer and I was back home, working in a restaurant in town.

'Be honest, Mum, it's not the lateness that's bothering you, is it? If it was Matt I was going to see, you'd be all in favour. You'd be kicking me out the door to see him.'

'Matt Thompson would come and pick you up – lovely lad that he is,' she quipped. 'I mean, would have,' she amended. She noticed me bristling. 'Ah, I'm not criticizing your choices, pet, you know that.'

'Good.' As usual, the mention of Matt brought out my bad temper. The break-up had been agony. We'd started going out in school – in fifth year – although we'd actually known each other since we were first-years, aged twelve. He'd walk me home if he didn't have training and we'd meet up at the weekends to walk Bobby and hang out, watching TV. We were one of the major school couples by the end of fifth year, in time for all the eighteenths. His name was Tippexed on my bag and someone had written 'Property of Mrs Thompson' on my history folder. I'd forgotten that.

Matt was easy-going and even-tempered. I didn't know, at that stage, the pressure his big-shot solicitor parents had been putting on him. All I knew was Matt didn't do the dumb stuff that the rest of us did and regretted. He drank, but not so much he was staggering and puking. He saved his energy for the rugby pitch and mostly was content to keep doing what we were doing. Early in sixth year I was beginning to rail against it – the sameness of everything, the predictability. And I hated the look I got from Justy every time I arrived at their house. A quick scan of what I was wearing, followed by the tiniest tilt of her immaculately blow-dried coiffure, signifying her disappointment. She'd given me two cashmere cardigans (Christmas of sixth year and eighteenth birthday) and, though I did wear them, I felt like an impostor. Matt never accepted there was anything in it – said then and still says I'm imagining it.

Now I understand how clothes and make-up work as

armour. Now I aim for the neat blow-dry myself and the trousers from Massimo Dutti and the well-cut mac, but it's too late for Matt's parents. In their eyes, I'm still lacking. I don't know, maybe Matt's right – I'm being paranoid. And paranoid Laura equals judgey Laura. Maybe Justy is only trying to help.

After Christmas in sixth year, I began picking fights with Matt – to test him, maybe, or just to feel something more – to make him feel more. I wanted him to choose me for being me. I wanted him to choose me over his stuck-up parents and their marble-floored mansion with intimidating place settings.

After the Leaving, while most of the lads were going Interrailing, he went on an art tour of Italy with his parents, followed by three weeks in a villa outside Florence. They invited me – but I knew they didn't really want me to come. Maybe Matt did. But I think they were relieved when I said I couldn't as I was working and saving for college. Richard, Andy and Simon – the rugby buddies – flew out, and they had a ball. Justy still talks about 'the boys'.

I decided college would be a ready-made fresh start for me. A place where I could reinvent myself and break away from my disappointing scruffy-schoolgirl image. I found myself hoping Matt would be unfaithful when he was away, and that we'd have to break up. Coward that I was.

But he came back tanned and smiling and ready to pick up exactly where we left off. And I waited all of one week in September, before finishing with him on a drizzly afternoon walk in Bushy Park, where even Bobby looked abashed. I went to Trinity to do psychology and sociology while he headed off to UCD. Matt was loyal and kind, as ever. He called in on Mum once or twice after Cian went to Canada. Bobby nearly exploded with joy any time he appeared on the doorstep. So did Mum, naturally.

Matt was gutted, but too decent to make it difficult for me. Justy was delighted. The following spring, when I bumped into her in SuperValu, she told me that even though he was *heart-broken*, he'd started going out with a really *gorgeous* girl doing medicine.

'She's on the varsity dance crew, too, can you believe it? *Contemporary* dance,' she'd gone on in the same awestruck tone. But I didn't care. That summer, I had other plans. I was going to Vietnam with Maeve and Lucy. So even though it stung a little bit to think of the gorgeous dancer doctor tucking herself under his wing, settling down into the front seat of Terence, his adored Honda Civic, enjoying his gentle good humour and frankly excellent kissing, it wasn't enough to make me go back. Even when I spotted them in Dicey's – we were out for a few drinks before heading off – I was able to smile and give a little wave. I was going to have an amazing summer of backpacking, followed by three more years in TCD, followed by a glittering career as a criminal psychologist. I wasn't too sure exactly, but still. And I was already more than a little bit in love with the new guy anyway – a singer-songwriter called Fiachra.

'How is Fintan anyway?'

'Mum, are you messing? You know his name is Fiachra.' She clamped my wrist and squeezed. 'No, sorry love, really – I just forgot. I'm not trying to annoy you. Come on, we'll have a cup of tea before Marie gets here, and you can tell me then.'

She got up and went to pick up the case, but I took it from her. Any effort now made her a bit breathless, and I wanted her well enough for her trip, not cramping my style here at home. We went downstairs to the kitchen to wait for Marie.

'I haven't seen him for a week 'cos I've been working and he's been gigging, which is why I wanted to go tonight. It won't even be that late – he said he'll be back by eleven.' Mum handed me a mug of tea.

'Look, I'm not going to lay down the law, I told you. You're eighteen –'

'Nineteen.'

'Nineteen. It's just you don't have to go, do you? He's not going to disappear into a puff of smoke if you don't go over there, is he? And anyway, who'll let Bobby out in the morning? He'll pee everywhere.'

At the mention of his name, Bobby got out of his basket and came over to Mum, stretching his arthritic legs. He licked her ankle with a serious air, just one lick, then sat looking up at us.

'I hate going away and leaving him.' Mum scratched behind his ears and Bobby closed his eyes in bliss.

'He'll be fine, Mum, I'll mind him. I'll be here.'

'But what about tonight?'

I sigh. 'Fine, I won't go now, if it makes you happy.'

'Thanks, pet.'

I sometimes think that was the last real conversation I had with Mum. It was certainly the last conversation where there wasn't a huge secret between us. And I wonder now, did she know or suspect that something had happened? I've only been Katie's mother for two and a half years but already it feels like I know her completely – like I can read her mind. When she was a baby, if she got hiccups, so did I. When she got wind, I had stomach pains – it was ridiculous. We did *Wuthering Heights* for the Leaving and there's a line in it where Cathy says, 'I *am* Heathcliff.' I remember thinking that was way over the top. But when I had Katie, that line came back to me. It's vast, the love you feel for them. It's not even pleasant. She's such a huge part of me, she *is* me. Or I am her.

Mum and Marie headed off in great spirits to the airport

and I fed Bobby and tidied the kitchen, thinking it was great that I wouldn't have to do it again for at least six days. I watched a bit of telly and ate half the chocolate biscuits. At a quarter to eleven, I sent a text to Fiachra:

Mindin dog c u in am xxL

Then I waited, worried that I shouldn't have put two xs. He'd think I was needy. We'd only been going out for a few weeks and I was desperate not to appear like the groupies he said trailed after them in pubs and clubs. I was different. I was tough and confident, completely self-contained.

At eleven fifteen I heaved a sleepy Bobby off my lap and he trotted after me to the kitchen. When I opened the back door to let him out, Bobby looked up at me, pleading with me not to make him go outside in the rain.

'Oh, all right then. Go to bed. But don't start whining at the door at the crack of dawn tomorrow, right?'

Aware that this was hardly the wild life I'd envisaged for myself with Mum gone, I turned off the lights downstairs and headed towards bed, trying not to feel defeated. It'll be good to have an early night, I told myself, getting into my pyjamas.

Dog cn sleep. Mind me! Xxx Fiak

I smiled. Three xs and he signed himself Fiak, his nickname. Before I could reply:

Wide awake n lonely

And then:

N horny

And then:

2nite R nite?

That was enough. We hadn't slept together yet but it was definitely on the agenda. Fiak was ridiculously good-looking – golden, tanned and slim. He wore loose jeans and baggy, faded sweatshirts with the sleeves rolled up to reveal his bronzed forearms. On his wrists leather bracelets clustered. His hair was always on the move, falling into his eyes and across his brow until he gathered it up with his ringed fingers and swept it over to the other side. The thought of access to that smooth, golden skin: the thought of his tanned hands resting on my hip or my stomach – I could picture it. I wanted it.

My pyjamas seemed ridiculous now. Who goes to bed at eleven forty-five when they're nineteen? I whipped them off, rolled them into a ball and fired them against the bedroom wall.

'Someone's gonna get some action,' I sang to myself, putting on the black thong with a lacey front, snapping the thin straps against my hip bones. I imagined his face, the 'wow' when I would unhook the black mesh bra, unleashing my boobs. It had worked with Matt; it would work with Fiak. I even allowed myself a glance in the mirror, when I'd put my jeans on. Lucy and I had been running and doing sit-ups in preparation for Vietnam and I was in the best shape I'd ever been and, anyway, I was nineteen. Don't overdo it, I thought, just a T-shirt and then the jacket for the bike. Outside, the rain teemed down, but I pictured Fiak's gratitude – I'd cycled through a rainstorm to see him. I reckoned when he saw me on the doorstep, rain running in rivers down my jacket, droplets shimmering in my dark hair, he'd be overwhelmed – no, moved. It'd be something we'd talk about for years afterwards. Then he'd say something like 'Let's get you out of these wet clothes,' and lead me into the warmth of his flat. It was perfect.

'Someone's gonna get some action,' I sang again. I liked it so much, I sent it as a text.

Redy 4 sum action?

Come n get it xxx

Bobby's claws clattered on the kitchen lino when he heard me in the hall getting my bike gear on. He whimpered.

'Go back to bed, Bobby. You're not coming,' I said.

Before I shut the front door, I heard his settling-down groans. Wheeling the bike from the side passage, I paused at the gate and looked back at the house. Two lights winked upstairs but everything was shuttered and snug. Thinking of Mum's dire warnings, I put on my reflective strip and snapped on the front and back lights.

I headed off for my hot date.

31. Jenny

'I want to see Mum and Karl. If I can't go home, when can they come in?'

Laura says nothing and I think she's a rubbish garda – she's not even doing anything. She's, like, staring at her page and sometimes she clicks the lid of her pen but she's not even writing. Niamh does her ahems every now and then and Laura doesn't even hear her. Haha, here comes the sun, I think. And also, everything's gonna be all right. Everything's gonna be all right. Dumb bitches know nothing.

There's a room that says 'Visitors' on the ward. It has a TV and magazines. Nobody goes there ever. It's empty. Maybe Mum and Karl can come in and be visitors and we will fill up the room. I see them get up from the sofa and they put Socks on a lead and they hold hands and they get in the car; no, not the car. That's wrong. They get the bus but no dogs allowed, only guide dogs. Socks can be the guide. But that doesn't last long because she does Serious Laura face then.

'Not yet, Jenny, sorry. It's not possible at the moment,' she says.

'But please, you can't keep them away! Please –'

I jump up and then suddenly I'm shouting and stomping around the room where I was nearly asleep a minute ago. Not cool not zen, dumb bitch. This is how they do it. They make you care too much. And I so want to see Karl – to see both of them. I haven't seen them since – since the day we sat on the sofa and had the hot chocolate. No, that's not right. Did we go to the shops or something? But that picture is pushed out of the way and now I remember other stuff. Everything was messy and it was raining or was I crying and – what happened? Why can't I remember? I run to the window and I think maybe I'll see them outside, playing in the snow. But it's grey and bare. No snow.

'It's going to be okay, Jenny.' She stands up and comes over to me at the window. We both look out like we might actually see them outside, under the tree or something.

'I want you to think of somewhere safe – somewhere nice where you feel safe. Okay?' She turns to Niamh and says, 'No notes, just leave the notes for now, I'm trying something.'

'Think of a safe place, somewhere you're really comfortable and calm. It can be anywhere.'

I try. I think of a treehouse high up in a huge tree. And the tree is on a little hill, beside a fast-flowing river. It's warm inside and there's a roof of woven willow branches and there's a cosy bed with a soft red cover and Minerva is there on her perch. And the rain patters on the willow-branch roof and the wind lashes the little circular window, but it doesn't get in. I can see the treehouse. But I can't get inside. I'm not in it.

'I can't.'

'Try to trust me, Jen? I really am trying to help you get better.'

She walks back to her desk – opens the drawer, takes something out – closes it.

Nice try, Laura. Not gonna work, no way no way. She sits down again and, from my left, a tutting sound from Niamh and I don't know what that means.

'Jenny, I'd like you to tell me a bit more about Stuart.' She pauses, puts on a 'don't worry, you're not in trouble' smile. 'I think you know where he is and you know what's happened to him.'

You can't trust her you can't trust her. She's going to wreck it all. Dumb bitch. All dumb bitches. Stupid, dumb bitch.

'So,' she says. 'Start again – with this.'

She holds out her hand and it's curled in a fist and I hold out my hand underneath. Her fingers unfurl and a necklace spills into my palm like cool water.

'You were wearing this when they brought you in,' she says. 'Start with this then.'

The owl necklace. Minerva.

I should have kept it in my treasure box, with my special stuff – not that there's anything special or worth anything in there. Just Dad's cufflinks and a ring they gave me for my tenth birthday – it doesn't fit now. And his black watch, which is waterproof for a mile underwater. I remember thinking that the three of us were going to be like merpeople, living in a little shell house a mile under water. I used to ask Dad over and over, 'When are we going to the underwater house?' And he started singing 'Octopus's Garden'. I remember that so clearly. I could see the little garden, the underwater house. It would be yellow, with shell flowers on the path outside. I really believed that. Dumb dumb dumb. Grow up.

'He thought I had a boyfriend. He thought a boy gave it to me.'

'Who – Stuart?'

'And he was like – "Where did you get that? Don't think I don't know what you're at." All that stuff. And I told him that wasn't it, but he didn't believe me. He tried to take it.'

But this is too hard, and she shouldn't ask me. I close my eyes and I try not to think about it, but it's like when they say, 'Don't think about pink elephants,' and all you can see is pink elephants. We were on the landing, Mum's door was closed and Karl was asleep and I thought it was okay – that nothing more was going to happen that day. It was over. For that day anyway. I was about to go into the bathroom and I was wearing pyjamas, the dalmatian ones, and you could see the necklace easily. And we were both whispering, like we wanted Mum and Karl to have sweet dreams.

And he said something like 'I don't want you wearing that' and he reached out to take it off me, or grab it or something. And I clutched it really tight in my fist and backed into the edge of the doorway and closed my eyes, like I could magic him away with a wish. And then he changed his mind. He stretched out his hand, but he didn't grab the necklace. Instead, he reached down inside my pyjama top and his hand began to creep down my bare skin like a living thing, never losing contact, never stopping – creeping and squeezing and pressing harder and harder. He took hold of my – of me. And he squashed all of himself up against me and we were both jammed into the doorway. His breathing was fast and shallow like there wasn't enough oxygen in the air for what he needed. And I couldn't see his face; my eyes were scrunched closed. But I could hear him with his head pressed into the door jamb above me while his hand squeezed and pressed and rubbed, my nipple trapped between his giant fingers – and it was disgusting. His smell was everywhere.

And don't tell don't tell this not ever not ever. It was disgusting – worse even than the stuff in the tower. At least that's dark and I'm not there, it's not me. It's not the real me. This was the first time he'd ever tried something like in the day with the lights on and Mum and Karl only steps away. And I wanted him to get off me but he didn't and I hated him then like lava – burning, raging, boiling. He pressed his whistling nose against my ear, his voice all muffled – 'You love this, you want this.' And I felt the silver necklace in my fist and I squeezed it tight. I hissed, 'Get off get off me,' and I shoved him. He'd been leaning against the door jamb and he lost his balance for a second and in that second I jumped into the bathroom and locked the door.

Laura is still waiting. Nodding like the dog.

'So he tried to take it?'

'Yes, but I got away – locked myself in the bathroom.'

I put my thumbnail in the grooves and trace her beautiful wings, her curved beak. And I'm so sad now. And the anger is coming back. It's danger danger danger. Sergeant Cleaver reporting for duty, sir.

'It's beautiful,' she says. Like she's so pleased we're chatting. 'So where did you get the necklace then?' Hah, nice try, but that's not happening. Be careful, sssh.

'Owls can see everything, they have full 360-degree vision,' she says. I told *you* that, Laura. She thinks I'm stupid.

She stands up and comes over to me, still talking, and she takes the necklace and motions for me to bend forward so she can put it on. She wears a lovely perfume – like green apples. Gently, she lifts my hair out of the way and fastens the necklace, and I think of Mum, because she was gentle, and the Sergeant Sharp Steak knife inside my chest twists.

'You could tell me what the little owl has seen, couldn't you, Jenny?'

And I think okay then, but it won't make a difference. Nobody can stop it. Even when they see it, nobody stops it. They don't know how. But I tell her one thing the owl saw.

'One time a man and a woman were walking along in the woods. A little boy was with them, and his big sister, holding his hand to make sure he didn't trip over branches. And high up above them in the branches of a tall tree, the owl was watching. Other people were walking in the woods, too, with their dogs and their children. And everyone smiled at each other as they passed by and said things like "Lovely day" or "Good afternoon" or just nodded.

'Then they reached the quiet part of the woods, and there were no other people. And then the woman did something, or maybe she didn't do anything, and the man drew back his fist and punched her in the side of the face and "Oh!" she cried and tumbled to the ground. And the little boy ran over and started to scream and cry because his mum was on the ground not getting up. And the big sister knelt down and tried to help the mum get up and tried to get the little brother to stop screaming because, even then, she knew it would only get worse.

'And in the middle of the screaming, a man with a bald head and a woman who was with him whose face was a crumpled page of worry, came walking over and the woman helped the mum get up.

'"Are you okay?" she kept on saying. "Are you okay?"

'And the first man said, "She's fine, she tripped." And it was going to be okay. But the bald man who was very brave said this:

'"She didn't trip. You hit her. I saw what happened. I saw it."

'And the whole wood held its breath. And the mum stood up and held her face and gathered her children to her and she said in a gasping voice – "It's okay, I'm fine. I'm fine. I just fell over. I tripped. Thanks so much for your help."

'And the worried woman took her husband's elbow and pulled him away. Though she kept looking at the mum with her eyes shooting out ropes for the mum to grab on to. But the mum looked down at the ground and she brushed the leaves off her.

'"I saw what happened," said the bald man. He kept saying it. And his wife stood beside him, clutching his elbow. "I saw the whole thing."

'But the man turned back and said, "Mind your own fucking business," and he grabbed the mum's arm and pulled her along until she was trotting and trying not to stumble. And the sister carried the little brother and tried not to look at her mum's bleeding face.'

I remember that day and how my legs chafed and rubbed as the piss cooled in the wintry air. I looked back and the bald man was following, though his wife was hanging back a bit. They watched us get into the car. They watched us drive away. And that night was very bad and Mum said to me with her face all puffy from crying, 'Oh, don't say anything to anyone, please don't, Jenny it'll make it worse. He won't do it again, he said he won't.' And it was like she was the kid and I was the grown-up because even I didn't believe that shit.

For days afterwards, I'd imagine the bald man and the worried woman coming to the house with the police. I waited for the doorbell. I was hoping and hoping. I thought the police would take Stu away in handcuffs, and he'd be shouting and roaring but you wouldn't hear him when they slammed the door shut. And then they'd drive off. Then the bald man would put his hand on Mum's shoulder and say, 'Come and live with us – bring the kids.' And his wife would smile and say, 'Yes, we live just by Bushy Park, it'll be perfect.'

'People say they will help you and all you have to do is ask – but that's not true,' I say. 'They can't do anything.'

'They can – we can, Jenny. Once we know about it, we can help you and it won't happen again. You'll be protected.'

'What's the title of the first track on the *White Album*?'

Her mouth opens a bit and she takes a breath. And I know then, when she goes, 'The *White Album*, did you say?' I know she lied.

Dumb bitch. She never listened to it. She's a liar. Worse than Mum, and I hate when grown-ups lie, and they're even thicker than kids and you catch them out.

And I think *yeah right, Laura. It won't happen again and I'll be protected*. How will you do that, Laura? Are you going to catch him and put handcuffs on him? You — no offence, but you don't look like you could sprint down to our house and catch him and, like, chuck him in a van. You're not going to be there when it happens.

'You don't know what you're fucking talking about.'

Haha, Laura. And she hates that and she's not Cheerleader Laura, but I don't care. It feels good. It's really quiet for a bit. So I add some more.

'You're a liar. You haven't a fucking clue, Laura. You don't know what it's like.'

But I maybe went too far because she goes red and her neck is all blotchy.

'You're too old for this bullshit, Jenny,' she says, and she's leaning forward and it's all frowns now. 'If I haven't a clue, how about you tell me? Tell me what I don't know! I'm tired of it. Where is he? And don't tell me the island. There is no island.'

Niamh comes over and sort of stands between us and I don't know who she's protecting, though she's looking weird daggers at Laura.

'Have you done something to him? What did you do, Jenny? Stop bloody wasting our time and tell us!'

'I'll tell you when he's dead,' I say, and realize that's a good plan. I can rest then, and it will all be over and I can go home.

'Stuart's not dead?' says Niamh. Up close, I can count the buttons on her shirt.

'Yet,' I say.

32. Laura

Niamh's on the phone, probably to the incident room. She brought Jenny back to the ward herself, told me to go and get a coffee. If she hasn't given Cig the heads up already, I'm pretty sure she's doing it now. I'm hiding out in the bathroom on the end of the corridor. I'm using the disabled toilet and I stand at the mirror, my hands submerged in the warm, soapy water. It calms me – the clean smell of the hand wash, the neat white box of clean white paper towels, the wall-mounted hand sanitizer. It's possible to wash your hands, dry and sanitize them and open both the cubicle door and then the bathroom door without once making contact with the woodwork.

I use more paper towel to clean the toilet seat and sit down. The dragging feeling has been niggling all afternoon – not as bad as usual – but insistent. Tiny claws scraping down, down, down – but when I check, there's no blood – nothing. I reach to get my handbag from the hook and pull it on to my lap, deciding to put a panty liner in just in case. Niamh's right about the Mammy tricks. Super-plus tampons and pads always to hand. I keep them in a Jiffy bag in the inside pocket of my handbag – and a pair of giant M&S knickers, just in case. Another Mammy trick.

I love the way some shops wrap your purchases in tissue or fancy paper, then place them in a bag with a bow. It makes even a pair of knickers look upmarket and expensive, as if you took ages choosing them and you spent a fortune. Some of them even throw in teeny soap pearls or dried flowers for good measure.

I can't remember where I'd got the set I was wearing that night. It wasn't Penneys or Dunnes. Maybe Knickerbox or even La Senza.

When you see the same knickers in an evidence bag, they don't look quite so classy. As the clear plastic bag is passed around a courtroom, their value changes. They're downgraded. They may as well have a note stapled on, saying: *This is the property of a slut with no self-respect who was out that night looking for some action and then changed her mind. You must acquit.*

In a recent case the girl's underwear was shown in court. His barrister said you had to look at the way she was dressed, that you couldn't rule out the possibility that she was attracted to him and open to being with someone. What does that phrase even mean? I couldn't get it out of my head – 'open to being with someone'. I see her sitting there, legs open like scissors. The underwear was a thong with a lace front. Open for business.

That's the adversarial system for you. I know how it works. I understand that everyone is entitled to a fair trial. I get it that the state failed to prove beyond a reasonable doubt that the girl did not consent to sex. I get it that they failed to prove that he knew that she hadn't consented. He said he stopped when the girl told him to. He said she wasn't crying *or anything*. So that's okay then, if she's not crying or anything? What's anything? I wonder. He said it was consensual.

She said it wasn't.

The question is, what did the thong say? Would they have acquitted if the underwear was a big square pair of M&S pants complete with period stains?

That night, it was windy as well as wet and some of the streetlights weren't working. My hair whirled and slapped across my face, making it even more difficult to see. With every few metres of road covered, I felt more and more stupid. Beside the little park in Harold's Cross, my front tyre caught against something – a pothole or a large stone – and I was thrown off the bike, landing on my right elbow and hip. I scrambled to my feet and picked up the bike. All down my right side ached and I knew I'd grazed my palms and cut my knee. I could feel the familiar gravel burn of playground tumbles as a kid. I began limping across the road on to the footpath, weighing up my options. The front tyre was punctured, so I'd have to wheel the bike home. It would probably take about forty minutes or more, but I'd be home and at least Bobby would be pleased to see me. Those same pyjamas I'd whipped off and flung across the room now seemed like the best outfit ever.

Or I could keep limping along in the direction of town and Fiachra. His flat was just off the South Circular Road, about fifteen minutes' walk. Maybe he'd walk halfway to meet me? I propped the bike against the wall, took out my phone, rang his number. No reply.

What would have happened if he'd answered? What wouldn't have happened?

A white van coming from the Terenure direction began to slow, tyres hissing. The indicator flashed as it crossed over and pulled up on to the path beside me.

'You look like you could do with a hand?' said the driver. He was maybe thirty or so, brown hair, kind of baby-faced. He smiled and got out of the car. 'What happened?'

'Busted tyre, it's fine.'

'Come on,' he said, taking hold of my bike. 'You hop in and I'll drop you wherever you want to go.'

'Oh, it's no problem. It's not far.' I hesitated. 'I'm grand.'

He ignored me, wheeled the bike round to the back of the van. I heard the creak of the doors and a slam. Then he walked round to the passenger side door and held it open for me, the perfect gentleman.

'Go on.' He grinned. 'I'm the best offer you've had all evening.'

And so I got in.

I don't know. Eighteen years later I still don't know what other way I could have played it. He chatted, turned the heat up full blast, offered me a cigarette. He asked me what I was studying at college, said he'd done commerce 'back in the day'.

'Isn't it lucky you ran into me, all the same?' he said. 'I had an important meeting that ran late. I'll drop you off.' The engine roared into life.

'Where to?'

I pointed and he did a U-turn, heading back towards Clonchapel. I tried to relax. I'd be home in ten minutes – there was no traffic on the road and we were lucky with the lights. But there was something not quite right. He kept turning to look at me, grinning. He reached down and squeezed my knee.

'You'll have to get out of those wet things,' he said. 'You could catch your death.'

I told myself not to be stupid. He's just a nice guy on his way home from work. There's nothing going on. I started wondering if I should offer him money – for the lift or for his time or whatever – to thank him. There was a box of chocolates on the dresser at home; I could run in and give him those. And Mum usually left a bit of cash in the drawer in the hall table, just in case.

We drove on empty streets, rain sliding down the windowpanes and the wipers thumping a rhythm. Then, in Terenure, after going through the green light, he began to slow down. Instead of keeping straight towards Rathfarnham and Clonchapel, he turned left, driving down the narrow laneway beside the bank. There were no houses, no lights. He came to a stop outside the railed-off yard behind the church. He switched off the engine.

'Now,' he said. 'We're almost there. We've just time for a little chat – get to know each other a bit better.'

I must have been staring at him. I couldn't think of anything to say. It was like there wasn't a script for me. Or maybe like the part had been written – but only one of us had seen it.

'Come on,' he said, leaning across to reach down beside me. There was a click as he undid my seatbelt and a lurch as the seat went back. I was on my back, looking up at him.

'It's not often I have a pretty girl like you in the car. I'll warm you up,' he said, taking hold of my jaw and applying a slobbery snog to my mouth and chin area.

'You should definitely get out of your wet things,' he said as he pawed at my shirt. He lifted it up and I remember being surprised that he couldn't actually see my heart thumping in my chest.

'Black bra?' he said. 'Naughty naughty.'

He kept talking – pretending that this was something fun we both wanted. 'Girls like you,' he said, shaking his head, 'you drive us guys wild. I bet you've seen a bit of action.'

I've no memory of the rest of the stuff he said, but I knew what was required. I tried to sit up and let him yank my shirt off. He balled it and stuffed it down in the footwell. I must have glanced out the window into the lane then – because I heard the clunk of the door locks. Why didn't I grab the handle? If I'd leapt out then and started running, I don't think he'd have caught me.

But I didn't. I lay there while he pawed at my wet jeans – they were welded on to me – and he struggled to get them off, roughly pulling them over my hips, becoming angrier as they jammed against cold, damp flesh. Eventually, he motioned for me to do it – like he was some kind of emperor – while he undid his fly. Shock had paralysed me, poisoned me, turned me into a puppet. I dug my thumbs under the waistband and yanked at the jeans, managing to get one leg out, one shoe off.

'You'll do,' he said, shoving my hands aside, dropping all pretence. Behind the front seat I'd seen a toolbox and, on the floor, a roll of tape. If he wanted to, he could change this script entirely.

He heaved himself on to the passenger seat on top of me, holding my head in place by grasping a handful of hair. He used his knee and his left hand to manoeuvre himself into position, shoving the thong to one side and scooping my flesh out of the way with his thumb, so he could get himself into me. A burning, stinging pain ripped through me and I knew there was blood. I couldn't move my head, I couldn't think. I – I don't know what I did with my hands – I can't remember. He was heavy – so heavy. Maybe I tried to push him away but – but there was no way I could.

I remember the cold steel of the gear lever under my right hand – I must have grabbed it to brace myself. I gripped this as though it was the only thing keeping me alive – as though it could save me. All my strength – all my resistance was focussed on the chilled metal.

His breath reeked of stale coffee and a fatty animal smell rose from his pores. He shoved, thrusted, drew back. I gripped the steel and scrunched my eyes tight. He grunted, thrusted, shoved, grunted.

Then it was over.

'Welcome to college,' he said. A bead of sweat from his forehead plopped on to my face. I felt my gorge rise.

'I need to get home, my mum –' My voice cracked. I could feel my legs beginning to shake. Somewhere in my mind, I knew it was really important to make him believe that this was consensual, that I wasn't screaming inside. If we stuck to the script of Nice Guy Helps Girl Home after Bike Accident, we could both walk away.

'Yeah, you must be knackered.' He grinned. 'Big night.'

He started the engine and we drove in silence on the empty roads while I struggled back into my jeans. I made him drop me outside the village, terrified he'd find out where I lived.

I did what you mustn't do – not if you expect to prove a rape charge, anyway. I flung the bike against the side wall of the house and took the stairs in twos in my haste to get into the shower. The compulsion to wash myself and to wash him off me was stronger than anything else. I felt as though I was bathed in his excretions – saliva, sweat, semen. My face burned where the dollop of his sweat had landed.

Bobby lay on the warm bit of the carpet outside the bathroom, blinking up at me. He wasn't used to being woken up at this hour, but he took his sentry duties seriously and he blinked at me with a weary despair.

I stood under the hot shower until the shivering stopped. Pink-tinged droplets of water ran down the inside of my legs and I took the shower head down, turning it up as hot as I could bear and squatting in the bath, so the water could scald me clean.

I stood and raised my face to the spray, blasting away the droplet, letting the hot water fill my mouth. I rinsed and spat to get rid of his taste. Rinsed and spat.

Rinsed. Spat.

A year later, in Templemore, we learned off the definition:

Under the 1981 Criminal Law Rape Act, Section 2, a man commits rape if he has unlawful sexual intercourse with a woman who at the time of the intercourse does not consent to it and at that time he knows

that she does not consent to the intercourse or he is reckless as to whether
she does or does not consent to it.

Even if I could have found him, if the guards had charged him, there's no way he'd have been convicted back then. He'd have just said I consented. Or that he didn't know that I hadn't. My word against his. My black bra and thong used as a licence.

And at some stage later – somehow – I took on the blame. I shouldn't have gone out that late. Mum was right. I shouldn't have gone alone. I shouldn't have been looking forward to sex. I shouldn't have worn a black bra. The thong. I brought it on myself – that's what I thought.

I never told Mum. What happened that night loomed between us like a massive boulder. To get past it, I'd have had to tell her that I went out, though I'd promised not to. I'd have to witness her hurt and her concern, her outrage on my behalf. I'd have to watch it sink in – the realization that her little girl, as she still called me, was raped in the front seat of a van, in the shadow of the church in Terenure, one leg still encased in her jeans, still wearing her underwear – somehow it was so much worse that he'd just shoved the thong to one side. I'd have to see how big a deal it was – how terrible – through her eyes. I'd have to change from Laura in Trinity doing psychology and sociology, to Poor Laura – Rape Victim.

I'm not taking on that role. I'm a guard and a mum. I'm sorted. I'm choosing my own bloody role. I'm a mum. Matt wants another baby – a little brother or sister for Katie. We're not exactly trying, but we're not trying not to either. I can't lie to myself. I'm in no rush to do the whole thing again.

What am I if I'm not even a good mum? I'm a mess – a useless mother – worse than useless, I'm dangerous. Who am I kidding? I can't control my own anxieties. I can't protect the one kid I have – so how the hell would I manage two? I'm a mess.

I thought I'd put that night behind me. I thought I'd dealt with it. All the work I did with Sam – the coping strategies that bring you back from the edge, the skills to deal with the anger and constant anxiety – it's all gone. Vanished. Sam's not here.

Now I want to find that guy and – and what? What do you want to do, Laura?

In Jenny's voice, in my head, I hear this: I want to smash his fucking head in.

I lean my forehead against the cool glass – make myself take a deep breath. I'm trembling.

33. Jenny

Niamh took me out of the Laura room and brought me back to the nurses. They take me to the dining room for tea. I'm scared of angry Laura with the red blotches, and she said 'bullshit'. They're not meant to swear. I keep thinking she's a teacher but she says she's a special police officer so she and Queen Not Niamh can curse all they like. Bitches.

Today it's bread and butter and sausages, then a slice of watermelon. It's all laid out on plates beside each other, so you know what you're going to have right from the start – no surprises. I suppose surprises are bad in here. But Catherine only ate the watermelon then she reached over and took another old lady's piece too. She saw me not eating and she pointed so I gave her mine. She ate that and gave me the thumbs-up. And then she moved on to the sausages, but she didn't eat them. She put them in her pockets.

And it makes me so sad to think of that because I remember Karl doing that with the Saturday pancakes. Saturday is Best Behaviour Day and we all pretend everything is Absolutely Fine – even Mum. Especially Mum. Stuart makes pancakes and we have to set the table and be useful and help and sometimes he's whistling and pretending that it's all great. Karl loves the pancakes; they're his favourite. Mum gets up and dresses in something nice because we all have to go down to the soccer field and watch Stuart play the match. Like a proper perfect family.

That day, already he was slamming stuff down on the table. Not good. Mum hadn't come down yet and I was putting out the cups and plates. Stuart yelled, 'Karl!' but there was no sign of him. He shouted again. Then he breathed in sharp, and I know that sound. I tried to get ahead of him into the sitting room where Karl was messing about with his Action Man – making him dive off the mantelpiece on to the ground.

'Whee! Splash!' Karl hadn't heard the shout.

'Karl!' Stuart stood right behind him. 'You come when you're called,' he said, grabbing hold of the toy. Karl's hand clutched at air and he stared, eyes wide. Then, like a tennis shot – blam, Stu hits him across the mouth with the Action Man.

'Get inside and eat your breakfast,' he said. 'Move.'

And I was hugging him and trying to wipe the blood with my sleeve, but he wasn't even crying. Like, even though he's only four, Karl knows we all still have to play the game and pretend it's okay. Especially on Saturdays. So he walked into the kitchen, climbed up on the chair and began loading pancakes into his pocket. And then he just sat there, saying nothing.

I stood right by the knives and, all by itself, like a spider, my hand crept along, inspecting the soldiers. I wasn't even looking, I was watching Karl. Paring knife. Boning knife. Carving knife. Bread knife. The little sharp one. And best of all, Sergeant Sharp Steak. This time, my hand came to rest on the carving knife. It snuggled against my palm like a pet. I squeezed.

Then Mum came in and it was like Act Two began. She was dressed nicely, just as Stu likes – jeans, little bomber jacket, long hair swishing, bright face on. She didn't notice me standing there, ready. She didn't notice Karl's cut lip. She stood waiting for Stu to say something. Like ten out of ten or something. Pathetic. And I hated her then, dumb Princess Piss-on-me. Doesn't she know you can't ever please him? It's not about pleasing him.

There should be better princesses – like Niamh Cinn Óir, not Garda Niamh – on her white horse, galloping over the sea to Tir na n'Óg. Or Queen Maeve, the warrior queen of Connacht. Maeve wasn't scared of anyone. She fought as fiercely as any of her soldiers. She was killed by a slingshot and buried facing her enemies. That's what she wanted.

'Right, I'm warning you – don't be late today. There's a lot riding on this. It's important to talk to everyone – like an adult.' He pointed at Mum's sleeves, which she'd rolled up. Idiot. We all know he hates that.

'Sorry,' she whispered, rolling them back down.

'And don't be late. I'm going down early to warm up.'

Then he left. I let go of the knife. When we heard the noise of his tyres on the gravel, we all breathed out. Right on cue. All at the same time. King Stu is in charge of how we breathe now.

'How long do we have to take this?' I took a plate of toast over to the table. Mum pretended not to hear. 'Mum?'

'Come on, sweetie,' she said to Karl, chopping a pancake into little pieces for him, trying to get him to eat. 'You love these.'

'Mum!'

'Don't shout at me, Jenny! I'm doing my best. He – he'll be in a good mood today after the soccer – you'll see. It'll get better. It always –'

'What if he isn't? Mum? You know that's just not true. It's bullshit! If it's not today, it's tomorrow or the next day or the next.' I slammed the plate on to the table and Karl jumped.

'No shouting! No shouting!' he yelled, hands over his ears, eyes scrunched tight shut. Mum hugged him close, covering his ears.

'Please, Jenny, let it be for now. Trust me – it's going to get better. I – it will. Trust me.' She smoothed Karl's hair and began putting on the baby voice he loves. 'How's wittle mousie going to pway football with no pancakes? Hmm? Just a wittle bite for wittle mousie, pwease?'

I knew then that it's down to me. No one else is going to make this stop. And I realized that if someone is in the way, you just have to step over them, push them aside. That's what Queen Maeve would do. She wouldn't question – she's not paralysed by fear.

I picked out Sergeant Sharp Steak – the carving knife is too big. I laid it in the thick pocket of my hoody and curled my fingers around it carefully. Cool, sharp steel.

'Ah, the Three Musketeers,' says Charlie as we passed the SuperValu. 'How's it going?' Mum gave him a little smile and we stopped.

'Hi, Charlie.' She patted her pockets, looking for coins, but she had nothing. She never has. She's not allowed her own money. 'I really have no change today, Charlie, sorry.'

'Not a problem – sure it'll do the next time,' he wheezed, adjusting the hood of his coat up around his ears. 'How's the man of the house?' Karl stared at the ground. 'Saying nothing? Good plan. Then they can't catch you out, heh heh.'

We walked on and Karl turned back to give a little wave. Charlie saluted. 'See yis later.'

Mrs Ambrose says all the nature is there, we just have to look for it. She says, 'Imagine the buildings all gone, no shops, no houses.' She says, 'Listen out for the birds and look past the buildings. Think what Ireland was like long ago when the Fianna thundered across the plains on their giant horses. When Queen Maeve ruled Connacht.'

It works – sort of. I put a blanket of thorny hedge over the big garage on the corner and I add more trees – a forest of oak, shading the houses, making them into cabins. Mrs A's house is all overgrown with trees anyway; it's hidden. We pass by it, but we don't look in. Even Karl knows it's a secret. A wagtail bobs across the path in front of us, then flits away.

'Look, Jen – waggytail?' I nod, remembering Mrs A showing us the bird book and pointing them out on the feeders in her garden. Robins are Karl's favourites, the wagtails mine.

'That's right,' I said, taking hold of his other hand.

'Well done you,' said Mum.

We walked on until we came to the Bottle Tower. It looms up from the ground, ugly and dark. Karl held my hand tighter.

'It's okay, the bad prince isn't there today,' I whispered.

'This is nice, isn't it?' said Mum, turning to smile at me. 'Just the three of us.' She stepped daintily around a big puddle, careful to keep her clothes clean.

'Yeah. It is,' I said.

And for a moment, I wondered about it – if I really went through with it and it was just the three of us. But I couldn't see that picture. Every time I try to picture it, Mum's standing in the way. She's crying at his feet, or clinging on to us, pleading and begging – doing nothing – nothing to save us. On the island, it should be me and Karl. Just the two of us – and Socks. The princess is holding us back. Princess Piss-on-me.

We reached the soccer grounds and stood together, posing like a proper happy family while Stu ran all over the pitch – tackling players right and left, taking shots on goal.

'Hiya, Melanie!' Val appeared and squeezed the two of us into a massive bear hug. Jack and Karl immediately started chasing each other around the place, squealing.

'Great to see you out and about, Mel.' She grinned. 'How are you doing?'

'Fine, we're grand. You know, watching Stu do his thing. He likes that,' said Mum, bright and cheerful – the Oscar-winning performance.

' 'Course he does,' Val said with a laugh. 'His very own fan club come along to cheer. Why wouldn't he?'

Val is the complete opposite of Mum. I can't believe they used to work together. It's like Val was allocated extra space on the planet when they were doling it out. Like someone said, *You! That woman there – have some extra world, you're going to need it.*

And Val definitely uses it all up. Val is noise and laughter and hugs. Val's hug is like your duvet got up off your bed and came over to snuggle you. Beside her, Mum looks like the stray sock you discover down the end of the bed – sad and empty. Within a minute and for the first time in ages, Mum laughed a real laugh. Out loud. She sounded like someone else. The match was nearly over when I realized that it was a bit too quiet. There was no sign of Karl and Jack.

'Mum? Val? Where are the boys?' They broke off chatting and started looking around.

'Oh, for goodness' sake – look! There they are – miles away,' said Val, pointing. They'd almost reached the boundary fence on the far side of the pitch, down near the running track.

'I'll get them,' said Mum, breaking into a run.

'Best woman for the job,' laughed Val, giving her the thumbs-up.

'I'll pick up their stuff,' Mum said, gathering up their jackets and toys. The whistle went and the players all began leaving the pitch. Stu jogged over.

'Hi, Stuart,' said Val brightly.

'Where's your mother?' he said, ignoring her.

'Mel's off with the boys, Stuart. Lovely to see you again,' she added, but he was already stomping off towards the dressing room.

'Oh dear,' said Val. 'Someone's a liddle grumpy.' She smiled. 'Sorry, I shouldn't tease, should I?'

And I felt a lift inside me – like being in an elevator. Just for a moment. Like plonking hot coal into a bucket of water, Val fizzes and crackles. If Stu touched her, if he went to hit her – she'd kill him. One mighty punch of Val's freckly fist blasting Stu into outer space. I smiled.

'That's better,' she said. 'I miss you guys,' she said suddenly, grabbing me into a one-armed squeeze. 'Do you remember when I'd come over to the flat and see you and your mum?' She shook her head. 'You must remember the lollipops? I always brought you –'

'Oh yeah! The cola ones!' I remembered.

'Those were happy times, weren't they? The singing –'

I knew she was being nice – but it hurt to think of it. I wanted to forget but at the same time I wanted to remember.

'Oh, and in case I forget,' she kept on, not noticing, 'can you tell Mel I have a proposal for her? It's about the shop. I'm thinking it's time I went back to work, now that my son and heir is in school – tell her I'd like to rent the shop – gonna reopen for business. Could you run it by her first – get her used to the idea, yeah?'

I must have stood there looking flummoxed because she shook her head in mock despair.

'Your mum and I were two shit-hot creatives, back in the day, you know.' she said, laughing.

I think of the bike shop, lying empty for years, slowly being eaten by dust, its broken windows and locked gate. Then I remember the course Mum wanted to do and hope opens up like a little flower, though she'd have to be smart – not tell him.

'Well, maybe not that shit-hot, but we were good. I've been doing an online editing course – I'm skilled up and ready to roll.' She laughed again. 'And I'd love to get Mel on board – she was brilliant.'

I imagined Mum in a business meeting, dressed in a sharp trouser suit and carrying a briefcase.

'I think that sounds great. She'd love it. I'll tell her,' I said. I get the full duvet hug for that.

Mum had caught up with the boys and they were on the running track, headed back. They were laughing and jumping – even Mum. Stuart appeared, looking stressed and jumpy. Beside him was an older man with grey hair who'd been watching the game too.

'Where is she?' Stu hissed at me. I pointed to the track. Mum was on the home stretch.

'Ah, this is your wife and daughter, Stuart?' said the older man, reaching out his hand towards Val, who shook it warmly.

'No!' said Stuart, as if the idea of being connected to chubby Val was shameful.

'Christ, no!' laughed Val, as if the idea of being connected to Stuart was even worse. The old guy roared laughing.

'Well said! I'm Tony – the big bad boss.'

'Val,' said Val. 'I'm a friend of the family – Melanie's friend. She's just down there, catching a couple of outlaws! Should be back any minute.'

We all looked to the track. Mum was beginning to tire.

'Come on, Melanie!' yelled Stuart. 'Lift your feet!'

He turned back to Tony. 'I'm always telling her to lift her feet –' He broke off and there was a collective gasp as Mum went sprawling on to the tarmac. She'd stumbled when Stuart shouted at her. Now she was struggling to get up.

'I've got this!' yelled Stuart, placing both hands on the fence and vaulting over it.

'The gate's just here –' began Val, but Stu was on a mission. He landed on the other side and began sprinting down to the track. I made as if to go to Mum, but Val put her hand on my arm.

'I think we'll let him do this one, will we? Knight in shining armour and all that?'

Stu reached Mum and hauled her to her feet. Then he lifted her and began striding towards the crowd, carrying her high against his chest. Whatever he said to Jack and Karl, they looked petrified, and they sprinted alongside him, trying to keep up. Mum was crimson with embarrassment, but Stu was enjoying himself – fully committed to the role.

It started in the car.

'I hope you're happy. I hope you're all happy now. You've made a show of me again. You've ruined everything. Christ's sake!'

'Sorry,' whispered Mum. 'I didn't plan it – I just fell.'

'It doesn't matter whether you planned it, don't be stupid!' he snapped. 'Why did you go running off on your own anyway? What were you thinking? All I ask is one day of your lives – all of you, one day, where you come down and – I don't know – act normal. Be normal. Is that too much to ask?'

Mum sat hunched against the car door, her head hanging.

'I told you today was important.'

Karl huddled in the corner with his eyes closed and his thumb in his mouth, rocking from side to side.

'I told you. I warned you.'

Stuart took his eyes off the road ahead to glare at her. Still Mum didn't move. Then he grabbed her chin, forced her to look at him.

'I'm sorry,' said Mum. 'I'm really sorry.'

I could see white where his fingers dug in.

'I'm telling you this, Melanie. You'd better not spoil again. You'd better not mess up the office party. So get yourself used to that idea. If you don't fall over or cry or witter on, talking rubbish, there's a chance, there's still a chance.'

'Okay,' she whispered.

'And that goes for all of you! It's a family day, so I expect my family to behave like a bloody family. Christ — is that too much to ask?'

We reached the house, and he got out first, slamming the door shut and stomping up to the front door. And we followed. I don't know why. I mean, now I wonder why. Why didn't we just turn around and, I don't know, leave? But we didn't. And when we got in the door, Mum got a shove and she stumbled into the banisters on her way upstairs to her room. She didn't come down again that night.

And later, there were noises from the room, like furniture moving, or heavy things falling. But I was useless. Even though I had Sergeant Sharp Steak in my pocket, I was too weak. I didn't go in to help her. Dumb bitch. Useless.

Bitch Nurse Barbara is on duty now for the evening shift and there's lots of people around in the dining room so she's on best behaviour.

'Will you not eat?' she says in the voice for Junior Infants. 'You're fading away.' I think about answering her, but I don't. You can say nothing here if you want. That's one good thing. Or you can say stuff that is crazy and no one believes you.

'When's the bus coming?' is what I say, and she runs over to me fast, looking over her shoulder to see if Catherine heard.

'Don't start them on that!' she hisses at me. 'Eat your tea like a good girl.'

34. Laura

'Seriously, what is up with you, Laura?' There's no trace of Niamh's teasing, no jokes, no smiles, no black humour. We're in the bathroom, where she found me as I came out of the stall. I try a grin.

'I know – sorry. I'm losing my touch.'

'No – no more shite. What the actual fuck is wrong?'

She lowers her voice, aiming for a softer tone. 'You're not a psychotherapist and we're not meant to be confrontational or – I don't know, doing that hypnosis shit you were trying.'

'It's a useful psychological tool,' I say. 'If I can get her to visualize a safe space, she can return to that any time the thoughts are too much for her.'

'That sounds good – in theory. And maybe it'd be good if we actually were psychotherapists, or hypnotists or whatever. But it's feck all use if you're rushing her and badgering her, desperate to get to the story.'

She puts her bag down beside the sink and turns, looking squarely at me, scrutinizing.

'Are you crying? Is there something wrong?' I busy myself washing my hands again, make a big deal of drying them and using the hand sanitizer, anything to avoid her direct gaze.

'No, I'm fine,' I say. 'Just tired.' *Him tired*, I think.

'Do you want to go on home? Leave Cig to me?'

She turns to go, but pauses with her hand on the door, giving me the no-bullshit look that's her other trademark. Why does she want to see Cig on her own?

'No way, Niamh! I'm fine, I just got frustrated, that's all.

241

Anyway, it worked, getting her angry – she told us stuff. She knows where he is. And he could be alive.'

She nods. 'Yeah, and we need to fill them in at the incident room. But the rest of it – how did we get that information? What about the court case, Laura? Remember those endless sessions? The role play, the mock trials – those fucking barristers grilling us?' She looks at my hand where, unknowingly, I'd grabbed her arm and was still holding on. I see her spot the raw skin.

'We'd months of it in our training and I'm pretty sure you did, too. And they kept on telling us that the most contested part of the whole process – the most contested part, Laura, is *this* part. These meetings. These meetings are bloody crucial. So, when they ask you on oath what did you say to the child during the clarification meeting to make her disclose this information – how are you going to answer?'

A livid flush of red has appeared at the neckline of her shirt; I've never seen Niamh so angry, not really angry. My heart is thumping.

'You're right – I know. But I need her to tell me – I need to hear her say it in her own words, so –'

'Exactly,' says Niamh, with a gesture of incredulity. 'That's what these meetings are for – so she can say it in her own words and you and I take notes and then – only then when the time is right and when she's ready –'

She takes a step backwards – as though not wanting to be tainted by my flaws. She has both hands up in surrender.

'You're going to blow this one, Laura, if you're not careful. What was it you said – oh yeah – *You're too old for this bullshit. Stop bloody wasting our time?*'

She does the air quotes, shaking her head.

'That's pressure. That's leading the witness. And any defence barrister worth their salt will know you've coached the witness. They'll sure as shit find out if you heckle her into saying stuff she's not ready to say. If any barrister – even a shit barrister – hears that, that dickhead walks free.'

She pauses at the top of the stairs and looks back at me. Softly, as if she were talking to a child, she says, 'We're meant to be surgeons. You're the one who told me that, Laura. You used to take pride in how smooth, how – how clinical – your interviews were. Cool and calm, yeah? We're meant to extract the information cleanly. We note the disclosures, then we record the interview, so the DVD speaks for itself – so the bastard pleads guilty.'

She ties the belt on her coat tight and hoists her bag further up her shoulder. 'The Super wants an update as well. Oh – and yeah – did Lab Larry get you?'

'No?'

'The blood on her shirt – it's not human. It's canine. How shady is that, right? She comes in covered in dog blood. Maybe she hasn't touched Stuart. Maybe he's just run off. Let's just cool the fucking jets, okay?' she says, stepping on to the top of the stairs. 'I'll see you back at the station. I'm going to make a few calls – see if we can talk to any of her teachers.'

Disgusted with myself, I count her footsteps on the stairs for as long as I hear them. If it ends on an even number, it'll be okay. What the hell is happening? I trained her. Yet Niamh is the one behaving like a trained detective, while I'm floundering.

I should know better. I *do* know better. She's right about the legal stuff, too. If I mess up at this point, the whole thing falls apart. The defence barrister will argue that her testimony was made under duress, that she was scared or we put ideas in her head or – or she made the whole thing up to get back at him for an imagined slight – or because he gave out to her for something.

The defence team will try to find a weakness anywhere. They want to get an 'in', a tiny black mark is all it takes – that will be enough to discredit your evidence and subsequently the whole process. In fact, they don't even need to discredit you; all they have to do is raise a doubt.

Tell me, Detective, when did you qualify as a Specialist Victim Interviewer?

How long was the course? What aspect of the course did you find the most challenging?

How did you do in your final exams? Did you pass on the first attempt?

Oh, you passed on the second attempt? I see.

What was the reason for failing the first set of exams?

Or perhaps they could use a different angle.

This job must be very stressful, or even upsetting. Do you find it stressful?

Have you ever had a situation where the accused was found not guilty, even though you believed him to be guilty?

What do you do about the feelings you are left with in situations like that?

Is there counselling available for gardaí? Have you ever availed of counselling services?

A good defence barrister is an artist; in a couple of brush-strokes, they will have conjured up an alternative, highly plausible picture. Perhaps it's one where the SVI is a cynical, neurotic, feminist man-hater, or a burnt-out, stressed-out do-gooder, or an under-achieving idiot who is incapable of doing their job, or – perhaps the most dangerous of all – an excellent garda operative who is simply mistaken on this occasion. They have read it wrong and allowed herself to be manipulated by the victim:

You know how teenagers are, members of the jury, and how family life can, during the teenage years, be fraught and full of arguments. Per-haps a disagreement arose over some unrelated issue? Perhaps the accused laid down the law too strictly or was too harsh and, while you may disagree with their parenting methods, have you been shown beyond a reasonable doubt that the accused is guilty of this awful crime?

A vulnerable child is interviewed at length in a highly stressful situ-ation, where they have, in effect, been sectioned. Might they not say anything at all to satisfy the interviewers, to secure their freedom?

I could bloody write it myself.

Niamh's right – I've got to get a grip. They piloted a scheme of mandatory counselling for guards working on high-stress cases a few years back and I know I'm entitled to free sessions. But I don't need help – or maybe I do but I don't want to be told I have to go for it. Sam understood. I could talk to him. And now he's dead.

Back at the station, the Super sticks his head out the door – catching us on our way to the incident room.

'Make sure you two call into me later – bring me up to speed on that case with the girl,' he says, inserting his finger into the collar of his shirt as if to loosen a noose. He has the door closed before we can reply. Niamh and I do matching eye rolls. That'll be an extra half-hour before getting home.

'Take the Solpadeine now,' says Niamh. 'Save time.'

I grin – glad she's back to normal.

In the room, Cig is looking at the jigsaw of evidence on the board: the timeline, the car, the knife, the Christmas photo, a map of the roads around Whiteash Avenue with a pin where the car was found, pics of the bloodstained clothes and now the family photo we got from Stuart's office.

'So, she's talking more now,' says Cig. 'What have you got?'

'She's still all over the place,' says Niamh. 'She's stalling.'

'What about this island? Any more on that?' Cig consults a sheaf of pages. 'We sent a team out to Dalkey Island. Nothing.'

'Right,' says Niamh. 'Look – I agree with Laura here. I don't think there's the slightest chance she really went to any island in a red boat. It's all cod – she's concocting a story – it's all delay tactics. Don't get me wrong,' she adds, sitting forward and gesturing a stop sign with her hand in the air, 'fair play to the lads for checking it out. Ye had to, in fairness.'

'In fearness,' echoes Declan, in a thick bogger accent.

'Fuck off,' Niamh says, smiling. She opens her notebook and flicks through a few pages. 'And I rang the school – got to speak to the Principal and, eh – a Ms Wilson – her English teacher. Nothing ringing any bells there, though the teacher said she is "distant and closed off", but nothing unusual was flagged up.' She closes the notebook, glances at me.

'I think she's playing the long game,' she says. 'And she's a class player at that. I don't think she's gonna tell us where he is any time soon.'

Before I can add anything, Declan interjects. 'The blood all over her top turns out to be from a dog, yeah? I say he killed her dog and she got even.'

'How?' I say, at the same time as Cig says, 'Where?', then he sighs and walks back to the desk, dropping the sheaf of papers on to the surface with an angry splat. It's no secret that Cig's on a short fuse. There's even a rumour that he did an anger management course before he was appointed to Inspector. He's even narkier than usual. I try to avoid eye contact.

'How does a fourteen-year-old kill or incapacitate a grown man and somehow hide the body? In broad daylight –'

'It was dark when the ambulance call came in,' says Sorcha.

'Did Uniform get to every house in the area?' I say. Mairéad consults her notes.

'They reckon so. First on the scene was the woman from number sixteen – the end of the cul-de-sac. She'd been at the shops. She knocked for a neighbour – she doesn't own a mobile – and they called 999. At that point, only the mother and son were in the car.'

'In the front passenger seat?' adds Declan.

Mairéad nods.

'I'm just putting this out there,' says Seán, warily. 'What if the dad wasn't even in the car? Maybe he's just gone off somewhere?'

'First off, we've checked airports and train stations, yeah?' says Cig. 'And the car is registered to him, so are you telling me now the fourteen-year-old was driving it?'

Seán shrugs, proceeds even more tentatively, 'In that movie with Julia Roberts – you know the one – she's trying to escape an abusive husband and she learns to swim so she can fake her death, by drowning and –'

'We have witnesses at the office party that saw them all getting into the car – all of them,' says Cig. He looks at me, nods. 'I want her in here tomorrow,' he says. 'Softly softly – just some questions. Maybe in this setting she'll abandon the make-believe. Do we have a FLO or a relative to sit in?'

'I contacted the uncle – Gareth,' says Niamh. 'But he can't get here till tomorrow evening.'

'She's beginning to trust me, though!' I burst in. 'I was getting through to her earlier. I reckon another session – if I had another hour or two with her, building rapport, getting her to trust me – she might disclose the rest.' I pause, aware that I'm sounding desperate – overheated. 'Not here, though – can't you see it'll freak her out?'

The glance exchanged between Cig and Niamh is so quick that I think maybe I'm imagining it. But I'm not. They've been talking about me. I take a breath and try to speak in a calmer tone. Niamh busies herself doodling on her notepad, avoiding eye contact.

'Fine,' says Cig, as though it's anything but. 'Talk to her in the morning and, if you get nothing, bring her in.' He turns to Declan. 'You guys take another run out to Clonchapel and the home address. See what you can turn up.'

It's nine forty-five before I'm putting my key in the door. Matt meets me in the hallway and, just for an instant, I'm swept with this crazy hope that he's going to pull me to him, holding my face with two hands, then he'll kiss me. We won't talk – because words will only mess things up in this scenario. And I won't be this twisted, injured, worried tangle of need and pain. We'll go to bed and I'll be strong and beautiful and whole. I'll be something beautiful in his eyes.

Then I notice he has his finger to his lips and he's wearing his track bottoms and slippers. How are we here already? And what am I thinking of anyway? I'm exhausted – pure jaded, as Niamh says.

'She's only just settled,' he whispers – and I hear the accusation. 'We thought you'd be home hours ago.'

'Yeah, hi to you, too,' I hiss angrily, dumping my bag on the chair and walking past him. I put the Sig in the safe, key in the code and head into the kitchen. He follows me down the steps and into the room, pulling the door closed gently behind him.

'I didn't mean that, you know I didn't.'

'Yeah. Look, it goes with the territory – as I pointed out to you and Justy when you all told me to put myself forward for Detective.'

'What are you talking about? That – that was your choice, Laura. I was just encouraging you. If it was up to me –' He stops.

'Look,' I say, too exhausted to fight. 'Fine – maybe it wasn't coming from you. But you know your parents – it's not enough for them to have a daughter-in-law a guard – Justy won't be happy till I'm the bloody Commissioner!'

Matt sighs. 'Not this again.' He moves towards the kettle, shaking his head. 'Mum thinks you're great. It's just her way. Do you want tea?' He starts placing tea bags in the mugs.

I can't do this. I'm so far from being who I want to be – no wonder he's weary of me. And Katie's already asleep – no hug to bring me back to myself, my best self.

'How was she?' I say, guilt gnawing at me even before he answers. 'Was she crying?'

'No,' he says, and I just know he's lying. 'We read Tiger Tame Tatee about five times and she fell asleep. She certainly loves that book.'

Even that makes me feel guilty; the story has a little girl and her mum at home one afternoon. It's mega-1950s – they're clearly waiting for Dad to come home from work. But before he does, a huge tiger appears on the doorstep, looking for tea. They give him biscuits and bread, but he's still hungry. He drinks all the tea in the teapot and the water in the taps. Every cupboard is open, every pot and plate has been used and discarded by the time the tiger leaves. Katie finds the picture of him drinking from the spout of the teapot hilarious – she clasps hold of her belly and chortles every time we get to that part. But what I think she loves best is the set-up – just a mummy and a little girl with nothing to do except keep the house tidy and wait for Daddy to come home. And when he does, there's no food left, so they go out to a café for chips – with the little girl in her nightdress. She adores it.

I ignore the tea and open the fridge. There's about three mouthfuls of Sauvignon Blanc left in a thumb-printed bottle. Not after last night. I close it again, overwhelmed by misery.

'I'm going to bed,' I say, not looking at him. 'Night.'

Day Four

35. Niamh

A muffled thump on the wall behind my head jerks me into consciousness. Six nineteen on the digital clock. Although I know it's ridiculous, I'm pure raging for the extra eleven minutes I could have slept if Lisa and Max – oh God, now I remember – the just-engaged Lisa and Max – if they hadn't decided to add a pre-work shag to their heavy schedule of fecking shagging.

I grab the pillow and fold it around my ears, blocking out the sound effects. Another thump and some creaking and then – thank Christ – he finishes. In fairness, Max never hangs about. Teaching sixth class will do that to you, I suppose. He's peppy – likes to get in early to the big multi-denominational school near Irishtown – steal a march on the kids. Lisa has the other extreme – a convent school close to the city.

They were both bursting with joy when I got back last night – still wrecked after the night before and only wanting my bed. But the champagne was out and there were fairy lights around the windows and candles lit – the whole flat was Instagram-ready – so serious toasting and drinking had to be done. Sure I'm delighted for both of them – I examine my conscience to see why I'm – what's niggling. I turn over in bed and look through the gap in the curtains to the pre-dawn Rathmines skyline. There's a streetlight just outside, glowing orange against the inky sky.

Suddenly, I've a pang for home – the proper darkness on the farm where you can actually see the sun rise. Dad would be up way before it gets light – around five – and there'd be footsteps and clanks and the lowing of the sleepy cows making their way in for milking. In Dublin it's traffic sounds that you wake to – or singing drunks returning home.

I sigh, my breath visible in the chilly air. The heat's not on yet. I decide I'll wait until I hear it come on. What's niggling is the normality of it – the 'Isn't that great news?' of the whole thing. Mam will be beside herself – everyone will. Lisa's like another daughter to her – from when we played on the same school team. I can just hear it – the warmth in Mam's tone, her joy in watching someone else choose the same path. It'll be 'Ah that's wonderful!' and 'We must send a card!' And she'll hug me – telling me to give Lisa and Max her best – then do that thing where she steps back, keeping her hands on my shoulders, her head tilted as she surveys me – measuring how far away from the ideal daughter I am now.

Giggles and thuds and the sound of running water tells me that the happy couple are sharing a morning shower – their room has an en suite. But even so, I can hear everything. Lisa's squeals go right through me.

To make it stop, I throw off the duvet and start getting dressed, deliberately making noise – shaking out the duvet, opening and closing drawers, humming tunelessly. I sit on the end of the bed, tying the laces of my Docs.

'I just want what's best for you,' she'd said – the classic line – and one Mam went back to over and over after I first came out. I'd waited and waited, hoping, I suppose, that they'd realize some day and it wouldn't be an issue. I finally told them after Christmas, the year I'd done the SVI training. I was twenty-four and I was fed up fielding questions about 'anyone special'. Plus, at that stage Ashley and I were still together – I'd even thought of bringing her home.

But it turned out that she'd never suspected a thing. My awkward debs with that poor fucker Darren, shitting himself in case he'd be expected to shift me, seemed to have thrown her off the scent. Straight at eighteen, straight for ever – that's what Mam must have thought, if she'd thought about it at all. And I can't blame her if she never thought about it – it's not been easy for her.

'I want you to have it all – like we have –' She'd put her hand on Dad's arm, squeezed – for strength or to get him to speak, I didn't know. 'Children – family life – you know?'

She'd tried, in fairness to her, to use the L word then – poor Mam.

'Don't lesbians – well – what about children? Have you thought this out, pet? Your dad and I – you know we love you and, of course – of course we still do,' she'd said, as if withdrawing that love was actually an option she'd consider. 'But – you can't deny it's not an easy life you're choosing – especially when you think of children.' She nodded, getting into her stride. 'Children need a father –'

'It's who I am, Ma,' I'd said, not showing the hurt. 'It's not a lifestyle choice. And gay couples do have children, you know.'

Dad had patted her hand and nodded – as if something were settled.

'Tina – we're going to keep the good side out for our girl. That's the way of it now.' He stood up and we both watched him. 'For Martin.'

The mention of the brother who had died before I was born meant the end of what Dad called 'chat'. He stepped towards me and pulled me into a hug. It was so long since he'd hugged me, I'd forgotten what it felt like. He's a big man, still a head taller than me, and he stroked my hair with a shiny leather palm. He smelled of the grain pellets we feed to the cows.

'You're grand,' he said.

In the poky kitchen, I rummage for breakfast. There's nothing. In the fridge, dairy-free yogurt sports a bloom of some weird fungus and there's less than a handful of oatmeal if I wanted – if I could be bothered – to make porridge. The happy couple must be planning on getting breakfast in Rathmines. Another ache twinges.

Dad's a great man for the porridge. He gets breakfast ready for her every morning – has done for thirty-five years. He sets out a bowl of porridge and, beside it, brown sugar in the same china sugar bowl they've had since they were married. He's a kind man.

Kindness and friendship, respect and love – if there's a magic potion, that's it, I suppose. I want the same – exactly the same. And more than anything, I want Mam to be okay with that.

'See ye later, Mr and Mrs O'Connor!' I yell, hammering on their bedroom door to announce the fact that I'm leaving. They may even get shag number three in ahead of school. Someone's thrown a half-eaten bag of chips over the bonnet of my car – hazards of on-street parking in Rathmines. I brush them off, scattering them for the waiting gulls. Before pulling out, I check my phone. Nothing much – just a text from Laura saying she'll see me in the unit ahead of the morning meeting. I sigh. She's off form – even the fact that she needs to send that text tells me she's wound up. It's a given – we're a team. Or I thought we were.

36. Jenny

It's warm in here this morning. Maybe they left the heat on. I think about sitting in Laura's chair, and Nurse Ella is on for the day again and I like her. She sees me going to sit there and she smiles. Then she says they'll be in to chat in about five minutes. Like we're having a lovely chat. But I don't give her the dagger look and she's not a dumb bitch. That's two people I don't give daggers to. Catherine is the other. Last night, I gave Catherine the watermelon, all of it. I felt sick and I didn't want to eat their dumb shit food.

In school, Amy and I have a buy-one-feed-two lunch plan. We buy one cheese-and-tomato-filled roll – it's cheese, to-mato, lettuce, cucumber in a French stick. We dissect the roll and she gets the cheese and lettuce and I get the tomato and cucumber and there's enough for two people. It doesn't work with the chicken-tikka wrap – too messy. And anyway, if Luke even smells the chicken-tikka wrap, he's over begging like a puppy. His favourite.

The following Monday, after the soccer game, we were in maths and I was sitting there – basically checked out, like on another planet. I was worried about Mum; she didn't even wake up when I went into her before school. The room was dark but, even so, I could see the bruises coming up. And the brown jar of tablets was beside her with the lid not put on right. And I was going to say something to her, but I didn't. I let her sleep. Dumb bitch Sleeping Beauty.

But then, in school I was thinking maybe she wasn't just asleep. I was kicking myself, thinking, why did I not try to wake her up? Why didn't I put the rest of the tablets away? What if she does something? What if she takes the pills – all of them? Whatif and whatif and, meanwhile, Luke was hissing at me, trying to get my attention.

'Psst! Watch out!'

Mussolini, our maths teacher, was striding down the classroom, pausing at each desk, checking the homework. I began rummaging in my bag. No sign of it. Then I remembered – it was at home, still sitting in the middle of the kitchen table. I'd forgotten to put it in.

'Here!' Luke hissed, shoving his pages into my hand.

'But what about you?'

'Don't worry, just take it. It's right.' I smoothed the sheets out and put them on the desk just before Mussolini stopped at my desk. He read them through quickly and nodded.

'Good,' he said. If I was really quick, maybe I could get the sheets back to Luke? But in another split-second Mussolini was already there, doing the Leaning Tower of Pisa over his desk.

'Where is it?'

'I'm really sorry, I did it and everything, sir. It's just that I –' Mussolini held up his hand, turned his back.

'Blah, blah, blah,' he said, waving his hand around. 'Detention. Lunchtime. Today. Room Five.'

'Sir?' I began.

'Quiet! Enough time-wasting. Turn to page one eight two.'

He marched the length of the room and I turned around to look at Luke. He was still grinning. He has one of those smiles which kind of cracks up his whole face, but in a good way. And he has nice eyes. Kind.

'Sorry, I mean, thanks,' I whispered. 'You didn't have to do that.'

'My pleasure.' He grinned again – more cracks. 'Just a little help from your friends, yeah?'

There's a group of kids in our year – Philip is pretty much their leader. They're the Goodtime Guys. Every weekend they're partying in someone's house, and every Monday morning they're laughing and chatting about it in the form room or in the dining hall. Laughing over the Snapchat stuff and tweeting. Luke could be one of them, easily. He's popular. He's smart and funny; he could spend his days hanging out with them.

And it's like everyone has a Thing – a hook. Philip and the yacht club; Chloe plays cricket or something for Ireland; Max is, like, a computer genius; Aimée (not Amy) models in her spare time.

What's my thing? Like, why does Luke even bother with me when he could be in with them and Aimée not Amy could be at his side, or he could be, I don't know, yachting at the weekend with Philip, the sea breeze whistling through their gleaming-white teeth?

My thing is what? The girl whose dad died when she was a kid. With the depressed look and the messy hair. The girl who can't draw but kept art so she could hang out with her one friend Amy (not Aimée). The girl who is quite good at maths but nothing special so who cares. The girl who knows random facts about The Beatles.

But what if it's worse and I *do* have a thing? A Thing. What if my thing is whispered behind their hands, texted underneath tables or, worse – discussed with their understanding parents? What if they can sense it, even smell it off me? See her? She's the one who's already been there, you know what I mean? They talk about a girl in fourth year who does blow jobs for cash. How do they know that? What do they know about me? Is that my thing?

He tells me I'm really good at it, like it's something I should be proud of. It's the one time he doesn't call me dumb bitch and he doesn't hit. When I was younger, he was like 'We have a secret' and 'You know I love you, don't you? This is how you show people you love them. You love me, don't you, Jenny? You're my princess. You know how I look after you and your mum and Karl? We all look after each other.' And it was dark in the tower. And he was nice to us all – Mum and Karl, too – once it was over. I pretended it was medicine. In the bathroom after I would clean my teeth ten million times.

They brought me back in here, but I don't know why. Why do they leave you alone in here with the ticking? Where's Laura? What about the chat, dumb bitch? I get up and walk over to the desk and I'm opening the drawers before I remember they're probably watching me. There's a square bit like a grid in the door and nurses look in on their way past. And there's a thing up in the corner; maybe it's a camera.

I look up at it and I yell, 'I need to go home now, you can't keep me here! I need to go home.' And then I look at it again and it's not a camera, it's a sprinkler. Haha. Luke is so going to love that.

I found him by the art room after lunch – which he'd missed because of detention. He was humming as I handed him the roll. 'Love Me Do'.

'Thanks,' he said, giving it the starving-dog sniff. 'Yessss! Chicken tikka. My favourite. How did you know?'

'Luke, it's what you have every day. Literally – every day.'

'True, well – thanks.'

Then he did The Grin and I started walking so he wouldn't see me blush. The blush is connected to eye contact, especially when combined with The Grin. There's probably an equation for that, too.

'Do you really hum Beatles songs all day, or just when I appear?'

'All day,' he said, through a mouthful of chicken tikka, 'in *case* you appear. I like to be prepared.' Grin.

We stood outside Mr Giles's room – I was already late for French.

'You could give me your number, you know? Now that we've shared a detention?'

I hesitated. To tell him about the no-phone rule would open up the whole thing – a crucial block in the Jenga tower of my life.

'We didn't share detention, Luke. You did it alone.'

'Ah, but you earned it.' He grinned. 'And I did it, so it was shared. A shared experience for us. Very special.'

He waited. What was I going to say – I'm not allowed to have a phone? Seriously – that's the rule. No way can Mum have one either. He says she doesn't need one. I have to walk Karl to and from school and Val's every day and then come straight home. Mum has to be there to let us in because, of course, I don't get a key. And she doesn't go out. He says if people need to contact us, can't they phone on the landline or call to the house? But no one does. I stood there like an idiot, saying nothing.

'It's fine,' he said, turning away. 'You'd better go into French. Wouldn't recommend another detention for us – fun and all as it was.'

'Luke – it's just that I –'

'No worries, it's cool.' He stopped walking. 'Seriously – it's cool. Meet you at the school gate at four, yeah?'

'Thanks.' I headed into the French lesson.

At four o'clock, he was leaning against the railings, face tilted upwards to catch the low autumn sunshine. Managing to look both cute and a bit of a poser at the same time.

'Have you time to come for a walk?'

I reckoned it up quickly. Shrugged – trying not to appear too keen.

'Yeah? Where to, though? I only have about half an hour.'

He laughed. 'Jaysus, busy woman! Come on – magical mystery tour!'

He literally sprinted off and I'd no choice but to run to keep up. He went out the school gate and then left to the games fields, past the rugby pitches and the junior hockey Astroturf, his tie flapping against the schoolbag hanging off one shoulder. Finally, he stopped outside the old cricket pavilion.

Panting a bit from the sprinting, he fumbled and fiddled with the lock. There was a click, and the door sprung open.

'*Et voilà* or something,' he said.

'How did you –'

'Dad showed me – an extra use for surgical instruments.' He pocketed something metal.

'I love your dad,' I said. 'First the cowboy hat and the ice pops – now this.'

He laughed. The sun had warmed a rectangle of light on the wooden floor and we both immediately sat inside it, leaning back against the faded boards.

'So . . .' he said. 'The Beatles.'

'Yep?'

'I've worked it all out, you know? Not easy.'

'Luke, I've no idea what you're going on about.'

'Wait, I wrote it down,' he said, rummaging in his pocket and taking out his phone.

'Okay – it starts "Do You Want to Know a Secret".' He waited. 'You say "yeah"?'

'Oh, sorry – yeah.'

'And I say – "Baby It's You".'

'Right.' I grinned. 'I see where you're going with this.'

'So, I say – "I Want to Hold Your Hand". And you say?'

'Erm, "Get Back"?'

'Haha, that's good. She crushes me, tells me I'm going "Nowhere Man", and then I say . . .'

'Erm, "Love Me Do"?'

'That's good – yeah. But no. I say, "Don't Let Me Down".'

'Nice one.' I can't help smiling.

He's beaming. '"Got to Get You into My Life",' he continues, his voice soft. '"Help!"'

I'm laughing so much – I could play this game all day. He sits forward then and turns to me. We're both laughing. Then, kneeling up, he reaches out and sweeps my hair back off my face. And he lets his hand stay there, resting along the side of my cheek. His hand is warm and my heart is thumping.

'"We Can Work It Out",' he says, and he kisses me, kind of getting the side of my mouth. And it's warm and gentle and dry – even if it was a bit crooked.

'Thought that might happen,' he says. 'Wrong angle.' He does a sheepish version of The Grin.

'No, it's –' I'm about to say – I don't know what I'm about to say. I'm tingling like I'm being rinsed through with liquid silver and melted chocolate – shiny, sweet and warm. But then he takes my face in his two hands and tries again. And we kiss.

Laura and Niamh didn't come in and Agency Nurse brought me back to the canteen for the morning coffee. They give you more tea and biscuits after the tea you have at breakfast. Like the whole day is a necklace made of meals with tea and biscuits the in-between beads. It's so warm in here; I just want to go to sleep. My head is resting on my hand and I am sorting out the biscuits on my plate. Then I eat the bread, even though it's got a ton of butter sliding around the top of it. All of a sudden there's a massive crash from the other end

263

of the table where Catherine and the sad old ladies are. One of them has thrown her plate on the floor.

'On your knees! You should be on your knees before me!' It's Mad Mary. Everyone calls her Mad Mary, but her name is Eileen or something. Some days she thinks she's the president and some days she thinks she's Mary from the Bible. Now she's yelling like crazy haha and it's really funny.

'I am the QUEEN OF HEAVEN! Get on your knees!'

She's wearing a fancy top with loads of glitter and I reckon, if you wore that top long enough, you might actually think you were the queen of heaven, haha. She's stretched up her neck and her chin is pointing to the ceiling, and if you had to pick one of them to play a queen in a show, you'd certainly pick Mary. And now I see that it wasn't her own plate she smashed, it was Catherine's. It's Catherine she's yelling at. The other old ladies – there are four of them – are looking up at her – like royal subjects, haha. But Catherine is not looking at her. She's eating her watermelon.

'FALL ON YOUR KNEES,' she screeches.

But Catherine doesn't even look sideways. 'Stupid bitch,' she says, taking another bite of watermelon.

And Mad Mary is going ballistic. So the nurses come over fast and nurse with red hair says, 'Come along, Your Majesty, let's go to the sun room,' and the two of them take her elbows and steer her out.

'Queen of my arse,' says Catherine.

37. Laura

Will this week ever end? It's only Thursday, but it feels like I've been on for a fortnight. A band of pain wraps under my jaw and around the back of my skull – I think I slept with my teeth clenched all night. Matt tiptoed to bed an hour or so after I'd gone and I willed myself to turn over, tell him I couldn't sleep, lean in for the cuddle – anything. Instead, I shuffled to the far edge of the mattress and lay there, dry-eyed and rigid, hugging my own misery to me like a favourite teddy. Katie was in at five thirty and I brought her downstairs. That was something, I suppose. When Matt appeared at six thirty, she greeted him like a returning war hero and I left them at it. I check the time on the dashboard – six fifty-five. My plan is to meet up with Niamh at the unit, make our plan for the morning interview, then head up to the psych ward afterwards.

The phone rings just as I'm pulling into the car park.

'Morning, Cig, I'm just about to –'

'Will you meet Darmody in the PoundCost shop in Terenure? Head there now, yeah? Armed robbery.'

'Oh – so you don't want me to –'

'Now,' he interrupts. 'It happened just as they were opening up for the day. One casualty – three raiders. They escaped – blue Audi. I've two uniform at the scene – can you get down there and get the details?'

'Right, sir.'

The morning is gone in interviews, report-writing and checking CCTV footage. I've barely drawn breath and it's gone lunchtime. Niamh's gone back to the station. I said I'd wait till she arrives before talking to the girl. My plan is to take a drive around Clonchapel; I'm itching to get there – see if I can find any clues we might have missed. Ahead of me, the Dublin Mountains huddle under a grey blanket of wet mist and, just for a second, I allow myself the Good Mummy fantasy. Imagine if I just went home, I think, let Sylvia go off early. I imagine Katie's delighted little face when she sees me home early – before dark – in broad daylight! Maybe we can go to the park, feed the overfed ducks that loiter near the entrance, waddling over to everyone in the hope of bread. Then we can come home, have half an hour watching *Peppa Pig*, snuggled under the duvet.

I shouldn't have thought about the park, because of the river.

Now it's in my mind. I see us in our raincoats down by the weir. I see myself the first time it happened. The classic. Katie had been crying all morning and I felt like I could do nothing right. Matt was in work. I'd tried feeding her, then changing her, putting her down, picking her up. I'd patted her tummy and taken her temperature. I'd rubbed teething granules into her gums and I'd sung to her. And still she cried. Everyone told us how lucky we were living beside the park. So I'd bundled her up warm and put her in the pram and we'd gone outside. The change in temperature did it. The cries had stopped by the time I'd done one round of the green, and I'd almost – almost – allowed myself a moment of thinking I'd done well. That I wasn't a completely shit mother.

But then, as we'd approached the weir, I'd slowed, then stopped. The muddy brown water churned and bubbled. There was a part not fenced off. I'd looked at the water and I'd looked at her perfect little face. I'd thought how easy it would be to let go of the handle and watch the pram roll in. I'd thought how terrible, sickening, unthinkable, it would be to shove the pram with all my strength into the swirling water. It was unthinkable, and yet I'd thought it. I'd pictured myself doing it. I'd thought about shoving my baby daughter into the roiling water.

I know what these are. I know these are intrusive thoughts and that they're the bastard offspring of my worst fears – thanks, Sam. But it doesn't stop me having them. They began to pop up everywhere. I started hiding the knives from myself – from her. I put them in a box in the shed. Just in case. She was a terrible sleeper, so I was up half the night anyway. But even so, when she did sleep, I'd have to creep in – risking waking her – to check she was breathing. I would check that she was breathing but I would also visualize holding a pillow over her.

How could my own mind betray me like this? I felt like her worst enemy. I felt like there was something rotten in me which could destroy her. On the worst days, I thought Katie's life would be better if I wasn't in it.

I went back to work when she was ten months old, hoping the work would help distract me, that it would save us both. And, sure, I was distracted. I hadn't a spare moment. Did it help me gain control of myself?

The jury's still out on that one.

A call comes through on the speaker. It's Matt.

'Oh hi, you're there,' he says. 'I was expecting to leave a message.'

'You could have texted me, then?'

'Well, yeah, true. But I thought I'd ring you. But you never answer your phone at work.'

'The clue is in the word, Matt,' I say, a flare of anger ignited. 'I'm in work.' I press down the guilt.

He sighs. 'I know you're in work, which is why I was going to leave a message.' He pauses for a beat. 'Are you okay?'

'I'm fine. Anyway, what was your message?'

'It was just that I have to work late. There's a problem with the client and we've to stay on for a meeting, so it'll be –'

'Fine,' I interrupt him. 'I think I can get back by six today.'

If I go home early, I can be there for bedtime then go back to the office later. I can do it. There's enough hours to be a good mum – I just have to be creative, that's all.

'No, it's Thursday, so it's five thirty.' He's using his extra-patient voice, the one for his difficult clients. It drives me nuts. 'Sylvia has to leave early on a Thursday, remember? She has a pick-up to do.'

He's right, of course. He's always right and he's annoyingly perfect. The fact that he's being so reasonable and patient makes me worse.

'I know!' I say, like a five-year-old. 'I'm a shit mother – why don't you just come out and say it.'

'What? No, you know that's not what I mean. Laura – what's wrong with you? I can arrange something, or we can ask Sylvia –'

'I'm going to sort it out. I am – I'm going to sort all this mess out, so don't worry. I'll sort it!'

I press the red End Call button just a second too early, hanging up on him.

Matt is an accountant; he enjoys order. He deals in columns of figures, transferring monies from this point to that, keeping track of decimal places, adding and subtracting, balancing. Even if he does have a difficult client, he's not responsible for them. He's not trying to deal with the worst aspects of their humanity. He just keeps track of the figures. His orderliness is the very thing I love about him. So why is it driving me mad?

I never told him about the thoughts. How could he understand? Where's his reference point for that? He's a nice guy.

An accountant. He's normal. He doesn't think about harming his daughter. He doesn't picture himself throwing her against a wall, her head smacking against solid brick. When she's crying in the middle of the night, he doesn't wonder about putting a pillow over her face. How can I explain the compulsion to think these thoughts to someone as straight and easy-going as Matt? I can't. So I don't.

And I never told him about that night. The thought of him knowing what happened filled me with shame. It still does. He knows I have panic attacks and that I used to see Sam, but that's all. That's enough. I didn't want him to see me wedged in a car seat while that bastard grunted away. As long as Matt doesn't know, as long as Mum didn't know, as long as no one knows, then it never really happened.

By the time Matt and I got back together, too much time had passed. And then Mum was sick, so that was enough pain, right there.

Matt's call has distracted me – I'm almost in Clonchapel. The plants on display outside the SuperValu shop sway and shiver in the chilly breeze. Even though it's the middle of the afternoon, the lights are on. I don't know if that's an improvement or not; sometimes, light makes the dark look darker. I drive past the shops and turn right, and then I see the Bottle Tower.

Jesus! The tower! *Bad things happen in the tower*, she said. And she'd drawn a tower.

I park on the path outside and get out of the car, hurriedly zipping up my jacket and wishing I'd brought a hat. It's freezing. I realize that I haven't looked at the tower properly in years, though I pass the strange, cone-shaped building often enough. It sits back from the road, behind a wall of grey stone, looming up into the skyline like a giant upside-down funnel. There's a wrought-iron gate, which is open, and two grand or wannabe-grand pillars topped with stone orbs. The November rain slicks against the ancient brick. It looks bleak.

Taking out my phone, I read in an online journal that bitterly cold and wet weather hit Ireland between 1740 and 1741, lasting for almost two years. Not much change there then, I think, clutching the phone against my chest, protecting it from the freezing sleet. Crops failed and livestock starved, leading to disease, famine and death. It says that 28 per cent of the population died – a much higher rate than during the Great Famine a hundred years later. *The Bottle Tower, also known as Hall's Barn, was commissioned in the 1740s to give employment but also to act as a grain store by Major Hall, who was inspired by the 'Wonderful Barn' of Castletown.*

I look up at the rain-lashed stone, trying to see it as a positive development, built to alleviate suffering. The article says it was modelled on grain stores in India, the idea being that the locals would never go hungry again, having a massive store of dry grain to fall back on. I read about the 'cantilevered external staircase' that winds around the building, giving it its strange corkscrew appearance. Most of the staircase has now crumbled away and the blackened steps clutch against the sides drunkenly – haphazardly.

I stuff my phone back in my pocket and step back so as to get a full view of the tower, half expecting to see a long-haired princess peering out of the tiny uppermost window.

A huge gust of wind catches me and I stumble, clutching at the wet stone to steady myself. There's no way of climbing the tower – access is blocked by overgrown shrubbery and, when I walk around to the other side, it leads to a brick wall. I gaze up at the blank stone. The woman found Jenny lying on the patch of ground outside Ely's Arch – frozen to the bone with the early stages of hypothermia. This landmark would be visible from the arch and from the village of

Clonchapel. And you'd be able to see this tower from the upstairs rooms in Jenny's house. Its brooding presence dominates the skyline.

The site where they found Stuart's car is about a quarter of a mile further down this road, although I know from the team that they didn't find anything else. They did house-to-house enquiries as well – nothing. Textbook quiet neighbourhood. But everything she's told us so far, it all points to here. It's got to be here – this island she talks about. I ring Niamh.

'I'm going to check something out,' I say, pressing the phone against my ear with frozen fingers. I can't make out what she replies, but there's a lot of squawking. 'I'm on Whiteash Avenue – did we ever find out what number was the teacher's house? Did anyone get to talk to her?'

'No – I don't think so,' says Niamh. 'No reply. Neighbour said she was in hospital.'

'Okay – well, I've changed my mind. I'm not going into Jenny yet. I'm going to have a nose around here – try to find that neighbour.'

There's silence – maybe she's buying it.

'What about bringing her in later? What will we –'

'What time does Cig want her?'

'He said four thirty, five maybe? Listen,' she says, her tone changing, 'how about you head home for an hour? I'll cover. I think we can both admit your head is pure fried, yeah?'

'Thanks for your concern, but I'm fine. I'm not a complete fucking imbecile.'

'What the fuck, Laura?' she says, her voice rising about three octaves. 'I'm trying to be nice here – I just thought you might enjoy an hour back home before it all kicks off later, when we get her in.'

'And I'm saying thanks for your concern, but I am grand.

And –' A burst of anger explodes in my brain. 'Why is everyone being so fucking patient and understanding with me, like I'm an idiot? Last time I checked, I outrank you, so I can make my own decisions.'

'Fuck. That was before you started acting like a pure dick. Go home to Katie and have a rest.'

She pauses. 'In fact – d'ya know what? – I'm taking over. Cig told *me* to bring her in. You're not even on board with it. I'll do it.'

I start the engine and her voice switches over on to the car phone. I miss the first part but I can kind of fill it in myself.

'I'll tell him you're talking to her schoolfriends. I won't shop you, okay?'

'Oh, gee, thanks.'

She sighs. 'Have a fucking break for a couple of hours, Laura. Right?'

She waits. And I make a plan of sorts.

'Right, sorry,' I say, sounding contrite. 'I'll do that.'

'She's probably resting now. I'm getting her in a couple of hours.'

I check the time; it's just after three thirty. I turn the car around and head back towards the hospital. I don't have long.

I pass our old house and, as usual, feel a pang at not seeing Bobby barking in the front window. Mum just let him – she said it deterred burglars. It was actually Bobby who got me and Matt back together. It seems that, for dogs, just like for humans, the early years are where the strongest memories and attachments are formed. Matt and I became a couple when Bobby was still only a puppy; he was certainly less than a year old. Bobby would go nuts when Matt appeared, barking and yelping, doing his downward-dog stretch and running over and back to the door, trying to get Matt out into the garden to play.

At weekends and on half-days from school, Matt and I would often walk to meet each other in Bushy Park; it's more or less midway between us. There's a bench in front of the children's playground, and that's where I'd wait for him.

Some Wednesday afternoons, we used to watch a gorgeous old dog playing with a balloon. It was crazy. The owner sat on the bench blowing up the balloon while the dog waited with a kind of weary-yet-patient look. The guy knotted the balloon then handed it over, knot-side outwards, to the dog – a retriever. The dog would take hold of the knot really gently between his teeth – it looked like he was smiling. Then he'd play for ages – releasing the balloon and nudging it into the air with his nose. It was surreal.

One time, Matt brought along a pack of balloons and we tried to teach Bobby. It was a disaster. Bobby bit through the very first one and got such a fright when it burst that he sprinted off into the woods. It took us twenty minutes, yelling and searching, to get him back.

When Matt and I broke up, I used to joke that Mum and Bobby took it the hardest. For Bobby, there was a lot of lying in his basket, looking up with a mournful expression. Meanwhile, Mum would do her infuriating Mona Lisa smile and say things like – 'It's not over till it's over' or 'We haven't seen the last of him.'

Then one rainy afternoon in April about five years after the break-up, I'd brought Bobby to the park. Mum had been gone almost six months, because I remember noticing the daffodils – her favourite flower – and thinking this was the first year I wouldn't be bringing her a bunch. By that time, I'd got used to Mum's voice in my head, making me do things I didn't want to do, slapping down my excuses. I still hadn't got used to the lurching realization that she was dead, whenever I saw or heard something I wanted to tell her. Once or twice

I'd even started to text her when I remembered. Anyway, that afternoon, I'd only brought Bobby for a walk because I heard her voice, clear as though she was actually standing beside me, telling me my skin was waterproof and to take poor Bobby out. And I was walking near the playground when out of the corner of my eye I saw Matt, in running gear, making his way past the tennis courts. Immediately, I ducked and turned back towards the woods, aiming to avoid him. But I'd forgotten Bobby.

Bobby had spotted him. Bobby had already started sprinting in his direction, bounding along on his short legs, barking and yelping frantically. So I had to follow. Then I had to sprint, too, because Matt hadn't seen Bobby and was almost out the gate, heading towards the main road. I yelled his name and he stopped. And the smile on Matt's face when he saw Bobby – and me, too, I suppose – it was just massive. He hunkered down, catching hold of Bobby's collar with one hand, petting him and scratching behind his ears with the other. He looked up at me, still smiling.

'Laura,' he said, making my very boring name, which I've always hated, sound like the answer to a puzzle.

'Matt,' I said, with stunning originality, and I blushed as if I were fifteen again, not almost twenty-three and a qualified garda. In my head, I heard Mum's voice saying, 'See?'

We took up exactly where we left off – meeting up at the weekends to walk Bobby, going out for dinner, hanging out with some of the crowd from school, who were delighted we were back together; people love happy endings. And it was all brilliantly simple and straightforward. I think, now, that a large part of the attraction for me was that, to Matt, I was still my best self. I was still Laura unblemished, undamaged – full of fun – with everything to look forward to. Back then, I thought I could have the happy ending, too.

At our wedding, Bobby walked us down the aisle with two white balloons attached to his collar. He never mastered the trick, though.

And so, I never told Matt about that night, and when the nightmares came, or the flashbacks, I'd put it down to stress at work or being overtired. Anything rather than tell him about the time I let a completely random guy take whatever he wanted from my body; let him slobber and paw me like a piece of meat; let him inside me – without a condom – and let him think he'd done me a favour. I'd had to get the morning-after pill, which, thank Christ, you could get from the Well Woman Clinic in town. I didn't realize the extent of the damage he'd caused. That he'd trampled the core of my being and torn it to shreds, like aggravated burglary – he'd pissed and shat and smeared himself all over me.

I can hide the anger, mostly. I've put it all behind me, mostly. But it's like a mug brimful of boiling liquid; the slightest jolt and out it sloshes, scalding the nearest people. And since Katie was born, it's like the mug is even fuller. Since this whole thing with Jenny – it's like I *want* to smash it into pieces myself.

If Matt knew what I'm about to do, he'd be raging. He's always going on about rules being your protectors, there to keep you safe. I know he's right. I know that what I'm about to do is way out of line. I've already gone beyond anything I could possibly dress up as part of the normal clarification process. What I'm about to do goes beyond even the reach of detective work. And I know none of this will stand up if I'm hauled up in front of internal affairs for breach of discipline. I know this. And I don't care.

She knows where he is and she knows what's happened to him. If I can get her out of the hospital, out of that room, I can get to her.

I'm going to bring her to the tower. I'm going to use the tower to try to get through to her. If I get to her, I get to him, is my reckoning. They'll be happy with that – or maybe not happy exactly, but they might overlook the other stuff.

I don't care. *I* need to get to him.

Craning my neck either side to see if any of the houses look particularly spooky, I drive along Whiteash Avenue. But nothing jumps out; bungalows that have doubled and tripled in size before the recession, 1930s three-bed semis, a large Georgian house which has been turned into apartments; the Dublin smorgasbord of properties arrayed along a winding kilometre of potholed road. I pass the spot near the cul-de-sac where they found the car – a scrap of garda tape flutters in the breeze, but nothing else. No spooky house, no teacher. No dog.

The abbey looms over all of this, on the hill above the town. Even the shade of red brick makes me shiver; it's a harsh shade of orangey-red, garish against the green hill on which it squats like an obstinate bulldog. The school closed in the late seventies and stood empty, except for a few remaining decrepit Brothers, until the whole site was developed into fancy two- and three-bedroom apartments a few years ago, when building started again. An apartment in Abbey Close will now cost you the guts of half a million, being so close to the Luas and the new bus corridor into the city centre. Niamh told me they'd named the old dormitory blocks stuff like Bishop's Walk and Abbot's Library. Apparently, the old school yard, where Michael and the other bedwetters stood in shame, holding their sheets up to dry, is now a herb garden. For Christ's sake.

Poor Michael. And Brother Fondie. I'm pretty sure there isn't a Brother Fondie block.

When he came to me, Michael was fifty-five years old with

a story of historic abuse perpetrated inside those red-brick walls, from the time he went in at age six, to his leaving nine years later. Intellectually impaired, breathing through his mouth, twitching and repeatedly slapping his thighs, with hanks of greasy hair falling across his forehead, Michael didn't look like the clients I'd imagined having. It was back in my early days as an SVI, when I thought I'd be rescuing five-year-olds, recording their testimony efficiently, ensuring they'd be taken into care or that we'd get a barring order in place or that, in some fabulous way, I'd be able to fix everything for them and there'd be no more suffering. I'd been prepared to be affected by the sad stories of small children. But nothing prepared me for Michael.

'Huhmichael' was how he said his name. Hearing loss meant that much of what he said was difficult to understand, and much of what I said to him had to be repeated. No one could tell me whether or not the hearing loss had pre-dated his entry to the abbey or been inflicted there. Getting thumped in the head could rupture an ear drum. It could possibly even have caused the brain injury.

'I can sign my name,' he said, before I'd closed the door.

'Oh! Wow – yes, that's great, Michael. Great.'

'I can sign my name.'

I'd taken him through the drill – telling the truth, saying 'I don't know', or 'I don't remember' if he didn't remember, and the whole time, he kept nodding and telling me he could sign his name.

Michael disclosed a litany – no, not a litany, a whole bloody epic of abuse from the Brothers. He'd been beaten with the strap and punched in the head. This was the same strap issued to every single Brother in the Abbey, although, in theory, there was meant to be only one Brother administering discipline, with one strap. Michael wet the bed constantly and got the sheet punishment on a daily basis. I asked him what he felt like when that happened, if it made him upset.

'Only babies cry,' he said. 'Michael doesn't cry.'

Michael received an education in humiliation and misery lasting nine years. And through it all, one of the teachers, nicknamed Brother Fondie, had paid him nightly visits.

'Give me a fondie. That's what Brother Fondie is always saying, and you have to do it or it's worse for you.'

Through the interview I learned that a 'fondie' covered pretty much any sexual act the Brother would like performed or permitted. When Brother Fondie asked for it, you did it. Because if you didn't do it, you got beaten.

The interview was done in an afternoon and, when it was over, I asked Michael if he was happier, did he feel better now he'd talked about it. I told him the school was closed and Brother Fondie would never be able to do those things to him or anyone else again. Michael's eyes shifted to the pages on my table.

'Will I sign my name now?'

After reading that harrowing report, I couldn't believe that no sanctions were ever imposed on the Brothers, these brutal men who took what they wanted from little children. There was no naming and shaming either – the order got permission to deal with the perpetrators privately.

I don't know why I'm thinking about this now. These are things I've understood and accepted; we can't fix everything for the victims. My job is to listen and provide a platform. My job, mine and Niamh's, is to record the video that sometimes – more than sometimes – often sends people to prison.

I'm a realist – this is the best we can hope for. It should be enough. We win by sending them to prison.

But this guy – I don't know – something has tipped the scales. They talk about Blind Justice – well, I want her to see.

Why doesn't she take off her blindfold and look around? That bastard has raped and beaten Jenny. He's probably been doing stuff and getting away with it for years. He has Melanie a prisoner. Even little Karl – his own son – isn't safe. I need to find him.

And then what, Laura?

I change gear and accelerate, moving into the right-hand lane for the hospital. I don't answer my own question. Because I don't know what I'll do if I find him. Or maybe I do.

38. Jenny

It was all a bit crazy after Mad Mary left. They took Catherine away, too, and one lady started crying for her mummy, and that is sad. And the nurse said to her, 'Don't worry, your mam will be in later,' but that is a lie. I told you. They're all in on it. When they noticed me, Nice Nurse – was it Ella or Eva? I can't remember, but whichever one. Anyway, she came over to me and she laughed at the way I'd lined up all the biscuits. Then she said all that same shit, like 'Are you not eating your lunch, Jenny? Not hungry?' But you could tell she actually cared. And I told her I'm not hungry, even though I am. But it's all full of drugs – they could put anything into the mash; stuff to make you sleepy, or the truth drug. I told you that already. Be careful.

Nice Nurse taps my elbow, but she waits for me to stand up. Not like Bitch Nurse, who always sort of pokes you. She uses her fob thing to open the door and then we're in the hallway. But we walk past the Laura room. And my heart starts to race because maybe Nice Nurse knows and she's going to put one of those jackets – straitjackets – or handcuffs or something on me.

'Where are we going? I don't want to go – where are you taking me?'

'We're going back to your room, Jenny. Okay?'

She squeezes my arm and it's friendly and she looks at me properly like I'm a real person. Or like there's a real person inside.

'It's just until the interviewers are ready for you again.

They're not here yet. Why don't you have a nap or something? Here.' She opens the door of our room and then she laughs. 'Look – don't wake her, okay?'

Catherine is asleep already and she's on my bed – not hers. And it's weird, because I hate this place and I want to go home and I thought I hated my bed. But I don't want to lie down on Catherine's bed. It faces the wrong way. But I like Nice Nurse because she makes it like it's our private joke and, actually, it is.

'Haha, okay, no worries,' I say, like Luke.

'Good woman,' says Nice Nurse. She smiles at me when I lie down on the bed.

'I'd say you've a little while yet,' she says, glancing at her watch. 'About half three or four. Do you want a magazine or anything to read?'

And I say no and, even though I hear the click when she closes the door which means the door is locked, I match her smile through the glass on the door.

I don't know if I sleep but I close my eyes and, it's weird, because I want to see Laura. I need to know is she still Angry Laura. Does she think I'm like Mad Mary and it doesn't matter what I say because I'm a joke dumb bitch? I didn't tell her about Luke and the kiss. Some things are spoiled if you say them out loud. And some things are a secret, haha, for ever.

But there's something bad about Luke. I don't want to remember it but it's going to come anyway, like when you know you're going to puke even though you don't want to. It's bad and I feel bad. There's a snake of shame still coiled in my body.

We were in the cricket pavilion again – a few days after. It was cooler, no warm patch of sunshine to sit in, though we sat in the same spot anyway.

'We could go back to my house if you want. It'd be warmer?'

'I've to pick up Karl.'

'He could come, too – what age is he? Little kids love me, you know.' He grins again. And I think, just for one day, I'd love to be Luke. To live in his head, where there's an answer to every question and something good is always just around the corner.

'I – we can't,' I say, feeling like a killjoy. Luke nods.

'Oh, well – some other time,' he says, laughing. 'When you've approved my CV.'

He rummages in his jacket and takes out his phone.

'So, I was doing more research – on The Beatles. Did you ever hear about their final concert? It was in London.' He starts to read.

'On a bitterly cold morning, 30 January, 1969, The Beatles played their final concert on the rooftop of the Apple building. John borrowed Yoko's fur coat and Ringo, too, wore his wife's red mac to keep warm. They started to play around midday and managed forty-two minutes before police shut it down. A crowd gathered on the streets below and secretaries and workers from nearby offices hung out of upper windows and crowded on to balconies to hear The Beatles play live. Traffic on Savile Row and neighbouring streets came to a standstill. George didn't sing much that day and John needed a prompt for some of the lyrics. The next year, the band split. The Beatles were over.'

He stops, looks at me. 'Do you want to know what they played?'

'Why did you do that?' I feel a falling inside, a tumbling, somersaulting feeling. A tray of glasses, cups and plates in free-fall. He has no idea.

'What do you mean?'

'I mean, why would you tell me about the rooftop and – and the end? When it all fell apart? Like, why would you think I'd want to know?'

And his face is so funny but not funny – absolutely zero zero smile cracks now. He's staring at me. Not smiling.

'It's – I – I'm sorry, Jen. I don't know. I didn't know you –' He stops, breathes deeply. 'I didn't know you'd be like –'

'Like what? What am I like?'

He doesn't answer and neither do I. It's out of my control. The glasses will smash, the cups are going to shatter. They'll fall to the ground and break into smithereens.

'I didn't know you'd be upset! I'm sorry – really. Can we not –'

He puts his hand on my arm and he takes hold of my face, like before. But not the same. And I want it to be all right but it's not all right. It's the rooftop concert. It's the end of The Beatles. It's not all right. Why did he tell me?

'Can we not do this? Can we just forget I said anything? I'm sorry, okay?'

And that would have been okay if we'd left it there. But Luke – Luke, he loves to help and he wants to be a doctor like his dad, so of course he goes on. Tries his hand at fixing.

'Is there something else, Jen? I mean, I've been meaning to ask you for a long time because you – I don't know. You look sad. You *are* sad. There's something – isn't there?' He waits a bit. 'You can – like, if you wanted to, you can talk to me? Let me help.' Then he does a sort of terrible impression of his usual grin.

'Help,' he says. 'Get it? Need somebody?'

And I think NO MORE TALKING NO MORE TALKING. I've got to stop him talking. I don't want him to know and I don't want to think. Shut up. And I know how you do that. This bit I know. I'm good at not thinking.

'It's fine, I'm fine,' I say in the calm voice for no arguments, like before. 'Nothing's wrong. I don't know – don't mind me.'

I take hold of his hand and I bring it back up to my face

283

and I put my arms around his neck. He goes to say something and I go sssh and kiss him even though he's still talking, and there's a clash of teeth. He pauses and I think, just for a second, it's going to be okay. I can do this.

Then I take his hand and I bring it down lower, inside my shirt, inside my bra, and I do a little sigh. Dumb bitch, sound like you enjoy it, can't you?

Quickly – like he got burnt, Luke jerks back. Pulls his hand out. Sits back against the wall.

'What the? I don't understand what just happened,' he says, and the burning starts. 'I really like you, Jenny.'

'But not like that,' I say – burning, burning, burning.

'Yes like that! Yes. But I can't – I mean, that was weird! One minute you're furious with me and the next – I mean, what the hell?'

I get up fast, button my shirt. Fix my hair. Grab my schoolbag.

'It's fine, I've got to go anyway.'

'Jenny? Wait?'

I run. I don't turn round. I can't bear it. I sprint all the way to Val's and pick up Karl, mumbling stuff to Val about being kept after school. And the shame burns and burns.

When we get in, Mum is up and dressed all nice. She's covered the bruises with make-up and brushed her hair and she's actually cooking dinner. And I so want to hug her and ask her stuff – the kind of stuff other girls can ask their mums; like what do you do when you've made a show of yourself and you threw yourself at the guy you like and he couldn't get away fast enough and you feel like you could die of shame?

And then I hate her I hate hate her because I can't ask her anything because she doesn't know fucking anything. Dumb bitch. And she knows about him and she knows about me and still she says nothing, not even 'Don't do that, Stu' – and

284

not even 'If you touch her, I'll kill you.' I look at Private Parer, but he's not sharp enough. He'd be no good – it has to be quick.

But I don't like thinking that and I don't go to the knife block. I don't do that. Not in this story. Instead I tell her what Val had said about the business and for the first time in ages – centuries – she perks up.

'We could do this!' She hugged Karl, grinning at me. 'We really could!'

And it felt like I'd given her something gift-wrapped. And I tried not to think of Luke's face. And I tried to forget that she knows.

And so later on, after a dinner where the food was perfect, and everyone did everything right and nobody annoyed him, she sat down and passed him over a small notebook with columns of figures in her neat handwriting.

'Stu? Val was thinking, I mean, I was thinking it, too, but Val was saying it first, to Jen. Oh, sorry, maybe I should start again.' Her words were already beginning to trickle down the drain.

He sighs.

'She – Val wants to rent the shop. She's going to start up again – you know – the video business? The building would be perfect, she says. So, we could make a bit of money on it? Rent it out, you know? To Val?'

She doesn't say anything about her working. She's dumb, but not that dumb.

Silence. He flicks the notebook closed without looking at it and stares at her until her hopeful face melts like wax.

'Not going to happen. Val will just have to open her business somewhere else.' He smirks. 'Although, let's face it, she might be better off opening a gym – do herself a favour. Har har.'

Karl looks from Mum to him to Mum to him. Then he sort of slides away from the table. No one says anything.

'Anyway, the shop is long gone.'

There's silence.

'It was sold – years ago.'

He looks at her like she's an idiot – starts to use his special voice. 'Private hospitals are expensive, Melanie.'

Mum looks down at her lap, fiddles with the notebook – rubs the edge over and back with her thumb.

'I took you in, you and Jennifer. You were in bits, weren't you? You said it yourself at the time. There's no way you were able to run the shop.'

'But when? How? I didn't sign anything – I didn't give permission –' She gulps down whatever she was going to say next.

'This is getting to sound kind of ungrateful, Melanie. You'd need to listen to yourself and think about what you're going to say next.' He fixes her with a look. 'I didn't need your permission; I had power of attorney. I'm your husband, yeah? Actually, I saved your life.' He pushes his chair back suddenly and we both flinch. He stands. 'But now I don't know why I bothered.'

He walks over to the mirror – talks to his reflection. 'I took them into *my* home. I put them in a lovely house, clothes on their backs and food on the table. And what do I get?'

Mirror buddy doesn't reply. Knife Squadron are still in the block. I had to put Sergeant Sharp Steak back in case they noticed. So, I don't have one ready. I haven't made a plan. Dumb bitch.

'Nothing. Nothing. Nothing,' he says, looking at us. 'Three big nothings. Three big zeros with nothing to contribute.'

And we sat there like it was true, like we believed it,

because none of us said anything – zero nothing nothing. And I thought about the shop and the day we'd sung 'Yellow Submarine' and Dad doing the 'Oh! Darling' slide on the floor. I thought about Sergeant Sharp Steak, wishing I had got him ready. Why had I put him back? I thought about being a dumb bitch who is also a pathetic wimp. Then I thought about Luke pulling his burnt hand back after touching me, and round O tears sizzled down my cheek, one by one.

I lie on Catherine's bed and look over at Catherine, lying on my bed. She has her dressing gown on still and she's on her side, facing me. Her two hands are folded one on top of the other, under her ear, exactly like the official position when you pretend to be asleep. She blinks. Maybe it's catching – like yawns. I blink. We do this for a bit. Until she closes her eyes and I think she's gone to sleep. And then I'm almost asleep, when she does a kind of evil-villain chuckle and my heart jumps. I bolt upright.

Catherine is sitting up, clutching a sausage in each hand, laughing and laughing.

'On your knees,' she says, taking a bite out of one sausage. 'Queen of Heaven,' she says, biting the other.

I was dreaming about the island. Socks came with us on the boat, and he was very sad, like as if he knew about the princess. We tied up the boat and Karl stayed playing on the beach, but I knew I had to do something. Something big.

There's a marsh around the tower – a moat of stinking black slime. I followed Socks and he jumped over the marsh, like he was showing me the way. But when I tried, I started sinking down down. And you know in dreams when your mouth is full of something and you're trying to breathe but you can't? Maybe you're grinding your teeth. Well, in my dream my mouth was full of the black marshy slime. I was drowning in it and I couldn't open my mouth to scream because more would get in.

Then I was climbing the tower, using the princess's long plait as a rope. It was like PE class where they make us climb the rope. That must be what I was thinking of. In the dream, I climbed and I slipped. But bit by bit I got nearer to the window.

And then I was in the tower room and it was huge. Like miles miles bigger than it looks on the outside. A freezing-cold wind rips through the windows and the room is bare. And like in slow motion, the room revealed itself. A bare wooden table and chair. Bare stone walls and, in the corner, a filthy mattress and a mound of dirty, ragged blankets. And all over the floor and in the air whirling are feathers – tiny white feathers.

And you know in dreams when you don't want to look because you know what you're going to see? I look at the pile of dirty blankets and they begin to twitch and move. And rats run out from underneath and then I see her – the princess. She sits up and, as she does, her tattered dress is whipped about by the breeze. The dress is a wedding dress, but it looks a thousand years old; it's a filthy grey colour and covered in grime. The wind is whipping up the feathers and stirring the tattered lace, up and up and round until it's like a snowstorm of feathers and lace. And the princess is a wisp of smoke, more of an idea than a person. I get a glimpse of her grey flesh – like something left behind on a plate. Nothing more. And her eyes won't meet mine and I hate her. I hate her. I don't want to save her because she's not worth saving. She's dead already.

I look away from the princess to the little owl. She's lying on the ground and she's dead, too, or nearly dead. She looks at me and blinks her big owl eyes and then her last feather falls out and is sucked up into the storm. There's a creaking noise and, for a bit, it's in my dream and I think it's a window or a door, even though the tower has no door. But then I sort of wake out of the dream and I'm looking at Catherine, asleep on my bed.

She's snoring loads – like a baby dragon or something, and the sound makes me happy and it takes me away from the tower. I think Catherine is the happiest person I've ever seen. She's still holding the half-eaten sausages.

I lie for more minutes on Catherine's bed. From this angle, I can see the door-window much better. I can see Nurse Ella take a sneaky peek in at us, but she doesn't come in. And I really want to go to sleep because I didn't sleep properly last night. I am so so tired. I didn't sleep last night, or maybe it was another night. I'm forgetting how many nights I've been here. Through the gap in the blind, I could see this star – crazy bright – so bright, it kind of looked fake. I thought maybe it was the one they discovered in 2004: Lucy. The astronomers named her Lucy because of the song.

Lucy's the biggest diamond in the galaxy. Thank you, Luke. Another fact found on the internet and handed over – the way a dog drops the ball at your feet. Maybe, haha, Dad is up there, you know, keeping an eye on me, organizing stars for me to look at. I just said maybe.

Yeah, dumb bitch. And maybe it's just a massive chunk of crystallized rock in the middle of the void.

Catherine's bed is comfy, even though it smells a bit of old-lady perfume. And I know I must have been asleep properly because something made me wake up – Laura's green-apple perfume snuck into my brain and pushed out Catherine's old-lady perfume. That's what woke me.

'Come on, Jen, wake up. We're going out,' she says.

And I don't know if she's here or if I'm dreaming her. Maybe we're on the island. Laura's eyes move quickly, side to side. She looks weird. Not shiny because you're worth it. Her hair is not tucked behind her ears; it's escaped. We're going to escape, too.

'Where are we going?' I say and, thump thump, my heart is listening very hard for the answer. You cannot trust her. This is the bit where she brings you outside or maybe into the car park. And there'll be gardaí all climbing out of vans and squad cars and they'll be wearing stab vests. That's what they wear. And they'll have guns and handcuffs. And one of them will be Niamh, but she'll be in her uniform. And Laura's going to say, 'I can't get any more out of her, she's all yours. Little bitch, she definitely did it. Take her away.' Niamh will say, 'Yeah, fuck it annieway. Take her away.'

'Come on, Jen,' she's saying. 'We're going to go together. Let's go to the island, let's see what we can find.'

And I don't think this is right because Nice Nurse Ella comes up whispering on her whispering feet. She doesn't make a sound.

'Sorry, where are you taking her?' she says, and she looks very worried. She likes me. She doesn't want them to handcuff me.

But Laura takes out her badge thing and she says stuff like 'We're bringing her up to the station for questioning. Just for an hour or so. It's been okayed by the Super – do you want me to call him?' And Laura is old, like thirty-something, and Nice Nurse is only maybe twenty-one or twenty-two. So she nods and says okay and buzzes open the door and then we're outside the lift.

We don't get in the lift, we have to go down the stairs instead, and Laura is holding my elbow. It doesn't hurt, but I don't like it. The stairwell is narrow and we go four steps turn a corner four steps turn a corner and on like that. It makes me think of the tower, but we are coming down not going up into the tower.

'It's okay, Jen,' she says, pausing on one of the steps just ahead of me. 'We're just going for a short drive. You're going to show me where the island is.' She steps down and stops again. 'And the tower.'

I think you could push someone down the steps easy peasy if they're below you and they're not very heavy.

In the car, I stare out the window because it feels like a hundred years since I was outside in the real world. We drive past the park and the SuperValu and my heart beats faster faster. And I think I could just open the door like right now when we are at the lights. I could jump out and run home. Mum will be there and it will all be all right. She'll be fine and her blonde hair will be clean. No blood. No more blood. I hear the click. She has locked the door. Dumb bitch, I told you.

This is how the dream ends. The princess is dead. Minerva was dead but, actually, she is like that other bird, the one that has to die first so it can come back alive. The phoenix. It's time for a new bird and a new princess. This bird has black feathers, black as smoke and pain and stabbing. This is the black crow, the Morrigan.

It's time now, too, for a new princess. No more sad dumb bitch with her long hair and her crying and smiling. None of that shit works. It's time for the Morrigan because sometimes she's a woman and sometimes the crow or even a wolf. She is the goddess of war and of battle. She will tear your flesh and stab and she could pull your eye out of its socket and laugh. She can be anything.

I saw her rise up from their dead bodies. And her hair flew

about, streaming in the wind. And she roared. She roared her loud roar and she found the prince where he was hiding, shivering in his seat. And she grabbed his head with her left hand. With a wide, high leap she fell on him. And she grabbed his hair with her left hand and with her right hand she butchered him slice slice across his throat.

Ssh – don't tell her.

39. Laura

It was easy enough to get her off the ward. They're short-staffed so only one nurse even noticed and she was easily dealt with. I flashed the badge and muttered something about bringing her back in an hour. Even so, my hands are shaking on the steering wheel. I grip it firmly to steady them. It's going to be all right. She's quiet, sitting curled against the car door, feet drawn up, head buried in her knees. It's only just gone four, so the traffic isn't too bad but already I'm wondering how the hell I'll get her back in time.

'Are you hiding, Jen?' No response. 'Is something scaring you?'

She huddles further down into the seat.

'We're going to take a look at the island – you said you'd show it to me,' I gamble.

She doesn't reply. I approach the tower from the north end of the road, furthest away from her home. It's already beginning to get dark and the showers of sleet which were forecast are beginning to splutter into action. She's muttering something under her breath and rocking, her head bumping against the windowpane. We park in the same spot where I was earlier, on the path outside the Bottle Tower. I switch off the engine and the temperature drops almost immediately.

'Do you know where you are, Jenny?' I bend my head, trying to see her face. 'Look, we're beside the tower. A girl was found near here the other day, did I tell you that?' The engine clicks as it cools and I start the car again, turn on the fan.

She's clenching and unclenching her hands, staring at her

fingers. For the first time, I get a little jolt of fear. Belatedly, I remember safety protocols from when you're on the psych ward. Things like not having objects that could be used as weapons easily to hand. Glancing at the pockets in the door of the car, I see an umbrella which is conveniently missing some of the plastic protective tips. In the cubby beneath the gear stick there're some biros with nice sharp points and a set of spare house keys. Shit – there's even a pair of nail scissors. If she tries something, she'll have plenty to work with. Shit. I lean back against the seat, pressing against the familiar heft of the gun.

I'm in this now. I need this. I realize I need to know the rest. I need her to know what happened for real – not just in her story. For real in real life in the real world which is full of dangerous bastards walking around, getting away with it.

'Jenny – I want you to listen to me. I'm going to tell you about the girl who was brought into hospital the other night; a fourteen-year-old girl. She was found very near here, at Ely's Arch. She was half dead with the cold and she'd nothing with her – no money, no phone, no ID. And do you know something else, Jenny? She was covered in blood. There was blood all over her clothes – a lot of it.'

Jenny has gone still. Now, she shifts in her seat, tucking her feet even more closely in underneath her. I notice she's not wearing shoes. She's in bootie-type slippers. Feck it – I should have noticed that. The silence deepens.

Psychotherapy is rooted in dialogue – that's another of Sam's catchphrases. I've got to get her talking again, get this stuff out in the open.

'So, first thing, of course, they tried to talk to her; asked her name, age, asked her what happened – but the girl wasn't speaking. She was in deep shock – it was almost as if she'd left her body. When that happens, when the person isn't speaking and their parents – they've nobody to speak for them – the medical team have to work with whatever's in front of them. The body becomes the witness. Do you understand?'

Jenny's eyes are closed and her hands lie flat on her thighs, like she's waiting for something. I go to place my hand on her shoulder and think better of it.

'Kind of like mechanics with a car,' I go on. 'A car can't tell you what's wrong with it, can it? So the mechanics check it out and do tests. It's the same at the hospital in the Emergency Department. If the person isn't talking, the body must tell what has happened.'

I keep my voice steady and even, like I'm reading a weather report.

'At first it was good news – even though the girl had a lot of blood on her clothes, it didn't seem to be coming from wounds on her body. That was good. But then' – I pause, checking her hands, checking she hasn't picked up anything that could be used as a weapon – 'then they found bruises – old ones and new ones, pretty much all over her. And this made them wonder. And so they did X-rays. And the X-rays showed that the girl had been hurt in the past – that she'd suffered broken bones.'

I wait while Jenny twists and untwists a long strand of hair, moves on to the next strand. 'They concluded that someone had been hurting this girl for a long time.'

A woman walks past the car and looks in, frowning. I make eye contact, nod. We probably look like mother and teenage daughter arguing. The woman smiles and hurries on.

'And then Ciara was called in. Ciara's the clinical nurse specialist who does the forensic examinations in cases of sexual assault. She's who they call when they suspect someone's been raped.' I wait, letting the word sit there. 'She has a special kit – the rape kit – to gather all the information. She finds out what happened and she gathers evidence so that whoever did this doesn't get away with it.'

I look at Jenny in the front passenger seat of the car, long hair falling across her knees, and I'm almost overwhelmed by déjà vu.

'Do you know what Ciara found?'

She is rigid, her knuckles clenched as though she's going to pull her hair out in chunks. Is it fair to do this? To confront her with the reality before she's ready?

What would Sam do?

I know exactly what he'd do because it's what he did. He sat there doing his nodding thing. It's a multitasker, that nod. It could be either calming or challenging. It could mean something like *That must have been awful for you, well done you for telling me.* Or it could mean *Really? Is this how you're going to play this? Do you really think you've finished telling me about this? You've got to engage, Laura. If you want to get better, you need to actively engage with this process. It'll need sustained emotional effort.*

I can't try the Sam nod because she's not looking. So I answer my own question. I want active engagement with this. I want a response.

'I'll tell you what Ciara found. She found evidence that the girl had been raped.'

Still, she says nothing.

'Jenny? We both know that the girl was you. Don't we?'

40. Jenny

I feel sick. And I don't want to hear any more about that fourteen-year-old girl. Dumb bitch. Paul McCartney was only fifteen when he met John. And John was sixteen. That means Paul was only one year older than me. And he was a genius. I wonder did they know when they met, like, did they recognize the genius in each other. Dad said they weren't individual geniuses but that when the four of them got together, that's when they became magic.

Luke's fifteen now. It was his birthday back in September. Amy and I went to the supermarket to get the drink for his party and she made me wait outside. She says I look too young. She'd got her cousin's ID and, obviously, we weren't wearing our uniforms. But still, she's right. I do look young. Anyway, she came out in less than five minutes with a whole six-pack of Kopparberg and four bags of Doritos.

'Watch and learn,' she laughed, zipping up her top. 'Job done. I can put these away. Distracted the guy on till six; no way he was going to make things difficult.'

And Laura is going on and on with the stuff about the dumb girl and Ciara. I am no way listening to that shit. Why does she use that dumb voice, like she's doing a safety demo? Or when they do fire drill in school.

The night of the party I said I'd planned to go to Amy's, that we were going to study for a test on Monday, but he looked at me weirdly. He just kept staring and staring. And I went red and he goes, 'Oh, I'll help with your test, Jenny.'

And dumb bitch Mum is all 'Oh, great, Stewie, that's so kind of you.' And. Yeah.

I told Amy and Luke that Mum was sick and I had to babysit. I always say that. They probably think she has cancer or something awful, and it's easier to let them think that. Is that really bad? I feel bad and I think Luke must have told his mum something like that, because she always asks about her. Luke's mum is so cool. She works in an investment bank or something. One time, I was at their house – it was nearly half-term and we were all going to the fifth-year play. Amy and I had called for Luke so we could walk up together.

'Great to see you, Jenny,' she'd said, looking up from the book she was reading. 'Get Luke to make you a cup of tea or something before you head out. Have you girls eaten? There's still some chilli left.'

And I'd had to close my mouth and try not to stare: everything about that exchange was amazing. The fact that she was just sitting there – her feet up on the coffee table – reading a book. The fact that she was still in her smart outfit for work, not caring if it was getting creased or covered in dog hair from their crazy shaggy dog Rocky, who's massive but thinks he's a lap dog. The lack of fear. The lack of tension. The fact that she looked so relaxed and happy. I was properly staring, I reckon, because she laughed a little embarrassedly. And I wanted her to be my mum. And at the same time, I wanted to be her – grown up, in charge. Safe. They live quite near here, but you can't see the tower from their house.

It's gone quiet and the only noise is the fan in the car. Maybe Laura's giving up on Nurse Ciara and dumb bitch girl. She looks like shit. Like she really needs a better mascara because the other eye has a big smudge now and her foundation is cracking. Laura needs someone like Amy to take her in hand. She rubs her eye and makes it look worse. She starts fiddling with the heating controls. It's roasting in this car.

Amy says curling your lashes makes the biggest difference to your eyes. She told me that when we were only first-years. We were hanging out in her house on our half-day and she was using the lash curler like a pro. I didn't even know what it was. Amy was so sophisticated, even then. I'm mortified; I probably follow her around like a puppy. She's probably sick of me.

'You should use that foundation – Flawless Fit or something. Or a primer. Amy uses a primer.'

And she's not even one bit grateful for the tip. Like, she says thank you, but she doesn't mean it one bit. And then she says, 'Would you like to hear what Ciara found?' and no no no because then it would be real. Would you like make-up tips, Laura?

But her sneaky brain stuff works; it's like she plants the thought and then you've no choice but to start thinking all the shit she wants you to think about.

I avoided Luke all day Friday and Amy, too, with her questions. But he was waiting for me at the front steps, with one of those big see-through umbrellas. He hooked it over us both, saying nothing. I thought I saw a glimmer of the grin, and he took a breath as if to speak, but I don't know what he was going to say because, next moment, everything went out of my brain like it was wiped. Bam. There he was; Stuart, sitting in his car just outside the school gate, tapping his hands on the wheel, smiling and nodding. I froze.

'You okay? Jesus, Jenny – you've gone white.' Luke turned to see where I was looking. 'That your dad – I mean stepdad?' I nodded. I could have said something. I think that was the time I should have said something? Maybe if I'd said, *Oh God, Luke, help me! I can't get in the car with him because of the stuff he does.* Maybe if I'd said, *No way. Don't let him see me, please. Hide me in this plastic umbrella.* Maybe. But dumb means you can't speak and I couldn't speak — my brain was racing and the words were gone. And dumb means you're dumb shit stupid. And I was both.

All I could think was maybe something bad had happened to Mum, or Karl. Why was he here? Luke was still staring at me — from him to me to him to me.

'What's going on, Jen?'

'Jenny! Thought you could do with a lift!' Stuart yelled, his head stuck out the window, teeth bared like a wolf. 'Hurry up — it's lashing, in case you hadn't noticed.'

The two of us were squished under the ridiculous umbrella. And the only words I could think of were 'oh God oh God'. And Luke began lifting the umbrella up over us both and made as if to walk over to say hi and I panicked and I said, 'Go. Just go.' And he stopped straight away, handed me the umbrella and ducked out into the rain.

'See you Monday,' he said, running off. And I walked slow slow slow to the car and stopped beside it.

'How come you're here?'

'I told you, I thought you'd like a lift,' he said, all innocent and kind. 'Get in.' He said nothing — not one word, for the ten-minute drive. Whump-whump. That was the wipers. Whump-whump. That was my heart. His breath was making a whistling noise. He was breathing fast.

When we got there, I got out of the car quickly and rang the doorbell. I needed to see Mum, even just a glimpse of her, even if she was still in her dressing gown or half asleep — I needed to see her.

But Stuart reached across me and put his key in the lock.

'No point in ringing the bell. She's out.' I actually stopped walking — stunned by this information.

'Yeah, I know – you weren't expecting that, were you? She's with what's-her-name, the chubby one. Viv or Val. They're out.' He flung his keys into the bowl on the hall table and I flinched.

'So,' he said, 'it's just you and me.' And he stood looking at me, weighing something up, breathing very fast.

'It's time,' he said. 'Up you go to your room.'

41. Jenny

Laura is going on on on in her special voice. She drones on and I tune it out. I look up at the tower. I hate it. I hate how you can see it everywhere, from everywhere. I can see it from my bedroom. And their bedroom. It's always there.

He closed the door and locked it. He took a deep breath, which kind of stuttered.

'Pull down the blind. Good girl. We don't want anyone to see you changing now, do we?' And I remember it sounded kind – saying 'good girl' – like he was pleased with me and I actually was a good girl. And I did the zombie sleepwalk like Mum. I did what he told me. I pulled down the blind, turned to face him.

'Stuart, I don't want to –'

He came over to me with his arms out and he was going sssh sssh. There was no shouting, it was best behaviour. He pulled the jumper off over my head, my arms rose up both together, stuck in the jumper, like a little kid's. He pulled me to his chest and it wasn't like the other time because this time I could hear his heart beating wham wham wham.

'Now the rest.'

And I know all the questions. These are the questions. Why didn't I run for the door? Why hadn't I shouted and screamed? Why hadn't I opened the window and yelled to a neighbour? Why hadn't I just shouted, 'No no no'?

And I still don't have answers to those questions because this is what happened.

I took off my skirt, shirt, socks.

'All of it,' he said.

I unhooked my bra and held it against me, watched the stupid tears roll down its peach cotton fabric. And he kept saying shit like 'You're a good girl – it's time. You're doing really well, you're beautiful.' And it was the kindest he'd been to me, ever. And he didn't call me dumb or bitch. I kept my eyes on the carpet, at the shipwreck of my clothes. Dumb, dumb, struck dumb. I said nothing.

And then it was different. Not like the other times – when we could both pretend it was something that wasn't real. Or when I look at the tower and I think about the princess while he is the wolf snuffling at the door.

This is different because it's like he's on a train and it's not going to stop. He's so heavy. He's lying on top of me, snuffling like a walrus. He stinks. There's something bumpy jamming into my spine underneath us – a book – maybe *Trauma* Ninth Edition? His hands are rough and big and sticky with sweat. They keep getting stuck against my skin and they're hurting, squeezing and grabbing. He's snorting in my ear, saying something – I don't know what. I don't want to know. His chin is covered in stubble and it scrapes my cheek, my mouth – burning. I have no breath, no strength.

I think of Sergeant Sharp Steak and the others downstairs in their wooden home. They're all ready and waiting. Reporting for duty, sir. But I can't get them. I can't move. I clamp my teeth and lips shut, and my eyes, too. I try to breathe without letting his horrible breath enter me. His nose is whistling in time to his frantic breathing and he – he tries to put his disgusting tongue, covered in cold slime – he tries to force it into my mouth. He doesn't say dumb bitch. He says, 'Good girl. Good girl. You're doing great' – like he's helping me with my homework. And one giant hand holds my head still and the other hand does the rest.

And I let it.

And – worse. I make the noises that make him hurry up but, all the time, she's screeching in my head – the little owl. I don't know how he can't hear her. Minerva is screeching but the sound stays inside. Dumb bitch princess lies there and now she is me and I am her and it's the worst because she says nothing. She makes ah noises because when she does that he doesn't hurt so much. And her tears fall but they make no sound.

The train smashes over the tracks and off the cliff and there's no going back now. This is how it is. He's the captain and the king and the prince and the bad wolf and he has won. He lies on me like he's tired after the train ride. But he's also smirking. Minerva the owl makes no noise – only blinks.

He gets up and buckles up his belt. Then he checks his reflection. He's humming something – I recognize it. 'Getting Better' – The Beatles. And just like that – in one second – I'm raging, even though it's too late.

'Don't sing that.' He turns around and he actually laughs.

'Jenny, Jenny . . . it's about time you gave up this Daddy obsession, you know? You're a big girl now.' He smooths back his hair, arranges his collar. He turns and smiles a sickly smile at me.

'A very big girl. A very sexy girl. You know exactly what you're doing, don't you? And don't think I didn't notice the boyfriend. You'd want to watch yourself there. It's not right to lead them on.'

And then I'm crying and he comes over to me, sitting huddled in the corner on the bed with the duvet pulled up round me. And, insanely, just for a second, I think he's going to hug and comfort me, tell me I'm great and beautiful and it'll all be okay. I'm sore – raw – stinging and throbbing with a pulsing pain.

'Enough,' he says, and his face is closed. 'Grow up, Jennifer. And face a few facts of life, yeah? One: your dad did not fall off a roof. Poor bastard killed himself. And two: I rescued you and your mum, took care of you and gave you everything. Now get dressed,' he says, as he closes the door. 'And grow up.'

My skirt and jumper are trampled on the floor, bra and pants strewn like rubbish. And then I notice Ringo, my old teddy who I've had since for ever, lying upside down on his head. It looks like he's had a nasty accident. He's fallen from a height. His neck is broken. Wincing, I get off the bed and pick him up. Moving like an old woman, I run the bath, hot hot. From between my legs, the red arrows trail their trails in the water.

Dad's final rooftop concert: #1

It was a bright and chilly January morning with blue sky and a brisk wind chasing over the rooftops. Dad heads out on to the roof armed with his tool kit, singing 'I'm Fixing a Hole' in a chirpy voice. As he drills the metal sign, his foot becomes entangled in the flex and he stumbles, only a small stumble, but enough to tilt his balance and, before you know it, before he is even aware of his mistake, he falls from the roof, down on to the concrete pavement below. He lies there, hardly a mark on him, calmly accepting the weakness which begins to engulf him. His wife and daughter, hearing the crash, run outside and kneel beside him.

'My darlings,' he says hoarsely, though somehow managing to smile, 'don't be sad for me. I didn't feel a thing. You know I'll love you for ever and be with you in spirit for as long as you live, and beyond.'

They nod to show they understand. 'Oh, darling,' and 'I

love you, Dad,' they say. They kiss him, they smile bravely and he just slips away. On the wind, on a radio somewhere, 'Let It Be' is playing.

Dad's final rooftop concert: #2

It was a bitterly cold January morning with sleet and wind flaying the rooftops. Dad, having been up since before dawn, unable to sleep, heads out on to the roof. He's exhausted. He thinks he's ruined everything. He's had enough and he can't see a way through this.

Nobody hears a thing. Nobody hears a thing. In fact, his daughter is still asleep when a neighbour starts banging on the door. The police are outside and she's told to stay indoors. But through the window she sees her mum, sandwiched between two police officers, being brought around to the courtyard at the back. She sees them huddle together around something on the ground. There's a shoe, lying incongruously on its side, all alone on the pavement. She recognizes it. It's Dad's shoe.

An ambulance arrives. Mum and Dad go off in the ambulance. Someone puts her in a car; she meets up with Mum in the hospital. Mum is crying, but it's too late, now. Later – it might be an hour or a day, she can't remember – they sit at Dad's bedside. He has bandages and a cage-type thing holding his head and chest steady. There is only a bit of cheek and nose peeping through, and closed eyes. A machine is making his chest rise and fall. Mum holds his hand. Jenny sits on her lap, though she's too big. She doesn't want to look at Dad. Nobody says anything. There's no music. He dies next day.

'I need to tell you something,' I say, and hahaha, Laura practically leaps out of the seat with fright.

'Go on.'

'My dad had the right idea. He killed himself. He jumped off the roof.'

I'm remembering other things. Sad things. It feels like they're queuing up, but not in order – the memories. Bang bang on the door. Little pig, little pig, let me come in. Where's Mum? 'Go and build your own house,' she said. 'You're on your own.' Bitch.

'Well done, Jenny,' she says, trying to look in my eyes and do the whole eye-contact thing. I close mine. I want to see Dad, the picture of Dad when he was happy, in the yellow submarine. Not the hospital picture when his mouth was open like a yawn with a plastic tube dragging down the side.

'It takes courage to accept something like that,' she says, but I'm not listening. Where's Mum? Why won't she tell me? It's been long enough now. Other pictures try to squash in on top of the submarine. Broken glass, and Mum slumped over like she's been shot. Her blonde hair is glittering with fragments of glass and what look like rose petals, but they're not rose petals, they're blobs of blood.

It's like a movie, but no way do I want to see the next bit and so I scrunch my eyes. But it doesn't work; the next scene comes anyway, and it's Karl. Little Karl curled up like Mousie, on the floor at Mum's feet. Why's Karl on the floor? Why am I seeing this picture? I'm remembering things, but they're like nightmare thoughts – I don't know if I really saw them. We were in the car. He was yelling. The knife was in my hand. No no no no I didn't do it. I wouldn't hurt them.

Would I?

42. Laura

The scream she emits is ear-splitting, shocking. In the confined space of the car, it bounces off the glass and metal and blasts into my skull, making it vibrate with the pressure. I jolt in fright, try to put my arm around her, calling her name, but there's no time; in a frenzied movement, she tugs the handle of the door and she's out of the car, running. The door lock must have released when I cut the engine. Shit!

Shit shit shit! I scrabble around, trying to get out. The belt of my coat catches in the door and I'm jerked backwards. It takes me another crucial second to open the door and release the belt and then I'm sprinting after her, through the stone gate and towards the tower. I'm cursing the wind, because I can't hear her footsteps over the freezing blasts shaking the trees and I don't know which way she went. The tower looms overhead, tapering towards the top, threatening and bleak. To the left, there's the high wall – overgrown with a thorny-looking hedge, so I head around the right-hand side of the tower, which leads me unerringly to – a dead end.

I double back, calling her, shrieking over the wind. My mind is somersaulting with the stupidity of what I've done. She's no coat, no phone, no money, nothing. Christ! She doesn't even have proper shoes. She's vulnerable and ill and I've put her in danger. Now I'm screaming, too. I bang on the door of the house beside the tower and, after what seems like ten minutes, an elderly man opens.

'I'm looking for a girl, a teenage girl – did she come

through here? Do you have a back garden or –' I whirl around wildly, trying to make sense of the geography of the place. His garden wall appears to join on to the tower wall, and both are covered in thick hedge.

'Can you get into the tower from here?'

The man is frowning, a step away from scratching his chin in a parody of 'bemused local'. His cardigan is buttoned up wrongly over what seems to be a vest, both straining over his large pot belly and, strangely, I'm worried about him getting cold. There seems to be a lot of exposed elderly flesh.

'You can't get into the tower through here, no.' He steps out of the doorway and closes the door over it. 'See there?' He points towards the corner wall. 'If you could get over that wall – not that you can, you hear me? But if you could get over it, you'd be in my back garden. And then there's another wall which, if you could get over that one – then you'd be on the golf course.'

He waves expansively: 'All of that back there, it's the golf course. It's huge.' He cocks his head to one side and grins. 'Have you an escaped golfer, heh heh?'

I don't laugh and the grin fades. He takes a step back and looks at me. I remember that I'm not in uniform; I must seem completely raving mad.

'Who is it you're looking for? Is it your daughter? Did ye have an argument or something?'

'No, she's not my daughter. She's –' I feel in my pocket, trying to find my ID. I haven't time for this. 'I'm a guard. The girl's a witness.'

'Oh right.' He turns and heads back inside, gesturing for me to follow. 'Come on in, so, and we'll check out the back.' We go into the house and are hit by a blast of warm air; the heating must be on max. Now I understand the vest.

'I'm just showing a ban-gharda the back garden,' he shouts into the front room as we pass through the hall. 'She has a missing witness.'

He turns to me. 'Herself,' he says.

Three steps lead from the kitchen into the walled back garden, which is L-shaped and surrounded by the same high wall, with only marginally less hedge growth. It's dusk and, standing in the middle of the garden, I do a full turn, searching.

'Sure she couldn't have got in here anyway,' he says. 'It's walled all the way round.'

'And your front door was closed? There's no other way into the back?'

He shakes his head. 'Not unless she can fly,' he says. We both survey the large space. It's not possible that she could have come through here. I've got it wrong.

'Thanks for your help,' I say, handing him my card. 'Ring me if you see anything, please. Anything at all.'

We go back through the house and he opens the front door for me.

'Good luck,' he says. 'I hope you find her.' I nod my thanks, sick at the thought of what I've done, how I've fucked up.

I race to the car; jump in, start the ignition, like a cop in some eighties cop show, and then it's as if I've been punched in the gut, literally. I exhale and slump over the steering wheel. What the hell have I done and where do I go now? She could be anywhere. Where would she go? I wish to God Niamh was here, but at the same time thank Christ she doesn't know – yet. If I can find Jenny and get her back to the hospital – I check the time; it's nearly quarter past five. Christ! What am I even thinking of? I have to find her first.

'Dad had the right idea,' she'd said. Oh God! What if she's going to try something like that?

Think, Laura! Come on! You got the Commissioner's fucking Medal, that's got to count for something. That means you've got a brain in there somewhere: come on, come on! There's a lump in my throat and I can feel the tears starting. Self-pitying, pathetic thoughts begin pressing in; about how fucking stupid I've been; how dangerous this is for Jenny; how I'm about to throw my career out the fucking window; about Mum; about how disappointed Matt will be when he hears. And when Cig finds out what I've done – I could lose my job. I *will* lose my job. And it'll be all over the media; another cock-up, another kicking for the Gardaí.

And worse, worse: what if I don't find her at all? What if that's it? She's run off, she goes missing? There were nine thousand people reported missing in Ireland last year alone. Or what if she's found dead and – oh my God, it will be my fault and mine alone. I was supposed to help her, but I've ruined everything. I feel like I'm about to throw up.

I take a breath, trying to focus, to remember my training; the scenarios we role-played in college. We'd be in groups of four and we'd have to act out a scenario – you're called to the scene of a crime and you've to take details, try to find out what happened, come up with a plan of how to proceed. I was always great at the strategy – I excelled at that part. Come on, Laura, what's the plan?

I know the missing-person procedure all right. The only problem is that I know it from the point of view of the guard. And right now I don't feel like a guard, I feel like the panicked mother. I've lost her. It was my job to keep her safe and I've failed her. With tears free-flowing now, I put the car in gear and start driving. I'll start at the beginning, I think, I'll go to her house.

43. Jenny

I'm running, running. It makes the screaming stop and it makes the picture go away. The picture is all wrong; the one where Mum has blood on her cheek and on her face and neck. It's dripping blobbing on to her shoulder on her good jacket – the pale pink one. In my head I can hear the wind screaming now. It's screaming *what have you done?* I'm going to keep running. I'm going to run home and then I'll know the picture is wrong. I just need to see Mum. I need to see them so badly. I didn't, I couldn't – didn't – wouldn't – haven't hurt them. I love her. I don't think she's a dumb bitch Princess Piss-on-me. But why can't I remember them – when I saw them last? Why can't I see it?

I'm sprinting past the shop and Charlie is yelling, 'Come here! Come here, love!' and people are looking at me weird. The lights around the plants bob and it should be happy but my heart is bursting.

And I turn and look back in case Laura and Niamh are following, in case there's a squad car nee-nawing its way, but there's not. It's not. I pass the arch but it's empty and no-body from school is on the footbridge. School's over anyway. It's nearly dark now. And then I'm running up the hill and it's the corner of our road and I'm hoping the stove is lit because that's what we'll do tonight. Mum and Karl and me. We'll sit in by the stove. I'm nearly there, so nearly there I actually slow down because you can – when you're nearly there.

Slowly, slowly I walk up the path to our house. Stuart's car isn't there, that's good. No lights are on, though. And I'm getting scared.

Then I see the shiny tape like the one you see on the news. It says 'NO ENTRY GARDA NO ENTRY GARDA'. It's across the front part and a ripped piece of it flutters at the side gate. I step over it and my heart is whamming inside my chest. I ring the doorbell and I can hear it from inside, like a ghost doorbell. If Mum was in bed, though, it'd take her some time to get up. I ring it two more times. Sometimes if Karl is in there on his own he peeps out the front-room window before he goes to get Mum. I look for him. He's not there.

I don't care about NO ENTRY GARDA, I open the side gate and run around to the back door. It's locked and it's all dark and now my heartbeat is like electric techno. This is wrong this will let the picture back in my brain. The one with the blood. And I'm freezing because I stopped running and I want to go in but, anyway, the stove is not lit and nobody's home.

And then I nearly laugh because of course of course! They're on the island! Now that it's safe and the prince is dead, Mum and Karl and Socks will be on the island all together, waiting for me. They're probably fed up waiting for me.

I turn around. I can go across the gardens at the back – get there even quicker. I run and now my heart is beating and it's happy beating. I'm going to see them soon.

And that lasted for a while, the happy heart beating. I change the running to a jog and I even say hi to Charlie. And he doesn't say, *How's tricks?*, he says, 'How are you, darling? I haven't seen you for ages.' But I don't stop. I can't wait to see them. Now it's all fixed and happy ever after.

He deserved it. It's the same in all the stories. You don't care if bad things happen to bad people. They deserve it.

I think back to the night before the party. Yesterday? No,

I was with Laura yesterday. It must have been before. It was the day he got me from school. That day. That day. Mum and Val had been shopping and Mum was smiling and even humming when she came back and she'd brought a pizza. And she asked him if she could get her hair done for the party, like he's King of the Universe and King of Hair, too.

And he goes, 'Oh yes, of course. You can meet us at the party, I'll bring the kids up. Wear the blue dress.' And she nods because she was still Princess Piss-on-me then, or that's what I thought.

'And Jennifer should wear something nice, too – now she's a young lady.' He smirked, folding a triangle of pizza over and shovelling it into his mouth. 'I bought her a new outfit. It's in the car.'

And I knew what it would be like. I could almost feel the seams pressing under my armpits already, because I knew that whatever he got would be tight on my chest and it'd be a skirt or a dress and it'd be short – and he'll look at me and tell me where to stand and what to do and – and I stared at him and that's when I saw his tongue, glistening in slime and pieces of food, quivering like a live animal in a cave. My stomach heaved and I lurched from the kitchen into the downstairs bathroom. The slice of pizza I'd been trying to force down exploded into the toilet bowl. Mum came in, held my hair, patted my forehead.

'I hope you'll be okay for the party, Jen,' she said. 'I've a surprise for you.' She stroked my back.

And I think – *I have a surprise for you, Mum.* And for him. I will wear his outfit because this is the last time. The squad is ready. Knife Squadron good to go. I will put Sergeant Sharp Steak under my pillow tonight – hah. And tomorrow, he will go in my pocket. Only Private Pizza on duty tonight and he only cuts pizza.

I'm nearly at Mrs A's house now and I'm hungry and cold. I can feel the happy heartbeats fading hurry hurry. I can't wait to get to the island.

He drove me and Karl to the party with him and he didn't even care if Karl could see or that it was daylight and other people in cars could see, too. He made me sit in the front and I was wearing the dumb bitch dress and the princess pants and my legs were bare. He rubbed his hand along my thigh like he was checking a side of meat, squeezing and pressing. I'd forgotten this bit – how smug he was. How it was like everything was perfect in his kingdom.

And it was the same at the party. He worked the room. Plant large grin on face – check. Hold hand of sweet little boy – check. Place arm around shoulders of charming stepdaughter – check. We were hauled through a sea of noisy people and all the time he laughed his loud laugh at nothing. Be seen laughing – check.

And boss Tony was all smiling and asking, 'Where's Melanie?' And Stu was saying stuff like 'You know women, har har har, getting her hair done or something.' And he's like a kids' TV presenter, all teeth and laughing, happy. Fake fake fake.

Then Mum arrived, but when I say Mum, I mean I knew it was Mum, but she looked completely and totally different – she looked amazing. She'd new clothes – jeans and boots and a silvery top with a pink jacket – she wasn't wearing the blue dress he'd told her to wear. My heart started pounding at that.

But it wasn't just the clothes; it was her hair. She'd cut it off – pretty much all of it. It was almost as short as Karl's – chopped, chopped.

I saw a movie once where the baddie was turned into ice. It started with his feet and then flowed upwards – knees, body, shoulders, head – until he became an ice statue. This was Stuart. He stared a cold, hard stare at her, like he could destroy her with his ice rays, and then he was beside her, grasping her elbow, hissing in her ear:

'What the hell have you done?'

Mum's hopeful smile vanished, blasted by the icy wind.

And boss Tony said, 'You look wonderful. You're a lucky man, Stuart,' and everyone was crowding around. Not good. Not good.

'Indeed I am, har har har,' Stuart said, but his eyes were chips of ice. And still everyone was gathering round, and then one of the women said, 'Melanie, do you remember when he rescued you after you fell, that time? When he carried you all the way up to the clubhouse?'

And her friend joined in: 'We were so impressed! Oh for a man like that!' and they're all laughing and Mum was scaffolding her smile in place, though the edges were slipping.

'You didn't hurt yourself that time, did you?'

Mum was all ready with the 'no no, I was absolutely fine' answer, I could see it, nearly on the tip of her tongue. But then Karl spoke.

'Dad was really angry. He said we were useless and Mum's eye was all black an' purple.'

Nobody said anything. The whole room was filled up with all the nothings people were saying.

'What? Oh yes! That's right, your mother had banged her face when she fell – and I wasn't there to catch her. Useless! Oh well,' he said, walking back to Mum and grabbing her shoulders. 'Like I said, it's all worth it. Anything for my princess.'

I moved closer to Mum; she was trembling. I put my hand in my pocket to check. Sergeant Sharp Steak. He's there. I can do this, I thought. Yes, I can. Oh yes, I can. But not here – later later. My hands were shaking, too, but I knew I could take care of that, too.

Your neck is full of veins and arteries, like railway tracks, like the Underground. And all the blood pumps through them, swishing and swooshing along. The heart keeps beating, keeps pumping the blood around your body, into your face and your brain – your hands and your legs and your feet. Round and round. The blood pumps and it helps you use your muscles so that you can move. You could run or jump. You could draw or dance or play music. Or you could stretch your fingers out to hold someone's face close and gently, gently, you could press your warm lips to theirs.

You could smooth a little boy's blond hair out of his eyes, away from the sticky blood. You could hold someone's hand and feel the blood pulse in the teeny-tiny blue wrist veins. And if you press your head against someone's chest, you can hear their heartbeat; boom boom-boom – faster, faster.

The blood pumps into your muscles and the muscles move your bones around – wherever you want them to go. If you want to make a fist, you squeeze the fingers tight, and a fist can smash into faces or ears or shoulders or soft bellies and it mashes everything up. You can press and squeeze and hold and hurt. You can tear and stamp and kick and knee and yes, you can bite.

And if you take a sharp sharp knife and make a cut in the vein – the one in the neck, I can tell you where, because I looked it up. If you make that cut, the blood spills out. It flows, spills, tumbles and rolls. Then it trickles and pulses and softer pulses you can hardly see – and then it stops.

And I knew then that I could do it and that I had to do it. I knew he'd drag us home now – before anyone said anything. I knew he'd get us into the house and lock the door. And once he'd got Mum and Karl out of the way, it'd be my turn. But this time, I would be ready.

I'm nearly there. I want to see the princess. I remember

how happy she was and her bony little shoulders as she hugged me, and the tears shining in her eyes, happy tears. And at her feet, the prince is dead. He wears a crown of ruby red and it's a shining sticky halo about his head. We step over him and we pick up Mousie and Minerva and they're not dead. Happy Ever After. That's what happened. That's what happened.

And I sit down beside the gate, hidden in the trees. Because maybe that's better. Maybe I need to wait a minute. I'm scared to see them in case it's the – the picture with the blood and Mum's head hanging down. I don't want to see that picture. I try to squeeze a new picture into my brain, with brain muscles. I can think in pictures. I like to do that, like John Lennon. He went to art college. Dad said you could always tell which of them had written the lyrics. Paul's told you a story but John's painted pictures.

Show me them, show them to me. But only a piece of picture – a particle comes into my brain. It's the bad picture. It's the side of Mum's face. Her head's bent. It's hanging down. Maybe she's just checking her nail varnish. I can't see Karl at all. Why am I seeing this picture? What have I done?

44. Laura

I've always liked this road – it's orderly. The houses are set back with cherry-tree sentries posted outside every second gate. Green recycling bins are lined up – it must be collection today – and everything about the street: the precise, square front gardens, the neatly pruned trees, the bins set with their handles conveniently facing outwards; everything suggests a calm, ordered state – contrasting starkly with my rising tide of panic.

As I pull up outside the house, the wind picks up and a lone plastic bottle sambas across the road, getting caught under the gate. The tech team were here the other day, and it's still sealed off. I walk up the path to the front door and ring the bell. Nothing. I try calling her name, shouting in through the letterbox, but the emptiness is total. The house is in darkness. I run around to the back door and rattle the handle, but of course it's locked. She's not here, Laura. She's run off and she's not here and it's all your fault – you stupid bitch, Laura. My phone rings. It's Niamh.

'Where the hell are you?'

'What do you mean?' I say, trying to delay her. 'You told me to go home for an hour or two. You told me to have a rest.'

'I mean, where the hell are you, Laura, and where the hell is Jenny and why the fuck is she not in the ward? What is going on? What the hell?' Her voice rises higher on each question.

'Look – it's not as bad as it sounds, okay, Niamh? She's –'

I stop, swallow and try to breathe. 'I was taking her to the tower. I thought she'd show me, I thought she'd tell me everything.'

Niamh says something I don't catch and I hear a male voice. There's a lot of clattering noise and some fake laughter from Niamh. Then she's on the line again.

'So that's Dr Connolly looking for her. She's late for her session. And the Cig – Cig is expecting me to bring her in for questioning after that.' She pauses to draw breath and, possibly, find a better location from which to yell at me. 'You brought her to the tower? As in, you took her out of the hospital without permission from anybody? Are you kidding me? Tusla has been on. They want to set up a meeting. If they get wind of this – Jesus! And, meanwhile, I'm standing here, lying my tits off and making jokes about you having brought her to the canteen, and all the time, all this time, you are undermining everything! You are out of line, Laura – you're so out of line you're in outer fucking space. Get her back here right now! Are you out of your mind?'

'I know, I know,' I gabble, 'I'm so sorry. It was dumb, I know. It was really dumb. I'll come back now – we'll come now, okay?' My nails are digging into the phone, I'm clutching it so hard. 'Please, just give me half an hour. Can you cover for half an hour? Thanks, Niamh, thanks. I mean it.'

I hang up before she can say no, or yell anything else. Shit shit shit.

I have to find her. I race back to the car and make a U-turn. They found her at Ely's Arch on Sunday night. Maybe she headed there.

The arch was once an entrance to Rathfarnham Castle's estate. Now, there's a main road and a whole load of houses separating the classical structure from the castle itself; it stands all alone on a patch of grass by the river. We were always told that it was built to celebrate the return of the Earl of Ely's son to the castle and, as a kid, I'd mixed it up with the Bible story of the prodigal son. I imagined the carriage trundling through the gate and the joyous parents waving and calling – she holding up her long skirts so she can run the quarter-mile to meet the carriage and he sprinting towards the gate, clutching a bottle of champagne. It appears completely random now, an unused piece of Lego far away from the main building.

There's no sign of her, but I turn and pull in across the road from the arch, parking on the footpath beside the bridge. It brings me back with a swerve of memory; we all used to cut through here after school. You could save yourself easily a mile and a half of walking if you cut down past the hockey pitches, over the gate and into the park. I get out of the car and head across the bridge, calling her, listening out for voices or the thwacks and yells of a hockey match in progress, but there's only the sleet-soaked wind. What the hell am I going to do if I can't find her? Niamh has reached the end of her rope – there's no way I can expect her to cover for me any longer.

Think, Laura. She can't have gone that far – not on foot. She's not at home, not at the arch. I think back to people she talked about, her friends Amy and Luke. Or maybe the child-minder, Val. I could call the incident room and get information on them – addresses and phone numbers – but I can't call the incident room because I'm off the grid and the Super or Cig will bloody kill me. And maybe, just maybe, Niamh will keep covering. Think. Think.

The first thing – her first communication with me, before she even spoke – was the picture of the tower. There's got to be more – there's something else about the picture, I'm sure of it.

She drew the tower first, then the sea. And then – then she drew a border of dark green leaves. She framed her entire picture in long, swirling swathes of leaves; she spent ages doing them. Each swirl had myriad swirls following the same trajectory. I hadn't paid any attention to it; I just thought she was enjoying the penmanship – almost like a handwriting exercise. She'd done a similar thing with the waves. But the picture – I rack my brain, trying to conjure it up, cursing myself for not taking a photo of it on my phone. In the picture, there's the tower in the middle of the waves, surrounded by a heavy hedge of overgrown foliage, forming a thick green arch.

I've seen that arch. There's a bungalow on Whiteash Avenue where the trees are so thick and the hedge so dense that they form a walled green archway over the gate. It's literally minutes away. I sprint back to the car and start the engine.

45. Niamh

Dr Connolly has followed me through the swing doors into the corridor. I hope to Christ he didn't hear the end of that. His frown deepens the closer he gets. I ram the mobile into my bag and head him off, stepping into his personal space. It works. The good doctor takes a fumbling step backwards.

'Communication problems!' I smile. 'Sure isn't that the way of it always?'

The edge of the frown lifts as he tries to smile. Bless him.

I thought I was picking her up, but my colleague is one step ahead of me.'

I look at my watch. 'So sorry about this, Doctor. We didn't mean to clash with you.'

I begin to turn away, taking advantage of his confusion. 'I'll bring her back soon – I'll go and pick her up.'

'Okay,' he says, uncertainly. 'Well –'

'Any word from ICU how her mam is?'

He shakes his head. 'No – I mean – no change. No further updates.'

'Lord have mercy on her, it's a tough one.'

Too much, maybe? But it works. He gives a nod of dismissal.

'Can you get them to page me when she's back?'

'Will do, Doctor.'

In the hospital's underground car park, I dither. Do I go back to face Cig's wrath without Laura, without our witness, or do I go and try to find them? I didn't like the sound of her – she's up to high doh. Maybe I could get them to check her location – all the station cars have trackers on them – but that'll blow the whole thing.

I drive up the ramp, through the barrier, then sit with the handbrake on, trying to decide. Left takes me towards Clonchapel. I could drive there and ring her to find where she is, or just look out for the car. If I go right, I'm heading back to the station to try and buy Laura more time. I'll get yelled at – but it won't kill me.

The guy behind me starts beeping – prick! I find myself very tempted to get out, show him the badge and yell at his sorry ass. I don't. Come on – come on! Decide! I head to where the ball is in play. I turn left.

46. Jenny

I can't stop shivering. It's so cold. All the time before – in the hospital, when Laura was saying 'You're in charge' and 'You're the boss here.' Well, it's a lie. I'm not in charge. It's like one day I woke up to find myself in the middle of this shitty story where bad stuff happens and keeps on happening and I go to school or home or the shops or wherever but always always and always it's like I'm on a path that I didn't choose – a path that loops back to where I started so that it's never-ending. And it's not just me – it's Karl and Mum, too. There was one time, only one time in my life, I was in charge. It was when I had Sergeant Sharp Steak from the Knife Squad reporting for duty.

We never got back to the house. I remember that now. In the front seat of the car, Mum hung her head in defeat or shame, or something. He was giving out, saying stuff like 'You're not fit for anything' and 'What did you do to your hair? You're a disgrace.' He reached over and grabbed her knee, pressed and squeezed. His knuckles whitened and Mum whined her princess whine and Karl started whining, too. Then Karl took off his seatbelt and started clambering into the front with her, whimpering, 'Mummy, Mummy' and stuff.

And my heart begins thumping and I lean forward in the seat, tilting sideways so I can reach Sergeant Sharp Steak and ease him out of my pocket. I hold him snug as a bug in the palm of my hand. I could do it now. I'm sitting right behind his head. I could stab and cut under the jawline – vena cava, carotid artery, jugular. Or I could ram it into his ear. But I wouldn't do that – I want the carotid artery or the jugular – to be certain.

And anyway, he's driving the car and Mum is crying and stroking Karl and we're on our way home. Home sweet home. We're near Mrs A's and the island. And that gives me strength. I can wait – not long now. In a minute in a minute when we take the turn and we go over the ramp to the quiet bit where nobody can see. That's when I'll do it.

And Stuart keeps driving and we take the turn and Karl keeps crying and we go over the ramp and Mum is going, 'Ssh, love, it's okay, it'll all be fine,' and wham-wham in my throat I feel my own blood booming and it will be fine. It will be fine because I will do it. Do it do it.

And I'm so close behind his seat I can smell his smell and the knife is slick like it wants to slide out of my hand, but no way. I bring it around the seat and it sneaks like a sneaky snake beside his shoulder and then – no! He locks eyes with me in the mirror and he turns his head and he's like 'What the fuck' and then 'No' and 'No!' Then I see a smudge of a blur of a something which looks like a dog on the road in front of us. The smudge is the same colour as Socks and the car's going fast and his head turns back and he's like whoa! And the car swerves. But the swerve isn't wide enough and the car hits the blur which is actually Socks – not a blur. And then there's a skid.

And then there's a sliding which turns into a smashing into the parked cars on the passenger side of the car, Mum and Karl's side. And I'm thrown forwards and it hurts my neck. Then the seatbelt hauls me back, roughly, like it's angry. Sergeant Sharp Steak has bounced out of my hand to the floor. And then it's quiet except for ticking metal.

I don't want to see this picture, but this is what I see:

Mum's head is slumped forward and it hangs down on to her chest. There's a big pole and it's smashed through the window and it's at her neck, like – like, right in her neck and it's killed her maybe. Her eyes are closed. She looks like she's checking her nail varnish. Except there's way too much blood. It's on her cheek, rolling down and dripping down her neck. A lot of it is on the airbag, too. Karl is crumpled half on her lap and his head is on one side. He's a bit underneath the airbag, like we were having a pillow fight. His eyes are closed. Maybe he's just sleeping on her lap. There's some blood near his ear and his hair is all messed up. I want to smooth it back. I remember now. I think they're dead.

Now now now I remember! I remember what happened and now a banshee's wail – a long moan of pain – sweeps upwards and outwards out of my body. I feel hot and sick and I feel the tears river-rolling down my cheeks. I scramble further back into the bushes, backwards like a crab, until I can't go any further. Then I turn my body over and lie, face down flat bury me, I don't care, on the damp ground. I press the howl into the earth and I don't care that grass and dirt and leaves are in my mouth. Mum is dead and little Mousie Karl. I remember now. And bitch Laura and bitch Niamh dumb bitches they didn't tell me. They're dead. They're all dead.

47. Laura

A slanting, sideways sleet slaps across the windscreen as I turn on to Whiteash Avenue, having waited for three light sequences. The wipers judder, struggling to clear the flood before the next batch is flung. I'm trying to calm down, but it's taking all my resources not to stop dead, leap out of the car and stand there screaming her name. Breathe and think. But I can't – I'm panting. She'll be here – she's got to be here. I pull up outside the house. She'll be here and she'll come back to the hospital and it will all be fine.

I get out of the car and look up at the gate. This is it. This is exactly what she drew as a frame for her picture. It's basically an archway made of trees where the foliage has been shaped to make a thick wall, almost like a castle. It's a couple of feet thick and it runs the whole way around the perimeter. The house is down a short path, completely dwarfed by the giant trees. It seems to cower. In the centre of the arch is a small, rusted gate, now swinging open in the wind.

I hurry through the entrance gate – running. Inside, it's quieter; the wind and sleet lessened by the shelter of the tree wall.

'Jenny? Jenny?' I'm yelling, looking all around for any sign of her. The only reply is the wind howling through the creaking wooden wall of trees.

The house is from another era, a single-storey building with a steep, slated roof and tall chimney, like the gate lodge of a grand mansion. On the western side of it, someone has tacked on an old-style conservatory, densely packed with overgrown plants, visible even in the gathering darkness. I approach the front door, noticing the side panels of stained glass just about held in place by rotted wooden strips. Tattered flakes of paint come away from the wood when I press the doorbell.

There's no sound. I knock, dislodging another shower of paint flakes. I try the door. It's locked. Uniform will have done house to house here, I'm pretty sure of it. It's very near to where the car was found. All the same, it's strangely quiet. There's a feeling of everything being untouched – like I've stepped back in time.

'Hello? Anyone home?'

I try to sound rational – positive even. I try to sound like I expect an answer. It's so dark – Jesus! Did I remember my torch? It's in the pocket of my jacket. Thank Christ. I breathe a sigh of relief and switch it on, but even its strong beam reveals nothing much through the glass. An empty hallway with a nest of post gathering on the rug.

A gust of wind penetrates the tree cover. Carried on it, like a code, is a distinctive smell. Something is dead.

'Hello?' I shout, as though now, with the addition of a smell, now I'll get some answers. Yeah, Laura, new information. The smell of death. It's coming from the left-hand side of the house, where the conservatory is. A chilly gust of wind wafts a fresh dose across my face. I follow it.

Some of my friends think that I see dead bodies all the time in my line of work, like I'm in some kind of Scandi noir drama. And I sort of let them think that – it's easier. I was one of the first on the scene when Larry O'Shea was gunned down. I've seen road deaths on the M50 and on back roads in Wicklow. I've brought people in to identify a body – done the whole 'lift the sheet off the face thing' countless times. It's not glamorous. Death is death. Same in Tallaght, Clonchapel, Dalkey or Killiney. People are snatched, stolen, ripped from their lives by blood clots and heart attacks, car crashes and farm accidents, holiday mishaps, brain haemorrhages and deep vein thromboses. People are stabbed and shot, strangled, suffocated, hacked or beaten to a pulp. It happens anywhere – everywhere: in cars, in living rooms and kitchens, parks and bathrooms, airports and bedrooms. Others are taken by stealth, inch by inch, like a slow rewind. They're nibbled and gnawed by disease in bite-sized pieces like the old Pac-Man game until – chomp – they're gone too. And still others are hell bent on doing it themselves, despairing or deluded, or just tired. They take control of the reins, calling time.

Mostly, I work with the living. I deal with living victims. TV detectives get the dead to talk, but it's my job to give a voice to the living as well. I swallow in apprehension, trying not to think what I might be about to find.

I trek through the long grass, my trousers getting more and more soaked. It's clear nobody has cut the grass or cleared any vegetation in a long time. There's a covered side passage leading into the conservatory. This is where the smell is strongest, this is where it's coming from. In spite of myself, I slow down. My hand goes to my phone – I should call this in. I don't know what I'm going to find, but it's not going to be good; I should definitely call for back-up.

And that's when I see I've five missed calls from Matt and a text.

Where are you? You meant to be home for 5.30? M

I stare at the message. Katie. Shit! The text came in at 17.38. I check the time – how did I forget to keep an eye on the time? It's nearly six. What? Panicked thoughts scramble over each other in my brain and I feel myself sweating – a wave of panicked heat. I forget Jenny and think only of Katie and me not being there for her. I'm bolted to the spot.

48. Niamh

As I approach the Dodder, my phone rings. I pull in, reasoning that if it's going to be Cig or the Super yelling at me, I'd better be off road. Plus, if I've to turn around and go back, it'll be easier to do it from the layby near the bridge, rather than any further along the road. I don't recognize the number – but the voice is familiar.

'Niamh? Is that you?'

'Yeah – sorry – who –?'

'It's Matt. Is Laura with you? She's not answering her phone.'

'No – she's out on a – well, actually, I'm on my way to meet up with her now.'

'Oh – but that's odd – are you heading to our place?'

'Now you're losing me entirely, man! Why would I be heading to your place?'

'She was meant to get home for Katie at half five – and you know how she is. She didn't show up, so Sylvia brought her with her – Katie, I mean. Like, that's not a problem, but for Laura –'

This is all being delivered at warp speed – so unlike Matt's usual quiet, laid-back manner.

'I spoke to her about an hour ago and she – well –'

I stop, realizing I'm about to tell him that his wife is AWOL with an unstable girl who may or may not have murdered her stepfather. But it turns out Matt's fears are worse than mine.

'Jesus! Where is she? What did she say? Where was she

331

when you spoke? I've been ringing and ringing and I'm meant to be in a meeting. I told them I had to step out for five minutes, but –' He stops and attempts to calm himself.

'What was she like when she spoke to you? I'm worried, Niamh. Really. She's not herself at the moment – she's really low. And the fact that she didn't get back for Katie – you've no idea – that's so unlike her. Especially as it means Sylvia will have to bring Katie in her car. You know she won't let anyone else put the child in their car?'

'I didn't know that, no –'

'She's completely irrational about it. We've had two years of it now – Katie can only go with us. She doesn't trust anyone else. Jesus!' He pauses for a second. 'She said she's going to *sort it out* – I've just remembered,' he blurts, his voice cracking. 'You don't think she'd do anything –'

'No! God, no!' I soothe. 'She's just stressed and stuff – she –' I break off, realizing that, in fairness, he's right to be worried. I'm worried. I didn't know that about the car. But I've been watching the obsessive counting, wiping, ordering, and it's like she's somewhere else half the time – or she's acting, that's what it is. It's like she's trying to pass herself off as what she used to be. And the pressure she puts on herself – Christ!

'Look – there's no point in both of us being on the phone when I could be out looking for her. She said something about the tower – she was checking something out. I'll head there. You go back – you said you had a meeting, yeah? Go back to your meeting. I'm nearly in Clonchapel, which is where she was when she rang. I have your number – I'll call you back when I find her.'

He hangs up. I try her number – just in case it's only Matt she's not answering. It goes straight to voicemail.

'Laura – it's me. Ring me, will ya? It's gonna be grand – sorry

I yelled earlier. I'm on my way to you now – I'll be there in a tick. Call me.'

I pull out on to the road and drive along the river towards Clonchapel, planning on heading to the tower, hoping to Christ that's where she'll be. And then a random, unsettling thought pings into my brain: Laura carries a personal-issue firearm – hers is a Sig.

49. Laura

I'm sprinting towards the front gate in full crazed-Mummy mode, like I've got to rescue Katie from certain death. My heart is pumping – it's somewhere in my throat. And then – and then I stop dead in my tracks. What the hell am I doing? There's no way I can leave here – not when I still haven't found Jenny and I've left Niamh covering for me and – and there's something rotten and dead a few feet away from me, behind that side door.

I stand in the middle of the overgrown garden, chest pounding. If I was on a battlefield, I don't think it could be hammering any faster. Images come flooding into my brain: Katie crying, toddling across a busy road, arms outstretched; Katie on her own in the house because Sylvia left and there's a fire in the kitchen and the smoke is snaking its way under the door of Katie's bedroom; Katie in Sylvia's car, not strapped in properly because Sylvia's never used the car seat, Katie screaming because she's never been in any other car except mine or Matt's and she presses the door handle and the door bursts open as Sylvia speeds up the motorway and Katie tumbles out into the path of an oncoming truck.

I'm panting – shallow little breaths. My vision blurs. I grab hold of my head with both hands and squeeze, like I'm trying to annihilate the images. Think! Think! What can I do?

Willing myself not to slide into full-blown panic, I dial Sylvia's number. There's no reply. She always turns it off when she's driving. So she's not driving. Breathe, I tell myself. Breathe. Sylvia is in charge. Sylvia will just take her with her in the car. It can't be helped. You're not there. So what? You've messed up, but nothing bad is going to happen. I keep saying it, willing myself to believe it. Nothing bad is going to happen. It's shit but *it's gonna be grand*, Niamh's words.

It takes physical effort to make myself turn away from the gate and back towards the house. There's a narrow door leading to the side passage and, behind that, the conservatory. It isn't locked. It creaks as I push it inwards and then bangs against the wall of the house, startling me. I use the torch to sweep along the length of the narrow lean-to. There's an old bicycle with a wicker basket and a sagging rusty chain propped against the wall, blocking the door at the far end. To the left, open shelves hold flowerpots and trays for cuttings, secateurs and trowels – gardening equipment from a bygone era.

The smell of decay is all around, hanging in the air – ripe and rotten. It's here – right here. I press my hand across my nose and mouth, trying not to breathe. There's a shadow at the end of the lean-to, near the bike. I can't see, I can't make it out with only the light from my phone, but I just know for certain that this is something that was once alive. And now it's dead.

50. Jenny

I see Laura, but she can't see me. She's running around and she has no Niamh with her. Bitch. Dumb bitch. She's smaller when Niamh's not there – and sadder. Dumb dumb dumb. She's nosing all around and she rang Mrs A's bell but no no she's not there. Even though she can't see me, I move back into the dark green wall. Further back into history. His story. Once upon a time there was a poor little princess who had no friends and no money. She was locked in a tower and she didn't know how to escape. Every night and any time he liked, the prince beat and hurt her. He took whatever he liked whenever he liked. And the princess did nothing to save herself and she did nothing to save Minerva and Mousie, her pets – dumb bitch. The prince hated them, too, and he hurt them.

But one night, Minerva got her chance. When the prince came stumbling into the tower, expecting to find the princess, instead he found Minerva. She pecked out his eyes so he couldn't see. Then she pecked a hole in his chest to let the evil blood spill out of him. Minerva killed him and freed the princess. And they lived happily ever after.

That's not right. One night the prince got angrier than he'd ever been before in his whole life. He smashed everything and he left the princess and Mousie and Minerva lying smushed on the floor, covered in blood. And it was going to be the end. But Minerva was like the phoenix rising from the ashes, rising out of her own dead feathers. Up she flew, getting bigger and bigger, her giant black wings blocking out the sun. Now she is the Morrigan, bringer of death and destruction. Goddess of war.

I remember now and it floats the memory on wings. Into my brain.

In the car, after the crash, it's so quiet; the only sound is the ticking metal. It's dark and it's snowing. A few flakes. They float down and down. It's like I'm the only person alive in the whole world or maybe I'm dead and this is after. I look at my hand. There's blood on my fingertips from where I stroked Karl's hair. I can't look at Mum or my heart will shatter. I don't look at him. I get out of the car and stand in the quiet. No other cars come by. The world is asleep.

It feels like I'm watching a movie but it's on a tiny screen far away. Mum and Karl are dead, but I can't feel that anywhere inside me — not my brain, not my heart. I walk to the front of the car and, look! There's the airbag with Stuart's head resting against it. I think *oh, he's dead, too*. And even though I should be very, very happy to see that, I feel the exact same — a cold bright star, far away.

I'm floating in the sky with the snowflakes and I'm also under water. I swim or maybe fly on and around, to the front of the car, and I look down. There's Socks. He's lying a bit under the car and a bit not under the car. He's on his side and there's a lot of blood on his sad old face. He looks like someone drew a picture of him. He doesn't look real. The streetlight is a square in his eye but he doesn't blink. I never noticed how old he was but now I see up close. I lift up his head and it feels so soft and also heavy. I lie down for a bit, to hug him and to blink with my forehead to his forehead because he likes that. His nose is still wet. His head is heavy. I blink. But he doesn't. The snowflakes melt on his nose. And then I pick him up because I must bring him to Mrs A — I must tell her what happened even though she's

337

going to be really, really sad. He's sticky with blood and very heavy.

I stand there holding Socks and I look around. The road is still quiet – this is the back road behind Mrs A's. Where is everybody? I hear cars hissing on wet roads but far in the distance. In another time. Socks is heavy and he's wetting my dress, but I don't want to let him go ever. I walk, a sort of falling over staggering walk, along the road until I come to Mrs A's gate. And then he's so heavy I can't open the gate and still hold him, so I put him down gently beside the path. His head rolls back and that's when I know he's dead and I feel a shattering inside but nothing comes out. The sharp broken pieces stay inside.

I open the gate and I pick him up again and we go up the path to Mrs A's. It's like I'm carrying a giant bear. I put him down gently on the doorstep and I ring the bell. Ding dong times maybe five or six. There's no reply. Nobody answers and the house is in darkness.

I can't leave Socks here but I don't know what to do so I pick him up again and, each time, he's heavier and sadder. I bring him round the side to his bed in the glasshouse and the door is never locked and we stagger in together, like we're dancing. And I put him in his basket.

It will be like he's gone to bed. Mrs A told me one time that Socks makes sure she's safely tucked up every night before he goes to his bed. She locks all the outside doors and he follows her like he's checking up on her. She goes into the bathroom and washes her face and brushes her teeth and he waits for her. She goes into each room, pulling down the blinds and switching off everything, and he follows her, too. She goes into her bedroom and he goes in with her to check for burglars. When she takes her clothes off to get into her pyjamas, he looks away because he's a gentleman. And when she gets into bed, he takes one last look, then he goes through the house into the side passage and into his own bed. And it makes me so sad because he can never do that again. I pet him and I pull the door over.

And now what do I do? What do you do when Mum and Karl and Socks are dead and you're fractured inside? The jagged pieces are spiking their spikes into your brain and into the quivering soft red jelly of your heart.

That's when I see him. He's not dead in the car because he's not dead. He's escaped from the island and he's killed everyone I love and now he's going to get me. He's shouting something but I can't hear it. There's blood running down his head and he's shouting and roaring. His face is an orange howl from the streetlight. I run across the garden. I run down and down and down the side part of Mrs A's garden, the vegetable part where it's all overgrown and the orchard part where the plums and the apples used to lie on the ground to make a wasp carpet, down to the end, past the lights of the SuperValu, down and down to the woods where the tall trees make the sound of rushing waves, down deeper and deeper into the dark part where nobody ever goes, to the shed. I know the way even in darkness. To the island.

He's behind me, snorting and snarling. He's yelling. He's getting closer. I have nothing – no Sergeant Sharp Steak, no boning knife, no carving knife or gouger, not even Private Parer. I run through the door into the dark inside of the island. I squint in the gloom, looking all around – books and more books and broken things and a chain and more books and the red boat propped up against the wall. And then I see Minerva. She is made of fierce hard stone and she tells me to be strong. Near the door, I see the digging spade. I take it in my two hands. I hide behind the door, my heart racing, pounding, beating, pulsing, thumping. He's very near. He's getting nearer. I hold the digging spade in my shaking hands. I hold my panting breath. He trips a bit on the step and he falls and – *do it! Do it! Do it!* I smash the spade down hard. I smash it into his head.

He goes down flat on to the floor. I don't have the knife and I haven't done the jugular or the carotid, but he's very, very still. It looks like he's never getting up. Never. Never.

But just in case, I drag him over away from the door and he weighs a million tons but I am fierce and strong. He sort of flips on to his back. I don't want him looking at me but his eyes are closed. And that's when I remember the boat. It takes a big heave, but I can do it. I am Morrigan full of strength. I push the boat over so it falls down on top of him.

Nobody can see him now – he's hidden underneath. Maybe his shoes will stick out like the wicked witch under the house, like Mum on the kitchen floor. But no. They don't. I block up the door with the statues and the books and the tables and everything and then I climb out the little window that only Karl used to fit in but I'm able to do it today and then I run far away into the woods at the back of the island. Far away.

I sleep in the woods for a bit because it's very late and dark. And when I wake up, I go to find Mum and Karl because I have something very sad to tell them, but now I can't remember what it is. And I go out on the road, but I can't find Mum and Karl – they're not at home and I can't find them and it's dark. So I go down to the arch by the river and I sleep.

I remember now. If Laura was asking me the questions now, I could tell her because nothing matters anyway. It doesn't matter and there's no shut up dumb bitch. He must be dead. And anyway or So-and-annieway, that's what Niamh says, now there is no need to hide because Mum is gone and so is Karl and Laura didn't tell me and I hate her. Dumb bitch.

Laura is sprinting round the back and I am hiding in the tree. I have found some long vines. And Spartacus and his slave army, they used the vines to escape. That's what Mrs A said. When they were trapped against a steep cliff and the Romans thought they couldn't get away, they braided the vines and lowered themselves over the edge. And I'm plaiting like them and like Rapunzel's plait, which was strong enough to climb. I will braid the vines into a rope and I know the knot you need to make. It won't take her long to find the island. I must be quick.

51. Niamh

The sleet is coming down heavily now, as though buckets are being flung against the windscreen. Not even midwinter, but it's pure freezing. Even the houses look huddled and wretched. It's cold enough for snow. I stop at the lights, already looking to see where I can pull in.

One time back home, I went with Dad to the top field to check on the ewes. There'd been a deep snowfall overnight and he was worried they'd have no water. I must have been only about seven or eight – I was just about strong enough to open the gate and pull the bolt across after he drove through. We broke up the ice and laid out the nuts on a tramline of snow and we were almost back at the house when I saw something – some small animal – flailing around desperately in the corner of the fence. I screamed at Dad to stop and jumped out. It was a kitten – a scrawny little tabby. Its back foot was snarled up in the wire. Another twist of wire curved around its neck and underneath its front paw. It was kicking and twitching and yowling all at the same time. Every kick tightened the wire around its neck.

Dad took out his pliers and began snipping. I tried to calm the little creature, reaching forward to stroke its forehead, trying to hold it still so we could free it, but it was wild. I yelled in pain as the kitten sank its teeth into the fleshy part of my palm and glared at Dad in outrage, as if he was responsible.

'Don't take it personally,' he said, snipping the last bit of wire off and sitting back on his heels while the kitten bolted off across the field. 'Hurt creatures can't be trusted.' He patted my hand, wiping away the two beads of blood I'd been saving to show the others at home. 'How was he to know you were helping him?'

I know Laura would laugh at this shite, but still. I'm thinking of that kitten – we never saw it again, though I'd gone back to the same spot for days afterwards with food scraps, still hoping for a happy ending where it trusted me and I brought it home to sleep by the stove happily ever after.

I can't believe Laura took the girl out – in her own car. Could you get a more confined space? She's hurt, sick, confused, distressed – but most of all, when I'm listening to Jenny, I hear her anger. She's almost the same size as Laura and – she'd have the element of surprise. Laura, I realize with a jolt, hasn't a clue when it comes to Jenny. She doesn't see a witness, possibly even a murderer. She only sees the injured kitten.

52. Laura

I'm so relieved when I see it's a dog, not a decomposing human corpse. Thank Christ! I bundle my scarf up over my nose in an effort to block out the smell. The side passage has a roof of corrugated plastic and it's sheltered from the biting wind. I look around for light switches but can't find any. Still clamping my scarf over my mouth and nose, I cast the light from the torch over the body. It's a big old collie, one of those farm dogs, and it has the toffee-coloured patches she spoke about. It must be Socks.

I step over him, making my way through the conservatory towards the back door of the house. It's locked. I feel under the mat and along the top of the doorframe for a key left out, but there's nothing. Another door leads into the back garden. Could she have come through here?

I should call this in. I'm waiting for Niamh's next irate phone call, or worse – Cig. I'm so far off the grid now, all bets are off. I've got to find her. She must be frozen – and that scream! It sent a shiver through my guts. I try not to think about the river – the black waters of the Dodder calling to her from down by the arch. Nothing else matters. I've got to find her. I step into the overgrown back garden, the narrow beam of white light puny against so much dark vegetation.

The garden is massive; it spans the full width of the house and runs down to a hedge of tall trees – the same ones which form the impenetrable wall in the front. And it's so dark. How can we be in Dublin, where every street is lit by the orange glow of streetlights, every star uplit? The darkness is absolute. I sweep the torch across and up, trying to assess the shape of the land. The grass is really long and there are channels criss-crossing all the way through it in different directions. I try to remember what day it is; the feeling of timelessness is so strong. It's like I'm stuck in another world. It's Thursday. I'm in South Dublin – just a back garden. They did the house-to-house on Tuesday, and this road will have been among the first to be done. I look all around, call her name again.

I stumble and slither on wet grass, my feet knocking against tree roots and stones. I'm slapped in the face by wet branches and I gasp in shock, thinking I'm under attack. It's like being in a Brothers Grimm forest – the type that grew for a hundred years while the whole palace slumbered. And I don't know why this is, but I feel Jenny's presence. I feel that she's here – close by. I feel like, finally, I'm inside her story.

'Jenny! Jenny!' I yell, aiming the torch systematically across the back of the house and all the way around the garden. It's so much bigger than it looks from the outside. I keep trudging through the grass, following the troughs, trying not to fall. About two thirds of the way down on the left-hand side there's an old wall which juts into the rectangle of grass. I head towards it and walk around the far side. It must have been built to give shelter to the small orchard behind it. Gnarled, overgrown apple trees cluster together in huddled rows and, behind them, other fruit trees – plum trees, I'm guessing – loom over the apple trees, like clawing fingers. I shiver, waiting for a witch to appear.

My phone pings with a message. I take it out in time to see 'Missed Call' glide noiselessly across the screen. I turn it off, worried it's going to run out of battery. The darkness settles on me, presses me against the stone wall.

'Jenny! Come on!' I yell towards the shadowed trees.

'Come back – let me bring you back inside. You'll freeze out here.' Only the groans of big branches answer. I reach the end of the garden, where the wall meets the trees.

'Come on! Jenny! Please!'

This is pointless. I turn and look back at the house, listening for any sounds, waiting for my eyes to adjust. The roads around here are ridged – so there's a constant roar of car tyres. And there's the wind and the groaning of branches. My eyes are a bit more used to the dark now, and there's half a moon visible behind the clouds. I turn back one last time to look. Where the wall meets the back row of trees is in shadow. But further away, in the corner, one shadow appears bigger than the others, and strangely square. And, now that I'm looking closely, I see that there are two rows of trees across the back, not one, as I'd thought. Between the trees is a narrow path, which means that where the wall meets the trees must be an entrance. An entrance to what?

I step into the path and I do what you do when you're on a path – follow it to the end. It's so quiet in here. I think of a line of poetry; something about the woods being dark and deep. A sudden shiver of wind disturbs the shadowed trees and I feel a lurch of fear. I reach around to the holster and take out my gun and – just like a training drill – I place back palm to back palm, torch in my left fist, right hand slotted on top, the barrel of the gun and the beam of the torch facing the same way. I should wait for back-up. I don't. I've drawn my gun without calling for back-up. There's no going back now.

At the end of the path, completely hidden and covered in ivy, is a shed. There's a door and a side window set into the brickwork and a bigger window at the back. I peer in the window, shining the torchlight inside. The beam jerks crazily from corner to corner – but I can't see clearly. There's something big – a large object – in the centre of the room. I try the door, undoing the bolt that has been pushed across. But it barely moves – there's something blocking it from inside.

I don't call out to her. I'm scared of breaking a spell. If I shout, if my phone rings, if reality happens, the spell will be broken. I'm scared to force the door, because I'm dreading what's on the other side – but I have to.

Without undoing the grip on my weapon, I shove my shoulder against the door with as much force as I can muster, and it budges a couple of inches. There's a scraping sound and something falls. I shove again, and again, until I can get my foot in. I see the leg of a piece of furniture wedged against the door, so I kick it and then, with a crash, I shove my way into the room and the makeshift barricade topples to the ground.

I'm in a – a cross between a boathouse and a den. Still holding the gun, I sweep the torch beam into every corner. There's an upturned boat filling the centre of the room. Under the side window there's an old sofa, swathed in rugs and clothing. A shaft of moonlight illuminates the wall facing me. It's lined with shelves on which is stored a crazy mixture of paraphernalia: small garden tools, a watering can and stacks of plant pots, bundles of twine, books of all sizes, some of them massive old-fashioned tomes, some garish paperbacks. There are old shoe boxes and biscuit tins and an old-fashioned kettle. Torchlight glints on glass decanters and, beside them, stacks of crockery. A huge rocking horse, its mane reduced to three or four little tufts of hair, is poised permanently in mid-canter by the window. A cloud passes over the moon and the torchlight seems puny by comparison. What is this place? My brain struggles to make sense of it all.

A glint catches my eye and I look down. A thick, dark stain

of something viscous – maybe engine oil or something – has spread in a small puddle across the centre of the room. I wish the moon would come out again – I can't see what it is. It's thick, greasy. There's a smell. My body knows before I do, because my heart starts racing and my mouth is dry. I place the gun down on the narrow window ledge beside the door and switch hands with the torch, bending down, touching the liquid warily. It's cold and gelatinous, kind of crusted on the top but liquid underneath. I bring my finger close and smell it; it doesn't smell like engine oil. It – I hold my finger to the light – it's blood.

And then – that's when I see the fingers – ghostly white – three corpse fingers curving upwards from under the edge of the – the boat. Because that's what it is. A boat, like in her story. It's all here. The boat – everything. I prop the torch down on a pile of boxes so it casts some light, and I bend down, bracing myself to heave the boat upwards.

53. Jenny

Ssh, Laura! Bitch! Shut up with your shouting. I'm trying to think. I practised this one so many times. It doesn't have to be a long rope; you can do it with a belt. My fingers are cold and I don't like the feel of the gritty ivy under my nails; it feels dirty. I will plait some more so it's long enough. I will slip it over my head like a princess's crown. I will bring it down until it's around my neck. I will attach the other end around that branch; it's not too far for me to reach. And then I will jump down. I remember now so clearly.

I remember it all now. I had it all planned and, even though it didn't happen like that, I would have done it.

I like this plan best because, in this one, Mum and Karl would be safe and they'd be fast asleep. And they wouldn't be dead. In this one, it's him coming into my bedroom during the blackest part of the night. I can see the tower through the chink in the curtain. He doesn't speak. He gets on top of me on the bed and I smell his stinking stink. His forearm is an iron bar reaching across my throat. If I move, if I make a sound, he leans harder and, with the tiniest adjustment, he can choke me. Smooth and sneaky, smooth and sneaky, I slide my arms upwards like angel wings up over my head. Sneakily, creepingly, my right hand slides under the pillow and clenches around Sergeant Sharp Steak. Reporting for duty, sir, and I say, 'Stand by, Sergeant. Stand by.'

He suspects nothing. In fact, he thinks I am surrendering. I do a sigh, though it makes me feel like I've already died, but I do it because then there's less squashing on my throat. My arm floats out from under the pillow and up. I pause. Just a short pause.

And then, really fast and hard and strong, I slice with Sergeant Sharp Steak whoosh from under his right ear in and down and across. Like a scythe. I get the carotid and vena cava maybe? Or even better – the jugular. Ssh, Laura, stop shouting. Let me finish. I'm almost done.

He roars, rears, falls, rolls. He's on the floor. Shuffling, snorting, choking, crying. Blubbing, panting, bleeding, dying. Blood and more blood, lots of clots. Blackberry jam and tomato ketchup and boiling lava – it would be hot, wouldn't it?

I wish I'd done it like that. I wish I'd done it the night before the party and then Mum and Karl would be alive. Dumb bitch. That part is true.

We did a Bible story in school about the little guy up in the tree looking down at Jesus passing by. And Jesus looked up because he knew he was there and called him down to follow him. And I thought that was mean – Jesus calling him out like that. Sometimes you're not ready to join in and you want to watch from very far away. You can choose.

It's starting to snow properly now, and it looks so pretty against the dark trees. My teeth are juddering together tic-tic-tic. And I've a pain in my shoulders from hunching them against the cold. The flakes swirl and eddy against the orangey street-lit sky. I can see the road below and the whispering cars driving by from up here on my branch. No one can see me. I see Mrs A's house and the side door open and I think a kiss towards it. Goodbye, Socks – Socrates. You tried to help us, me and Karl. I don't think Mrs A really needed anyone to walk him, I realize suddenly. She wanted to show us the island kingdom so we could read all the stories and dress up and ride Niamh Cinn Óir's white horse and fix everything. She wanted us to have fun and play in our make-believe world. I think she knew we didn't want to go home to reality.

Socrates was right. What's real is what you believe. There are no lights on in Mrs A's house, I realize. She must have gone away.

The snow drifts down in sticky postage stamps. It's covering the path and the treetops. I picture it floating its white kindness over the bike shop and the roof where Dad took his own life, over the houses and the parked cars, over the castle and the tower, over our car with Mum and Karl tucked up fast asleep inside. I wish I'd tidied her hair, brushed it back off her poor face. I don't hate her. I'm not even angry with her now. It was like, with every fight and every put-down, she got younger and younger until she was the little girl and I was the grown-up. She couldn't change anything, she couldn't protect us, but it wasn't her fault. All her powers were gone. He took them.

The snow covers Mum and Karl's glass coffin car. I'm so sorry, Mum. I couldn't save us either. I'm sorry.

If I don't do this now, my hands will be too cold and it will be too late. I pull the knot tighter and shift myself along the ancient branch. I think of Amy and Luke. They were good friends. But now, this branch, this twisted vine, all the snowy trees – they're my friends.

Not you, Laura. Laura didn't come out yet, she's going to find him soon. It won't be 'Poor Jenny, you're the boss, you're in charge.' Now, she'll know I'm a murderer. She'll hand me over to the other gardaí and they'll take me for questioning and I'll be sent to prison dumb bitch.

And another wish is sneaking in slippety-slip like a snake – dumb bitch Laura. Dumb bitch you go girl Laura with her shiny hair and her dumb bitch face full of hope. She gets a pay packet and she gets money and she thinks she does a good job but she's full of shit. She lies her dumb bitch lies 'I will help you' and 'It won't happen again' and 'You'll be safe.' And she lies her own lies and she is full of cracks and red marks from her hurting. They are all full of shit and full of lying. Laura's gone quiet and stopped her shouting. She must have found him by now. I pull the plaited vines sharply between my hands. They're strong. I make the knot and then and then, haha, dumb bitch, I climb down out of the tree, tippy-toe so slowly. Because you have to be so quiet when you're sneaking.

And I will bring Laura, too, because she is a dumb lying bitch and it's all fake. She can't help me and she can't help anniewan, haha, not even herself. I will do it for her first and then me and happily ever after.

54. Laura

There's a scraping sound and a mighty crash as I heave the boat over, right way up. There he is – Stuart. His eyes are closed and deeply sunken. His mouth is open, frozen as if in the middle of a cry. From under the back of his head, a dark thought bubble of sticky blood emerges, black in the moonlight. I should call it in. Still training the beam on him, I fumble in my pocket for my phone, my hands shaking. And that's when I see it in the narrow beam of torchlight – an infinitesimally small movement at the base of his neck. Trembling, I hunker down and press my fingers against the cold skin, feeling a faint flicker of a pulse. Christ! He's still alive.

I pull my hand away as though burned and sit back against my heels. Now I must call it in. I should call an ambulance, cover him with blankets and try to keep him alive till they get here. There's bound to be water in the house. I should break in the back door and run into the kitchen, make a mixture of sugared water or something and drop it into his open mouth, keep him alive until the ambulance crew get here. It'll take them at least twenty minutes minimum. I should do it. Quick. Hurry.

I stand there doing nothing. After I call it in, I should go back outside and find Jenny and I should call Niamh and tell her the truth, tell her how I fucked up. That would be the right thing to do. But that's not what I do. I don't do that.

I put my phone back in my pocket and I get to my feet slowly, my body blocking the beam of moonlight so he's in shadow. I look at Stu – motionless, on the brink of death. And I don't even think about Jenny or where she could be or what could be happening. I don't think of Katie and Matt. I just look at him.

I think about the rape – about him pinning me in place by the hair and shoving my knickers to one side – all part of the consensual experience. His smirking – *welcome to college*. I think of Jenny at fourteen lying there in silence as she's stitched. I think of her silence and her cunning. She was right to play for time and stall this. He's taking one hell of a long time to die.

I think of all the stuff Jenny's told me, and what Ciara found in her examination: the bruises, especially the older bruises, the torn flesh, the swollen tissue, the lacerations, the broken bones that have thickened along the cracks. I think about him throwing the coffee mug, about little Karl getting hit with his Action Man, and Melanie's frozen rictus smile in the family photograph. And then I think of the others; terrified women and children getting beaten and thumped and stabbed. I think of Baby X who died of Shaken Baby Syndrome six years after her father inflicted the injury; the boy who screamed, 'Daddy, we can get you help – just don't do it!' even as his father tried to strangle him; the murder-suicides; the femicides; the endless and ongoing brutality and sense of entitlement.

I think about women getting killed when they decide to leave him, or when he decides to kill himself and wants to take her with him. Women killed for infidelity or burning the toast. Women killed for wearing the wrong clothes or for confronting him. Women and children killed for no reason at all.

If he dies now, or sometime in the next few hours, is that such a bad thing? My job is to protect and serve. If I let him die, I've failed in my duty and broken my promise – to him.

But if I let him die, I'm making sure he will never hurt anyone again. I'm protecting the community. Sometimes you have to do harm to do good.

That's how I'll frame it. He needs to die for the greater good. But even as I think this, I know it's window dressing.

I want him to die because he deserves to die. Even looking at him splayed on the floor, his head caved in, inches from death, I am not moved by him. I am angry. I want to punish him for Jenny, for Melanie and Karl, for all the women and children who are casualties of men's narcissism, entitlement, rage and immaturity. I don't want to save him. I'd like Katie to grow up in a world with one less bastard in it.

And then a thought pops into my head. I don't know where it comes from – but for some reason, I remember Katie and Liam and the naughty-step incident. When I wanted to slap Liam, to see him properly punished, Katie wanted something else. Katie, at two and a half, believes in a better world, where people do bad things because they're tired, where people are forgiven and where being the forgiver is in itself, healing.

What Shauna said about maithiúnas – I remembered, afterwards, the meaning behind the word. The word 'maith' means 'good' but it can also mean 'absolve'. If you forgive someone, you are making good. The phrase doesn't specify which someone is being made good – because both victim and perpetrator stand to benefit from forgiveness.

I don't want to forgive him; he hasn't earned forgiveness. But if I let him die, then he has been killed by Jenny and I don't want her to become a murderer.

There's a tiny shift. I don't want him to die. I want him to be well enough to go to court and stand trial. I want him to go to prison for what he did. I want him never to hurt another person again.

I want Jenny to live – fully. I want her to make her video statement so her story is heard in its entirety. I want his defence team to watch it and realize that they haven't a hope – he must plead guilty. He must. We must – Niamh and I – we must nail this one. Fumbling in hurry and cold and terror that now he'll die and it'll be too late for Jenny, at last I take out my phone, ready to call it in.

And that's when I see her in the doorway – like something from a horror film, the combination of malice and innocence. She narrows her eyes – measuring – taking in the whole scene lit by the moon. There's something ancient and cold in her gaze, ice shards splintered from a glacier. She's holding something dark and vegetal – for a mad moment I think she's trying to give me a pile of brambles.

'I made crowns,' she says. 'Put yours on first.'

55. Laura

'Jenny, there you are!' I say, and I hear my own fear. She's still framed in the doorway, her face ashen in the beam of the torch. 'I – I was worried about you. You must be freezing.'

She says nothing.

'Come on – let's go back to the car and get warm, shall we? I –' I falter. She's staring at me.

'Is he dead?' she says, her voice full of hope. She takes another step towards me. I step backwards, trying to avoid the blood.

'No – he – Jenny, I have to make a phone call, okay? What's going to happen now is I'm going to call this in and they'll come and take him away and he –'

'He's not dead? Dumb bitch dumb dumb dumb he will kill you. He'll kill us both – it's all his fault!'

She takes a step inside and – Jesus! My gun is on the window ledge right beside her. Has she seen it? She glances down at him, her hair swinging across her face.

'Why is he not dead? Why didn't you do it?'

'Look – we're going to get back in the car and get warm, okay?' I put my arms out as though to shepherd her out. 'We can sort everything – we'll get some food, a hot drink, yeah? You need to leave this to me – I'll sort it, I promise.'

I tilt the phone so I can see the keypad, dial the number. Her mouth drops open in disbelief. There's a click as the phone is answered, then it dies. At the same moment, my eyes slide to the Sig – she follows my gaze.

Jenny moves first. She drops the vines, twists and grabs

357

the gun by the muzzle first. I freeze. Now, she's holding the gun in two hands, as though cradling a doll.

'Jenny, I want you to listen to me, okay?' I swallow, placing my phone down on a box and reaching my hands, palms up in supplication, pleading with her.

'You need to give me the gun,' I say, stressing the 'need', willing my voice not to shake. 'I know it doesn't seem like it now, but it's going to be okay, everything is going to work out.'

She doesn't answer. She turns the gun over in her palm and rights it.

I swallow, sick with panic, trying to stop my eyes gliding towards the body – trying to hide my fear. There's no movement, nothing. He could be dead already.

I scour my brain to find the right words. Fucking words! Why aren't they better agents for us? Why can't they do more? Why can't they work harder?

Mesmerized, I watch her turn the gun towards her face. My hands are in shadow. I scan right and left to see if there's anything I can use to knock it out of her hands.

'Jenny – don't do this. I swear – it's all going to be – this will end and –'

How do I do it? Convince her that she'll be okay and this night will be a distant memory. Tell her she's young and she's had barely a taste of the world – not enough to decide to leave it. I want to tell her about college and falling in love and nights on the lash with your friends and hangovers and getting fit and getting out of shape; slobbing around doing nothing in your PJs and running marathons. I want to tell her about working with your best friend, about birth and babies – about holding your child to your heart and kissing the top of their head. It is all ahead of her – it's all there – like clean towels folded and ready.

'Jenny, please trust me. I know you're on the edge of an abyss – trust me – I know. But –'

She closes her eyes.

'Jenny – Jen, listen, okay? Listen for a little more, please. Please! Your mum, and Karl and all these people who care about you, the friends you told me about, Amy and Luke, they're all here for you. Jenny – I – it really is all ahead of you – good things, really good things. Better times.'

She opens her eyes and I feel a shift, even before she turns the gun towards me.

'Dumb bitch you think I am so dumb. Lies. Mum's dead. And so is Karl. And –'

'They're not dead – oh God! You think they're dead? I swear it, Jen. I swear it!' I'm whimpering. 'They're not dead. They were injured, but they're going to be okay, both of them. Jenny, I was with your mum – I saw her, she's going to be okay.'

'You're lying. Dumb bitch lying dumb lying bitch. You're so fake. All of you. You make up anything – anything you like – to make us do what you want. You're a liar.'

She takes a breath and, in that breath, I dig for truth – for my truth – for something to show her – like a treasure.

'I'm not lying, Jenny. I swear I'm not lying. Jenny, please! I know a bit of what you're going through. I know what it's like to want to die.'

I'm full-on sobbing now, big ratchet sobs rising out of my chest. Katie's face – my little Katie and Matt are floating beside her and my heart is cracking.

'Please, Jenny! You've got to believe me – I – I was raped when I was nineteen. I never told anyone – even now – not even Niamh – I felt ashamed and used and dirty. I thought it was my fault.'

Snot and tears are mixing on my cheeks and I wipe them

away with my sleeve. 'I never told my mum. My husband – Matt still doesn't know. Nobody knows.'

I look down at Stuart's motionless body.

'Jenny – please listen. I swear I'm telling the truth. I bottled it up inside – and I see now that you're right – it's just more lying. Seeing you, seeing how brave you are, how you tried to save your family – you've made me realize that I have to tell, even now, all these years later. We both have to tell our stories – so that it stops happening.'

She's still gripping the gun in both hands, still pointing it at me. I realize that there is, after all, a moment of truth.

'I became a garda to protect life – all life. Even his.'

I glance at Stuart's limp body, my breath stuttering.

'I have to call an ambulance – I have to try to save even this bastard's life. I'm asking you to give me the gun so I can do my job and keep my promises. But Jenny – I swear to you – we will send him to prison – you and me. And you'll be free and you and your mum and Karl – he'll never hurt you again. I swear it.'

I step towards her, my eyes trained on hers – those watchful owl's eyes.

56. Niamh

I wait, just outside Laura's line of sight, my gun trained on Jenny. I watch her lower her arms, the gun dangling loosely in her fingers. She hangs her head and allows Laura to take the weapon. I exhale.

Only then do I deactivate the trigger and holster mine.

They're hugging and crying when I step inside the shed, Laura almost as much as Jenny.

'Thank fuck!'

'My phone's died. Call it in,' hiccups Laura.

'Already done,' I say unnecessarily, as we hear the wails of the siren.

I envelop the two of them – skinny wagons that they are – in the traditional post-match hug.

'Bring it in, bitches,' I say, squeezing them so they gasp. We stand huddled together by the dusty window, casting giant misshapen shadows on the book-lined stone walls. I'm hugging them so tight I don't know who's shaking, who's sobbing. I only know it's over.

The ambulances arrive and take first Stuart, then Jenny away. I'm going to follow Jenny.

'Bring her to see her mum first,' says Laura. 'Swear.'

'I swear,' I say, walking over to Laura and clasping her little heart-shaped face in my hands. She's covered in mud and dust and a combination of dried tears and snot. I plant a big kiss on her forehead.

'You've never looked more beautiful, bitch. You're gonna be grand.'

Epilogue: Four months later

Laura

'Sure how was I to know it wasn't his real name?' says Niamh, for the tenth time in twenty-four hours. She sniggers.

'It's not funny. She'll probably never speak to me again,' I say, taking my keys out of the bag and unlocking the front door of the interview suite.

'Well, that might be no harm – your Gaeilge's not up to much, in fairness,' she snorts, unrepentant.

Niamh had been over at our house the day before, hanging out with me and Katie on her day off. Matt's at a conference so we had a girls' afternoon. Midway through the fourth showing of *Peppa Pig's Day Out*, the doorbell rang. Shauna was on the doorstep, dropping back a book I'd lent them.

Always friendly and eager to be nice, Niamh had asked her about the wedding plans.

'And how's the little fella? Damien?' There was silence. My mouth opened and closed. And in that moment, before I could fix it, Shauna understood. Something closed in her features.

'As in son of Satan? He's grand. Yeah – thanks for that,' she said.

'His name is Liam! Niamh!' I said, grinning and eye-rolling at Shauna as if to say how dumb can your friends be.

'Oh, right! Sorry,' said Niamh. 'So how's he doing anyway?'

'He's fine, thanks,' said Shauna, lips pursed. 'Slán.'

'Slán! Bye now! Thanks soooo much for coming over to drop that back. You needn't have,' I wittered. Mortified.

'She'll see the funny side soon,' says Niamh. 'It's hilarious.'

The spring sunshine is doing its best to heat up the interview room and, just for a second, I realize I'm actually looking forward to work this week. I'm so relieved they let me stay in the unit. Everything is laid out, ordered, clean and calm. I have a feeling of, I don't know, hope or optimism or something. And I'm excited to see Jenny.

'Nine thirty start or nine thirty you told her to come in?' Niamh says, handing me my earpiece.

'Start,' I say. 'Sorry – it's just that –'

'I know, yeah. That's cool. Sure it won't take long to explain and she's doing much better now. She knows what she's about.'

She turns and heads out into the control room. On the earpiece, I can hear her humming 'Galway Girl'.

'Jesus, could you be any more of a bogger?'

'What? It's a great song,' she says, starting the song again, louder this time. 'Here, what's the story with her mam?'

There's some rustling and banging as she sorts out the folders and our question notes. It will be Niamh's job to keep me on track when I'm running the interview.

'Melanie's doing well. There's talk of her coming out in a week. She managed a couple of steps yesterday. And Karl home – well, out. They're both staying with Val, for now. Tusla were okay with it.'

'Cewel,' she says, giving it full-on accent.

I roll my eyes.

'I fecking saw that, bitch!' she says, coming back into the room. 'That's casual racism, actually. I could report you for that. You're not allowed to mock people from Tipperary.'

'I retract it completely,' I say, 'so don't report me. I've enough on my plate, thanks.'

She grimaces. 'Ah Jaysus,' she says. 'It turned out okay didn't it? You acted to preserve life – and you did that.'

'Yeah,' I say, keeping my tone light. It still hurts.

I was suspended pending the GSOC investigation. Even I can't believe what I did. From this remove, with everything calm and sorted, I can't actually comprehend the risk I took with Jenny – removing her from the hospital and bringing her to the tower. Then there was the fact that I entered that house without back-up, with my weapon drawn. That was off the scale. If they heard that Jenny got hold of the gun and turned it on me, I'd be finished. But that never emerged – thank you, Niamh.

As it is, I'm lucky I still have a job. Or that I'm not property manager in some station in the back end of nowhere or rostered for duty in Phoenix Park. The carefully constructed professionalism – the career that I'd worked so long and hard to achieve – everything got flung out the window that night.

But I'm still in the DDU – still with Niamh. Thank fuck, as she'd say herself. I'll talk about it in the next session; I'm attending the psychotherapist, and not just because it was mandatory. Jenny was not the only one who needed to tell her story. That's how it goes.

Matt has been amazing. I realize that by not telling him I'd effectively shut him out of my life. It was as if I didn't trust him enough to love me once he knew what had happened. And the counsellor has helped me understand that, in thinking like that, I'm buying into shame and blame. As if I were somehow responsible.

Matt says he knew something had happened, way back when we had met up again in our twenties, but he didn't know how to bring it up.

Jenny's getting better, too – although it'll be a long road. They're hoping it was a temporary psychosis and that with counselling and vigilance and support she'll make a good recovery. I know she's already had a good few counselling sessions and will have more during the coming months. But she wanted to get this video evidence done – she's determined.

Stuart very nearly died. If it'd been another few moments, that would have been it. As it is, he's been left with serious side effects. He's been discharged from hospital, remanded on bail, and the trial is coming up in September.

We're going to nail this video, Jen and me and Niamh. He's going to plead guilty as soon as he sees it. Job done.

Jenny

'Are you sure you don't want me to wait for you?' Amy says, stamping her Doc Martens into the gritty footpath in an effort to get warm, although it's not even cold. 'They've got to have a waiting room, yeah?'

'No, it's grand, go on,' I reply. 'You were really good to come. But I don't know how long it will take, so you'd better head off.'

'And do you have to come back a few times and give more evidence and stuff?' She zips up her coat and stuffs her hands into the pockets.

'No, Laura says they have to do it in one session. They can't film me more than once.'

'That's good.' She pops in some chewing gum to disguise the smell of the cigarette she had on the way over. 'Suppose I'll see you at school then, yeah?'

I nod, the mention of school giving me a swish of anxiety in my stomach.

'See ya later,' she says, walking back towards the bus stop.

Today is the day for the truth. When I first went back to school in January, the stares were like something concrete. I used to hate being invisible; now I'd welcome it with wide open arms. I've worked out quips to help with the uncomfortable silences; I tell people I was in rehab or in the States on a shopping trip. But mostly, I just tell them the truth; yes, I'm the girl who bludgeoned her stepfather half to death. Yes, he'd been abusing me, my mum and my little brother, for a long time. That shuts them up.

I've been thinking about truth – because maybe it's not overrated. Maybe it's everything. Your truth belongs to you and you alone. No one else can tell it. It might be a tangled mess of all the hurt, pain, love and dreams – but it's yours. It's you.

John Lennon said who's to say that dreams and nightmares aren't as real as the here and now? Like Socrates and his two realities. Socrates kept asking questions to get to the truth. For this he was sentenced to death. Think about that, Laura. Hah.

The woman in reception reminds me of Mum – the same blonde hair, the same edginess, similar mannerisms. We're living with Val for now, but when Mum gets out and we get the legal stuff sorted, we're going to find a new place just for us, the three of us. Mum's put her name down for the videography course. She can't wait to get out. We're going to go shopping, she says; we've got to look good for when she's doing job interviews.

Niamh and Laura come into reception together.

'Group hug, Jenny. Deal with it,' says Niamh. There's a squish of shoulders and long hair and the faint scent of apple perfume. When they release me, I spot Laura's bump. She sees me noticing.

'Oh, wow! Erm congratulations,' I say. Laura begins to thank me, but Niamh butts in.

'What? Oh Jaysus! You think she's preggers, do you? So embarrassing. She's not pregnant, she's just got really fat.'

She roars laughing.

I'm so embarrassed. My face flames and I try to think of apologies. Laura grabs my arm and steers me away from her.

'Don't mind her, Jenny! I am pregnant – thanks for the congrats. Niamh's just being a complete idiot,' she finishes, loudly, bringing me into the interview room.

They show me the whole set-up. Laura and I are in one room with a camera and microphones. Laura wears an earpiece so she can hear Niamh, in the control room. Niamh will keep it all on track, so I don't forget anything. So I can tell the whole truth.

The boathouse was full of Mrs A's books. All the legends were there: fairy tales and Irish folktales, Greek legends and Bible stories, too.

I think my favourite character of them all is Minerva, the owl. Minerva represents Athena, the Greek goddess of wisdom – oh, and strength, courage, inspiration, justice, arts, crafts and skills. She kind of covers the whole lot.

Minerva perches on Athena's shoulder, lighting up her blind side with her huge eyes. She can swivel her head fully around, which means that nothing is hidden. When nothing is hidden, you can speak the whole truth.

This morning, in the interview with Laura, I will tell the truth and, later, when we go to court, I will tell the truth again.

The truth will lock him up. And maybe it will set me free.

So I'll stand there and I won't be scared. Nothing will be hidden.

Acknowledgements

Thank you, Faith O'Grady – fantastic and most aptly named agent – for believing in this story and for setting the adventure in motion. Thank you to the amazing and brilliant Patricia Deevy at Penguin Sandycove, whose passion for story and sharp eyes for inconsistencies keep me always striving to do my best. To skilful editors Sarah Day, Natalie Wall and all the team at Penguin Random House, heartfelt thanks for your painstaking work. I am thrilled that Laura and Niamh have found their home in your hallowed halls – it really is the dream.

So many people have helped in the writing of this book. I apologize for shamelessly bombarding you with emails and phone calls and what I call Quick Questions, which turn out to require long and detailed answers! Massive thanks to the expert team of Danni Cummins, Mary Fallon and Deasún McNally, who provided information about the work of the Gardaí from all angles, including special victim interviewers, detective work and scene of crime investigators – and who were generous and creative with all their advice. Any mistakes are absolutely and entirely my own.

I'm fortunate to have family and friends who work in a variety of medical arenas, including psychiatric, general and emergency medicine. The following people have been pressed relentlessly for information and assistance. Huge thanks to Avril Browning, Joan Love, David Walsh, Keith, Adrienne, Conor and Heather Perdue. Sincere gratitude also to neurological consultant Professor Colin Doherty for advising on head injury.

Writing friends Clare Harlow and Gianna Pollero, thank you for always being ready to read the next bit and for the wisdom plus encouragement combo. I would never have got to the end without you. Thanks to everyone at Curtis Brown Creative, especially my friends from the classes of 2016–19 and tutors Catherine Johnson and Jake Arnott. Thank you, inspirational teachers from way back: including Jill Wigham, Noelle Tracey, Colin Polden and Robert Dunbar. Here at home, thanks and hugs to writing buddies Ger Meade, Aileen McGee, Ger Mills, Elizabeth Murray, and Juliette Saumande. When's our next meet-up?

I would be lost without the sisterhood of Joyce Perdue and Debbie Allen, who have had my back and inspired me since the dawn of time. Heartfelt thanks, too, to my other sisters in the Order: Mary Buttanshaw, Birgit Schmidt, Pauline Baldwin, Anne Walsh, Ali Kemp, Felicity Mills, Louise Courtney, Rachel Sterling, Liz and Jackie Morris, Hazel Perdue, Carolyn Good, Sheena Hunt, Gill Brislane, Anna Lynch, Rachel Pyper, Taryn Barling and Sophie Warnock – who always ask how's the writing going, even though there's a real risk that I'll answer. Thank you, Hazel for allowing me to use a small part of the legendary Spike's story. Thank you, Linda Mullen, for keeping the show on the road and Ashling Hendrick for keeping it real.

I'm so grateful for my sibling tribe. Huge thanks to my brothers Keith and Con for unstinting support, encouragement and advice. Four kisses and endless gratitude to the best sister anyone could have – Adrienne. You are my rock. Daughters Jess and Sara – thank you for making everything clear, for the inspiration, and for more than you will ever know. Angus, for the listening, the hiking, and for not minding the endless hours of solitude, thank you. Yours are my crucial coordinates.

Finally, but most importantly, thank you for reading this book. I hope you enjoyed it.

WHEN THEY SEE ME
GILL PERDUE

COMING SUMMER 2023

The gripping second novel in the Shaw and Darmody series.

An au pair disappears in the heart of suburbia. When her body shows up, all eyes are on the only witness to her abduction: a two-year-old child.

Detective and expert witness interviewer Laura Shaw knows she is needed. But in the aftermath of a case that nearly broke her, Laura questions if she can continue to do police work. Her partner, Detective Niamh Darmody, is on the case, but without Laura to rely on, she's struggling too.

When the discovery of a second body blows all their theories out of the water, Laura and Niamh must accept that the killer is poised to strike again.

All they know is that he is tantalisingly close, hidden in plain sight.

But they won't see him – not until he wants them to . . .